Abo⸱

When Helen retired, she dec␡ ␡gy which would see her through ␡␡ all the tasks she'd never finished and t␡ ␡which she had put on hold while raising a large f␡ ␡working full time. One of these projects was to try her hand at a novel. In the past her writing experience had been academic, as a professional in the education world.

She began writing *On the House* in December 2012. This book came about following extensive research into her family history where she made a sad discovery. One of her ancestors volunteered for Wandsworth workhouse, where he hanged himself in 1863. What could have prompted such a desperate act? This led her to fascinating research about living conditions, regulation and control in nineteenth-century workhouses. In Victorian England, provision of welfare for the poor was a fractious political issue which divided opinion, as it still does today. But, while those issues are integral to the story, the events that unfold in this Suffolk workhouse in the early months of 1838 are considerably more graphic, as her synopsis describes.

Helen enjoys all aspects of historical writing: developing the strands of ideas, researching and discovering the different perspectives of her characters. The Lawes and Hudson trilogy is now complete and she has grown to like her two protagonists. She hopes you will too.

ON THE HOUSE

ON THE HOUSE

HELEN MASKEW

This edition first published in 2017

Unbound

6th Floor Mutual House, 70 Conduit Street, London W1S 2GF

www.unbound.com

ISBN (eBook): 9781911586272
ISBN (Paperback): 9781911586098

Design by Mecob

Cover image: © Shutterstock.com
© Textures.com

To Roger

Dear Reader,

The book you are holding came about in a rather different way to most others. It was funded directly by readers through a new website: Unbound.

Unbound is the creation of three writers. We started the company because we believed there had to be a better deal for both writers and readers. On the Unbound website, authors share the ideas for the books they want to write directly with readers. If there are enough who will support the book by pledging for it in advance, we will produce a beautifully bound special subscribers' edition and distribute a regular edition and e-book wherever books are sold, in shops and online.

This new way of publishing is actually a very old idea (Samuel Johnson funded his dictionary this way). We're just using the internet to build a network of patrons for each writer. Here, at the back of this book, you'll find the names of all the people who made it happen.

Publishing in this way means readers are no longer mere passive consumers of the books they buy, and authors are free to write the books they really want. They get a much fairer return too – half the profits their books generate, rather than a tiny percentage of the cover price.

If you're not yet a subscriber, we hope that you'll want to join our publishing revolution and have your name listed in one of our books in the future. To get you started, here is a £5 discount on your first pledge. Just visit unbound.com, make your pledge and type HUDSON17 in the promo code box when you check out.

Thank you for your support,

Dan, Justin and John
Founders, Unbound

Super Patrons

Contents

Foreword

There was a hanging today, although it was more of a strangling – demonstrating the practical difference between being hung and being hanged. A hanged man will have a regulation knot and a measured drop through a trapdoor to ensure a cleanly broken neck for a swift exit. All this is officially overseen by the services of a professional hangman, a doctor to certify death, and a chaplain to pray the man's soul into heaven.

This was not official. Just a home-made plait of odds and ends of rope; a stocky bundle dangling from its noose, slowly swinging this way and that under its own momentum until finally coming to a stop, like the pendulum of a clock whose mechanism has run down. Having expended all its energy, it hung still in the sweet May air; the supreme imperative of gravity by which the body should reach the earth only denied by the stout hook to which the carefully measured rope was tied, and the resulting tension as it pulled against the beam.

A wooden crate had been kicked away by feet clad in poor, thin shoes. The legs, arms and body were straight as an arrow, but the head hung down impotently, chin on top of chest. The neck was squeezed by the rope, turning the skin beneath purple. The face was the same hue, as was the tongue that had protruded through the lips, grotesque and swollen. No colour could be determined from the bloodshot eyes that bulged expressionless. The man was of average height and build, dressed in meagre grey clothing, cotton shirt, jacket and trousers – grey in every particular. *Ecce Homo*. What would lead a man to end his existence this way? Undoubtedly this is a house of misery, where all dignity has been extinguished and nothing is left but black despair.

Part One

Edgar Lawes's Account

Seddon Hall, Suffolk, 1838

Chapter 1

'Edgar, you know there's nothing sentimental about me. As a practical man I've always tried to live out my morality in actions not words.'

I sat by my father's bed and watched as the man of whom I was fondest in all the world peered at me over his spectacles as he lay propped up by numerous pillows. His face was grey, although his breathing was regular and still strong enough for him to form his words coherently. But the doctor had already told me it would only be a matter of days before there would be no more conversations.

'I've been privileged to live in an age of wise men – the new prophets who aren't frightened to express enlightened ideas – even against established and embedded prejudices. The Scotsman David Hume's that kind of man: a good philosopher who thought our knowledge of existence can only come from our experiences, something with which I fully agree – any man of logic must.'

'I know you do, Father, but why don't you rest and take your ease for a while? Besides, perhaps it's not the time for philosophical debate. There'll be plenty of opportunity for that later when you're well.'

'You and I both know that's not the case – I've spoken to the doctor and he's been mercifully frank with me – no placatory bedside nonsense. No, there are things I want you to know. What better time for a man to be reflective than on his deathbed? I want to be certain you understand the precepts on which I've tried to live my life. I'm not necessarily expecting you to adopt them all but I do encourage you to consider some of them as options.'

'A few minutes, then I insist you sleep for a while.'

He leaned forward and gripped my hand with his thin pale one. 'Listen then! Bentham's principle of "the greatest happiness of the greatest number" – that's what I believe myself, the combination of social equality with freedom of the individual. Lately I've been wrestling with ways to achieve it but I fear there's no more time for me, but I might persuade you to follow that principle in your own life.' I nodded and squeezed his soft, cold hand. He went on: 'You and

I've been soulmates since your mother died and I've tried to be a good protector and counsellor. It's my view that children should be taught by example not exhortation. I've always hoped I've given you good guidance, but tried to do it through my own behaviour.'

'Father, you have been – are still – the wisest and kindest counsellor any son could have. There's no one else I would ever seek out for advice.'

'I'm glad, but never be afraid of listening to others, Edgar, although you must always keep a discerning mind – and most important, a loving heart. For myself I face the end with equanimity, since I believe there's nothing beyond it. But I'll tell you this – even as a non-believer in the afterlife, if I'm wrong, Edgar, I'll surely have questions to answer and to ask; unfortunately if I'm right I'll never know. How frustrating for a man who prides himself on his logic!'

His voice faded away as he fell into a deep sleep. There was no sound in the room other than the quiet ticking from the longcase clock; from outside could be heard the dribbling winter song of a robin just below the open window. The room was full of the man and his interests – curios, paintings and mementos from his few travels. On his bedside table was a pile of books set aside to be read, but in my heart I knew they would never be opened.

As his only child, my father's death radically altered my way of life, since, at the age of twenty-seven, I became the inheritor of Seddon Hall, an estate of some size, with a position in local society to match it. I was already a Justice of the Peace with considerable local power as one of the county's legal officers and general administrators. My father had always determined that deeds not words fuel progress and so I began to cast around for additional ways in which I might be part of the spread of Jeremy Bentham's 'greatest happiness'. I considered entering politics, but the Member of Parliament for Suffolk was firmly established. In any case we shared certain Whiggish political ideas, besides the fact that he was a distant relative. With a minor aristocratic background and correspondingly useful connections, I was now what was understood as a man of standing and had that ultimate benefit of independent means – time. I was also unencumbered by domestic considerations since matrimony had as yet escaped me, although as a full-blooded bachelor, considered reasonably good-looking, as kind friends assured me, I'd not lost hope in that direction. Only on one occasion had I felt myself really drawn to someone, but had prevaricated, missed my chance and left the field open to another. The numbers of young women my age in my immediate circle were few and, as a result, I was considered a real catch by their mothers, whose persistence I managed with great difficulty.

Seddon estate was centrally placed in the county and twelve miles from Ipswich. Suffolk is an agricultural county through and through, farming a mix of sheep, cattle and arable, the soil well drained and fertile. My land was well managed and profitable under the regular and sustained supervision of my father's bailiff, Samuel Saunby, who'd been with the family since I was a small boy. His intimate knowledge of all aspects of its running, at all times conscious of my father's wishes as to how tenants and workers were to be treated, required no substantial oversight on my part and so I decided to continue as my father had and leave him to it. I also ran a racing stud on a very small scale but with good-quality animals. For this I relied on the expertise of my stable manager and groom Harry Valentine, whose knowledge of horses exceeded anyone's in the county. With such expertise in both land and equine matters my presence was sometimes more of a hindrance to them than a help. With all this in mind my instincts told me it was an appropriate time to take stock of how the 'greatest happiness' can be achieved and what I might contribute to it personally.

My father was a voracious reader with a substantial library, and once I'd put away my law books from Cambridge I took full advantage of the contents of its shelves. It was an eclectic mix, mostly devoted to works of philosophy and science, but with poetry and novels as new additions. I found works by Wordsworth, Byron, and a new writer – Benjamin Disraeli – who my father insisted 'was one to watch'. But my father's last conversation drew me back to Jeremy Bentham whom I'd read but forgotten. The philosopher had been dead for six years but his utilitarian morality and ethics were undiminished. In the year that Bentham had died, the Great Reform Act of 1832 had enfranchised more men than ever before. Last year, for the first time for over a hundred years, a young woman of eighteen became queen; between the reign of Queen Anne and the newly crowned Victoria there had been five kings of varying quality.

Times are certainly changing and increasingly there are those who strive to propel the country into more enlightened thinking. Questions of conscience have arisen over the enthusiasm with which industrial progress is being achieved, and at what cost to the individual well-being of the workers who service the great engine of technology. Social change is surely accelerating. New ideas and processes are accepted by some, but for the critical mass I suspect there are many questions they would like to have answered about their futures, as would those of us encouraged to think for ourselves who ponder over the wider social effects of mechanisation.

But at this time these national concerns, crucial as they were, didn't answer my immediate problem: how to put this luxury of time to profitable use in the search 'for the greatest happiness'? It was a casual meeting with a friend that set me on a path to achieve my ambition. But until that point I had no idea how, within weeks, I would become involved in matters and experience events that previously would have been unimaginable.

Market day in our small town of Seddon: even by late afternoon it was still crowded with local farmers and dealers, their mothers, wives and daughters, as well as pedlars, tinkers and providers of sundry services who are always attracted to the town on such a busy day. After my morning sessions at the magistrates' court I crossed Seddon's main street and was almost bowled over by a small terrier-like man who was looking over his shoulder and not where he was going.

'I beg your pardon, sir!' he said and raised his hat. 'Why, it's Mr Edgar Lawes; good day to you!'

'Good day, Ted. You seem in an almighty hurry and somewhat distracted.'

'Indeed. I was looking to the clock to see if I had time for a drink before loading up and driving home. It seems I have – perhaps you'd join me in the Fleece? It's a piece of good luck meeting like this, Edgar, for I was going to seek your opinion on a matter.'

My father was particularly careful to keep his circle of acquaintances as wide as custom allowed and I followed his practice, making a point of moving socially among all my neighbours and keeping my ear to the ground. Edward Lake was a man I counted as a friend and one I respected for his openness and fair dealing. He owned Rushie Farm, two hundred acres in the adjacent parish of Maiden Lindsey.

My curiosity piqued I said, 'I was thinking of taking drink so, yes, I'll join you Ted,' and followed him across the road and into the inn.

The Fleece Inn was a respectable house: one universal bar, clean and plain with wooden floors and walls. As it was now well into the afternoon the place was only half full and we had no difficulty finding a quiet corner well away from the fire. Badly ventilated, the flue gave back puffs of smoke every now and then, leaving a faint haze as it dispersed around the room. Ted Lake had his own pint tankard that the landlady selected from a row of others hanging above the bar, filling it with the house ale from a large jug; I took a brandy. Being late winter the light was poor and besides the smoky atmosphere the small windows were an additional bar to visibility; our eyes took some time to adjust to the gloom.

'So, Ted, what've you been about? Sarah and the boys are well I hope?'

'They're all thriving, Edgar, thank you. The boys are growing apace and I tell them they're costing too much to feed and will soon have to look out for themselves! But of course they'll stay on the farm as long as we can make a go of it. I couldn't afford to lose them; they're excellent workers and earn their keep.'

'And are you making a go of it? Is the farm still profitable?'

'As usual – like everyone else we have our ups and downs. This cold spring hasn't helped with the wheat, but the four of us soldier on. Sarah does more than her share of hard work. We're lucky.' He took a pull at his ale and leaned forward, elbows on the table; he suddenly seemed pent-up and more akin to a small canine on the scent than ever. 'But never mind that, what I want to tell you is I've put myself up as a candidate for a place on the board of guardians for the union workhouse. I'm quite excited about it; it's the first time I've stood for any public office.' He took a gulp from his tankard, his face animated and his brown eyes bright. A small, neat man with regular features, his was an honest physiognomy full of life and open to all emotions, which passed across it like waves on a pristine sandy shore.

'Why on earth do you want to get involved in that? I'd have thought you had enough to do running the farm.'

He relaxed a little and fell back on his bench. 'I'll be honest. If I'm elected, it won't do me any harm as far as business is concerned and it moves me into local politics, which I'm interested in – what with the new franchise and everything. I don't think I'll have a problem getting in. My reputation's pretty solid; I pay bills on the nail.'

'That doesn't answer my question: why you would want such a thankless task; aren't the poor always with us?'

'I can't argue with that – poor bastards! Anyway, I've always had mixed feelings about them. At first I thought "it's all their own making"; if I can make a go of things – feed my family, pay my way – why can't they?'

'Plenty of people think the same, Ted.'

He leaned forward again, even more animated. 'Maybe, but recently I've had second thoughts. Deep down I know it's impossible for many of them to get out of their poverty. What's true is that no money means no hope; if a man can't feed his family, whether it's his own fault or not, what becomes of his wife and children? I only pay lip service to Christianity – attendance at church is a means to an end for me – but I don't like the idea of "suffering little children".'

By now I was really interested; something in the man's fervour caught my attention. 'So you've had a change of heart – something must have prompted it,' I said.

'It's all come about through an incident I heard of last year. Jake Gray, a tenant on a neighbour's land, lost an arm in a ploughing accident. He's a hard worker, with a wife and three children, paying a few shillings a week rent. When the accident happened they were just about managing, no debts but no savings either. Neither had they any security in their tied cottage; consequently they were almost immediately put out by the landlord so he could get another worker in. Within three weeks the whole family was in the Seddon workhouse with no hope of discharge. This was a man who'd worked for the same farmer for twenty-three years. I know Gray – he's a decent man.

Why is this allowed, I ask myself? Who has the right to make such a man's life so miserable?'

I took a sip of brandy as I digested this story. It occurred to me there was a touch of the radical about Ted that didn't seem to sit comfortably with a solid yeoman farmer.

'So, Ted, what would you have done in this situation?' I asked.

'Firstly, I wouldn't have turned them out immediately; I'd have given them time to approach any family they had, or get help from their neighbours. I would also have given him a few weeks' wages to tide him over. My wife could have found work for his wife in the house and I'd have employed both his young boys on my land. Between them there would have been enough to pay rent on a small cottage I could offer them. I could keep him going until there were better times on the land – as there always are.' He put down his tankard. 'Another drink?'

'I'll get them,' I said, and stood up and went to the bar. Returning with the drinks I said, 'This is all very well, Ted, and I admire your altruism. But presumably these actions weren't open to your neighbour and so, as you infer, he callously abandoned five people to the workhouse. In his defence one could argue that he needed the cottage to house a worker who would be employed on the same terms and who most certainly was himself in need of a house and labour—'

'But there must be other ways of going about these things, Edgar.'

'As I see it, it's the classic horns of a dilemma. Your condemnation of your neighbour is, I suspect, as much about the indecent haste of the eviction, as the act itself.'

'Maybe so, but I was stirred by the level of unconcern shown by the farmer. When he heard of the family's destination he simply shrugged and commented: "Well, that's all right; at least they'll be under shelter." It was then I thought something should be done.'

'Hmm, certainly seems a callous attitude. But it still doesn't explain your desire to become practically involved.'

'He got under my skin at the time and I certainly wasn't impressed by it. Anyway, it was about then that candidates for the board of guardians were being sought, so I thought it the right time to throw in my hat.'

'But what has your story about the tenant farmer got to do with you joining the union guardians? What good can you do for someone like Jake Gray?'

'For a start I may end up making a difference to the inmates' conditions. There's also the fact it won't do my reputation in the district any harm.' He hesitated for a moment before adding, 'Besides, I've other concerns that it won't do to talk about here.'

Now I was really intrigued, but he seemed uneasy as he made this last comment and I instinctively avoided pressing him further. Instead I moved on to practical details. 'So tell me, do you know how much of your time it will it take up?'

'It's not onerous: fortnightly meetings at fixed times – generally in the morning. The guardians are supposed to visit the inmates regularly and inspect the buildings and facilities. So really it's not going to interfere greatly with my running of the farm.'

'I know how the place works, Ted. I've had to read through the Poor Law. Have you?'

'Not exactly read it – just got the gist, and I've heard rumours. I think they need people on the board who might start asking some hard questions and I intend to do just that.'

The inn was now beginning to fill up as people completed their business and sought refreshment and the warmth of a good fire.

'Well, I admire your candour. I can't blame you for wanting to improve your situation locally. I just wonder if there aren't easier ways to do it. Why not local politics? Why not stand for mayor or even parliament?'

'You know that's impossible. Those offices are mostly inherited – or fixed by the local –'

'Gentry? You mean the likes of me?'

'Well, yes. I don't say you were personally involved in managing it, but one of your relatives is the member for Suffolk – and it's been kept in your family for generations.'

'Well, given the new Reform Bill he might not be for very much longer! But getting back to your proposal and these hints at "other concerns", what are we talking about here?'

'Look, I'd rather not talk in public, Edgar; these are matters that need investigation and may show people in a bad light. Besides, you never know who's listening. Will you have another drink?' I nodded and he made his way back to the bar.

Now loose talk from whatever quarter was risky and taverns in small towns were not good places for questionable conversation. It was only four years since six Dorset labourers were sentenced to seven years of transportation to the penal colony in New South Wales for administering illegal oaths in a private house. But Ted had roused my curiosity. When he returned I said, 'Tell me, what could possibly cause serious concern in Seddon Union – apart from the fact that we need such a place in this day and age?'

He frowned and for a moment he looked uncomfortable. 'Look, Edgar, I'll be straight with you. You know as well as I there are great changes under way. Since the Reform Act many people are seeing opportunities for progress. Myself, I think it's been going on since the revolution in France but, as I've heard, you're a reader and follower of ideas and must know what current thinking is on these things. I don't give a fig for Shepherd and his ilk; I'd like to see their power diminished. It's all built on false premises of land, money and custom. There's nothing about Shepherd that shows any real personal integrity; his motives are self-seeking and I'd go so far as to say dubious. That's all I'll say.'

'Strong stuff, Ted!' I said, raising my eyebrows. Shepherd was clearly not a favourite with the farmer. 'But tell me how Jack Shepherd fits in to the workhouse system. I've never thought him a man likely to be interested in the poor.'

'He isn't, but chairman of the union guardians gives him a certain standing in the county. I'm sure that's why he canvassed for the job in the first place.'

'Like yourself?'

He smiled. 'I suppose you could say that, Edgar. But don't think me that much of a hypocrite; I want to investigate how the place is run, that's all. Shepherd gets on all the committees because he likes the sound of his own voice and, more than that, likes wielding power over others.'

I knew Shepherd as a boorish, self-satisfied man, who, as Ted pointed out, got himself installed on to every committee in the district, ran the Seddon hunt as if it was a military campaign and treated his servants and tenants with equal distain. He dined out on his war stories, but whether he'd really fought alongside Wellington (always using his sobriquet 'Nosy') no one had ever dared to challenge him publicly.

'I certainly don't think of you as a hypocrite, Ted. Far from it, you have a refreshing candour and I appreciate you being as open with me as you dare. But do you know exactly how Shepherd runs the place?'

'As I've been told, meetings are brief and decisions mostly go through on the nod. Shepherd has the thing nicely organised to suit his own arrangements, especially around his hunting and shooting schedule. He turns up and conducts a rapid meeting in the boardroom, talks briefly to the master who runs the place and leaves as soon as he can.'

'You could say he's being efficient with everyone's time. The guardians all have other things to do I'm sure.'

'But they have other things to do as guardians. I can't be sure, but I don't think anyone on the board has actually spoken to any of the inmates, although there's supposed to be a visiting committee that can report any of their complaints to the board. I've been told none of the committee asks questions, other than how much can be shaved off the running expenses to keep the rate down.'

'You seem to be hinting that the union is mismanaged and that it's down to Colonel Shepherd as chairman?'

'That's what I want to find out, Edgar. I want to ask questions no one else has the courage to. Some of the guardians are his employees or tenants. They're not going to be the grit in the oyster.'

'And you intend to be that? It sounds risky to me and hardly going to endear you to the likes of men such as Shepherd.'

'I'll manage it, Edgar,' he said, his mouth forming a hard, determined line.

In the course of the next half-hour and a few brandies I managed to squeeze out of Ted much more about the composition and politics of the Seddon guardians. The farmer was standing with a corn merchant of the same parish, Will Faulkner. Will had apparently been persuaded into it by Colonel Shepherd's land agent, George Stenning, who was himself a guardian. Both Ted and Faulkner were standing unopposed.

Lake became more voluble as his consumption of liquor increased. It was fortunate that we were in a secluded booth, mostly in shadow and well away from the crowded bar area. In a lull in the conversation I thought I might take the opportunity to draw it to a conclusion but in his impulsive way Ted surprised me. 'Edgar, would you consider using your position as JP to join the board?'

'That's unexpected, Ted!' I replied. 'I'm not sure what I think about the whole business of the union. I'll confess I've given it little mind. Reading the Poor Law it seems to me the whole thing is over-regulated; your hints at mismanagement seem unlikely.'

'Will you at least think about it?'

'Yes, I'll do you that courtesy, Ted.'

'That's all I ask.' Leaning back on his seat again he shook his head and said, 'Mark me, Edgar, if things don't alter there'll be trouble. The aristocracy – yourself excepted of course – the aristocracy can't continue to run things as though nothing's changing. Progress is coming whether they like it or not and the likes of Shepherd are going to get a shock.'

It was evident he was reaching that stage of steady drinking when the zenith of organised eloquence begins a rapid descent to the nadir of unstructured ramblings and I recognised it was definitely time to conclude. Fearing we were in dangerous territory I got to my feet and said, 'Well, Ted, what you've told me is very interesting and I hope we can talk some more. As I promised, I'll certainly give it serious thought.'

'I hope so; there's much more I have to tell you.' He grabbed my arms. 'I – we – need someone like you, someone of your standing to –' he faltered, at a loss for words at last.

I nodded, took up my hat and we pushed our way together through the crowd and out on to the street. He was swaying slightly as he walked towards his cart. I hoped his horses knew their way home unaided.

Riding home my head was filled with the conversation. I was as aware as my neighbours that there had been significant changes to the ways the problems of the poor were now addressed. Until this point I'd not troubled myself overmuch with the union's affairs, other than when the regulations might involve the local magistrates' bench. Like most rate payers I was content to contribute through my poor-rate and pay to let others manage arrangements for the destitute.

The new Poor Law Act had been in operation for four years and our local reconditioned union workhouse was up and running under the new regulations. As I had mentioned to Ted, as a JP I had been obliged to read the document from cover to cover. It was freely available for anyone to read but the majority of the poor of the parish on whom it had most impact were illiterate and for those who could read it was the most indigestible document: pages of obscure and difficult parliamentary legal text. What it boiled down to was that all the small local parish poorhouses were to be amalgamated into one large establishment. No union was to be placed outside a radius of more than ten miles from each parish, considered a day's reasonable walking distance. In essence the new unions were, as poorhouses had always been, voluntary institutions where those who had reached a point of destitution from which they saw no return could seek shelter and relief. Unlike any penal institution or mental asylum, the inmates were therefore equally free to leave.

There was no possibility of anyone being unaware of the existence of our new institution. Converted from a rather charming old country house whose owner had been made bankrupt ten years previously, it stood on the edge of Seddon. It had been purchased with monies raised from the closure of individual workhouses in the seven surrounding parishes, the building having been extended to meet the requirements of the 1834 act. Rationally speaking, its loathsome reputation probably exceeded its actual potential for misery. Those likely to be most affected combined a few facts with an ingenious mythology to designate 'the House', as they termed it, a place to be viewed with fear and abhorrence. It clearly suited those administering the Poor Law for workhouses to be viewed in such a way. After all, they were primarily intended as a deterrent to those regarded as 'the undeserving poor', those who were presumed to have intentionally avoided any kind of work. For my part I knew of no worker locally who would deliberately put himself out of employment with the expectation that he or his family should be fed, sheltered and clothed, effectively by his neighbours.

The encounter with Ted had set me thinking about those who live hand to mouth. Who were these people? How did it come to pass that they were forced to throw themselves on the charity of others? I say 'charity', but of course it was a tax on us all. I cast my mind back to what I'd read and been taught about the Poor Law. The rationale behind it went back centuries. In the days of Good Queen Bess there were so many vagrants, homeless and unemployed that they were perceived as a social menace. The Elizabethan authorities quickly apprehended the power and danger of suppressed anarchy. Mob violence has always been a bogeyman for any government and at that time, to draw its sting, strict rules of movement were instigated, ameliorated only by parish handouts – just enough to keep the belly active and the heart docile. Almost four hundred years later the government had decided to rationalise the system.

As a magistrate, I could be an unelected ex officio guardian with the same duties as those elected but with the additional power of right to visit at times outside the official meetings. It crossed my mind that Lake knew this and might be setting me up for this very purpose – someone who could visit at will. I remembered his enigmatic comment; I'd yet to discover what his 'other concerns' were, but I cast this thought to one side until such time as I could quiz him again.

I tried then to reflect honestly why I would want to take on this particular office. Without doubt I had a high standing with most in the district; as a landowner I rubbed shoulders on a fairly regular basis with fellow farmers and those of the middling sort. I also met the widest cross-section of the neighbourhood in my weekly court work, where I saw all kinds of scoundrels and petty criminals, many of whom had fallen on hard times and, desperate, had tried to take the criminal route out of their difficulties. There were also the natural-born rogues who couldn't help themselves and fell into any illegal ways of trying to make 'easy' money. These I might safely consign to prison or, if the crime was serious, send them to be tried at the assize court where they might be transported to the Antipodes, or hanged. But it wasn't the function of the magistrate to condemn someone to the workhouse; that was something people did for themselves out of desperation.

By the time I arrived home, had dinner and taken my usual brandy in the library I was seriously thinking I might take up Ted's request. It would be as much out of curiosity as anything else, but the man had hinted that all was not well at Seddon Union and I was intrigued enough to want to see for myself. Besides, the term of office would only be for a year and not more than twenty or so meetings. Surely this was nothing onerous for someone who had time on his hands. It took me the rest of the evening and a second brief perusal of the Poor Law Act to make up my mind and, not one to show irresolution, I penned a letter there and then to William Harbey, clerk to the union, offering my services. Some days later I received a written acceptance. I was scheduled to take up office in the second week of April.

In the interim I was curious to hear and gauge the attitude of the inimitable Jack Shepherd. Bracing myself for a tedious hour or two, I invited him to dinner with the express intention of quizzing him. Jack Shepherd was a man of local standing and a height to match; at the age of almost sixty he still had a military bearing. He liked a drink and the resultant venose mapping of his rubicund cheeks and nose was one of which a cartographer might be justly proud. His bellicose background was reflected in a voice that in musical terms was double forte. We met occasionally on the hunting field, but other than that our social interaction had been somewhat restricted. As a rule I didn't seek the company of those men for whom a battle is the be-all and end-all of existence. On this occasion I welcomed him with as much warmth as I could muster and we chatted over dinner. To begin with I deliberately steered the conversation towards the gossip and trivia of small-town life.

He may have been a first-class snob who tried to keep himself aloof from the common herd, but he was also sufficiently small-minded to speculate on the peccadilloes of his neighbours, which according to him ran from suspected adultery to vicious assault, to say nothing of egregious incidents of poaching that exercised him more than any of the other deadly rural sins. His parochial exposition continued throughout the meal until we moved into the library.

Pouring him a copious brandy I settled in my chair and immediately got down to the real business of the evening. 'Jack, before I take up the post of guardian, I'm keen to acquire as much knowledge of the working of the institution as I can. My practical knowledge is limited to what I've read in the Poor Law Act itself, which is so hedged about with legal niceties that I can't see the wood for the trees, so to speak; hence my recourse to you as chairman. You've had the supervision of the place since it first opened; I imagine you've a thorough understanding of how things are done. Are there any particular aspects I should be aware of from the start?'

'Harbey's told me you're joining us. I must say it'll be a pleasure to have someone of your standing and class on the board, someone who's sympathetic to the fact that we're all busy men with many responsibilities and often a shortage of time. I pride myself on keeping meetings short, to the point and with as few interventions as is possible.' He took a pull at his drink and leaned back with an air of smug satisfaction which grated on me. 'The workhouse runs itself. The master and matron have firm control of day-to-day issues and trouble us very little. We're quite small as boards go, which allows things to tick along nicely. I've got everyone to agree to fortnightly meetings as I consider that adequate to our size and scope.'

'So how are the meeting constituted? Are there specific items to be covered? What would my role be?'

He leaned forward and his mouth formed a smile that showed teeth yellow with age. 'It's not onerous, believe me. I do everything I can to discourage long-winded discussion. There are some on the board who like the sound of their own voices. A little power seems to go to their heads.' He tossed back my fine brandy as though it were the cheapest stirrup cup and continued. 'As ex officio you have the same responsibilities as the rest of us: setting the poor-rate; checking the finances are in order and that only those who are entitled to relief get it; and reporting on the state of the buildings. As I said, we have very little trouble with the arrangements.' Again he smiled bleakly, this time with his lips pressed together; the surface veins on his cheeks aggregated into a single mass of rosy pink, and with his slightly hooked nose it flashed across my mind that he bore a distinct resemblance to Mr Punch.

He sighed. 'To tell the truth, most of the rate payers care little as to how it's distributed. For them it's "out of sight, out of mind". The fact is they have to pay it but are content to let us on the board manage matters.' He relaxed back in his chair, confirming his casual approach. It was evident that he placed great emphasis on the efficiency of the master and matron who, as far as I could judge, had a free hand in the daily management. It was also clear that he wouldn't encourage too much questioning by members of the board.

Despite his insouciance he did appear to have a general understanding of how the institution worked, and I had no difficulty in picking up useful information on the current state of affairs. I asked him how many inmates the House accommodated. 'We have forty-seven in all,' he explained. 'Twelve men, fourteen women, nine boys and six girls between the ages of seven and fourteen, and six children under seven, including two babies.'

I was taken aback; the colonel's precise knowledge didn't square with his casual approach to running the institution as Ted had described it.

'I'm impressed with your accuracy, Jack.'

'Hmm, well, I like to know what I'm dealing with, Edgar; birds in coverts, hounds in kennels – you can't manage things unless you know the numbers. We have a slight problem with shortage of space and at present two boys are housed with the men. It's not normal procedure – they should sleep separately until they reach fifteen – but we have no choice. Children under seven sleep in the women's section.'

Over another brandy he steered the conversation back to local matters of parish politics and petty crime, in particular his perception of an increase in poaching and who were the likely villains. He stayed for a further thirty minutes, then, since I didn't offer him another drink, he stood up to take his leave.

'You'll pick it up in no time. There's nothing onerous about the office. Sometimes it's depressing when one considers how some people can't manage themselves, but we have to put that to one side and concentrate on doing the best for the rate payers – something we all feel strongly about.'

After he left I mused on the conversation, particularly his parting remark. If that was the board's priority, obviously guided by him, then it could be presumed the welfare of the inmates came a poor second. But until I had sight of what was the full nature of welfare and concern in the place, it wouldn't do to leap to judgement. What was certain was his vague and almost dismissive approach of the role of the guardians, but I also reflected that he was right about the lack of interest shown by the majority of the rate payers, myself included. We were guilty by default in our ambivalence towards the running of the union. It was a necessary evil for all concerned – those who supported it financially, and those who were supported by it against all their inclinations. Clearly the Poor Law with all its ramifications was universally divisive.

Chapter 2

On Monday, 16 April, after Easter Day and two days before the first meeting, an agenda was delivered by hand from the union clerk with a list of members of the board attached. Out of the fourteen guardians listed, six of us were novices. The rest had been members of the board since it was first constituted and I considered I knew half of them pretty well.

The comments are my own short assessments. Excluding myself:

Colonel Shepherd – landowner in his late fifties, ex-military, had been JP. Largest landowner in the area of Watfield, and hunt master for years. Generally not popular with any class – the workers on his estate find him tyrannical and he applies the game laws with an excess of zeal, which is bitterly resented by those who endeavour to supplement their meagre diet with the odd rabbit or partridge. Chairman.

Thomas Bennett – furniture maker in his thirties. Has a large workshop in the village of Brent Eleigh and employs at least eight men. Does well over a wide radius in a chair and table kind of way and turns out furniture of varying quality according to price. Is careful with his money and gossips speculate that this is how he can afford to live in a newly built and comfortably sized house on a prime piece of land on the outskirts of his village. Vice-chairman.

Thomas Lewis – butcher and shopkeeper in his late forties with property in Seddon town. Superficially a genial man. Colonel Shepherd is a good customer and Lewis is utilitarian. I imagine he would always toe the party line when it came to a vote.

Hugh Bradshaw – gentleman. Hugh is a well-respected widower in his early sixties and has a large, stylish residence in Hadleigh some six miles from mine. An avid bibliophile, he has an extensive and well-maintained library that he keeps stocked with an eclectic mix of literature. He is a Tory through and through, but of the old style – scrupulously honourable – and although our politics sometimes clash I am often invited to dine, especially when he needs to make up numbers. He lives with a less elderly sister, Deborah, who manages his house and most of his affairs with a firm hand. He is affable, but no fool.

George Stenning – estate manager. I know he is forty-four since it was revealed during a recent case I heard. Stenning is Shepherd's land agent. Along with the gamekeeper he is the scourge of local poachers, showing no mercy when he catches them – they are straight before me on Monday mornings. A man with little humour, but nonetheless sharp and clever and, I think, honest.

Robert Bignell – lawyer of Seddon who manages a substantial local practice. I imagine he is the youngest of us and could not be more than twenty-five. He has built up an impressive list of clients, mostly farmers and shopkeepers. I occasionally come across him at the magistrates' court, but he never deigns to defend the type of rogues that Stenning seeks to have prosecuted.

James Keen – general stores owner in Seddon. In his mid-fifties and someone else who appears to be running a very profitable concern. His premises have recently expanded into an empty cottage next to his shop. He purveys all manner of foodstuffs, household necessities and clothing to the whole community in and around Seddon.

John Newton – fiftyish, a cloth merchant. He deals in a wide variety of woollens and cottons and has the monopoly locally for supplying tailors, dressmakers and upholsterers, including Thomas Bennett. Operating from the village of Naughton, three miles from Seddon, he employs about nine or ten men and women. He lives above the shop, which in all is a large property. His landlord is Colonel Shepherd.

Ted Lake – successful farmer from Maiden Lindsey, well respected, good tenant, some education, politically aware and tending to radicalism, which is just about tolerated since up to now it has never actually come to anything. Well liked, but regarded as headstrong by the more staid in the community. Newly elected.

Will Faulkner – middle-aged corn merchant with a business based in Seddon; of 'good standing' but dull as ditchwater and with an obsession for everything frumentary. Indeed it is impossible to have a conversation with him unless it allows for a minute analysis of the state of the current corn market and a prediction of future disasters, both natural and economic. Lives in Wattisham, but I have had a discussion with him at the Seddon Corn Exchange. Newly elected.

Michael Jameson – shopkeeper and landlord of the Fleece Inn in Seddon town. Decent chap who runs a good alehouse. Not built like a typical mine host, rather attenuated and looks a little pinched. He has a reputation for parsimony and if he were a woman would be categorised as 'shrewish'. It is his wife Annie who fronts the business and provides the necessary cheer and welcome, the essence of a well-run tavern and shop. Newly elected.

James Edwards – innkeeper of indeterminate age; my guess is that he is younger than he looks. Keeps the Bay Horse in Cross Green and is said to be thriving in spite of competition from two other taverns in his village. Not well known to me. Newly elected.

William Marchant – tenant farmer in his late twenties with aspirations. He holds about a hundred and fifty acres

in the parish of Kersey. We have met on market days and
discussed agriculture. He inherited the farm from an uncle
who ran it down, but Marchant has done well with it
and earned a reputation for shrewdness and good business
sense. Shepherd is his landlord. Newly elected.

Also, **William Harbey** – clerk to the board and in his forties. He is another Seddon solicitor and doubles up as the
board's treasurer. A paid official, he is on £45 per annum
for his clerical duties, but as treasurer, according to the regulations, he is entitled to any profits 'left on his hands from
time to time', which is delightfully ambiguous. I come
across him occasionally in court and have never heard anything unfavourable about him or his practice.

The new board has met. I had determined that throughout this
account I wouldn't bore my reader with the minutiae of its protocols,
but rather endeavour to describe the atmosphere of meetings and the
interplay of its members. When a group of men of a certain style
and social connections meet in the capacity of decision-makers, with
complete power and control over those they consider inferior in every
way, they must clearly disclose many of their prejudices, especially
those which obviously colour their arguments and inform the way
they vote.

The meetings always took place in the workhouse itself in a
room set aside for the purpose. It was at least a three-mile drive from
my own property and since it was a drizzling April day I used my carriage. My coachman pulled up in front of a pair of large, plain iron
gates, with a lodge house on the left at the end of a solid eight-foot
wall, which I knew encircled the place. As I alighted I gave my driver
instructions to return for me in an hour, for Shepherd had estimated
the first meeting would take no more time than that. A large bell was
attached to the gate frame from which hung a rope. I pulled at it and
a few seconds passed before out of the lodge door bounded a lithe
young man of about twenty-five or so, of medium height and with a
mop of unruly brown curls. He wore a simple uniform of plain black

jacket and trousers. Arriving at the gate he peered at me through the ironwork.

'Open the gate, please. I am expected – Mr Lawes, one of the board of guardians. I'm here for the meeting.'

'Yes, sir. You would've been welcome to bring in your carriage and drive up to the entrance.'

'No matter; I'm minded to walk, but thank you all the same.'

'Just go straight up to the main doors and ring the bell. Most of the board have arrived already.'

'And you are?'

'Porter, sir.'

I nodded. 'Well, Mr Porter, I shall look forward to learning about your position here.'

'No, sir, I mean I'm the workhouse *porter*. My name is Lodge – Fred Lodge. It's a strange stroke that I found employment as a *lodge*-keeper – quite a coincidence you might say.' I waited in silence while he opened the lock with a large key. He pushed one of the gates open and it made a large arc outwards. As I walked through he immediately pulled it shut behind me and I heard the key turn again. Clearly there were stringent checks on ingress and egress, even for bona fide visitors such as myself.

I strolled up the well-weeded gravelled drive and my first impression was of a large, reasonably maintained and not unattractive building, which was three storeys high with a central front door over which was a rather fine pediment. Two substantial wings corresponding in height had been recently added on either side, each with their own separate entrances. There were a few small outbuildings and stabling next to the lodge house. As I arrived at the front entrance, before I could reach up to pull the bell, the door was opened by a man of singular dimensions; his girth seemed almost in proportion to his height, which must have been a little less than six feet. The consequence on his constitution of permanently bearing such weight was evident in the hue of his face, which flushed a dangerous puce after exertion, returning to a pallid grey as soon as he was at rest. His chest wheezed and his gasps became more pronounced as he spoke. He was dressed plainly in white shirt and neck-cloth, black coat, brown trousers and boots. He seemed courteous enough as he held out his hand.

'You would be Mr Lawes, sir?'

'Indeed. Good day to you Mr... ?'

'Calman – John Calman. I'm the master here. Let me take your hat. The rest of the board are gathered in the boardroom. I'll show you the way, just follow on.' We walked through the front lobby, which was decently furnished with a couple of upright chairs, and a mirror above a good oak occasional table where he deposited my hat and gloves. There were some pastoral prints on the wall and overall the impression was as one might expect of any average country house. We passed through a pair of doors that opened on to a large hall some thirty-feet long by about twenty wide, where the atmosphere and furnishings changed dramatically. I became conscious of lime-washed walls devoid of any decoration. An unpleasant smell of stale food hung about the place. I recognised immediately that the two wings of the House were strictly separated by this central area and anyone entering or leaving either side would do so by different entrances.

In spite of the reverberation of our boots on the wooden floor, I became conscious of an intense silence. For an institution that housed four or five staff and almost fifty inmates, among whom were young children, it was completely noiseless. The stillness of the place left me with an impression of abandonment, like a ship from which everyone had strangely disappeared. Stacks of folded wooden tables and benches rested against the walls, and there was an open fireplace at the further end. Although it was early April and the air was still spiced with the chill of winter, the grate was empty and unused. Two large sash widows at the end of the hall were clearly ill-fitted since there was a notable draught blowing across the whole area.

With scant time for any further observation I was ushered through the hall and into an ante-room at its far end. This was altogether different; evidently once a substantial dining room, it was wood-panelled and with a good coal fire burning in the grate. A long mahogany table was furnished with eighteen chairs, one each at the head and foot, eight on either side. There were two French doors at the south end that opened on to the gardens beyond. A small table with a chair in the corner held numerous books and neatly piled papers, along with a pen and an inkpot. I presumed this was for William Harbey, the clerk who would take the minutes. In the opposite corner was an occasional table on which had been placed a tray with glasses and a decanter of sherry. Next to the tray was a covered salver. Colonel Shepherd was standing with his considerable backside to the fire talking to three others; the rest stood about in small groups. Shepherd came across as I entered.

'Lawes, glad to see you! Last to arrive, but no matter.'

There was no handshake or further hint of social niceties. He turned to the others and signalled he was ready to start. Everyone took their place and the pecking order was interesting. With territorial imperative, the eight who'd been guardians previously went automatically to chairs they'd obviously occupied before. The newcomers, myself included, stood back until it became clear which seats were left vacant. The master, matron and relieving officer waited until all the guardians were seated, then took the remaining chairs. Shepherd sat at the top of the table. He cleared his throat to bring us to order.

'For the newcomers we generally start proceedings with a short prayer. Reverend Patchin—' He signalled to a youngish man, a slight, sallow-faced figure sitting at the end of the table in clerical garb and spectacles. We bowed our heads and he intoned a few appropriate requests to the Almighty that we might all prosper in our decisions. As I recall there was nothing specific asked for the inmates.

I'd already ascertained from Ted Lake that the agenda for every meeting was the same, and this was confirmed when I received my own copy. But for this first meeting of the new board it was necessary to elect a chairman and vice-chairman. Shepherd was unabashed in assuming his re-election should be a foregone conclusion. It was at this point that I took note of how the board was politically constituted. Of the fourteen of us present, eight had been guardians since the union was formed four years previously, five were newly elected and I was an ex officio member. This election was conducted swiftly with a simple show of hands. I glanced at Ted and could see his face was troubled; in fact, it was more like contained fury. I felt uncomfortable. I had no liking for Shepherd, but was cagey about making any kind of protest so soon in the proceedings. This was an impolitic time to be making challenges to the status quo, especially from a newcomer. When it came to the vote I'm ashamed to say it was unanimous. Even Ted, probably for the same reason but clearly reluctant, put up his hand. The previous vice-chairman, Thomas Bennett the furniture maker, was also returned unopposed.

Shepherd moved swiftly on to the business in hand. For the benefit of the new members he gave a brief résumé of the state of the workhouse: numbers and classifications of inmates and information about the union staff. After the minutes of the previous meeting had been read, briefly discussed and signed, we opened discussion on the second item, which was setting of the poor-rate. This too was taken at the gallop. Admittedly the rate was pegged according to the rules, taking into account the ability of local rate payers to pay, and the estimated needs of a budget to ensure the efficient running of the House. Shepherd argued that it was unnecessary to alter the rate in any way, as there had been little change during the year in either the taxpayers' means or the institution's requirements. Again he was unopposed; the committee assented through a series of grunts, taps on the table and nods of approval followed by a unanimous show of hands.

And so it went on: each item smoothly dismissed with as little effort as possible. Even discussion of the accounts was exiguous. The books had been audited and were presented by the clerk. It was simply a question of examining the final tally. Did income exceed expenditure? Of course it did. There was a general atmosphere of self-satisfaction as these well-presented figures, beautifully inscribed in the workhouse books, were passed quickly between us for examination. We then moved on to the master's report. Again, on the surface it seemed as though all was in order. As the books had been balanced so was Calman's report. According to him there had been no untoward events to disturb the peace of the House, and certainly no complaints from the inmates. The chief relieving officer Thomas Carrick, whose role was to collate all the requests for parish relief from the six other parish relieving officers and present them to the guardians – in effect a gatekeeper – reported that no officer had reported new requests for either outdoor-relief or admission over the previous fortnight. But, since the government had now suspended outdoor-relief for the able-bodied destitute, he expected there would be new candidates for entry to the House in the near future. The union surgeon had sent his apologies as he had been called away urgently on a case, so there was no report from him as to the state of the inmates' health. But the Reverend Patchin assured the board that the souls of the inmates were well nourished and that the short services every Sunday were attended by all as required. And that was that.

Shepherd was right. The whole meeting was completed in fifty-five minutes, just time to have a glass of sherry. Harbey did the honours and placed the trays on the table; we helped ourselves to a glass and a Bath Oliver. A few lingered to talk some more, but most of us walked out together through the main hall. As before, there was no sight or sound of any inmate. The oppressive soullessness of the place hit me and I began to feel how the institution would bear down on anyone condemned here for a substantial length of time. As we were filing through the main door Lake touched my arm.

'I'm going round the back to the stables to collect my nag. Then I'm off to the Fleece – can you join me?'

'I'll meet you there in half an hour.'

I had no hesitation in taking up the man's offer. There were many aspects of the last hour that I'd found disturbing and puzzling. I was interested to hear if his views matched my own. The lodge gates were open and my carriage was waiting on the road. There was no sign of the porter, although two small children were playing on a bit of garden. I presumed they were his own.

Arriving at the Fleece Annie Jameson was behind the bar and clearly her husband hadn't arrived back. She was all affability and poured me a brandy. The place was empty.

'I take it the meeting's over. Mick said he wouldn't be long. Colonel Shepherd told him it wouldn't take longer than an hour. One of the reasons my husband decided to stand was because it was unlikely to demand much of his time, and it's good for business. He'll have quite a standing in the town now he's a guardian.'

As Lake hadn't yet arrived, and not wishing to engage in small talk or to be questioned about the meeting, I moved over to a table by the front window. Some minutes later I saw the farmer on his grey trotting up the street. As he dismounted an ostler took the reins and disappeared with the horse into the tavern's stables. Lake entered and I rose to buy him a drink. 'Well, you were right in every particular,' I said when I returned.

Eagerly he asked, 'Well – first impressions. What did you make of the meeting?'

'It was as you said it would be: short, efficient, superficial. I began to wonder why we were bothering to attend.'

'Exactly! Look, Edgar, I'm not that well acquainted with you, but you've a reputation for fair play. It's one of the reasons I'm keen for you to get involved. I need someone objective to ascertain what's going on up there.' He looked around and seemed satisfied we wouldn't be overheard. 'But before we get down to exchanging views I'll fill you in with what I know.' Leaning forward conspiratorially, in a low voice he said, 'About four months ago Fred Lodge the porter came to see me; he'd been in the job since last May. He's the wife's nephew and I've known him all his life. An exceptionally sharp young man – nothing, as they say, gets past him – useful in a lodge-keeper! He told me he was concerned about several things. First, he'd picked up that the food the inmates are getting is really poor and, secondly, that some of them are often physically badly treated, the children in particular. He's uneasy about other aspects of the running of the House as well.'

'Hmm, are you sure this information can be trusted? Why didn't he go straight to Colonel Shepherd?'

'Certainly he can be trusted! I swear he's as straight as a die. Needless to say I questioned him closely. It was obvious that he has no trust in Jack Shepherd or any other member of the board. He came to me because we're close, hoping I could make it official somehow. I think he thought I'd even approach you as the local JP. But I realised that what was wanted was hard evidence of any wrongdoing, and how better to collect it than to become a board member myself? That's how I came to put myself up for election; there never was any self-interest. At the time I wasn't sure of your motives and whether I would be able to trust you. In all certainty everything I've seen this afternoon assures me that Fred wasn't exaggerating. There are things going on in that institution that are at least oppressive and may even be illegal.'

'What do you want to do about it? If you're right then it's a matter for the Justices. You say you need "hard evidence" but getting it will be difficult, if it exists at all. In my experience people who are wilfully committing acts of ill-treatment, or crimes of any sort, usually take great pains to cover their tracks. For example, if there's fiddling of records or accounts, you may be sure they'll be well hidden.'

'Not necessarily. Don't you see? The speed and superficiality of the meetings ensure no close scrutiny by the board of either; Colonel Shepherd has the thing as tight as a duck's arse. You must have noticed there's no time allowed for questioning. Now, either he's complicit in the wrongdoing, or his style of chairing meetings and his anxiety to be off and doing other things plays straight into the hands of the officials running the place. What's needed is a change of chairman. I was in a fury when he was voted in again unopposed.'

'Come, man! You could've opposed him yourself and at least stirred up a discussion.'

'I can't dispute it. But, as it was my first meeting, I didn't think it was wise for a newcomer to show his radical credentials too soon, so I had to bite my tongue and let it through – besides I've got a reputation as a bit of a firebrand!'

'Well – I'll admit – my behaviour was just as reprehensible; I felt the same way. My first impressions, as you asked me, were that the conduct of the meeting left much to be desired; it was certainly superficial, and insufficient time was given to the accounts. Calman's report on the inmates was uninformative and lacked any detail. Patchin's just a time-server.'

'Good – you agree. I judged you as a man of perception, but are you willing to embark on an investigation "to right the wrongs"? Or are you simply a man who reads enlightenment literature, nods approvingly while quoting it, then wrings his hands but won't get them dirty trying to bring those ideas into practical effect?'

I was stung by this, and my immediate reaction was to tell him to go to hell. I wasn't going to be bullied into actions that I suspected could be deemed as hare-brained and might recoil on us both. But he had a point and 'deeds not words' reverberated in my head. Ted Lake was undoubtedly a radical, whereas I was an intellectual, priding myself on a cool approach to problems using logic as a device with which to solve them. Lake saw wrongs to be righted as black-and-white issues that must be tackled through action not intellectual concepts. In this instance, however, he had generated some emotional response in me; his idealism was infectious and I found myself agreeing, not wholeheartedly, but in part converted to his cause. But I would wait and see what he proposed before I threw my hat fully into his ring. At that moment, before I could answer he flashed a warning look; I looked up to see one of the board members bearing down us. It is a weakness of mine that I can't remember names and, although we'd been introduced only an hour or so before, it quite escaped me who this was. Ted stood up and offered the spare seat.

'Good afternoon again, John! Take a seat.' The man was tall and well built, in his fifties and well dressed in a coach cape, with a tall beaver hat in one hand and a beer in the other. Affability was evident in his face, but on closer inspection his eyes were narrow and close together, which gave an after-impression of shiftiness. Half ashamed of making such an immediate judgement about someone of whom I knew nothing, I held out my hand. In order to ascertain his surname I re-introduced myself.

'Edgar Lawes, good afternoon.'

'John Newton. Ah yes, the local magistrate. Good to have you on board and on the board as it were. How did you find the meeting? I suppose the most important issue is the one we covered today, which is setting the local rate.' He certainly knew his priorities. 'Everyone wants to keep that down as much as possible and we do our best to leave it at the same level each year. We—'

I intervened, having no wish to hear a repeat of the mantra put out by Shepherd. 'What happens when prices rise and the cost of relief fluctuates – as it must, given the poor harvests and upheavals of the last decade or so?'

'Well – we look very carefully at costs and see how we can adjust them. The most important thing is to keep the rate as low as possible otherwise everyone will be up in arms. No one likes paying taxes.'

Ted swallowed the remainder of his drink and in his forthright manner said, 'Well, gentlemen, it's time I was off. See you both in a fortnight.'

With no wish to be left alone with the cloth merchant I gathered up my coat and downed my drink. 'I also should be elsewhere. Sorry to rush off so soon, Newton, but, as Mr Lake said, we'll meet again in a fortnight. Good day to you.'

I followed Ted out of the inn to find him standing by my carriage. 'Newton's Shepherd's man and supplies the inmates' clothes; he makes a pretty penny out of it, I'm sure. Just one of several who see an opportunity to line their pockets, but I can't prove it – yet. Can we talk again, before the next meeting and somewhere less public?' he asked.

'Look, Ted, I appreciate your concerns, but it's too early for me to make judgements about possible corruption and malpractice, which I think is what you're saying. Good God, man! We've only been to one meeting. I can see you're right about its cursory style; perhaps there are things that should be aired and examined more thoroughly. But maybe Shepherd does have a sense of what's going on and is satisfied to allow them to continue in a way that suits him. It doesn't mean there's anything necessarily untoward.'

'If I could assure you that my nephew Fred will furnish us with evidence that things aren't right, would you be prepared to help me do something about it?'

I hesitated. 'I can't make any commitments until I've really thought through all the possibilities. I'll compromise with you. Come and dine with me next week and I'll listen to what you have to say – but no promises. I've no wish to get into a fight with Shepherd, or the rest of the board unless there's a reason to do so.'

'Thanks. Send a note about a day and time – good day!' He turned abruptly towards the stabling at the rear of the inn. I climbed into my carriage and the driver flicked his whip.

Keeping my word, I invited Ted over the following Wednesday, exactly a week between meetings. In the same way that I'd approached Colonel Shepherd when he dined with me, I kept the conversation over dinner to local and wider issues. Although I trusted my servants to keep their mouths shut, I made it a rule not to talk about any confidential matters in front of them – mostly to preserve their integrity. I had no wish for servants to overhear any loose 'gossip' about the workhouse. The union was a source of apprehension for many of them as it was. Most labourers and domestic servants in the district knew of someone, either a family member or a neighbour, who'd been sufficiently down on their luck to have recourse to poor relief, or even a place in the House.

I sent for a bottle of brandy and we settled in the library after I'd dismissed my manservant Foster until it was time to lock up. I had been careful in controlling the amount of wine we'd drunk at dinner. I'd seen first hand Ted's dubious capacity for holding his drink and I was looking for a lucid account from him as to his campaign plan. We were both therefore comparatively sober.

'Now, Ted. You're certain about your nephew as an honest source of evidence?'

'He's spying things out for me.'

'I asked is he reliable.'

'He's right on the inside, knows how the place runs intimately, has access to some documents, and is willing to attempt to get hold of others. I have to trust you with this information, Edgar. You should know that he might be prosecuted – most certainly lose his job if he were found out.'

'Divulging information isn't a crime, unless he gets paid for it, but he clearly runs the risk of being turned out of his post. If you're so sure there's wrongdoing then of course I'd never divulge your source. But as I'm a magistrate you see my position. I would be condoning an employee to spy on his employer. Do you really want to encourage him to be acting so recklessly?'

'It was Fred who came to me in the first place. We discussed all the risks, but he wanted to go ahead anyway – simply because he felt it was the right thing to do. I trust him totally – I was the one who acted as surety for him when he answered the advertisement for the post. He, his wife Amy and his two young boys occupy the lodge – you would have met him on your way in. This is why it's important to keep his name out of it. If he's thrown out, then he'll never get another job with accommodation. Irony of ironies they could end up as inmates in Seddon Union – although of course our family would never let that happen.'

I was intrigued that this young man with a family, who had found himself a permanent post with good accommodation and prospects, would want to put it all at risk. Either he was a radical off-shoot of the Lake family or Ted in some way had manipulated or even bullied him into cooperating. The last I dismissed; radical and passionate he might be, but Ted was no tyrant. I determined that Fred was a rare case in our age of hard men, hard money and hard machines – a man with an acute and active conscience. How unusual it was that a simple workman, probably with little general education, although literate to a degree, should be exercised by the wrongdoing he was allegedly witnessing, to the point that he was prepared to expose himself to the ultimate risk of losing all he had achieved. I mentally chided myself for my condescension. Why wouldn't he want to oppose oppression? So I probed a little further.

'He's putting his position at risk and you've put up a bond as surety for his carrying out his duties. Surely, you're gambling that also.'

'As I said, it took him months before he decided to come to me, worried about the general running of the place and the treatment measured out to the inmates. When I first heard about it I could hardly believe it, misguidedly thinking the guardians are there to ensure the inmates are treated properly and the properties well maintained.' He leaned forward conspiratorially. 'Fred told me, apart from the board's monthly tour of the premises, that no inmate's seen individually by any member while they're in the building; no guardian actually interviews or even speaks to any of them; it's almost as though they're invisible. The monthly tour is preceded by a general sprucing up and the inmates appear clean and tidy, so they pass Shepherd's military inspection. The rooms and dormitories are sparsely furnished but clean, so there's nothing untoward as far as the board is concerned.'

'I've read the regulations. The guardians are supposed to set up a visiting committee so that inmates can have access to them to voice their concerns. There was no mention of it at the meeting.'

Seeing his glass was empty I replenished it sparingly and threw another log on the fire. The room, which had become gloomy in spite of the oil lamps, was immediately lit up again. I could see Fred's face had become even more animated.

'As we are such a small union, the colonel decided a specific committee was unnecessary and that the information supplied in the master's report would be sufficient.'

'So you are saying that there's been a breach because there is no such committee? As I understand it there's supposed to be a regular report from the guardians on the state of the inmates to be entered into a separate log.'

'Another one of Colonel Shepherd's shortcuts. He simply has the master's report copied out once a month into the visitors' book.'

We moved on to talk about the union's paid employees and Ted was able to help me compile a list of the eight officers currently employed, who was who and what he knew about each of them, adding some local gossip:

Master: John Calman. Responsible for the admission of paupers and overseeing all aspects of the running of the workhouse. About forty years of age. Previously a sergeant in the local rifle brigade. Not connected with Colonel Shepherd, although appointed by him – probably through the old-soldier network. His annual salary amounts to £35 and his wife receives an additional £10. They are provided with apartments, coal, candles and rations and live above the main building. They have no children. A regular in the Fleece and invariably drunk by the end of the evening. In spite of his size he is weak in the face of his wife's temper and always seeks to placate her.

Matron: Jenny Calman. Thirty-three years old. Responsible for the running of the women and children's quarters and all domestic matters. Becomes intemperate very quickly when any obstruction to the smooth running of the institution occurs. Has a very tight grip on the organisation of the inmates, particularly the women and children, who apparently fear her more than her spouse. In her youth was probably regarded as pretty. Always plainly dressed in black, relieved only by immaculately starched white cotton apron, collar and cuffs.

Overseer: Robert Enderby who is responsible for collecting payments of the poor-rate. The brother of Jenny Calman, he also stands in for the master when John Calman is elsewhere. He is paid £25 a year and lives in town. A drinking companion of his brother-in-law, he is doted on by his sister. At thirty-plus he is still unmarried but with a reputation as a philanderer. Heavy drinking has ravaged what were once handsome features, but he still manages to attract some of the more dubious types of women in the town.

District Medical Officer: Matthew Burgwin is a new-comer to the district, in his early twenties and newly qual-ified from London. He has an annual salary of £35 and is responsible not only for the inmates but also treats the poor within the union district with the authority of the board. That is not to say that he is prohibited from enhancing his salary by treating elsewhere, even though his is a full-time appointment. His youth, good breeding and sympathetic looks have made him a popular bachelor in the district, par-ticularly with the mothers of daughters with marriage in mind. Lake considers him 'an innocent abroad', in spite of his metropolitan roots.

Chaplain: Reverend Peter Patchin who preaches a ser-mon to the inmates every Sunday and on holy days throughout the year. He is also supposed to catechise the children once a month and reports at the meetings of the guardians on the moral and religious state of the inmates. A dour, short-sighted man in his late twenties and unmarried, he is steeped in Church of England dogma. Because he has a reputation for long-windedness and repetitive moralising it is said he recently failed to obtain a lucrative living that had become available in a local parish. He is permanently on the lookout for a living of his own. As official chap-lain for the workhouse he is entitled to sit on the board; he also receives an annual salary of £25 in return for religious duties comparable with those of a parish clergyman.

Porter: Fred Lodge. Young man in his mid-twenties, married with two children. The post requires him to be lit-erate and to keep accounts and he is paid an annual salary of £12, plus a new suit of clothes once a year. He has been porter and lodge-keeper since 1 May last year and, as Ted Lake suggests, is not happy with what he is discovering. I can only take Ted's word that he is to be relied upon, but until he proves me wrong I will suspend my disbelief that he is prepared to risk all by exposing any wrongdoing he is aware of.

Assistant Matron: Amy Lodge. Wife of Fred, she holds the position of nurse for which she receives £7 a year. She deputises as matron when Jenny Calman is absent from the workhouse. Mrs Lodge shares her husband's concerns about the treatment of the inmates, especially the women and children, and does her best to ease their suffering with little acts of kindness, which are very much appreciated by the recipients. She has had a very good basic education and notably writes in a beautiful hand.

Chief Relieving Officer: Thomas Carrick is the highest paid officer at £85 a year. One of seven parish relieving officers he is the link between them and the board. These are powerful men who are authorised to deny outdoor-relief or admission to the House. All those in need must apply to their RO whose responsibility it is to check their qualification for admission; Carrick collates all the requests and presents them to the guardians. It is on his advice at each of their meetings that they approve or deny the application. A man in his middle years, Carrick lives in Kettlebaston, three miles from the workhouse, where he has a small holding of land that he works with his two sons. He appears to have a fair reputation, although he is looked upon with some apprehension by those in his neighbourhood, who for obvious reasons are not anxious to make his official acquaintance.

Before the lights dimmed any further I rang the bell and asked Foster to bring in more lamps. Fully relaxed by the cheerful aspect of the library, plus the effect of the brandy working its way to his tongue,

Ted was keen to elaborate with extra chit-chat about some of the officers. But I was anxious to pursue something else that had been playing on my mind. Ted's apparent radicalism had come from somewhere, but his background as a yeoman farmer didn't strike me as particularly fertile ground for many of the ideas he was expressing. Obviously comfortable in one of my armchairs and very willing to talk, I thought this might be a good time to find out a little more about him. So, firstly, I asked about his education.

'My mother taught me to read. One of my earliest memories is of sitting by her side in front of the kitchen range listening to her stories and songs. As I grew older she taught me my letters using the Bible and a battered old copy of Foxe's *Martyrs*; gruesome but gripping, she made the stories intelligible to me. I was a fast learner and by the age of nine could read fluently.' He sipped at his drink and half smiled to himself. 'Both parents encouraged me to take notice of what was going on in the wider world by reading copies of the weekly broadsheets, which came via the mail coach and were posted up in inns and taverns for all to read. By about the age of ten, as soon as I was fluent and understood everything in the weeklies, I made myself a regular purse of money by reading out news reports to those who had no such skills – charging a penny an article; I was much in demand. Keeping up with current news and events is a habit I've continued. I know you're a man who likes his philosophers, but I follow interpreters of events and those who are trying to make change through actions.' He paused as though recollecting. 'There's one particular journalist whose writing I really admire, Ambrose Hudson. I call him a "crusader". He's exposed incidents of bad employment practices, particularly in the textile factories up north where working conditions for women and children are dire and mostly illegal. I first came across him when my father showed me a report Hudson had posted of Henry Hunt's speech in 1819 in St Peter's Field, Manchester, and the events afterwards.'

'There'll be few people who don't know of that.'

'I know Hudson's now in his middle thirties, so that must have been when he was just starting out as a very young journalist. I think it was his first piece. You may remember reading about it?'

'I was nine at the time, but my father told me of it later. As far as I know some fifty thousand people gathered in St Peter's simply to hear Hunt speak and to demonstrate for parliamentary reform.'

'The problem was they were carrying banners with revolutionary slogans, although there was no disorder until the magistrates lost their nerve and ordered the militia to arrest Hunt. When the crowd tried to stop the soldiers from reaching him, the Hussars drew their sabres and eleven people were killed in the panic.'

'I've read about it subsequently. They called it the Peterloo Massacre. But was it worth eleven lives?'

'Well, according to Hudson, who was present and witnessed everything, the crush to hear Hunt was a factor in the number of deaths, but the blame lay squarely with the Hussars who should never have drawn their swords. I remember he wrote that the overriding emotion that day was fear. Fear of the soldiers by the crowd, fear of the crowd by the soldiers and the authorities.'

'But surely this is what happens when men mobilise spontaneously – order must be restored otherwise, as in this case, people are maimed and even killed.'

'No one set out for it to happen. But we must have the right to express ourselves, whatever the outcome. "Orator" Hunt – now there was a man who was never frightened to speak for the people. Did you know it's only three years since he died?'

'I think I read he died in his bed. Sixty-two's not such a bad age.'

'He's a great loss – we need people like him who can speak plainly to the people and aren't afraid to press for change. That's why I admire Hudson. He goes to places others are nervous about investigating because they don't know what they might find. People like him try to prick the national conscience.'

I admit I was surprised by Ted's stance. It was evident he'd been brought up to question the status quo. He was on the fringes of a growing movement that sought to challenge habitual conventions and opinions in a very practical way.

We continued agreeing and disagreeing over current events, politics and ideas for at least an hour until it was so late I felt obliged to get one of the stable hands to drive him home in the dog cart, leaving his horse overnight in the stables to be collected the next day.

After Ted left I sat for a while and considered our discussion and my next move. It seemed that I should make every endeavour to gain access to the inmates. I had the right to demand entry to the workhouse, something denied to the other guardians who legally could only be invited in by the master. The problem was how to achieve such access without putting Shepherd's nose out of joint. He clearly had a very territorial attitude towards the supervision of the House, and would be unlikely to stomach any untoward interference, whether or not it was legally enforceable. I decided to bring the matter up at the next meeting and to request a tour of the building and casual conversation with some of the inmates, 'in order to acquaint myself fully with the mechanisms of supervision'. I would compromise by suggesting that the master or matron accompany me and choose those to whom I should speak. Although I wouldn't be free to roam or engage with any inmate privately, I could at least gauge the ethos of the place and, from the very choices made by the master, could indirectly ascertain more about the inmates he ignored than those he selected. In terms of Fred Lodge, I decided to leave him to Ted. I had no wish to increase any risk to the man or his family and judged that the time wasn't yet right to involve him in any practical investigation of my own. That needed to be planned carefully and with Ted's total involvement. Reining in my thoughts at this point, I reminded myself that we'd no evidence of any wrongdoing. All that had transpired was a too-brief meeting, and lack of scrutiny of the substance. Ted had given me pen-portraits of the main protagonists, but in terms of their personas, his assessments were entirely subjective, much of it based on local tittle-tattle. The demand for hard evidence was clear. The next meeting was in seven days and I needed to keep a cool head to prepare for it.

Chapter 3

Succumbing to custom and occupying the same seat as at the first meeting, I found my place at the table, near the bottom with George Stenning on my right and Hugh Bradshaw to my left. Shepherd and the clerk ran through the usual agenda. When we reached the fourth item I waited until Calman had delivered his report then made my move.

'Point of order, Mr Chairman!' I saw a flicker of annoyance cross the colonel's face. He sat back in his chair. 'You have our ear, Mr Lawes.'

'As a newcomer, I'm very keen to get to know the workings of the place, its buildings, meet some of the inmates – see how things work generally.' I left it vague, casting my fly casually but expecting a bite.

He frowned. 'Well, as you know we're due to have our monthly visit in two weeks – that would be an excellent opportunity for you to see how it all works. We think it's better for the smooth running of the House that there aren't too many intrusions. It can be disruptive for the officers to have streams of visitors arriving unannounced.'

I seized my chance. 'I had no intention of simply turning up unannounced. I thought I could make an arrangement with the master today to make a visit entirely at his convenience – when he would have time to escort me round the building. I'd also be happy if he selected any of the inmates who he thought would be willing to talk to me – in his presence.' Shepherd shot a questioning glance at Calman. It was difficult to read the response in the master's face since his fatty jowls obscured his eyes and I was left with the overall impression of a face like a grey steamed pudding that gave no indication of its contents. Some of the board were clearly taken aback by my suggestion; Ted Lake tried to catch my eye, but I deliberately avoided his – I had no wish to involve him. I knew he would volunteer to accompany me if I gave him any encouragement, but this was a visit I wanted to make entirely on my own. I was, in military terms, seeking to reconnoitre the lie of the land prior to engagement.

There was a brief pause before Calman turned to the chairman and wheezed, 'I see no reason why Mr Lawes shouldn't visit us, sir, if it's within the terms he suggests. Since he's a Justice, under the regulations I can't deny him entry and neither would I wish to. The most convenient day and time for me would be next Monday, sir, ten days before the official board visit. If you could make it by eleven o'clock, my wife and I will be doing one of our daily rounds of the building, so that will be no inconvenience to us at all.' Unfortunately Monday morning was inconvenient for me because of my responsibilities in the magistrates' court. I suggested that the afternoon would be acceptable, and we agreed I would visit at three o'clock.

I don't know why I was surprised at the ease with which my request was accepted. Calman was right; he couldn't deny a JP entry. Shepherd signalled to the clerk to enter details of the arrangements in the minutes. He moved on swiftly to the relieving officer's report and, with his customary brevity, the rest of the agenda. The most interesting aspect of the meeting was who left with whom at the end. I noted that Colonel Shepherd and Calman remained behind with their heads together, presumably assessing my intervention. Just before I rose to leave, Hugh Bradshaw put his hand on my arm.

'Edgar – have you come across the writer Charles Dickens?'

'No – can't say I've heard of him. What's his area?'

'He's a novelist – writes stories.'

'Not really my sphere of interest.' I tried not to sound disdainful. 'I leave novels to the ladies. Jane Austen and all that – too sentimental for my taste.'

'No, no, no! He's quite different to Austen, although I'll take issue with you there – she's not sentimental at all, very sharp in fact. You shouldn't be so dismissive! But to the point: my nephew Frank put me on to Mr Dickens, who has his stories published in monthly instalments in *Bentley's Miscellany*; a clever sales technique that will make him plenty of money, I think. Dickens's background is journalism, so his stories are backed up by his own observations and experience. Knowing I was involved with the union, Frank thought I'd be particularly interested in his current story, *Oliver Twist*. It's all about workhouses – very harrowing and thought-provoking. I've got all the back editions at home; I'll send them over if you like. In my opinion it's a damned good read and gets into the guts of what being destitute means.'

Not wishing to seem impolite, but inwardly groaning at the thought of spending time on mawkish – and probably badly written – works, I agreed to have a look at them. Hugh was an eclectic reader and I had no way of knowing what he considered 'a good read'. He said he'd arrange for his man to bring them over.

We caught up with the rest at the front entrance where James Edwards and Michael Jameson had stopped to have a word, presumably in connection with their shared business interests as innkeepers. William Faulkner was trying to engage Thomas Bennett in conversation, but the latter seemed anxious to be off and was soon out of sight down the drive. A couple of newly elected members took time to address me; one asked if he might join me on my visit, but I was able to persuade him firmly but politely that this was an ex officio visit and not open to anyone else. Ted was clearly anxious to talk, but I'd other things to do at home and I wasn't going to be drawn into a conversation that would surely result in him giving me unwanted strategic advice. Trying to keep this enterprise official, I told him I'd make a full report to the board.

Just before three o'clock on the following Monday afternoon, I duly presented myself at the workhouse. The master was already waiting for me at the main door. Behind him stood his wife, Jenny, and my first impression was of an oval face with even features and large, brown eyes. At one time I'm sure she'd been considered pretty, as Ted Lake had observed, but close scrutiny revealed hardness within those eyes, and a mouth that was compressed and unsmiling. She was of average height, verging on the thin, and dressed in black, apart from white collar and cuffs and a close-fitting cap that completely covered her hair. There was a tension about her, as if she was on permanent alert for aggravation. I understood how she had come to dominate her fat, lazy husband, whose original military mien had obviously been diluted by years of post-martial over-indulgence. It was an open question which tendency had provoked which – his slide into physical decline or her embrace of waspishness. They greeted me politely and, as had been agreed, they were both to accompany me on my tour.

The master explained the routine. 'We're obliged to do two tours of the workhouse every day, one at eleven in the morning and the other before nine at night in the winter and ten in the summer. The first is to check the cleanliness of the wards where the inmates sleep, the second to ensure they're all in bed and that the fires and candles are all out. My wife superintends the female side, and I look after the men's accommodation.'

Mrs Calman looked particularly sour and said, 'We have, of course, completed our rounds this morning. This inspection is over and above what we are normally required to do.' She pressed her thin lips even further together in obvious disapproval of my intrusion.

We didn't enter via the main lobby; instead Calman marshalled me round the side of the building to a main door in the left wing. From the small lobby inside the door there were stairs leading off to the left. We ascended to a small landing with a door into the male dormitory, which had floors of rough wooden planking and lime-washed walls like the hall. I counted sixteen wooden bedsteads arranged in two rows of eight on each side, with about two and a half feet between them. I knew there were twelve men and two boys accommodated here so there was clearly space for two more admissions. My first impression was of the starkness of the room; since there was no furniture other than the beds, there was nothing to cause disorder. I was also immediately struck by the rank smell of urine. I could see that the mattresses on the beds were actually palliasses filled with straw, and my first question was how often they were changed.

'One of the young boys and a few of the older men are chronic bed-wetters,' said Calman. 'In autumn, after the harvest, we have a good supply of straw, but by this time of year our stocks have run out, apart from what we need for bedding for the animals. If mattresses are soiled, the inmates have to lay the straw out to dry before packing it back and reusing it.' I noticed some remnants of straw around two of the beds.

'Has there been no move to provide flock mattresses with some kind of protection?'

His wife intervened. In a clipped voice she said, 'Wool mattresses would be very expensive, sir – a significant outlay to start with and no guarantee that they would not be equally misused.'

We walked through the dormitory, which had a fireplace with an empty grate. The windows on the left side were all barred and with open shutters. Six double-candle sconces were placed evenly round the room, which, by my estimation, would provide a meagre light for its size. The whole dormitory was depressing in its functionary orderliness. It was simply a place for the men to be horizontal for ten hours; certainly sleep would be difficult. I was reminded of my boarding-school days. I knew the problems of sharing a large dormitory, but at least we had sufficient light to see by, and our beds had reasonable space between them and were fitted out with decent mattresses and warm bedding. Here there were just two neatly folded blankets at the bottom of each bed, all ready for inspection. We moved to the end of the room, where I could see a further set of stairs that obviously led above the dormitory. But the master turned to leave via our original entrance. I indicated the staircase. 'Where does that lead?'

'Storerooms, sir. They run the length of the dormitory. The board had once considered using them as dormitories for the boys, but it was decided to divide the equivalent space on the female side rather than go to the expense of opening up a whole new ward. We house a few large items of furniture there. Shall we move on to the work-rooms downstairs?' I was most anxious to meet the inmates and saw no real benefit in investigating surplus tables and chairs – they could wait for another time. But I thought perhaps the board should find a more productive used for the roof space some time in the future.

We returned to the ground floor and entered the workroom: a large rectangular area that corresponded exactly in proportion with the dormitory above, again with a wooden floor and limed walls. But here there was at least a small fire that was burning wood, and a store of logs was piled up in a corner of the inglenook. Again, my immediate impression was of the smell. The room was reasonably warm and an odour of stale clothing and bodies pervaded the atmosphere. A haze of dust hung in the air along with a stranger smell; it was soon clear where it came from. As we entered, men and boys rose to their feet from the forms arranged around the sides of the room. As they did so bundles of rope that they had been unpicking into individual strands fell to the floor. By the side of each man was a straw bushel basket, into which they were dropping the dusty fibres. Jenny Calman read my raised eyebrows. 'Oakum picking, sir. The shipping companies send us their old hemp rope and the inmates unpick it. We sell the bits back to the companies and they mix it with tar. It's used to seal the linings of ships – I believe they call it caulking.' I signalled to the men to sit down.

'Is this their only occupation?' I asked.

'It's all that's available to us. Some unions go for stone-breaking, but there are no quarries around here. Oakum picking is all we have – apart from domestic and outside work. The inmates are never unemployed.'

'It seems a very repetitive, unstimulating kind of activity.'

'The inmates are not here to be entertained,' she said crisply. 'Remember, sir, the workhouse is here as a deterrent to the would-be idle. The commissioners have laid down that the purpose of these institutions is to provide the minimum of subsistence and to encourage those who might decide not to work when they are well able to think again. Rate payers like you, sir, expect a fair return on their taxes. The cash from oakum picking goes back into feeding and housing the inmates and helps reduce the rate, or at least keep it down.'

The men were rhythmically untangling, picking and pulling at the pieces of rope, seemingly oblivious to their audience. It appeared as though even in the most stultifying tasks we humans could make an ordered approach to production. It reminded me of the working arrangements in the new textile factories, where machines now controlled the rate of work. In this setting these men had found their own mechanical pulse.

I felt sure that the Calmans were trying to guide me on and I thought it time to remind them I had also come to talk to some of the inmates. I was immediately aware of a young boy, about twelve or thirteen years of age, sitting at the end of the bench. He was fully aware of me and as I looked at him I saw a pair of angry grey eyes returning my gaze defensively. I stood in front of him and the master immediately was at my side. 'How old is this boy?' I asked him.

'Fourteen, sir.'

I turned back to the boy. 'My name is Mr Lawes – and yours is?'

'Samuels, sir – Peter. I'm thirteen, sir.'

Mr Calman intervened. 'I'm not sure you would want to speak

to this boy, sir. Samuels is very refractory. He's just had twenty-four hours in isolation for lying and swearing at the overseer.'

Samuels went red in the face. 'I didn't lie.' He almost spat it out.

Calman turned to me again. 'Oh, he did, sir! Mr Enderby said he called him a bastard – begging your pardon, sir – and I'd prefer to take the word of the overseer against a little liar like this.'

'I didn't call him a "bastard",' shouted the boy in frustration. 'I called him a fucking bastard.' There was a sharp gasp from the matron, who flushed with anger and looked shocked. The master took a step forward and seemed prepared to take his rod to the boy there and then.

I restrained his arm. 'Why did you call him that?' I asked Samuels.

'Because he clouted me round the head for nothing; just came into the workroom and hit me. When I asked him why he done it, he said "because he could" and I was "looking insolent". I lost my temper and called him – those names,' he ended lamely.

The master became defensive and hastened to shut the boy up. 'Yes! Yes! We know what you said, and you were correctly punished for it. It says in the rules – which if you could read you'd know about – that anyone over twelve using obscene language and especially to an officer is to be punished by confinement in a dark room and given bread and water.'

'But,' I protested, 'you said the boy is only fourteen – although he disagrees. Whatever age he is it seems a harsh punishment for one so young.'

'Thirteen or fourteen – according to the rules he's old enough.' Calman looked triumphant and self-satisfied, knowing he was on absolutely safe ground, backed by the power and written authority of the Poor Law commissioners themselves.

As we were speaking I noticed that one of the men raised his head from his unpicking and appeared to be listening intently. Although he was sitting down, I judged him to be of well above average height, possibly in his late thirties. There was something in his face that induced me to level my eyes to his. They were clear and brown, responding to my challenge with one of their own. Behind them was intelligence and a judgemental awareness of my presence – I was being appraised as I was scrutinising. 'We agreed that you would select someone who would talk to me – perhaps it would be convenient now?' I approach my assessor. 'Good day, I'm Mr Edgar Lawes, newly appointed to the board of guardians. You are… ?'

He stood up and faced me. 'Henry Millhouses, sir.' He continued to look me in the eye, but any further conversation was cut short as Mrs Calman stepped forward and firmly intervened.

'We thought that Jacob Fearnley would be most appropriate, sir. He's been here for four years and knows the place. He's not perhaps the brightest of men, but should be able to talk about our routines and daily activities.' Jacob Fearnley looked up at the sound of his name. A short, swarthy man, with a pock-marked face, probably in his late fifties, he was sitting at the end of a row of six men. As I approached him he stood up and a pile of rope and oakum fell off his lap. He was clearly nervous and I tried to put him at his ease by helping him pick up a few of the greasy pieces.

'I'm Mr Lawes, Jacob – one of the guardians.' If he'd been wearing a cap, he would have doffed it. Instead he put his knuckle to his head as if in salute. I wondered if he'd once been a sailor.

'Sir?'

'Tell me – do you remember when you first came here?'

'Not rightly, sir.'

'Matron says you've been here four years, in fact, since the House opened.'

'Well, sir, if that's what she says it must be right. Time passes and every day's the same. I think that's a good thing – keeps you safe.'

'Do you think you'll ever leave?'

'Leave, sir? Don't know, sir.'

'Can you remember why you came here?'

He frowned as he recollected. 'I remember I was working in a smithy until I'd nowhere to go. I was told to come here and that's all I remember.' I was about to ask him if he was happy, but realised in time how fatuous that would be. Instead I enquired whether he was comfortable – another very middling sort of question, but I couldn't think of another. He considered for a minute then said slowly, 'Comfortable? Yes, I would say so. I've food to eat and a bed to sleep in. I don't have to worry where they come from; they're always there.' I wanted him to tell me how he was treated by the officers, but with

Calman and his wife within earshot I had no opportunity. Instead I asked him an open question, hoping he might let something interesting slip. 'What do you like about being here?'

'As I say, sir, we're looked after. The master makes sure we have all we need. We get breakfast, dinner and supper – which, as he says, is more than most people get outside. They give us our clothes too, sir.' I looked at his garments, which were all grey – shirt, jacket and trousers of thin, poor-quality cotton.

'What about this oakum picking – don't you find it tedious?' For the first time he looked thoroughly bewildered and I realised that the concept of tedium was probably unknown to him. 'I mean, isn't it too much of the same thing?' I still didn't think he understood me.

'The work's good. We're indoors in the dry.'

I chanced my luck: 'And the bad things?' Jenny Calman's head jerked up like a sentry-goose.

'Can't think of anything, sir. What else would a man want than what we're given? I've no complaints.'

In anticipation of further awkward questions, the matron signalled to Fearnley that the interview was over. He went back to his seat and his relentless picking. She drew me aside.

'He's typical of the inmates here. You see the problem, sir – he's become used to this way of life and because of that he's now unsuited to life outside. He'll remain a drain on the rate payers until he dies here,' she said with a sniff. 'That's the weakness of the workhouse system.'

'Well, thank you for letting me talk to him. He doesn't seem to have any complaints. I shall be interested to talk to the female inmates.'

'Unfortunately we won't have the time this afternoon, sir. If you want to see the rest of the building, any other interviews will have to be done another day. After we've visited the female ward I have to supervise the workers in the kitchen who are preparing the evening meal. It's not convenient for you to inspect the domestic arrangements now, sir, because it would be a distraction. Perhaps you could satisfy yourself as to conditions in the kitchen during the monthly visit by all the board next week.' I caught what I recognised as defiance, covert but just about perceptible. However, her face betrayed no emotion other than empty politeness. I knew she was wary of me and I wondered whether she realised my motives were more than curiosity but hadn't yet worked out my intentions. One thing was sure, I wouldn't underestimate her; even at this stage of our acquaintance I appreciated that she had a particular variety of cunning.

In order to reach the female accommodation it was necessary for us to return to the front door and walk round to the opposite side of the building. I was propelled forward into the capricious April air round to a corresponding door, which led to an identical layout. The dormitories here contained twenty-four beds, eight of which were small cots for the children. There was an absence of any touches of comfortable domesticity: no womanly touches such as ornaments or pictures, certainly no evidence that young children slept here. It was unremittingly bleak. We went through to the top floor where the older children were accommodated. Again there was the acrid smell of stale urine from a single bucket at the end of the dormitory for the children to use in the night. The long low-ceilinged room was partitioned by a thin plaster wall with a connecting door to provide separate dormitories for girls and boys. There were seven beds in each, with blankets neatly folded at the foot of each mattress. There was no fireplace here – possibly a blessing since any conflagration would have been fatal for everyone as there was only one exit down the stairs we had entered by. As in the adult accommodation there was just a bed for each child, with a small space between it and its neighbour. Walking back down the two flights of stairs to the ground floor I mused that the starkness of these living quarters was a reminder that the workhouse system allowed no softening or sentiment, even for young children who were innocent of any responsibility for their families' situation.

Although I wasn't to be granted an interview with any of the women I was anxious to see the conditions in which they worked. Like the men, all the women and children were dressed in grey cotton garments with thin boots and occupied with the same task. The only difference here was that some had their young children with them. As an unmarried man without nephews and nieces nearby I had little contact with small children and found it difficult to assess their ages. A couple of them, who might have been four or five, were putting the shredded oakum into baskets. Two little ones, barely on their feet, tottered among the piles of hemp rope; one grasped a handful of stray oakum, which it automatically put to its mouth. Restrained by its mother with a resounding slap on the hand, it wailed out and sat down plumb in the middle of a pile of fibres. Its face turned red with frustration and the tears pouring down its cheeks, coupled with the mucus from its runny nose, were mixed with dusty fibres that clung to its face and hands, streaking them with a grey backwash – like a water-colourist's preparation for a wintery scene. The woman took the child in her arms to soothe it – partly from motherly concern, but also in response to the matron's gesture that the child should be controlled.

My recollection of the regulations was that children under the age of three could stay permanently with their mothers, but those between three and seven should be placed in a nursery during the working day with one of the female inmates entirely separate from their parents. It seemed that here there were no special arrangements for these young children, but that they were actually employed in oakum picking alongside the women. I resolved to investigate the rules and not only about where they should be during the day. I was sure they should be having some kind of schooling.

Anxious to hurry me away, Mr Calman moved to the door at the rear of the room, which led to the domestic area at the back of the building. We walked through the kitchen, which was occupied by five women preparing supper. A brief scrutiny as I passed through revealed that some kind of soup was on the menu today. I remembered what Fred Lodge had told Ted about the poor quality of the food. Quantities of what looked like oatmeal were being poured into a large vat of water suspended over a range. A good-looking woman of large stature, whose name I later discovered was Rosa Hines, was peeling and chopping potatoes, which she threw into the mix. What most struck me was the silence. Experience of my own kitchens, although occasional, was that they were welcoming places where the cook, kitchen and scullery maids chatted and gossiped easily together. Here, apart from the noise of utensils, chopping and pouring, there was silence: no conversation or talking of any kind as one might expect between women in that warm environment. Whether this was the rule of the workhouse, or whether these women were just silent from the sheer misery of their condition, I didn't know. Perhaps they were simply intimidated by the Calmans. I stood awkwardly at the entrance and couldn't bring myself to break the silence, being unsure of what the consequences might be. We left through the scullery and were immediately outside in a covered yard. Beyond this paved area was housing for animals, most likely pigs. Further afield was about two acres of garden, which ended at the perimeter wall, where I could just about see some young boys hoeing a vegetable patch.

The matron walked me round to the front of the main building. It was almost as though, relieved that I was leaving, she recognised she might have been too frosty with me and in an effort to redeem herself smiled with closed lips – her thin mouth grimacing, giving the appearance of a new moon that had slipped its moorings and found itself surprisingly horizontal.

'I hope you've seen enough, sir. If you missed anything, I'm sure you'll be able to make up for it at the board's own visit.'

I made a corresponding effort at politeness. 'Thank you for your time; it has been interesting – and informative.' She watched me as I walked round to the stabling at the back of the lodge house. The weather being dry but cool I'd ridden over, partly for the exercise and also because I didn't want my coachman to be waiting around since I'd no idea how long my visit would be. I had plenty to think about as I rode home and plenty of research still to do.

There was a tray full of correspondence waiting for me when I returned to Seddon Hall. Alongside it was a large parcel, which I presumed correctly had come from Hugh Bradshaw. True to his word he had immediately sent over a dozen back-copies of *Bentley's Miscellany* with a note to say he would send the rest in instalments after he had read them himself. Ted Lake had sent a note asking to see me 'urgently' and there was a report from Sam Saunby, my bailiff, which I made my priority. As I explained, he ran the estate so efficiently and with such extensive and historic knowledge that I could safely leave him to it. His report was fairly standard, but he reminded me that I had promised to ride the bounds of our land with him the following week. He had questions about some of the tenancies and other matters that he needed to discuss. There were some social invitations also: a dinner with a distant cousin and his family who lived in a neighbouring county, which meant an overnight stay, and an evening of cards with a friend with eligible daughters, a frequent occurrence for a bachelor of independent means.

I dealt with the correspondence, thanking Hugh for his thoughtfulness and promising to let him know what I thought of Mr Dickens; accepting the invitation for cards with my neighbours on Thursday week; declining the dinner with relatives on the grounds of a prior engagement – which was true as an overnight stay would have meant me missing the next board meeting. My decision brought home to me how rapidly involved and absorbed I had become with the workhouse and its inmates. A month ago I wouldn't have given up the prospect of a good dinner with pleasant company for an administrative meeting. Then I turned to Ted's request. Should I report my visit at the board meeting first, or put him in the picture immediately? On reflection I thought the latter course was fairer. After all, it was Ted who had really got me into this, and he deserved my trust and confidence; I knew we were on the same side. The board's visiting day was ten days away, so we had plenty of time to meet. I scribbled a note suggesting he came to the Hall on Thursday at noon.

After an early dinner I spent the whole evening reading through the regulations again, particularly those concerning the children. I was right – they should be provided with education. The rules clearly stated that boys and girls were supposed to receive each day *at least* three hours of reading, writing and arithmetic and a good dose of 'the principles of the Christian religion'. Other duties of the schoolmaster were to provide 'such other instruction as may fit them for service, and train them to habits of usefulness, industry and virtue'. It seemed that the children in our union workhouse were being denied this provision and were being put to work instead. Ideally someone specific should be employed for this purpose, but the regulations didn't exactly stipulate what qualifications were required, neither did they specify age, unlike the clerk, treasurer, master and relieving officer who all had to be over the age of twenty-one.

I also investigated the rules concerning sleeping arrangements. Again the articles were very clear. It was the responsibility of the matron to ensure that 'all the beds and bedding be kept in a clean and wholesome state' and for her to supervise the washing and drying of all linen, stockings and blankets. There was no prescribed provision of flock mattresses, but I felt that the spirit of the regulations was being tested with the current use of straw palliasses. Clearly, all this was driven by cost-cutting – the place was being run 'on the cheap'.

It took me almost a couple of hours of reading and extrapolation of special points into my notebook before I felt I had anything near a full appreciation of how the regulations were being ignored. I didn't have to look far to guess why the board was slack and transparently negligent; the members were mostly selected and endorsed by Jack Shepherd, either through close acquaintance or because they had some financial obligation to him. Those with no connection were professional men and well-placed artisans with responsibilities for employees and probably obliged to their banks. Unlike me, they would have little leisure for a detailed examination of the regulations and would take the format and outcomes of the board meetings as customary practice. I didn't imagine that even Ted Lake would have stretched his mind to absorption of the legal documents available. The source of his concerns was emotionally charged, not emanating from parliamentary edicts. By the end of the evening I felt sufficiently confident that I'd mastered the major points and could challenge the board on several issues. I concluded that Colonel Shepherd's lack of rigour was probably not malicious in its intent. Rather it appeared he was disposed to laziness and taking the easy option. It made me wonder why he'd been willing to take up the chairmanship in the first place.

Ted arrived punctually on Thursday at noon. I'd provided some light refreshment, which we took in the library. As before when we had dined together, I was careful to have only one bottle of claret brought up. With a plate and glass comfortably at his elbow he plunged into questioning me immediately. 'So, what happened? Did they let you roam freely? What were your impressions?'

'They were both quite obliging – at least Calman was; his wife's a different matter. She verged on the obstructive. However, they escorted me where we'd agreed.' I described what I'd seen and, rather than voicing my concerns at that point, waited for a reaction. I wanted to see if he could, with a clear head, echo what I was thinking without any prompting. He didn't disappoint. 'Firstly, this business of the children working with the mothers – that can't be right. I'm sure they should be elsewhere and looked after while the mothers are working.'

'Correct. As we heard at the first meeting there are twenty-one children in all but no suitable provision for them as far as I can see. According to the rules the little ones should be in a nursery and the older ones should have schooling. The toddlers are scrambling around on the floor among all the dust and dirt of the oakum. The sleeping arrangements are also questionable. The children under seven sleep in the women's section. There's a shortage of space in the children's dormitory for the older boys so two of them are in with the men. I understand that this is permissible as long as the board agrees. I can see the master has a difficulty with overcrowding, but I don't think the arrangements are satisfactory. Besides, he told me there's space up aloft of the men's dormitory for another ward for the boys if necessary – although it's used as a storeroom at present. Again, it was a matter of cost.'

'Even though your visit was brief and obviously heavily super-vised, you've come away with clear evidence that there are serious breaches of the regulations. The fact that the children aren't offered any chance of school or training is irrefutable and something the board can't ignore. I'll be interested to hear what Shepherd has to say about that.'

'Hold hard a minute. Before we consider confronting the board we need to be sure of all our facts. Because I didn't see any children being taught, it doesn't mean that they don't receive some kind of education at some time during the week.'

'Well, set your mind at rest. I know there's no teaching going on. The children are put to work around the place, mostly outside with the livestock and in the garden.'

'I suppose Fred Lodge has been keeping you informed?'

'While you've been flexing your official muscle, I've been talking to Fred who's been passing on some of what he's noticed. By the way – he's relieved you're going to help us.'

I was immediately discomforted about the depth to which Ted had assumed I would want to be involved. I was also somewhat annoyed at the speed at which he was moving; he had no right to tell his nephew anything about my intentions.

'Look, Ted, let's clear the air here!' He looked puzzled and I went on, 'It seems to me as though you're trying to draw me into a conspiracy with Fred without fully consulting me first. I admire your eagerness and I'm fully sympathetic with your passion that things should be put right—'

'Well, that's good!' he burst in. 'We can work—'

'Together, but at my speed. Look, we're dealing with some difficult characters. Colonel Shepherd's no fool; he's got a status outside the union to protect, although he's clearly sloppy. Once we start unpicking things it'll have a damaging effect on him socially.'

'Well, he'll get what he deserves then! I've no scruples about damning his good name.'

'Clearly,' I said dryly. 'Then there's Mrs Calman, who's certainly not to be underestimated; she's obviously the most powerful officer in the place, and her husband would back her to the hilt if there's the slightest criticism of her actions.'

'Like Shepherd, they must take their chances. If they've been doing wrong, they must pay for it.'

'That's a tough stance for a radical, Ted!'

'I see things as black and white; we either have justice or no justice—'

'I understand your position, but let's also consider your nephew Fred. From what you just said you've mentioned my name to him.'

'What about it?'

'Fred Lodge seems a decent sort, and obviously his intentions are honourable – he's risking his job after all. But I wish you hadn't told him I would help.'

Ted made himself at home with my claret. 'Why? You've already promised you will. Besides, he needs to know we have someone with clout on our side.'

'I would have liked a little more time to prepare.'

'What's to prepare? Stop prevaricating, man! We're all set up – an inside man, someone to act as a go-between, and you and I to make sense of it all.' My hackles began to rise; I didn't like being hectored in my own library and there was a prickle of annoyance on the back of my neck at what I perceived as lese-majesty. Then I realised I was behaving exactly as Shepherd would. Ted was right; I'd come too far and already discovered things that needed challenging. Nonetheless, I would rein Mr Lake in – for all our sakes.

'Look, Ted, this is the beginning of a serious investigation, but one which must be tackled systematically. If you were a lawyer, you'd appreciate the need to collect evidence first before jumping to conclusions, plunging in and involving others in risky actions. I know you think I'm being over-careful, but if any of this gets out before we're ready to expose our findings, there's time for those we might implicate to cover their tracks. We must have a watertight case to take to the board. Have you also considered the politics?'

'What do you mean – politics?'

'Who'll line up with whom if it comes to a vote of no confidence in Shepherd? Even worse, will we be supported if we insist on some kind of formal enquiry? All of them have a lot to lose socially, and we'll surely come under scrutiny as well. It'll put the whole district under observation. Could you take the pressure? It might be a matter of different board members taking opposite sides. Weigh up the possibilities – who would be Shepherd's men, who would we have to persuade, and who would be for us?' I wanted to be sure that Ted Lake would moderate some of his impatience. My lawyer's training would be necessary from now on – not only to think through any legal issues but also to provide a secure base for our operation. 'Now that I'm implicated in this I want you to assure me you'll not undertake anything without discussing it with me first. No rushing off on your own pet cause. As I said – we must be systematic about it – unless anything untoward happens in the meantime. There aren't any other hares you've started running without telling me are there?'

'No, no – be assured I'm as concerned to keep Fred's involvement secret.' He looked me squarely in the eye. 'I'm not stupid – I know you have reservations about my impetuosity – my wife does too! – but I can assure you I'd never put any of us at risk. Can't afford to be out of step in this small community! My whole object is to get to the truth about the running of the place – recklessness would be self-defeating.'

'I'm glad to hear you say so – and never underestimate the opposition. As I say, they've a lot to lose.' We finished the bottle and I sent Ted on his way.

That evening I took out the first three instalments of *Oliver Twist* and sat reading until Foster came to enquire tactfully whether he should lock up. Hugh was right. They were beautifully written and thoroughly engrossing. So much so that an idea occurred to me, triggered as I was reading an early episode. I would produce a 'twist' all right, but a literal one.

Chapter 4

The board was due to meet the following Wednesday morning at nine thirty in order for the regulation monthly visit to take place before the full meeting. I arrived by carriage ten minutes early and made my way round to the back of the building. Other guardians were riding in or dropping off from carts and cabs. When I returned they were assembling in the lobby where I counted ten of us in total; Shepherd was there with his estate manager George Stenning. We waited a further five minutes for stragglers. The last to arrive was the innkeeper, James Edwards, in a flurry because his horse had gone lame the day before and he'd had to borrow a neighbour's mount.

Gathering us all together Shepherd, with Calman in tow, led us round the left side of the building to the men's quarters. We began the tour up on the first-floor dormitory, which was exactly as I had seen it and still with its heavy odour. Some of the newly elected guardians looked awkward, as though they didn't know exactly what they should be looking at or for; after all, there was nothing to see but beds, mattresses and blankets. They lingered around the entrance waiting for a signal from Shepherd. He cleared his throat and nodded approval to Calman. We made our way down the stairs to the working area.

This was different from my experience the week before. The floor had been swept and was clear of much of the rope and oakum. The men and boys, including Peter Samuels, were lined up for inspection. I also recognised Jacob Fearnley and Henry Millhouses, who was last but one in the line. Colonel Shepherd led the way down the ranks, followed by a file of guardians. Nodding to a couple of the inmates the chairman took in their general appearance – which was spruce and clean – all traces of dust removed from faces and hands. Their clothing, grey as it was, was also clean. No attempt was made to engage them in conversation, but Shepherd stopped at the end of the row and addressed all the men together as though they were on the parade ground.

'Now, men, we're glad to see the institution is continuing to provide you with all necessary food and shelter. You appear to be well looked after by the master and matron. I can see there are no problems here. Three meals a day, clothing and bedding – all provided by the rate payers. In return we expect you to work hard, love God and obey the rules.' I was standing close enough to Millhouses to try to read his expression, but his face was as blank as Jacob Fearnley's; there was no flicker of response.

We moved on through the kitchen where Mrs Calman was looking almost flustered. She cast a glance in my direction, but then returned to supervising preparation for the midday meal. There was a cursory inspection of the kitchen table and the range, and one of the guardians picked up a wooden bowl and proceeded to inspect it. Another went over to the stewpot hanging over the fire, sniffed at its steam, wrinkled his nose briefly and moved away. Others stood aimlessly waiting for the cue to move on.

The rest of the inspection continued in much the same half-hearted way until we had completed a full tour of the building. The women and young children received the same exhortation from the colonel as the men. The older children were lined up in the large dining hall where they were told of the dire consequences of misbehaviour. Mr Calman looked appropriately fierce as the punishment book was presented to the colonel. I had no prior knowledge of it and made a mental note to investigate its contents as soon as possible. It was an oversight on my part – of course there would be an official record of any punishments meted out. My own experiences of beatings at school should have prompted me to think about the methods of control and use of physical punishment adopted in this institution.

According to the book, one boy had that day received six strokes of the cane on the hand for 'persistent lying'. He was hauled out of the line and placed in front of the colonel who, ignoring the boy entirely, directed his remarks to Calman. 'How old is this boy?

'About eight, sir.'

'Lying is an abomination.' He turned to the boy. 'Do you know what an abomination is?'

'No, sir.'

'It is something we will not tolerate. What were you lying about?'

Calman intervened. 'He denied he'd wet the bed again. He said someone changed their wet mattress for his. I know he's a bed-wetter, colonel.'

'Lying's bad enough, but bedding is expensive. Don't you know you are living off other people's money?' The boy looked confused and terrified. A rabbit caught in lantern light came to mind.

'Mr Calman, if the beatings don't stop the offence, what other methods have you at your disposal?'

'Only beating, sir; he's too young for isolation and the bread-and-water diet, sir.'

'Then the beatings will have to continue until he learns.' The boy was returned to the line.

The silence was oppressive; the air in the room was almost breathless as no boy dared moved a muscle. I looked for signs of response on the faces of the guardians, one or two looked uncomfortable. Ted Lake obviously – with a blush of anger on his cheek. Hugh Bradshaw and Michael Jameson looked distressed, but thrashings are accepted practice; we'd all been victims of them at home and at school. Nevertheless, to my mind the persistent beatings as prescribed by the colonel were over-rigorous and not appropriate for a young boy and certainly not for the offence.

As the children filed out to their appropriate sections, we took our places in the meeting room at the end of the dining hall. There were the usual procedures. The chaplain led the prayers, the clerk presented the accounts and Calman gave his report. All was in order, the visit declared uneventful and Calman was congratulated on keeping an orderly house – like an innkeeper in favour with the local bench. We came to the end of the proceeding and on to Any Other Business.

I drew a deep breath. 'I have an item, Mr Chairman. It stems from my own visit last Monday week. I'd like to give a brief report.'

'Go ahead, Mr Lawes, I see we are about to be enlightened.' I was unsure whether this was a criticism of my reputation or a piece of heavy sarcasm.

I ignored it, rose from my seat and went to the door. Turning to the members I said, 'But first – if you would bear with me for a moment—' I left the room briefly and within seconds returned with three of the women from the kitchen. Rosa Hines carried a large tray with sixteen wooden bowls and spoons. Another small, thin woman, Edith Smitherson, struggled with a large soup pot; the third, who I'd been told was called Aggie, balanced between her hands a wooden platter on which was a flat grey object. I indicated that they should put them down in front of me. As they left, Mrs Calman entered the room. 'Excellent! Mrs Calman. Please join us.' Unsmiling she took the place next to her husband.

The colour mounted in Shepherd's face, which soon became flushed with anger. 'Look here, Lawes! What is all this?'

'I simply wish the board to sample the midday meal given to the inmates. After all, as you remind us so often, we're paying for this food and consequently should be monitoring its standard. The question is are we getting value for money?' There was a concerted muttering as I began to ladle out the grey watery mixture from the pot into the bowls, taking care to add an odd lump of vegetable to each one.

'Pass this round and tell me what you think.'

In frozen silence the bowls and spoons were passed from hand to hand round the table until everyone was provided for, but as there was no move to the spoons I set the example by taking a mouthful of the watery, lukewarm, unseasoned liquid myself. I admit I had to force it down, but tried to retain an air of unconcern as I looked round the table.

'Come on everyone, eat up!' I said encouragingly. 'We're privileged to be breaking the same bread as the inmates, aren't we Mr Patchin? What does it say in the Bible?'

Patchin looked intensely uncomfortable, but slowly picked up his spoon, dipped it into the bowl and fished out a piece of potato. Hugh Bradshaw on my left took a spoonful of liquid and manfully swallowed it. Gentleman as he was he betrayed no emotion, other than a slight grimace as the sour concoction hit the back of his tongue. Ted Lake, pink with suppressed laughter and surprise, joined in with gusto, taking down spoonfuls of the wretched mixture without a murmur. While the rest fumbled with their spoons I took a knife and cut up the grey loaf on the wooden platter into sixteen pieces. I passed the plate round.

'We must have bread with soup,' I said. 'Help yourselves.' Biting into a piece, I immediately tasted chalk.

I looked round the table to ensure that everyone had at least tried both the soup and the bread. Shepherd remained with his arms folded, his soup untouched. 'I don't know what you're trying to achieve here, Lawes, but this is good food going to waste!'

'How do you know, colonel, when you haven't sampled it? Do try the bread – I think you'll find it, shall we say, not quite what you're used to.'

'Damn it, man! This is an outrage! We do everything we can to keep these people fed and clothed. We're not running a country house with qualified cooks. This is the poorhouse. People know what to expect when they get here. They must take what is given and be—'

'Satisfied? If you would but try this... this... whatever it is... you would know that it's definitely not satisfying. If you sampled the bread you'd recognise it as having been adulterated with chalk. I've had rogue bakers up before me for that very thing and I had no hesitation in giving them very large fines. This food is, to quote you, an abomination.' He remained silent, his face purple. I wondered whether he was about to lose his temper. Casually waving the ladle over the pot I looked round and asked, 'Would anyone like some more?' Immediately appreciating the Dickensian reference Hugh Bradshaw spluttered into his spoon.

The Calmans meanwhile had obediently sampled the fare. Mr Calman was extremely discomforted. His wife tried to retain her composure, but I could see that she was seething. Of course she knew what I was about. I had arrived early for the purpose and visited the kitchen to prepare the presentation. When I asked her to make ready the food and utensils she had at first refused, saying that it was unprecedented for any of the guardians to interfere in anything connected with the kitchen. I asked directly if she was prepared to deny the legitimate request of a visiting JP and under which authority she might do so. She had no answer and I raised my eyebrows and faced her down, which shut her up. Her demeanour at the table was inscrutable. She had obediently taken a few sips of soup and a mouthful of bread. She now sat, hands in lap, waiting for my next move.

I looked at her directly. 'Matron, would you ask the ladies in the kitchen to come and collect up the dishes please?' She immediately left the room and in seconds Mrs Stuart and Aggie returned. They poured the remains of the bowls into the soup pot and piled them on to a tray. As they left I observed they had a spring in their steps and I couldn't be sure, but I might have seen a brief smirk and a heaving of shoulders. Mrs Calman returned and took her place again.

'Good – I'm glad you're remaining with us. I think the board need an explanation of what they have just enjoyed – or not. What exactly has gone into this meal, and is this the normal standard of workhouse fare?' I looked round the faces at the table. Colonel Shepherd remained with his arms folded. His face was expressionless but I could see by the set of his head and shoulders he was furious and, better still, discomfited.

As there was no immediate answer I went on. 'The soup can only be described as disgusting. The flour in the bread has plainly been adulterated with alum or chalk. The board needs to know where this adulteration took place. It's inconceivable that it was done by the inmates themselves in the kitchen. Rather I believe it was done at source. In other words the miller sold it to us in this state. If this is the case, then the board – and the rate payers – are being cheated.' I looked directly at the master. 'Which miller supplies us?' He looked at his wife before clearing his throat and answering with a wheeze. 'Raston of Bury St Edmonds. We've had a contract with him since the House opened... sir.'

'So, our inmates have been eating this foul bread for four years, and presumably none of the guardians has thought to ever taste it before it was served. I imagine the inmates are in no position to complain.'

Shepherd intervened. 'Look here, Lawes – the contract was agreed in good faith. Raston is known to some of us and his was the best tender. We always look out for the—'

'Rate payers' interests. Yes, I know. But on this occasion they've been short-changed. The man's been robbing them blind.'

Will Faulkner the corn merchant put up his hand. 'Raston isn't reliable, Mr Lawes; I had brief dealings with him and heard he sometimes give short measure. I didn't want to be associated with him and moved across to Johnsons of Ipswich and I've had no problems with them for the last three years. I've been very pleased with the quality of their grinding – their flour is said to be very fine. In fact, they use—'

I quickly moved the discussion on before Will had a chance to bog us down in the finer points of milling. 'Thank you, Mr Faulkner, that's very useful indeed. My suggestion is this, Mr Chairman. In order to ensure the board receives value for money in its purchasing we set up a sub-committee to look at all aspects of supply, tendering and ordering of food. It can make a full report to the board on its findings. If there's such blatant and regular adulteration of flour, what other mischief might suppliers be up to?' Shepherd looked mutinous but I ignored him and asked for candidates. Ted raised his hand immediately, along with Will Faulkner, John Newton and the farmer William Marchant. I continued: 'Mr Chairman, I suggest that each be formally proposed and seconded and that the members of the committee should elect their own chairman.' Shepherd nodded resignedly. It was also agreed that the board's treasurer would provide them with copies of relevant orders and receipts. Having settled matters thus far I went on: 'As far as the existing sacks of flour now redundant in the kitchen are concerned they can be consigned to pig swill; the pigs won't discriminate at anything thrown at them from a bucket. I also suggest financial losses caused by the affair are logged in the accounts. If we can prove that Raston has made money from cheating we'll take appropriate legal proceedings against him.' There was a low murmur of approval from some of the men round the table. 'As for replacing the adulterated flour, can we leave it to you, Mr Faulkner, to arrange for a new supplier pro temp?'

'Certainly,' agreed Faulkner, 'I'll get one of my men to drive immediately to the miller of Kettlebaston; I know his flour is of good quality because—'

Again I was forced to shut him up before his enthusiasm for the task overwhelmed us. I went on: 'As a temporary measure, I suggest we buy in six hundredweight bags until a new permanent source of supply is arranged. Is that agreeable to all? Shall we take a vote on it?' There was a slow nodding of heads but everyone looked at Shepherd first. His mouth was set in a hard straight line, but he could see the way things were going and gave a brief nod of assent. Slowly everyone's hand went up, including his.

The matter was closed. The clerk was having difficulty keeping up with recording all the arrangements and we gave him time to enter them before proceeding. Then, in an effort to regain control of the meeting Shepherd asked whether there was any other business, looking straight at me in expectation that there was bound to be something else. I did not disappoint him.

'I would ask the board for time to discuss the matter of the children's education. I would have raised it today but I feel it's worthy of more time than we can give it now. Besides, I think it deserves to be itemised on the agenda separately as a standing item. I would like that entered into the minutes.' The board members looked at each other. If they'd been totally shocked by this morning's proceedings, they were clearly bewildered that I would press another matter so quickly. Feeling that I had ridden my luck as far as I wanted to, I leaned back in my chair. Taking his cue, the chairman nodded to the clerk to record my views and closed proceedings.

As the meeting was breaking up Ted commandeered the members of the newly formed sub-committee and got them to agree when they would meet. He caught me up as I was walking round to the stables.

'Well, damn it! That was unexpected. You certainly play things close to your chest. Why didn't you tell me what you were going to do?'

'I only thought about it last evening; perhaps your enthusiasm for action was infectious! But your committee will be important. Interesting that Newton volunteered. He supplies cloth – whether to the union or not I don't know. But we'll find out. Faulkner's a good chap and at least knows his corn! I've got a nasty feeling about all of this. Your nephew mentioned poor food to you and who knows what tricks the suppliers have been up to.'

'Believe me, Edgar; I'll make sure we get to the bottom of it. I intend to get myself elected as the committee's chairman. One thing though, this makes things easier. We needn't ask Fred to do anything underhand, like copy the accounts; this new group will need to see them. I can't wait to get my hands on them. Do you think we'll find anything untoward? You don't think Harbey's on the fiddle?'

'My guess is no. William Harbey's a straight man – besides, he has a professional reputation to protect. I don't think he'd involve himself in fraud or cheating. Neither I might add would Shepherd.

He's simply lazy, as well as obsessed with the poor-rate and being popular with the tax-paying voters. He was genuinely shocked today – not just at my antics, but at the thought of a serious misuse of funds. He knows that he's ultimately responsible for the supervision of this place. That's why he didn't oppose my suggestion.' We left it that we would be in contact – perhaps meeting up for a drink at the Fleece during the following week. He agreed to give me prior knowledge of what came out of his committee meeting.

As I reached the gates Fred Lodge was waiting to lock them.

'Well done, sir! It's already all over the House what you did. The inmates are beside themselves. But the Calmans are on the warpath and your name's mud.'

I leaned across my horse. 'How quickly things get about in a place where people are supposed to be cut off from each other!'

'Don't be surprised, sir. Anything of importance is fed out one way or another. The women in the kitchen got the story through to the men almost immediately. There are ways and means which we know nothing of – and long may it stay that way.'

'Fred, I'd like to come and see you and meet your wife. You can tell me exactly what your suspicions are. I know you pass information to your uncle but I'd like to hear your views for myself. Next time I'm here I'll call on you. Don't worry, you won't be in any trouble; everything will be above board. I'll tell Colonel Shepherd that I'm continuing to find out what everyone does here so that I can get things in perspective. He can't argue with that.'

Fred nodded, but looked doubtfully at me. 'As you please, sir. But I'd rather you didn't mention it to the colonel – or any of the rest. Also, is there any chance we could meet somewhere else – perhaps at my Uncle Ted's place?' He lowered his voice. 'I wouldn't feel comfortable with you coming into the lodge – none of the guardians have visited me before. It would look strange. Knowing how keen you are to get at the truth they might wonder. But wherever we meet my wife will be delighted; you've become a bit of a hero in our house, sir.'

'Ah – that's something to be discouraged. I'm only carrying out my duties. I want us all to be responsible for any changes that should be made. I take your point about Colonel Shepherd and the Calmans.

I'll be seeing your uncle in a few days and I'll arrange things with him. Now I must be off! Good day to you.'

The week ahead was crowded with appointments. The magistrates' court was in session on Monday and on Tuesday my estate manager Sam Saunby had arranged for us to ride out together to look at the estate and discuss various matters connected with tenancies and our newly purchased piece of woodland. Then there was the invitation to cards with Lady Somerset and her marriageable daughters, Esther and Miranda, on Thursday evening. In view of Fred's concerns I sent Ted Lake a note suggesting it might be more appropriate for all three of us to meet at Rushie Farm. I didn't specify a date or time for the meeting, but left it with Ted to coordinate a day convenient to us all – if possible before the board meeting on Wednesday next. Ted was well aware when the magistrates' court sat; he replied quite swiftly by note, suggesting the coming Saturday at midday, which suited me well. I took out my notebook and began to formulate some questions I might ask Fred, particularly those touching on matters that he had seemed reluctant to express.

The court sitting was run-of-the-mill. Before me stood the usual display of drunkards and petty thieves, but today the list was lightened by the appearance of our regular town trollop, Mary-Ann Wilcox, or Merry Mary as she was more familiarly known. A woman of uncertain age and celebrated reputation, she was persistently up before me, a pathetic sight in her shabby clothes hanging over a fleshy body topped with generous-sized breasts; through a gap-toothed grin she always spoke for herself, the excuses for her behaviour ranging from the strange to the ridiculous. Sometimes she pleaded lack of memory; once when accused of wanton behaviour in a public place she said she'd done nothing wrong. 'I only gave him a little tickle at the back of squire's monument because he said he needed cheering up like.' The crowd in the public gallery were inevitably on her side – why not when some of them were her regulars? With no other means of occupation she certainly provided a 'service' within the parishes, which was a problem for the more strait-laced in the community. But if it hadn't been her someone else would have stepped in to fill the need. Colonel Shepherd would have been proud when she insisted from the dock, 'I'll be no drain on the poor-rate. I'll pay my way and God forbid I'll ever ask for assistance from the House'.

On this occasion she had been caught fair and square by the Reverend Patchin. Walking home through the churchyard at about midnight he had come across Mary and a farmhand indulging in casual congress, flat out on the large tombstone of a member of a very respectable family. Patchin wasn't asked what he was doing in the churchyard at that late hour, but, being a man of the cloth, it was assumed he was on legitimate church business – nothing to do with the widow Neal who, it was rumoured, held out hopes of making herself a vicar's wife. First thing the next morning he'd reported Mary to the constable who arrested her and brought her before me. As usual the other half of the business arrangement was never charged; in fact, it remained anonymous. I fined her the minimum, as on all previous occasions, and gave her the customary warning about the possibly dire consequences of a repeat offence.

My trip with the estate manager next day was more straightforward. Whippet-thin, Sam Saunby was as bald as an egg, with the exception of a few wisps of ginger and grey hair, which laced his collar. His once clear blue eyes were now becoming rheumy with age, but this didn't detract from their brightness. He was a countryman through and through, with an encyclopaedic knowledge of estate management. For years he'd steered us through the good times and bad – poor harvests, low milk yields, as well as gradually introducing new farming methods. I always enjoyed my monthly ride round the estate and I think he did too – exchanging ideas, thinking about the future. But today I could see there was something else on his mind.

After visiting three outlying farms and exchanging pleasantries with the families we rode over to our newly acquired beech grove, dismounted and took a rest. The day was warm and bright, one of those days that smelled sweetly of early summer. Skylarks were singing over a field of young wheat and hedgerow birds were chattering and scolding, protecting their territories. There was even a cuckoo calling from a far-off oak wood. Sitting on a fallen trunk we stretched out our legs and Sam filled his pipe. Obviously wanting to get something important off his chest he came straight to the point.

'There's a difficulty with one of the tenants, Mr Edgar, sir.' He maintained with me the deference established between my father and himself and, although we had ridden out together round the estate since I was old enough to undertake a day's riding, he'd never presumed anything other than a master-servant relationship. I'd moved smoothly from being 'Master Edgar' to 'Mr Edgar, sir'.

'Old Peter Simpkiss has told me he's getting too old to manage his piece of land. I've noticed that he hasn't been on top of the work for a few months. It took him much longer than it should to plough three acres for the new barley. The problem is he's no family here. Neither of his children wanted to take on the tenancy and have both left the farm. His daughter's emigrated with her husband and family; his son's moved to become shepherd to a big flock over in Norfolk. He's nowhere to go in the village when he gives up his acres. He's been a very good tenant – ran his land well and paid his rent every Lady Day – never missed. On the other hand we need his cottage and farm. I already have someone in mind to take it over. But I know you'll want to treat the man fairly.' He fell silent and sucked at his pipe.

I was suddenly confronted with the same dilemma that Ted Lake had described when he first talked to me about the tenant thrown off his land. In our area dispossessed farm labourers were top of the list of entrants to the workhouse. Ted's example hadn't been unusual – and owners couldn't afford to be sentimental. But I'd seen the effects of homelessness first hand, the demoralising and degrading conditions its victims were forced into. There was a moral choice to be made. I wasn't minded to throw a man off his land because he was old, but needed to keep the estate farms economically viable.

'Mm – I see the problem.' I said. I felt certain that Sam would have thought not only about the problem, but also the way out. 'Have you any ideas?' I asked.

'Well, I've contacted his son in Shipdham to see if he has room for him with them, but his wife's expecting another child and they're already overcrowded.' He hesitated. 'I do have another idea – pretty radical and not cheap. It was something your father and I were considering, although it was only in our heads when he passed away.'

'Go on.'

'This isn't a new problem, but up to now we've always managed to provide some sort of accommodation for old labourers in this situation – mainly by using lodging houses in the villages. This is successful because everyone knows each other and the landladies are generally sympathetic. But I'd like to see a more permanent solution – one which your father was considering. That is that the estate might build something like almshouses where our old tenants without family could be accommodated for free and for the remainder of their lives. We wouldn't need many as this situation doesn't arise frequently.'

'As I understand it, almshouses are built and run by the church, and have been since the Middle Ages. I don't know that it's our place to provide such charity for our workers,' I said doubtfully. 'We wouldn't be popular with the other estate owners once we'd set a precedent like that. Free housing is an innovation too far, I'd have thought. Anyway, I'm not sure what qualifications ex-tenants would have to show to be eligible.'

'A tenancy for life on this estate would mean just that. It would be understood that all tenants without family to retire to would be guaranteed a place to live for perhaps a peppercorn rent. As I say, my experience is that there wouldn't be many of them.'

'You mean they would be living for free? Wouldn't that give all the tenants the idea that their old age was taken care of automatically as a tenant of the estate?' As soon as I heard myself I thought of Jack Shepherd. That was exactly the kind of argument he would use – immediate suspicion that people were getting something for nothing.

'In a manner of speaking that would be a risk. But we could operate a strict test of their means, which could include length of service, loyalty and scrupulous payment of rent on time over the duration of their working lives. The property itself would be an asset to the estate and it would also allow us to plan ahead. We would know which tenants would be moving out and when. I think overall, while it'll need capital to set up, the long-term rewards will outweigh the initial outlay – your father certainly thought it a good idea.'

'But, as you say, there wouldn't be many needing such help; most have families to go to. That means there must be times when the properties would lie empty – that would be a waste of money, surely?'

'We could use them to house casual workers on a short-term

lease. If they were in full-time work, they could pay a market rent. Useful at harvest time particularly.'

'You've obviously given it a great deal of thought – as I might expect.'

He smiled and continued. 'I will confess there's some self-interest in my suggestion too.'

'Go on!'

'You may not realise it but I'm coming up to seventy next Christmastide. I can't continue working forever, and you'll be wanting to get someone else trained up to run the estate.' I shook my head in disbelief. I'd never really imagined Sam as old – he'd always been hale and hearty, never a day's illness and as efficient now as he had been in his forties. I couldn't imagine being without his company and advice.

'But you have a family. Your daughter's always badgering you to go and live with her.'

'Well – I like my independence and I'm not ready to be a burden on anyone else, let alone Emma. Since my wife died ten years ago I've managed very well for myself. But I'd like to think I could have a small house of my own to see out my days in my own way and in peace and quiet.' I reflected that Emma Williams was a loud woman with a noisy household in which numerous children of all ages constantly moved in and out. Sam was a quiet thoughtful man and liked his own company.

'You're suggesting I build a few of these almshouses and you could take one for yourself.'

'Oh no, sir! I've a little property lined up over in Boxford. In return for overseeing his accounts the landlord's willing for me to have a life tenancy. It'll suit me fine – still keeping my hand in, and secure. Michael Revel's a friend and we regularly play chess together.' I felt a little hurt and also rather ashamed. I knew Sam was a private man, and I'd rather left him to it to manage the estate, but I would have liked him to talk these things over with me first before making arrangements like this. I realised how little I knew of the man outside his position as estate manager. Plays chess! Well, that just reminded me to stop making assumptions about the people around me. It was my own fault. I'd never really got to know him beyond our professional relationship, and he wasn't one to presume above his station.

'So where does the self-interest come in?'

'I'm lucky because I can be sure of my future. Most farm tenancies are carried over, generation on generation unless the estate is sold. Your father and grandfather have kept this estate profitable, and I'm sure you'll do the same. But there are a few like Simpkiss who are the end of the line and have nowhere to go. I'd like to be part of a legacy that protects such men. I know your father would have felt the same because we spoke about it before he died. At that time it was just an idea and that's why he didn't talk to you about it. He did ask me to raise it with you when I felt the time was right. Well – as I intend to retire soon the time *is* right.' He looked at me expectantly.

'I see – you've given me a lot to think about and I certainly will. It would be a good idea for you to make some calculations and also consider where we might build such places – if we decide to.'

'Already done, sir. I have them in the estate office and can show you any time.'

'I might have known that would be the case. Bring them over to the house one day next week. As far as Peter Simkiss is concerned he can stay in his cottage for the time being and you can arrange for one of the other farmers to give him a hand, someone who has lads he can spare; the estate will pay their wages.'

'Very good, sir and thank you; I'm glad we've spoken.' He tapped out his pipe and we remounted, riding on in silence. As I'd told him, he'd given me something else to think about.

On Thursday evening I presented myself at Lady Somerset's for an evening of cards. The house was elegant late Georgian, but with unfortunate modern embellishments, which in the level of their ostentation competed with its owner. The rooms were so stuffed with furniture it was not easy to move around without bumping into something. Fortunately on this occasion there were only a few of us, enough to squeeze round three tables of four at whist. I knew all those present. I was pleased to see Hugh Bradshaw, but without his sister who didn't venture out so much these days. Robert Bignell the lawyer was also there, as was the surgeon Matthew Burgwin. Like me, both were in their late twenties and unmarried. Bachelors were fair game for the Somerset daughters Esther and Miranda, neither of whom was physically appealing. Esther was sharp-featured with a receding chin, and Miranda, although slightly more presentable, was running to fat even in her early twenties. She clearly followed her mother, also generously proportioned. I always made a point of avoiding any situation where I would be alone with either daughter, being fully aware of Lady Somerset's intentions – my own were not to be manipulated into any dangerous liaisons.

As I entered the drawing room the chatter ceased and eyes were on me. Lady Somerset came across with her hand extended.

'Good evening, Edgar! My, you have had a busy week. Mr Bignell has been telling us all about the events up at the poorhouse. We're all dying to hear more.' I was taken aback. Somewhat naively I'd not considered my actions would have become subject to general gossip. I waved her comments away and muttered something about it being of not much interest. But she pursued it.

'I hear Colonel Shepherd is most displeased and thinks you're interfering in things that you shouldn't. I invited him here tonight, but when he heard you were coming he declined. So you see, you naughty boy, you almost wrecked my table arrangements!' If she'd had a fan she would have been flirting behind it. A fat old woman trying to behave like a coquette is embarrassing and I squirmed inwardly.

'There was nothing remarkable about it, I was simply demonstrating a point I wanted to make in a practical way. There was no intention of annoying Colonel Shepherd and I'm sorry if he's taken offence.'

'Apparently you made him look ridiculous. Now tell me, what was it all about? You know, Edgar, you're acquiring a reputation for being somewhat of a new *radical*.' She whispered the word behind her hand, as though she was expressing something filthy. I'd no wish to enter into a discussion with her about my politics and knew it would be fruitless to try to start a debate with a woman for whom hardship was the purchase of one less ballgown than normal. I put paid to the conversation by reiterating that I had no intention of belittling Jack Shepherd – I was just trying to get at the truth. In the end she gave up quizzing me and retired somewhat huffily to organise her tables. We settled down with plenty of food and drink on hand as Amelia Somerset was well known for her hospitality – probably why she was so self-contentedly obese. She'd been a widow for twelve years and I remembered her as a svelte young woman when she first arrived in the town as a bride nearly twenty years ago. She was comfortably off and her daughters would be financial catches for some. But it would not be me.

I was paired with Robert Bignell and we faced Miranda Somerset and Hugh Bradshaw. I confess my mind was not on the cards. I should have known better than to be surprised that news had travelled round the town so quickly; the information exchange in small communities is extremely efficient. I wondered what Shepherd's next move would be. I'd clearly rattled him and he was the type of man who would retaliate if he thought himself humiliated.

During the course of the evening several of the guests approached me trying to glean more information that they could then carry to their next social engagement. I was unforthcoming and also watched what I drank. Several brandies were enough to make me more loosed-tongued than I should be. Hugh Bradshaw was also circumspect, just gave me a wink when I was being interrogated by a particularly nosy woman from Eastham who had strong views about the place of the poor. She thought they should do away with workhouses altogether and ship 'the indigent' out to New South Wales where they could 'do some real work and stop being a burden on hard-working people.' Bignell was particularly anxious to get me on one side after cards were over and we fell into groups over the supper table.

'You certainly brought the meeting to life, Edgar. It was worth tasting that filthy food just to see everyone's reaction. I've never seen the colonel so nonplussed. But tell me – what was the point? We could all see the food's not particularly appealing – but at least the blighters are getting fed – and for free.'

I was irritated. The total lack of sympathy and imagination of those in charge, or their ability to put themselves in another's place was depressing. But why should I be surprised? For the majority of the population life remained, as Thomas Hobbes had put it, 'nasty, brutish and short'; as for the wealthy, our privileges are tightly protected. Rich and poor – their paths rarely cross; there's minimum social interaction between us. Outside the big cities there is little tradition of philanthropy, other than from the Church, which always expects something in return. A few resolute men, such as William Wilberforce, who did so much to abolish the slave trade in our empire, and the champion of the poor, William Cobbett, were notable exceptions. Bignell, Shepherd and the rest were expressing the view of the majority who held power, certainly in our closed-minded Suffolk society.

Finally, frustrated by the recurring theme of resentment towards people who for the most part couldn't help themselves and of whose struggles little was known by most of those present, I curtailed my visit and left with Hugh Bradshaw, who always departed from social occasions at least half an hour before everyone else.

'Edgar! I haven't really had a chance to say – well done! I take it Mr Dickens was your inspiration? I appreciated the reference! Can't remember when I last laughed so much. Deborah was delighted when I told her; she's no time for Shepherd. He courted her once, y'know, and she turned him down – recognised straight away he was a bully. Well – you certainly put a shot across his bows. What's next in your armoury?'

'I'll just keep digging. I'm convinced all's not right. Ted Lake will get to the bottom of the supply business, I'm sure. My strategy is to take it one step at a time.'

'Best idea!' Climbing up into his carriage and holding firm to his ordnance theme, he said, 'Remember, always keep your powder dry!'

Chapter 5

Apart from my court commitments and board meetings, at this time I was mostly engaged in estate business with Sam, especially discussion about the new almshouses, which I was not quite yet persuaded to sanction. Having looked into it, setting them up might be more complicated than Sam realised. They would possibly need to be run by a trust rather than simply owned by the estate; in that way the residents would have much more long-term security. But Sam had done his homework and produced some figures that I would need to study in further detail.

Just before eleven o'clock on Saturday morning I set out for a leisurely hour's ride to Rushie Farm. There had recently been rain, but although it had been heavy the May sun was just about warm enough to draw out most of the moisture, leaving the paths and bridleways damp but firm. Ted's place was about a four-mile ride across country, six if I stayed on the tracks and avoided the shortcuts, which were by this time of year becoming overgrown with young nettles and brambles.

The ride gave me chance to recollect events; I did much of my creative thinking while on horseback. I'd ridden all my life and was able to anticipate my horse's response almost before he made it. Jogging quietly along, I considered the events of the last two months since my drink with Ted in the Fleece in March to the last eventful meeting of the board. By now I was certain that Jack Shepherd was not implicated in any wrongdoing. His reaction to my exposure of the quality of the food had been one of anger but also bewilderment. But that was almost as culpable. His lack of close inspection of the accounts, the responsibilities of the officers and the treatment of the inmates were all derelict in the extreme. But there was no evidence as yet of any actual fraud on his part. The obvious mismanagement was predicated on his insistence that the poor-rate had to be set at the lowest possible charge to protect the rate payers. The dereliction was that the needs of the inmates came a poor second.

Beyond the workhouse, the reaction of local society to the paupers in the House, from Lady Somerset's card-playing crowd (the circle I confess I most move in) to customers in the Fleece, was unsurprising: the poor should take it upon themselves to find work and not rely on handouts from their hard-working neighbours. Most of the wealthy took the view that there would always be winners and losers, and as long as the losers were kept at bay life could continue in the traditional age-old way. They might see a way of giving more alms in the church plate to salve their consciences, but 'out of sight, out of mind' was the prevailing abstraction. Those of the middling sort – solicitors, merchants, farmers and especially anyone self-made, were even less sympathetic. They had a critical approach to the poor, reflecting that because they had been able to sustain economic security through their own efforts – good, solid hard work – why shouldn't others do the same? They conveniently forgot that they had the benefit of education to varying degrees, which allowed them to have control over their lives through the choices they could make. As for the working poor, they lived in ever-present dread of having to condemn themselves to the House. Always at the whim of landlords and employers, they had no security either financial or emotional. They were invariably just one step away from abject penury.

For our farm labourers this had not been helped by the introduction of machinery. I'd recently sent Sam to Sussex for a few days to see one of the new threshing machines in action on a relative's estate. He came back and reported with some enthusiasm, 'It was certainly impressive, in size, function and noise! There's no doubt, sir, it does the job in half the time of two men. That's why their use is spreading, even though there's a lot of resentment from the labourers who lose their jobs as soon as a machine comes into the yard. Remember Captain Swing, sir; all that rick and barn-burning in Kent when they tried to introduce machinery?'

'Not helped by high levels of unemployment as the soldiers came home after the wars. It was a fact that arson was soon replaced by machine breaking across many southern counties.'

'The authorities were very ruthless. As I heard it, in the following year nine men and boys were hanged and about as many labourers transported to New South Wales, although there had only been one man killed, and him by the yeomanry.'

'Well, Sam, since the upheavals in France our government has always been provoked into overreaction by its constant fear of revolution.'

'Indeed, sir, but it seemed very harsh to me.'

Here was another dilemma for a landowner with a conscience. Should I embrace the new methods, which would surely be economically advantageous to the estate, or should I consider the workforce and continue to provide manual work in order for them to feed their families? I was able for the moment to shelve the decision as to whether to introduce new machinery since Sam was still working out its potential and its impact. No doubt we would have to have a conversation and make a decision before the harvest in August, but my instincts were to wait at least another year. I had to admit to myself that my involvement with the union was partially influencing my decision, and also that of Sam's proposal for the almshouses. To support my workers and relieve any necessity of them having to enter the House had now become somewhat of a crusade since I had seen first hand the conditions they would face if they were unfortunate enough to have to volunteer themselves.

As I rode through the Suffolk countryside, with the early shoots of spring crops greening the landscape, I saw wisps of smoke rising from the other side of a hedgerow. Hearing voices I peered over the dazzling green hawthorn hedge to see a tinkers' campsite. Having just crossed the Seddon Brook I knew I'd arrived on the very edges of Ted Lake's land. Unlike most of his neighbours, Ted had always welcomed the tinkers and year on year the same family returned at this time to a site he'd designated for their use. It was a mutually agreeable arrangement. Ted allowed them free access to wood for their fires, any rabbits they could snare, and milk, vegetables and bread from the farm. In return the family did odd jobs for him, fence-mending and helping with sheep shearing. As a constant if seasonal presence, they also provided some security against rare intruders, besides being crack shots against foxes. They would stay for the harvest and then move up to Lincolnshire for potato picking in the autumn. Garth O'Brien, the head of this Irish family, respected Ted for his welcoming stance, and Ted's trust in the O'Brien family had never been abused. The presence of the tinkers was, however, contentious. Colonel Shepherd, who shared Ted's boundary, abhorred their shooting of what he regarded as his foxes, which should be left for decent gentlemen to hunt. His estate manager, George Stenning, was also convinced that the stock of game in the coverts was reduced from what it should be between the middle of May and September, but his keepers couldn't trespass on to Ted's land; if a few fat pheasants ended up stewing over Garth's fire, no one could prove from whence they'd strayed.

My horse immediately caught the scent of others and whinnied. As I looked over the hedge I could see a large man in brown trousers and jacket, with a grubby shirt and greasy cap, who was banging out a piece of metal on an anvil. He was working in the middle of a circle of wagons, plainly painted and with brown-canvas coverings. Several sturdy ponies were tethered to trees in a small copse close by. Garth's womenfolk were preparing a meal over three fires. One of the women was cradling a young baby and, hovering around the wagons, were seven or eight scruffy children with dark hair and large deep brown eyes, which immediately gave away their ancestry. Hearing the horse the man looked up and I recognised his brown, withered, weather-beaten face.

'Good morning, Garth!'

He put down the hammer and the base of a large saucepan, and walked slowly towards me, still peering and screwing up his eyes, although he had his back to the sun. I realised that his sight must be going and he couldn't see me clearly.

'Who is it?' He peered at me suspiciously. Tinkers are more used to abuse than pleasantries.

'Mr Lawes, from Seddon Hall. I see you're all back.'

He doffed his cap. 'G'day, sir. Yes, we arrived a week ago. Mr Lake's still a good friend to us. Never refuses. We like to stick to places we know we'll be welcome.' He peered up at me, still trying, I think, to remember who I was.

'Well, I know Mr Lake appreciates your help. Where are your sons and brother?'

'Out hoeing for Mr Lake, sir.'

'Are you still able to make a good living for your family?'

'We live off the land, sir, and it always provides. We've done it for generations.'

'Long may it continue,' I said. As there was no response and in order to forestall the awkward silence now we'd run out of things to say and before we got on to the weather, I wished him farewell and jogged on.

It occurred to me that this was a family that, while it stuck together, would never be in fear of the workhouse. It was a mutually dependent and self-sufficient unit. Admittedly Garth and his dependents relied on the liberality of certain landowners, but it was not charity they received, rather like for like – space to live in return for work. In that sense they were not unlike labourers with tied cottages, but in one major respect their situation was totally different. They weren't tied to a permanent habitation and therein lay their security from homelessness. A labourer would lose his house if he lost his job. When the work ran out for the O'Briens they simply harnessed up and drove to another location. I would like to have asked Garth whether he had any thought about the workhouse, but something prevented me. It was surely an irrelevance; I could no more see the O'Briens asking for union help than I would myself.

As I was a mile off Ted's farm, I turned my thought to the man. Sam Saunby had filled in a few details for me. Having lived in the area for nearly seventy years there was very little that Sam didn't know about the parishes and the people in them. When I had gently probed for information Sam was able to give me a succinct background, which greatly helped explain some of the contradictions in Ted Lake's character that had struck me since I'd made his deeper acquaintance.

As Ted had told me himself, he'd been quite well educated at the local grammar school. It was his mother, Marie, who'd given him and his brother David their love of learning. Sam informed me that David had left home, trained as a solicitor and then taken a small practice in Ipswich.

'Mr Lake senior married Marie, a woman with money and brains, in a love match. She was a lady of some spirit, sir, and ignored the wishes of her father, insisting on a marriage to George Lake. Eventually, as her father had always encouraged her to think for herself, he could hardly deny her the demands of her own mind. Marie came with a sizeable dowry, which George Lake immediately used to buy the freehold of Rushie Farm, then he built a fine farmhouse for his new wife.'

It was well known locally that Ted's father was a stout supporter of the Methodist church and that it was only on this point that he and his wife disagreed. To his sad regret, she professed herself agnostic and wouldn't attend chapel with him. When the boys were young they went off to chapel with their father, but as they grew older they were given the choice of attending. David remained a committed non-conformist, but Ted confessed to me that as a young man he had veered towards atheism. Now in his late thirties he was, like his mother, agnostic. As he had already told me, it was she who'd introduced him to the delights of reading, but both parents taught him to have a mind of his own, to question and not take the entrenched opinions of others without scrutiny. He also inherited his mother's lively, impetuous character and his father's looks. George Lake had been a man of medium height and slim build – his sharp face topped with an unruly mop of light brown hair. Ted's similar lack of physical beauty was more than made up for by his open and friendly disposition; his smile lit up and modified otherwise pointed features. He had a quick and active mind.

Ten minutes late, I reached the track that led directly to the farmhouse. Four-square and solid, unlike Lady Somerset's property it had no unnecessary augmentations: just plain brick, sash windows and a Georgian pediment round the main door. Its only ornaments were pots of spring flowers, which lined the front of the house. Ted's wife Sarah came out to meet me, and her eldest son Walter took my horse.

'Good day, Mrs Lake – and you, Walter! Apologies for my lateness but I stopped to have words with Garth O'Brien who I see has returned as usual for the summer.' Like her husband, Sarah was not blessed with overly good looks – but her smile dazzled and made up for any imperfections in her face.

'Good day to you, sir. Ted and my nephew Fred are in the dining room where I've laid out some food for you. Can I say, before you go in, how grateful we are that you take such an interest in what's happening up at the House. At the moment I feel it's all on Fred's shoulders to deal with and he's only a young man, sir, and with a family. I'm worried about the risks he's taking.' She touched my arm. 'Do

what you can to protect him, sir. From what he's told us already there
are some wicked people in that place. I don't know what they might
do if they found out he was spying – which is what he's doing after
all.'

'The first thing I must do is to hear what he has to say. But
believe me, Mrs Lake, Ted and I are fully aware of the risks to Fred
and that's partly why we're meeting today – so that we can find ways
for him to continue digging for the truth, but at the same time to
ensure he's protected. We'll take all steps to see his family isn't jeopardised, or his post.'

She led me into the house; I'd visited on a few occasions previously and remembered it as well decorated and furnished in a solid
country style. There was evidence of good-quality wooden furniture
and comfortable chairs, some with cushions hand-embroidered with
skill. The whole house was perfumed with beeswax and lavender
polish, and the plain floors glowed with its regular application. We
walked to the rear of the house and she opened the door into a sunlit
dining room. Ted and Fred were sitting at a large walnut table that
was strewn with papers. On the large oak sideboard were cutlery,
glasses and china and a cold collation.

The two men rose and extended their hands. Fred had put on
what I presumed was his best suit – not the one allocated by the union,
but a good black worsted jacket with a high collar, and light breeches.
'Welcome!' said Ted. 'We were just catching up with family gossip
– a glass of wine?' I nodded and he poured what looked like a good
Burgundy, confirmed when I took a sip.

'You obviously keep a good cellar, Ted – who's your vintner?'

'A merchant in Ipswich; he deals directly with a chateau across
the Channel. The old vineyards have recently been replanted since
the damage done to the land in the revolution. I can let you have his
name.'

I took a seat at the table and looked at Fred. I thought he was
tense, and for a young man had unexpected shadows under his blue
eyes. In an attempt to put him at his ease I expressed my appreciation
of his personal courage, and that I understood that he must be under
somewhat of a strain. Ted nodded in agreement.

Fred took a gulp of wine and said, 'I'm just trying to do what's right, sir. As soon as I entered that place I knew there were things happening that were plainly wrong. Before I applied for the job I had to read up on what the duties of a union porter were and I also took the trouble to find out what every other officer's responsibilities were, to make sure I never trespassed on anyone else's patch. I'm sure you've looked at them yourself, sir. They're very clear and precise, which makes it easy to establish when they're broken.'

His uncle intervened. 'It would be a good idea, Fred, if you told us, as briefly as possible, your experiences since you took the job.'

'I moved in about a year ago to replace the first porter employed by the union who left – I never found out why. I soon became acquainted with my duties. Would you like me to list them? You probably already know what they are.'

'I know Ted has read them through, as I have, but just give us the gist again – to refresh our memories.'

'Well – I keep the gate – that's recording in a book who comes in and who goes out. I deal with new admissions and place them in the receiving ward. It's my job to search all the male inmates entering or leaving, especially for liquor. At nine in the evening I lock all the outer doors and take the keys to the master, and at six in the morning he gives them back again and I unlock the place. Sometimes I have to stand in for Mr Calman when he goes out and Mr Enderby, the overseer, isn't available. My wife does the duties of a nurse and stands in for Mrs Calman when she's not on duty. She—'

'Excellent – very succinct,' burst in Ted. 'But now tell Mr Lawes what you've found. Perhaps you should tell him firstly about some of the inmates.'

Fred turned to me, frowning slightly. 'I thought you'd met some of them, sir – on your visit a couple of weeks ago?'

'It was a very hurried inspection because the Calmans were anxious I didn't linger. They selected one man, Jacob Fearnley, who seems to have been incarcerated for years and wasn't very enlightening.'

Fred continued. 'As you both know the House is almost full. We have just under fifty men, women and children and no likelihood of any of them moving out in the near future. Some, like old Fearnley, came in from individual parish workhouses when the union was first formed. The oldest inmate is Christmas Davey. She's been in a work-house of some description for at least thirty-five years. No one knows how old she is, her records were lost many years ago, but I worked it out that she has to be at least eighty because she says she remembers seeing one of the first mail coaches pulling into Ipswich when she was a girl. According to my old dad they first appeared around 1760 – that makes her born around 1756, if her memory's right – but many inmates lose track of time, particularly those who stay for decades – one year rolls into the next. The newest arrivals in Seddon are the Alfrey family, three of them – Richard, Emily and their daughter Caroline, aged fourteen. Also a single man – Henry Millhouses. They all volunteered themselves in March.' He took another pull at his wine and I took the opportunity to ask him to tell us something about their stories.

'Alfrey's very typical of most of the inmates. He was a leather dresser in Boxford – cleaning hides. Unfortunately he had an accident and lost his job. To cut a long story short, the family was thrown out of their cottage and forced on to the parish. He's taken it badly, especially being separated from his wife and daughter, both of whom, I might add, are exceptionally good-looking – although the longer they stay, the more their looks will fade. "House sickness" we call it. I've been concerned about him – he seems very morose.'

I pressed Fred further. 'Tell us about Henry Millhouses. A single man you say – widower or bachelor?'

'Bachelor, thirty-seven years old. There's something different about him. He doesn't strike me as your run-of the-mill pauper. For a start, he reads a lot.'

I was puzzled. How could an inmate of the workhouse with its absence of books 'read a lot'?

'What do you mean? How does he do that?'

'Well, sir – I mean he reads the Bible. When he first came in and I had to supervise him changing into workhouse garb, he had a small leather-backed Bible with him. Now the rules are clear – new inmates must hand in any personal possessions they have on them. These are stored with their own clothes to be reclaimed if and when they leave. It's quite unusual for anyone to bring in a Bible, although not unheard of. As he'd made a special request to keep it I immediately asked the master if it was within the regulations – not being sure myself. Mr Calman saw no reason why he shouldn't keep it and Millhouses carries it around with him all the time. I often see him taking it out of his pocket and reading sections to himself. I don't think he's any kind of evangelist – he certainly never engages any of the other inmates in talk about religion, although it's clear he can quote texts, like he did with the parable of the loaves and fishes – but I think he was being what you'd called ironic. He muttered something about "too many bad loaves and not enough good fishes!" when he entered the dining hall for his midday meal.' He paused to take a drink. 'There's another thing.'

'Yes?'

'He looks different. Even though he's obviously poor and his hands certainly show signs of manual work, there's something about his manner I can't describe; it's as though he's out of place. He's a tall man, handsome you could say and not yet damaged by workhouse food and conditions.' My mind went back to my visit two weeks previously. I remembered a thin man taller than most of the others with a pair of clear brown eyes in a well-featured face that had looked straight into mine. He had struck me as exceptional in comparison with the rest of the inmates. Fred clearly had the same impression.

'What's this man's history – do you know?' I asked.

'He came up from London where he'd been working, but like Alfrey lost his job. He was a labourer in carpentry and, as he couldn't get another job, he had to tramp back to his parish in order to claim poor relief. Both his parents came from Kettlebaston but they're dead and he's homeless. Thomas Carrick investigated his family connections, state of health and financial means and was satisfied he met all the requirements for admission. When Millhouses arrived he had no money on him at all – just his Bible. While I was overseeing his admission I noticed he has a local Suffolk accent.' As Fred paused, his uncle rose to the sideboard to claim the claret jug, from which he replenished our glasses. Ted had heard Fred's account in silence but now, with his customary impatience, he asked his nephew to move on and divulge what he had observed at the House, and why it had worried him.

'There were three things that really concerned me as soon as I arrived. He turned to me. 'The first, which you have obviously picked up, sir, is the quality of the food. The diet for Seddon's inmates is poor and doesn't follow the allocations laid down in the rule book, where the amounts are set out most clearly. As you've found out, sir, the flour's been adulterated. Although I don't have any part in the ordering of food, I supervise its delivery and took away a couple of samples of the flour because it seemed a funny colour. When my Amy made it up into a loaf we could both taste the chalk. The same for the milk, which is sent over in churns from an outlying farm; no one checks on its quality. I've tasted it and there's no doubt it's been watered. That's why we were so glad when you showed everyone at the meeting. Now it's out in the open, things can only improve; anyway I—'

Ted intervened. 'They certainly will now our committee's started to examine bills and receipts for produce supplied. Will Harbey's account books are models of neatness, but you can be sure we'll be giving them thorough scrutiny; Fred's no mean book-keeper himself and I've passed copies of the accounts to him to see what he makes of them.' He indicated the papers strewn on the table. Obviously they'd been discussing them before I arrived.

'Good! That can only throw more light on the matter. Now, Fred, what's your second concern?'

'This is the most serious and involves the punishments. Again – the rule book's very strict about physical punishment, especially of the children – but I'll come on to them in a minute. You'll have seen in the regulations that there are over twenty offences for which the inmates can be punished. Some of them are really petty – like making a noise when silence is ordered, or playing cards or dice, or being in the wrong part of the building according to their class. Also, if they're thought to be insolent or so much as swear at the master or matron, they'll be punished by being isolated in a separate room with a bread-and-water diet for up to forty-eight hours. There's no corporal punishment allowed for adults. If their offence is really serious – like theft or wilful damage – they must come before the magistrate.'

'To my knowledge there's not been one appearance of an inmate from the workhouse before my bench, certainly not in the last two years,' I said. 'Now let's talk about the children.'

'At the moment we have twenty-one children up to the age of

fifteen, six under seven including the two babies. The youngest children are supposed to be in some kind of nursery while their mothers work, but, as you've seen on your visit, Mr Lawes, there's no provision and they stay with their mothers – or if they're orphans or bastards – are looked after by any of the women.'

'What about their education? They appear to have none, which is a clear breach of the regulations.'

'You're right, sir. But the children in Seddon are either working with the adults, or mostly sent out to the union smallholding. I know that in other unions pauper children are often indentured out as apprentices, but there's never been any move to do that in Seddon. At one time the board considered hiring a teacher, but then said it was too expensive. They approached my Amy, who has a very good hand at copy-book writing, to see if she'd be willing to teach a few of the younger children their letters, with a slight increase in her wages. She was very happy to do it, but I think Mrs Calman raised objection.'

'Why?'

'She said it would take Amy away from her nursing duties, but she also stands in for the matron when she's away from the workhouse. I think Jenny Calman thought that if Amy had any extra work it would interfere with her own timetable. She must've made a good case because the guardians withdrew their offer.'

I said, 'This is something I *will* take up at the next board meeting. What else has disturbed you, Fred?'

'It's how the children are punished, sir. Both the Calmans are very severe. Male children as young as seven are flogged with the official rod approved by the guardians. Often it's for the same offences as the adults, who can't be thrashed. These beatings are supposed to be entered up in the punishment book, which is then shown to the board at their meetings. But I know that what's written up doesn't always tally with the actual punishment and the offences are often exaggerated. For instance, Calman comes down hard on bed-wetters, or any child who attempts to steal food. I think eight strokes of the rod on a nine-year-old boy for cussing at another boy is very harsh. I think both the master and matron enjoy it.'

I remembered the hands of the small boy hauled out in front of us at the monthly board visit. His palms and fingers were streaked red and purple from six strokes of the rod. His offence was bed-wetting and 'lying' about it.

'Have you seen any beatings yourself, Fred? We'll need eyewitnesses to prove that they're excessive. After all, it's well within the regulations for the master or schoolmaster to administer floggings when a child breaks the rules.'

'I did see Mr Calman raise his stick to a boy and cut him across the legs. Another time I saw Mrs Calman dragging a small girl by her hair into a cupboard and lock her in. She was there between the midday meal and eight o'clock in the evening – missing supper because she was sent straight to the dormitory. I don't know what she did – but according to the regulations no child under twelve can be punished this way. As for what else goes on when we're not there, I can't say, sir. Sometimes the inmates let slip things, but always say they don't want it to go further. I think they're frightened, sir. They're certainly not willing to have any complaints put before the guardians.'

We had talked for over an hour when Ted suggested we should stop for refreshment. He called in his wife, who uncovered dishes of cold meats and cheeses. While we were eating I asked Fred if there was anything else about the House he could tell me.

'It's more a general feeling about the whole atmosphere in the place, sir; I think it's fear and a kind of hopelessness.'

It was all very vague, with nothing specific – just a deep despair in the place, made worse by the lack of comfort, warmth and hope; all immeasurable, but features that make fundamental differences to everyone's living conditions. Undoubtedly most of the inmates had exchanged one set of bleak domestic situations for another, but at least there was usually an absence of physical fear where they'd come from.

He confessed that it was having a bad effect on his family. 'If it wasn't for the fact that we live separate from the main house, we'd find it hard to stay. As soon as I enter the wards and workrooms I'm overwhelmed by feelings of disgust. Amy and me – we feel helpless, sir. There's nothing we can do to change things and improve conditions for the inmates. What makes it worse is that we have two children of own living freely on the outside. We feel guilty about the suffering of all the children on the inside.'

Finishing the food, I felt we'd come to a natural halt in our deliberations. It was now well after two o'clock and we'd covered much ground. I personally had a better grasp of affairs in the workhouse and Fred's account had been of real practical help. He had obviously discovered areas of bad practice with which we could challenge the board. The next thing was to work out a plan of attack. Ted's scrutiny of the accounts would be a useful starting point. Before we went our separate ways we made the decision to wait a week or so for the sub-committee to come to some conclusions and then we would incorporate concerns over education and punishments into a comprehensive report to the whole board.

As I waited for Ted's son to bring my horse, Fred waylaid me. 'Thank you for your time, sir. I'm sorry that I might have seemed vague and can't give you much in the way of what you would think of as good evidence, especially with you being a lawyer. We try to do little things for the inmates – help them when we can. Amy's always good to the children and they love her for it, but she can only do it when Mrs Calman is away. We're really hoping you'll be able to do some good.'

'I hope so too, Fred. Please believe me when I say that I'll do all I can to protect you, but you must continue to keep a record of what you see.'

'I will indeed, sir.'

I leaned over and shook his hand. 'The inmates are relying on you!'

I had much to think about as I rode home. I took the shortcut, through briars and fresh undergrowth, which still took me back to the O'Briens' camp. Across the hedge wafted the smoke from the fires and the aroma of cooking meat. I could see the women busy with their pots and the younger children playing together in and out of the wagons. An almost idyllic sight – but I also thought of the hardship they suffered in bad weather when they had to work in fields with fingers frozen as they harvested vegetables, or foraging for food and fuel for themselves in snow and heavy frost. But generation after generation of them had rejected the idea of giving up the independence of travelling life with all its hardships. Perhaps they were wise. As Fred had told us, the majority of the inmates in Seddon were there because they'd lost access to secure accommodation.

This led me to think about Sam Saunsby's almshouses project. The security of a roof over his family's head is probably the most important gift a man can give them. Now it was time for me to act on my beliefs for 'the greatest happiness for the greatest number'. By the time I reached home I'd decided to go ahead; after all it was a simple 'yes' or 'no' decision. I knew Sam would be a happy man when I told him my answer would be 'yes'.

My manservant Foster was waiting for me at the door. 'You've just missed Colonel Shepherd, sir. He was very anxious to see you and, as you were not at home, he wrote a note for you.' He handed me a sealed sheet and I took it into the library to read it. I half guessed its contents. In fact, I was surprised I'd not heard from him sooner; it had been over two weeks since my little tasting session at the board meeting. His comments were, as expected, straight to the point:

Saturday, 26 May

11.30am

Mr Lawes,

I would like to have spoken to you personally, but understand you are otherwise engaged. I have waited until now before I confronted you concerning the events that took place at the last board meeting of the guardians because it was my hope that you might have done me the courtesy of approaching me personally to explain why you took the extraordinary action you did, and your insistence on the participation of the board in what I can only describe as 'theatricals'.

It is important that things are made clear between us as to who is responsible for the efficient administration of the Poor Law in this union. As a gentleman and a professional man you must appreciate that, as chairman, I have overall charge of the board of guardians. I am distressed that you appear to be challenging some of the precepts by which we run the union, particularly our rigorous attempts to keep the poor-rate at an acceptable level. Your actions may have significantly undermined that intention. I am sorry to be so direct, but I am concerned that you understand where I stand. As I say, I would have preferred to discuss this with you face-to-face. Perhaps you would do me the courtesy of either visiting me at your convenience, or responding by letter. In any event I remain:

Your humble servant,

Jas. Shepherd (Colonel, Rtd)

That was me severely admonished; he couldn't have been plainer. I was minded to ride over and have it out with him 'face-to-face', but I had much to do before he could be fully confronted with my concerns – and evidence. In fairness I felt he was right in the fact that, as chairman, he was due some kind of explanation, so I decided to invite him to Seddon Hall on the following Monday, late afternoon after the court session. It would be politic for him to understand my motives at least, even if I wasn't yet prepared to share our concerns in depth. I scribbled a note, which I gave to Foster and asked for it to be delivered straight away.

I spent Sunday afternoon in my usual fashion preparing for court on the following day, having attended morning service at Seddon parish church. We were subjected to one of Reverend Patchin's interminable sermons – his usual choice of Old Testament text, this time taken from Deuteronomy 30 on the benefits of obedience to God. He was officiating for our rector who'd taken a tumble from his horse and broken an arm. There was no doubt Patchin was somewhat embarrassed by the office of union chaplain and had expressed as much to other members of the board. Indeed, he was outspoken in his view that it was somewhat beneath his dignity to be preaching sermons to the lowest class of congregation and catechising their offspring – some of whom were bastards.

One or two of those bastards and their adult companions were in the congregation that morning, occupying two pews at the very rear of the church and presenting a uniformly grey appearance. I understood this was a monthly occurrence and the arrangement was that, as long as there was a quorum of at least ten inmates requesting participation in a Sunday service, then the union was obliged to provide an escort. Whatever the inmates' motives, there was never less than a dozen attending each month. On this occasion Jenny Calman, severe in shawl, black bonnet and dress, tempered only by her customary pristine white collar and cuffs, was supervising from the end of the rear pew, thin bloodless lips pressed even more tightly together, eyes darting this way and that, and frowning at any child who moved out of turn.

My motives for attending services were mostly noblesse oblige. As master of Seddon Hall it was expected that I should be an exemplar for the estate workers and the wider parish, but my religious beliefs were ambivalent. Although raised within the teachings of the Church of England, my father's intellectual curiosity and the encouragement of his son to think and question all dogma had left me profoundly agnostic.

Patchin droned on and I mentally drifted off to consider the events of the last few days and the reaction to my revelations at the last meeting. The word was now out in the general district that the inmates were being poorly fed. Although the majority of folk in the union parishes would rather have nothing to do with the workhouse themselves, there was always an underlying feeling of sympathy for those unfortunate enough to find themselves incarcerated there. Their attitude was: 'There but for the Grace of God...'

As the service came to an end I followed the chaplain out into the sunshine with the congregation streaming behind us; the paupers brought up the rear. Most people stayed behind for town gossip and news from their neighbours, but the inmates formed a regimented pairing and shuffled off in a subservient file, heads bowed, eyes to the ground. They were ignored by the rest of the worshippers who were well used to their monthly presence. The matron caught my eye as she came out of the church porch. Saying nothing, she gave me a short bob as she gathered up her flock. I watched them round the corner of the building and then cross the churchyard to the lychgate that led to the road. From there it was just over a mile's walk across three fields of pasture back to the workhouse. It said much about both Jenny

Calman's ability to control the group single-handedly and the cowed state of the inmates, including three young children who, it might be expected, would want to run and gambol in the sunshine. But they clung to their mothers' hands, already habituated to a sense of subjection absorbed from the atmosphere of the House. Their submission and her authority were inextricably linked; the paupers were scared of her temper and power, and Mrs Calman fed on that fear.

Jack Shepherd arrived at the Hall the next day promptly at four o'clock. Foster showed him into the library. Neglecting social conventions he refused both my hand and a seat. Drawing himself up he drew breath to deliver a clearly rehearsed speech.

'Now – look here, Lawes, you must have got my meaning from my letter. Things just can't go on like this. I appreciate you have certain powers as a JP, but there are ways of going about things. I need to be kept informed about anything you find untoward in the running of the union. Damn it, man! I'm the chairman after all and you made me look pretty stupid.'

'Mea culpa – but in fairness I told no other members of the board what I was about. I felt that we all needed to be jerked into a reaction, hence my demonstration. I had no intention of trying to undermine your position. If you feel that was the case, then I apologise wholeheartedly.'

'Well – you damn well did! Of course you know it's all round the parishes and—'

There was a tap on the door and Foster entered with the post tray.

'Excuse me for interrupting, sir. Two letters have arrived, one for you and one for Colonel Shepherd from the master at the workhouse. The porter has brought them. When he heard that the colonel was here he said it had saved him another journey over to Watfield. Would you both come to the House as a matter of urgency? The man's still here, sir.'

'Urgency! What "urgency"? The master's probably exaggerating some minor problem. I think he has an inflated sense of his own importance.'

Pots and kettles, colonel, pots and kettles! I thought.

Shepherd went on. 'Unless it's absolutely necessary I won't go. I'm busy this evening with hunt business. Read what he has to say, will you? I'm sure it's not important.' The gist of the letter was that there'd been an unfortunate death at the House and it was very important that the colonel and I came straight away. I handed him his letter, which I imagined more or less replicated my own. He scanned the contents. 'What does he mean – unfortunate? Why does he want to involve us? Surely it's a matter for the medical officer and the coroner. It's most unusual for the chairman of guardians to be involved in what's probably a routine matter. The inmates die fairly frequently – there are some very old men and women living up there. The master's fully aware of the procedures to be followed, which are very straightforward. No – I'm not minded to ride over at this time of day – it can wait until Wednesday and if really necessary be discussed at the next meeting.'

'I think we should have Fred Lodge in here to find out exactly what this is about. After all, as you say, it's unusual for you to be called out for a routine death. Foster, bring in Mr Lodge, please.' Foster disappeared and quickly returned with the dishevelled porter who, aware of his dusty appearance began brushing down his breeches. He looked nervously at Colonel Shepherd who barked belligerently at him.

'Now look here, Lodge – what's this all this about? It's very inconsiderate of the master to expect me to ride over this evening. Can't it wait?'

'No, sir, it's an emergency, sir.'

Trying to calm Fred, who was looking flushed and ill at ease, I offered him a seat and told him to take his time.

'It's not a routine death, sir. It's a suicide. One of the inmates has hung himself in the yard.'

'Good God!' Jack Shepherd looked firstly alarmed and then exasperated. 'Do we know why?'

'It's too early to say, sir. Mr Calman only found him about an hour ago. He's been cut down and laid out in the dining hall – the suicide I mean. Mr Enderby's gone for Mr Burgwin and Mr Ollington the coroner.'

'Who is it?' I asked.

'Richard Alfrey, sir. He came in March with his wife and daughter.'

'I presume the wife's been told?'

'Yes, sir. I believe Mr Calman let Mrs Alfrey see the body as she was so distraught. The master laid him out so that he looked quite normal – well, as normal as he could under the circumstances. Will you come straight away, sir – and you, Colonel Shepherd? The coroner and surgeon will probably arrive after you.' Given Shepherd's earlier disinclination to be at all involved I took the initiative and forced his hand.

'We'll both ride over now. Tell Mr Calman to leave everything exactly as it is – including the place where Alfrey hung himself. We must check that this is a genuine suicide.'

Shepherd raised his eyebrows. 'What d'you mean – genuine? What else could it be? You're not suggesting foul play are you?'

'No, colonel, but when there's an unusual death it's best to cover all possibilities. I'm sure the unfortunate man, for whatever reasons, decided to end his miserable existence by his own hand. But we should investigate fully' – I looked at him squarely –'with no shortcuts.'

'All right. The three of us will ride over together – shouldn't take us more than twenty minutes.' We were saddled up and off in five, Fred's small Welsh cob doing well to keep up with the colonel's hunter. As we approached the House, Amy Lodge came out with the key and swung the gates open to let us in.

Richard Alfrey's body was laid out on an old stable door on a trestle table at the far end of the dining room. He'd been covered with a blanket and, although evidently not a tall man, his feet, clad in the institution's thin regulation-issue boots, were hanging over the end. Mr Calman was standing centrally behind the table, like a surgeon waiting to perform an operation. He was wheezing as usual and his face was its customary colour of putty, but there was a flush of excited pink on his quivering cheeks, reminding me of a junket livened up with a spoonful of strawberry jam. The man I knew to be Henry Millhouses stood nearby looking quite unemotional.

Calman turned back the blanket to reveal Alfrey's face. The

noose, now loosened, was still round the neck, which was heavily bruised and reddened from the actions of the rope. Alfrey's mouth was open and his swollen, a purple tongue protruding from between the lips. His eyes were also open, bulging and bloodshot. My immediate thought was that this could not have been a pleasant sight for his wife.

'Henry Millhouses found him this afternoon, about three o'clock, hanging from a beam in the yard next to the area where we keep the crates of old rope for the oakum. Millhouses lifted him so that I could cut him down. He'd obviously knotted together lengths of junk rope to do the job, sir.' There was no question that Alfrey was dead by hanging and this was soon confirmed by Matthew Burgwin who had just arrived with the coroner. We all walked outside to the yard at the back of the main building to examine the place the man had been found. There was a piece of slack rope hanging across a high, thick cross-beam in the corner. One end was tied to a stout hook screwed into the wall; the rest of it lay over the beam, from where it dangled impotently, its end cut trim where Calman had cut Alfrey down. On the ground under the rope was a crate, which the man must have stood on while adjusting the noose and then kicked away.

We stood for a few moments in a more or less respectful silence, but which was soon broken by Jack Shepherd who wanted to know what the next move should be. The coroner said to save time and for convenience sake he would hold an immediate inquest, as the cause of death was clear and everyone involved was present. He would take statements from Millhouses, the master and possibly Mrs Alfrey. There might also be inmates who could throw light on why he had decided to kill himself, but there was no doubt that it was suicide and the death certificate would record such a verdict. Privately I thought it might be difficult for Emily Alfrey to cast any light over her husband's state of mind. They'd been separated for three months. It was more likely that one of the male paupers would have an accurate account of Alfrey's recent mood, but I could see that Jack Shepherd became fidgety when the coroner suggested interviewing the inmates. In his usual hasty way he wanted the whole matter closed as soon as possible and could see no advantage in involving them.

The body, still on its stout door, was carried off to an unused stable to be placed in a workhouse coffin. The coroner expressed the hope that burial would be swift – which should present no difficulty since suicides had no funeral service and were buried in unconsecrated ground; it simply required a work detail to dig a grave somewhere in the pasture beyond the churchyard wall. We left the coroner to open the inquest and to take his statements in the boardroom from those most closely involved. Mrs Calman offered us some refreshment, which we declined. Having no further involvement with the matter, Shepherd and I left, he reminding me that there would be an ordinary meeting of the board in two days' time. I noticed his emphasis on 'ordinary'.

But the Wednesday board meeting was anything but 'ordinary'. There were no absentees and the regular officials were all present, including the relieving officer who had a list of new applicants for poor relief. Matthew Burgwin the surgeon was there to give a report on the general health of the inmates, and also to be questioned about the state of mind of Richard Alfrey. The Calmans sat in their usual places near the end of the table. John Calman seemed ill at ease, particularly when he caught my eye and I wondered if he expected me to be more incisive in my questioning of him than had probably been the case during his formal interview with the coroner. In her usual tight-lipped way Mrs Calman revealed nothing of her inner feelings. She was calm to the point of iciness, her eyes lowered and avoiding contact with any board member. Her dress was as usual stark in its neatness; the pure white collar and cuffs reflected hours of work with scrubbing brush, starch and iron by one of the female inmates responsible for the laundry – a woman who no doubt was doubly careful about the attention she gave them.

There was a significant feeling of expectation in the air – in complete contrast to the usual smug atmosphere that generated from an embedded self-satisfaction. Today the members were alert and ready to participate. There were three extra items on the agenda. One was the coroner's report to the board concerning the suicide of Richard Alfrey; the second was a preliminary report from the new 'procurement' committee; the third was an item included at my request on the provision of education for the younger children. The minutes of the previous meeting were agreed and the chairman ran through the standing items as swiftly as he dared.

Thomas Carrick reported that there had been three applications for admission and that some of his fellow relieving officers were in the process of checking their circumstances. It seemed likely that they would fulfil the requirements and should be admitted sometime in the not too distant future. This was agreed and we passed on to the master's report.

John Calman's report was, in its usual way unremarkable, except for the death of Richard Alfrey. But Colonel Shepherd advised him that the board would be discussing that as a separate item and it would be more appropriate if he omitted any references to it at this point. I noticed that some members of the board who previously seemed to pay scant attention to the master's report were now sitting forward in their seats and taking some notice. The farmer William Marchant, for instance, was obviously listening more carefully than usual, as was Robert Bignell. Whether my intervention and discoveries at the previous meeting had at last alerted them to their responsibilities I couldn't know, but the atmosphere round the table was one of a sharpened interest in what was going on.

After Calman's report the surgeon spoke about the general health and welfare of the inmates. Again, there was firmness in his delivery as though he was more confident to report what he saw rather than what the board wanted to hear. Burgwin was a young man and this was his first post. Up to now he had been swayed by the colonel's bullying tactics and smoothed his reports to satisfy the board, but recent events in the House might have caused him to reconsider. He was not an unintelligent man and while he was slowly building a practice in the parishes, his reputation was not yet made and he had clearly come to the realisation that his present involvement with the union might result in serious risk to his integrity. If there was a crisis there would be little time to jump ship before he was implicated along with the rest. Building on the evidence of the quality of nourishment provided, he commented that some of the inmates were underweight, and the allocation of milk for the children might be increased. It was a start, I thought.

We came to the first additional item, that of Richard Alfrey's death. Colonel Shepherd had a copy of the coroner's report, which was brief. 'There had been no foul play. The inmate, Richard Alfrey, aged thirty-six, a leather worker from the parish of Boxford, had deliberately taken his own life for unknown reasons. The man's widow, Emily Alfrey, aged thirty-two, could throw no light on her husband's recent state of mind as she had not spoken to him since they were separated when they entered the workhouse together almost three months previously. One of the inmates, Henry Millhouses, had discovered the body. It was the master who was the first official to be called to the scene; he had cut down the body at approximately three in the afternoon of Monday, 28 May, and could offer no information to enlighten the enquiry. The official verdict was "suicide by hanging while temporarily mentally deranged".' This was replicated on the new official death certificate, which had just come into use the previous year.

Shepherd was ready to move on, but to my surprise his estate manager George Stenning, who was usually most obvious for his lack of involvement, leaned forward in his seat and asked to put a question to the master. With no option, Jack Shepherd acknowledged that he had the board's attention.

'Mr Calman, you say you have no idea why this man took his own life, yet you came across him daily. You must have noticed something in his manner that could have suggested' – he paused – 'something… different?' He left his question hanging in the air.

'Sir, there are about fifty inmates in the union – I can't be expected to understand what each is thinking – let alone likely to do.' Calman's chest heaved under the pressure and his dumpling cheeks began to flush. 'The man had never said much, kept himself to himself, although I know he sometimes talked to one inmate, Henry Millhouses – but I presumed that was because they came in at the same time.'

'In that case, Mr Chairman, do we know what Millhouses said to the coroner during his enquiry?'

Colonel Shepherd looked bewildered – whether from the shock of his right-hand man actually disrupting the smooth flow of his meeting, or simply because he had no answer. 'No idea, George!' he blustered. 'Although he found the body, there was probably nothing to say. It was obviously a clear case of suicide by hanging with no one else involved. No need to make a song and dance about it.'

'Good God, colonel!' exclaimed Ted Lake, explosive as ever. 'This is the only way we might get at the truth. Perhaps we should have Millhouses in here now and ask him. We might at least be able to offer some comfort to the widow.'

'I see no reason to interfere with an official verdict on which the coroner and surgeon are both in agreement. This simply muddies the waters. We want the man buried as soon as possible.'

'No one is seeking to overturn the verdict, colonel – we just want to be able to tell his widow why he did it.'

Jack Shepherd began to bluster again. 'Perhaps the man didn't know himself – perhaps he came to the end of his tether.' The unfortunate comment was not wasted on Ted who muttered, 'He certainly did that all right.'

Ted's argument was sound; Mrs Alfrey deserved an explanation if there was one. Also, if there had been any negligence on the part of the union itself then it might come out at the same time. I suggested that we could put it to the vote as to whether Henry Millhouses should be called. There was a general murmur of agreement from the members. The Calmans exchanged glances; John Calman was squirming, but his wife's face was as inscrutable as ever. The colonel recognised defeat and called for the vote.

This was a new and significant departure for the board. Admittedly we had held a vote on the constitution of the new procurement committee, but that had been uncontentious and singular. Votes were normally not taken – standing issues were always agreed unanimously. When I had first received the information about the members the politician in me had estimated where the balance of power lay. In other words, who would support Jack Shepherd and who would oppose. I had calculated that eight of them, because of their connections, would always support the chairman. Of the other six, three of us were most likely to oppose and the others might swing either way. But there was something out of kilter in this meeting – prompted by George Stenning's unique intervention. I became aware of a sea change in the atmosphere, which I attributed to cracks that were beginning to appear in the solidarity of support for the colonel's style of chairmanship. The more astute board members were beginning to see that cutting corners in administration might be convenient in terms of time and effort, but there could be consequences when slackness of supervision led to serious breaches of the regulations, in this instance the most serious case of an unnatural death, which must be accounted for. There were punishments for guardians' 'misdemeanours', which could amount to an appearance in the magistrates' court and fines. Discretion being the better part of valour, the board hedged its bets and voted nine to five to interrogate Millhouses. The master pulled himself out of his seat and went off to fetch him.

Seen alone, away from the crowd of inmates, Henry Millhouses presented as a tall, well-proportioned man in his mid-thirties. He was verging on the thin and had assumed the House pallor – a direct consequence of poor diet and lack of regular fresh air – but that didn't in any way detract from the alertness in his eyes and face. He stood composed before us and seemed in no way intimidated. Colonel Shepherd wrested back control of proceedings.

'Now look hear, what's y'name – Hillhouses?'

'Millhouses, sir – Henry Millhouses.'

'Millhouses – yes – well, what we want is for you to tell us what you know about the man Alfrey and why you think he hanged himself.'

'I imagine he hung himself because he couldn't face another day here.' I noticed his subtle correction of Jack Shepherd's misuse of grammar.

'I understand from the master that Alfrey spoke to you a few times – is that correct?'

'We had a few conversations while we were oakum picking. It's the kind of boring, repetitive work that lends itself to idle chat among the workers.'

I picked up an almost imperceptible subtext of critical irony, not a device regularly employed by the labouring classes. It led me to intervene. 'Did Mr Alfrey ever give you any indication that he was so deeply in despair that he was considering taking his own life?'

'He talked mostly about his wife and daughter who were in the women's section. I would say he was as deeply depressed as any man – or woman – in this establishment. I only knew him as a fellow inmate

– indeed we came into the workhouse almost on the same day. What kind of a man he was on the outside I couldn't say. He told me he was a leather dresser from Boxford; he'd lost his job and with it his home and had been forced on the parish' – he paused, turned his head and looked the colonel straight in the eye – 'his history was no different from the rest of us.'

Ted Lake raised his hand and the colonel nodded for him to speak. 'If you knew him for a few months, were you aware of any significant change in his demeanour before he took his life?'

'He seemed particularly distressed about a week before but I had no chance to talk to him so can't report what it was that had upset him, even if he'd chosen to tell me – which he might not have. He didn't always want to converse; it depended on his mood. But I can tell you he must have had something very serious on his mind because the night before he killed himself he had a nightmare that disturbed the whole dormitory. In the middle of the night he screamed out several times and sat bolt up in bed in a sweat. He'd woken some of the men and they were angry. I called out to him to calm him down and he went back to sleep. When I asked him about it the next morning he denied he'd had any bad dreams and so I didn't pursue it further. I think he felt rather ashamed and humiliated when I told him he'd woken the rest of us. I had no further conversation with him after that.'

Colonel Shepherd looked relieved. It seemed certain that Henry Millhouses could provide no new evidence as to motive and that the verdict and death certificate could remain unchallenged. The burial could go ahead, probably on Friday. He did the board the courtesy of asking if there were any further questions and even George Stenning – who had set all this in motion with his questioning of John Calman – shrugged and shook his head. Millhouses walked out accompanied by the master and the board settled down to its further business.

The interrogation had taken up some time and there were still two important items to discuss. Colonel Shepherd was forced to concede that my request to examine the provision of education for the children was considered to be of substance enough to warrant a full discussion with adequate time provided, and I agreed it could be postponed until the next meeting when it would become a priority on the agenda. Ted Lake, as chairman of the sub-committee, was ready with its preliminary report on the cost and quality of the food provided for the inmates. By this time in the proceedings I hoped it would be short.

As it turned out he could only report that Mr Harbey the clerk had been very cooperative and let them keep the order books for several days. Ted, with Will Faulkner, John Newton and William Marchant had met twice and delegated different concerns so that they would not duplicate any of their work. Their first task was to match orders, invoices and receipts, particularly for staples like flour and meat, which they found to be in exemplary order, complimenting the clerk on his efficiency. The colonel looked relieved, but Ted went on. 'Our next task will be to consider the commissioners' regulations regarding the diet of the inmates, which are clearly laid out as to quantities and type. In view of the discovery the other day we want to investigate whether they are receiving sufficient and of what quality. With your permission, matron, we would like to come into the kitchens at some time and look at the stores.'

Jenny Calman's hands remained in her lap and there was not so much as a twitch of her lips. Her face remained impassive as she inclined her head and said, 'Certainly, sir. If you would care to tell me when will be convenient – I suppose you wouldn't all want to inspect us at the same time – it might make a busy kitchen rather crowded to have you all there at once.'

Ted Lake looked at the others. 'Two of us will come as soon as we can arrange convenient times between us.' He sat down and the matron remained as she had been throughout – unruffled and fully composed.

The meeting had overrun its normal fifty minutes by another forty and most of the board were looking at their watches and wishing to be elsewhere. Colonel Shepherd drew it to a conclusion and only a couple of members stayed for sherry and biscuits. I was relieved that Ted immediately sought out Jenny Calman to make his arrangements with her. I didn't want to stay for a long evaluation of the meeting, which I could see would result if I remained any longer. With other considerations on my mind I went swiftly round to the stable and collected my horse.

I trotted down the drive to the gates to find Fred Lodge waiting for me. He was ill at ease and distracted, showing none of his usual prompt and business-like activity. He stepped up to me. 'Mr Lawes, sir, I wonder if you would be so good as to step inside the lodge for a few minutes and have a word with myself and Mrs Lodge – it's a matter of great importance, otherwise I wouldn't trouble you.' I was intrigued because previously Fred had made it clear that a visit to his home by the guardians was a novelty and one that he didn't generally encourage. I dismounted and tethered up and Fred called his eldest boy across to watch the horse. I followed the porter into his lodge, ducking my head at the low door, and was shown into a neat parlour where Mrs Lodge was standing – looking equally apprehensive.

'Good morning, Amy! So, Fred – what is it? How can I help?'

'This suicide has caused Amy and me a lot of concern, sir. As soon as we heard about it we knew something wasn't right. We've talked about it for a long time and then decided the best thing to do was to write it all down – that is what we know and think – in a letter as a kind of record. You're the one person we know we can trust, both to keep it confidential and to know what should be done.' He took a small package from the parlour table and handed it to me. 'I think it would be best if you read it in private. It's beyond us to do anything. We thought you being a JP would know what was best. Please remember, sir, it's only what we've heard – we've no real evidence.'

'Well,' I said, 'thank you for your trust. I'll do as you say and read it at home. Obviously depending on its content I might well have to take action. But I'm very aware of the awkwardness of your situation and I'll do my best to make sure you're not implicated, at least as far as I'm able. In the meantime try not to worry – difficult I know! For now, I thank you for your confidence.'

'Thank you, sir! As I say, you were the only one we could think of to tell.'

I wished them both good day and promised we would speak again soon.

As I rode home I considered what the letter might contain. Several possibilities crossed my mind – perhaps it was foul play after all. This I dismissed immediately as there was no evidence to show how anyone could have murdered Alfrey in that way, unless it had been mob-handed, which was impossible given the solid evidence that all the inmates and officers of the union had been fully engaged and within sight of one another at the time the act took place. It seemed more likely that it was connected with Alfrey's motive for killing himself and those reasons I could not begin to conjecture. But it was certain that Fred and Amy had been badly shaken by something – enough to risk committing it to writing and into my hands.

Arriving home there were various business matters and some correspondence for me to deal with and, although I had not forgotten about the letter I had no opportunity to read it quietly and in peace until after dinner. As I was dining alone there were no formalities and the meal was over in half an hour. I took a decanter of port into my study, settled in my armchair and took the sealed letter from the occasional table. It was addressed to me in an excellent style and hand and I presumed that Amy Lodge had written the jointly composed effort. There was no doubt that Fred had been at pains that morning to demonstrate how much he relied on her opinion. I opened his letter, which was startling in its detail.

The Lodge,

Seddon Union Workhouse

Tuesday, 29 May

Mr Lawes, sir,

For some weeks we have deliberated as to what way we should report our concerns about the running of the House. The recent death yesterday of one of the inmates has led us to finally take action. You are the only person we can tell about our serious unease, although you might wonder why we have not informed our uncle, Mr Lake. We fear he would be rash and want to take immediate action, but as we have yet no evidence to support our concerns – only what we have been told and surmised from that information – that would risk a scandal without a verifiable foundation and the perpetrators would never be brought to justice.

Mrs Calman and her brother the overseer Robert Enderby are guilty of committing wicked acts against the female inmates. They collude together, or rather Mrs Calman is in thrall to her brother and cannot deny him. You may have heard of his reputation as a womaniser, but we fear it goes far beyond that. The women are not safe when he is on the premises. Worse still, neither are the young girls. Enderby and his sister have a system whereby he alerts her to the woman or girl he wants, and she provides the means of access. She has given him a key to the women's quarters and a particular room in the attic for his use where he takes the females she procures for him. The women are powerless to complain. No one will take the word of an inmate against the master or matron, or any other official. Some of the women have dubious pasts themselves and are not regarded by anyone in authority as either respectable or honest.

You will want to know how we know. As porter and assistant to the matron, we have regular dealings with the inmates and have got to know most of them to some degree. When Mr and Mrs Calman are absent we are responsible – unless the overseer is available – for the running of the House. On those occasions when we are in charge Enderby is invariably off the premises and we take the opportunity to talk to the inmates. It took many months before they began to trust us, but three of the women have told Amy that the overseer has viciously assaulted them and they know of others who have suffered the same treatment but will not speak of it. They were willing to expose him because they found out that he had started going for the really young girls – some as young as eleven or twelve.

At the risk of being indelicate, this is rape, sir. There is no other way to put it. The three women who approached us all maintain they were forced, but their concern is mostly for the female children. None of the inmates have faith in the board of guardians – indeed, none of them have ever spoken to any of the members. They were given a glimmer of hope that for the first time someone is taking their side when you confronted the board about the food.

We have told them we will do all we can to expose this outrage and this is a first step. We are certain that the suicide this week is connected to these wicked acts; information from one of the inmates would confirm it. But it seems to us it is all part of a pattern of ill-treatment that is underlined by an evil force in the place. There are many other concerns we could describe: the harsh treatment of the very young children, inappropriate punishments, spontaneous beatings, poor food and conditions etc., etc. But I know that your own investigations, which are under way, will eventually bring these to light. In the meantime, please use this information to take whatever action you consider necessary.

Although we would ask you to have regard for our situation, if you think the welfare of the inmates requires it, feel free to use this letter in any way you think fit, regardless of the consequences. We have discussed the possible effects of our revelations but are willing to take the consequences for the sake of the women and children. We are both sorry that we did not bring these matters forward earlier.

With the greatest respect we remain in confidence,
Your humble servants,
Frederick and Amy Lodge

I sat quite still for a minute when I reached the end of the letter. My immediate response was one of admiration for them both. It was clear they were willing to risk all in pursuit of the truth and 'doing the right thing'. I made a promise to myself that I would do all I could to keep their names out of any future investigation, if it came to that.

It took some time to absorb what Fred and Amy were alleging.

What I'd heard and knew of Enderby would lead me to suspect he was certainly capable of such outrages and probably more. But where was the proof? Rereading the letter, I weighed their conclusions in the balance. As a lawyer I recognised they were entirely based on hearsay evidence, inadmissible in court. The probability was that it was true, but if it came before a jury the accusers from the House would be most likely considered unreliable witnesses on account of their social backgrounds, as the Lodges had pointed out. Such witnesses would be torn to pieces by a defending counsel, who would immediately cite their previous lifestyles as dubious in the extreme and their word not to be relied upon. Obviously we needed confirming evidence. It would be impossible to prove that the alleged locus of the crimes actually existed as such. The room in the attic could simply be a hideaway for Enderby when he came back to the House drunk, although it would appear to be an inappropriate place for him to bed down – up in the roof space where the children slept. But that did not mean he used it for vicious purposes. Any physical evidence of assault from the women would also be very difficult to produce unless it was examined immediately after the event. As for evidence of collusion in criminal activity between the overseer and his sister, that could never be established unless one implicated the other, which would be most unlikely. An investigation based on all these impossibilities would certainly put Fred and his wife at considerable risk. I didn't underestimate Jenny Calman or her brother, and knew they would do everything in their power to prevent exposure. If they had the slightest hint that their activities were under scrutiny, they would most certainly try to destroy any evidence and probably seek to physically damage their accusers.

The suicide might be a distraction and unconnected to the serious allegations made against Enderby and his sister. The significant point in the investigation that had followed was that no one had come up with a motive for Alfrey's act of self-destruction. Even the short interrogation of Henry Millhouses at the board meeting had provided very little detail, other than Alfrey was considerably morose during the week before his death. But it would need a significant and prolonged enquiry to establish a connection between the man's suicide and the Lodge's allegations. Colonel Shepherd was certainly not going to allow the board to waste any more time on it unless I presented Fred and Amy's letter. In that case I would be opening up a new dimension, one which implicated House officials in serious crimes. The ramifications were too great to be contemplated lightly. Unless there was absolute proof, Fred and Amy would probably lose their positions, and Enderby and his sister would most likely escape justice. The board would be thrown into confusion and my position, as the instigator, would become untenable.

I could understand why Fred had been reluctant to involve his uncle. Given Ted Lake's volatile personality his response would have been to confront the alleged villains immediately and attempt to give them both a horse-whipping, then the game would have been up and justice ill served. The Lodges were wise to be circumspect, but they needed to maintain that discretion. There was always a possibility that they might lower their guard in relief that someone else was involved. I needed to caution them to remain careful in what they said and to whom they spoke. It might also be that the women's hopes had now been raised and their expectation was that action would be taken and the matron and the overseer served with appropriate justice. If the Lodges or any of the women became loose-tongued all hopes of that would be dashed.

Having come to no great conclusion as to my future actions I locked the letter away in my desk drawer, finished off the Old Tawny and went to bed.

Chapter 6

Three days later at about four forty-five in the afternoon I heard hooves and wagon wheels on the gravel drive, someone dismounting and then a frantic knocking at the door. Foster answered it and brought young Fred Lodge into my study. Dishevelled from a fast ride, dusty and red-faced, he was in such a state I immediately ordered a brandy for him. Only when he'd swallowed half of it did I say, 'Whatever's the matter, Fred?'

'An accident – Enderby – the overseer – dead in the pigsty – no bits, all chopped off and the pig has made a meal of him.' Gabbled out at such speed, at first I could make no sense of it. He went on: 'Mr Calman sent me in the pony and trap to get Colonel Shepherd, but you're the closest and I thought it would make more sense for you to go and see what's happened. I'll go off to fetch the colonel now. Will you go, sir?' I had a distinct feeling of déjà vu. It had only been a few days since he'd ridden over from the workhouse with the news of Richard Alfrey's suicide and insisted that we rode back together to investigate.

'Of course, but just calm down and tell me what you know.' It was not very much. The overseer had been found half naked in the pigsty only about three quarters of an hour before. The two boys who routinely fed the pigs at four o'clock had found his body.

Although I felt sorry for Lodge and would have liked to let him stay a while and gather himself, it was imperative that the surgeon should be called, and of course Jack Shepherd must be informed. I told Fred to take a horse from my stables and ride to Burgwin then on to the colonel's. He could ride back to the workhouse with Shepherd and I would take the trap back to the House immediately. I particularly wanted to arrive first and have a look at the scene where this 'accident' had taken place. I was soon on the road and arrived within twenty minutes.

Amy Lodge opened the gates for me and I could see immediately that the place was in uproar. The main front door was wide open and as I alighted one of the boys climbed up on to the trap and drove it round to the back. Calman appeared at the door. 'My wife's been put to bed, sir, struck dumb by it all. It's a bad business. She saw the body, sir.' His face was uncharacteristically pale.

We walked into the hall and I went over to the corpse, which had been carried from the pigsty in the same manner as Richard Alfrey's, on a shed door that now lay on a trestle table. Calman winced as I drew back the bloodied sheet and exposed the overseer's body fully. It was naked from the waist down and what lay in full view was as gruesome a sight as I'd ever seen. No wonder Mrs Calman had to take to her bed. It was now obvious why Fred's garbled account of Enderby's 'bits' was so shocking – they had been either chewed off or 'chopped off' as he'd described. I calculated that Enderby's body had been in the sty for a good few hours and during that time the pig had done a thorough job. There was evidence of savage incisions on other parts of the torso but the face, although filthy, was largely untouched, the dark hair matted with blood and straw. Mercifully Enderby's eyes were closed. Calman replaced the sheet and I ordered two sensible-looking men to stand by the doors and let no one through. I went into the boardroom to wait for the surgeon and Colonel Shepherd. As for overall supervision of the place, it said something about the iron control that was exercised over the inmates that none of them had seemed to stir from their customary docility, which was fortunate as there was no one immediately available to carry out their office.

Hearing Burgwin had arrived I went into the dining hall to meet him. He was flushed from his hard ride and looked younger than ever. I ordered the two men to leave and after they disappeared the surgeon took off the sheet and began to examine the body. I was not sure how much surgery Matthew Burgwin had been involved with. He was too young to have been in any wars, even recent ones. I supposed he'd seen and dissected cadavers during his training, but it was evident that he was shocked beyond belief at the state of Robert Enderby's body. I told him that pigs could be extremely vicious under certain circumstances and there was evidence here of the boar's bloodlust. The legs and lower torso were covered in long gashes, some of them wide open and deeply incised with jagged edges. The crotch area had been particularly mauled and chewed at; this seemed to be the primary scene, or the first cut. According to the witnesses there had been no signs of

Enderby's private parts in the sty. I conjectured with a shiver that the pig had probably eaten what would have been tasty titbits. Between us we turned the body over. Carefully examining the back of the overseer's head, Burgwin showed me where it had received a massive and possibly fatal blow. He pointed out small fragments of skull that were just visible. There was no question that Enderby had been severely struck over the head before being mutilated and thrown into the sty.

As we were making our examination Colonel Shepherd stamped into the hall, came across to the corpse, cast his eye over it in the same manner in which he probably scrutinised a savaged fox and brusquely asked Burgwin if he could tell how long the man had been dead. The surgeon could give no definite answer and said we would have to wait for witness statements to ascertain when Enderby was last seen. Shepherd grunted, turned on his heels and entered the boardroom; Matthew and I followed him. At this stage I believe Shepherd thought, or at least wanted to think, it had all been a terrible accident, that the overseer had fallen into the sty while semi-drunk.

But Burgwin was adamant. 'In my opinion the genitals have been deliberately carved off with a very sharp butchering knife and the wound on the head has been inflicted with a heavy object. There's no denying that Mr Enderby has been murdered.'

I cut in. 'As to the motives for such a barbarous act, there will have to be a full investigation by the coroner. He'll need to call witnesses, some from beyond the walls of the workhouse.' I saw Shepherd's face contort and knew that the last thing he wanted was for an extensive enquiry, possibly with outsiders coming in, to uncover who knew what.

He looked me squarely in the eye. 'See here, Edgar, as a JP can't you get to the bottom of things quietly and report to the coroner without outsiders coming in?'

'I don't think that's possible as Coroner Ollington will have to hold an inquest. I'll ask him about the protocols of my involvement in any investigation, but it might not play to the rules – after all I'm involved with the supervision of the institution – and who guards the guards, Jack?'

'Hmm, I'm sure there are procedures to be followed, but I think an internal investigation would be best all round. Let's try to keep it within the walls of the place.'

'I see your point and we are on the spot with local knowledge. But eventually wider authorities must be involved; the constable must be informed of the incident as soon as possible.' I told Shepherd I would ride over to discuss possibilities with Ollington in the morning. One thing was certain: the news would be spreading fast throughout the villages through parish-pump gossip.

Unlike London, which for the last nine years has had its own metropolitan police force, local arrangements for matters of law and order in our small rural parishes are very ad hoc. We have a constable for our district, but no 'lock-up' and no official body to investigate serious crimes, other than JPs such as myself. This particularly nasty crime would require full investigation, as much as Jack Shepherd might resist it. As promised, I consulted the coroner, who felt it wouldn't be improper for me in these early stages of enquiry to try to get to the truth and see justice done – clearly there was no one else. He offered me any help I wanted and I said I'd probably call on his expertise at some point. I wanted to get matters moving as soon as possible while memories were fresh and witnesses uncontaminated. The febrile atmosphere in the workhouse left me suspicious that some kind of obfuscation might take place; some of the inmates might easily be bullied into false testimony.

There was also the most important fact of Fred's letter and in what respect, if any, the Lodge's allegations were connected to Enderby's murder. The women concerned had not offered any evidence other than what they had been told or experienced themselves. They had been unable or unwilling to provide precise details of dates, times or locations. It was their word against the Calmans and Enderby, and he was now in no position either to defend himself or to be a witness. I was unsure at present what the response to those complaints should be, who I should involve and when I should raise the matter. If I called Fred Lodge to give any information at the proposed enquiry, I would have to cite his letter. That would put him in the position of key witness as to motive for the murder, but would be a breach of confidence on my part. Enderby and his sister were obviously hated by all the inmates, men and women, and I could see that this had a significant bearing on why he'd been killed in such a manner.

The problem was when and how to question the women concerned without arousing the Calmans' suspicions. I was assuming that John Calman was involved, but perhaps that was a mistake. As Jenny Calman was in awe of her brother, so John was equally daunted by his wife. Perhaps she considered him too much of a fool to include him in any conspiracy with her brother. I would give Calman the benefit of the doubt for the present but, as I had already decided on first acquaintance, I would not underestimate Jenny Calman's capacity for deviousness.

I didn't attend the formal inquest on the Monday morning as I had cases in the magistrates' court to hear that I could not avoid. As it was reported to me later, Daniel Ollington opened the inquest in the boardroom at the House. Colonel Shepherd and many of the guardians were there. The coroner explained that he was initially concerned with the timing of events and the cause of death. Any motive for murder, if that was assumed, would be investigated later. From my perspective this was ideal as it meant I need not reveal to the coroner Fred's allegations in evidence.

According to Ted Lake, Ollington handled the inquest well. It was an open inquest and there were plenty of curious onlookers from the town. Questioning of various witnesses left the court with some clarification as to the timing of events on that Saturday, which, in some instances, placed the victim precisely, although the times recorded were not exact for the most part as many of the witnesses had no timepieces available to them. The report I received later was structured thus:

10.00: Robert Enderby, on horseback, was let into the workhouse through the lodge gates by Fred Lodge, who reported that he looked the worse for wear and smelled of drink. Although it was officially his day off Enderby had agreed to oversee the inmates while the Calmans were out for the rest of the morning. The porter took the overseer's horse round to the stables, while Enderby was let in through the main door by Jenny Calman. He told her he was going up stairs to their accommodation to clean himself up.

10.15: The master and matron left the premises together in the pony and trap.

10.30: Enderby came down stairs and passed through the dining hall into the kitchen where there were five women preparing the midday meal. One of them, Edith Smitherson, said he told them he was going to check on the boys working in the garden. The boys were at the bottom of the vegetable garden, out of sight of the pigsties. They said that Mr Enderby had not come down to see them at any time during the morning. No one had left or entered by the wall door at the bottom of the garden that morning while they were working there. The door had remained locked as it always was.

11.15: The women in the kitchen reported that, from the windows, they had seen the overseer return to the main building.

Midday: The Calmans returned and Mrs Calman sought out her brother. The women in the kitchen were taking gruel to the dining hall. She enquired as to where Enderby was and was told that he was last seen from the kitchen window returning from the garden to the main building sometime around mid-morning. As no one had access to a timepiece they could not be more accurate. He had not been seen since. According to Mrs Calman she stayed to supervise the midday meal, thinking her brother might have left the premises again – he was wont to come and go as he pleased. It was his day off in any case so she was not unduly worried that he had not turned up during the afternoon.

4pm: Two young boys, Peter Samuels and William Tuttle,

went down to feed the pigs at their regular time and found the body. They ran back in an hysterical state to find the master. Hearing something of what had happened, the Calmans rushed down to the sty with the boys to find the mangled remains of Enderby, naked from the waist down and face up among the straw and dung. The boar was very reluctant to let go of his prize so he had to be coaxed out with a bucket of peelings and some strokes of a stick. Fortunately the commotion had brought out a couple of the male inmates, one of whom jumped into the sty to help remove the animal. Once the sty was clear the two inmates manhandled the body between them, one inside the sty, one out, until it lay on the grass. They took the shed door off its hinges and laid the body on it, covering the indecent half with a large apron taken from a hook in the shed. The master took his wife back to their apartment and the two men and boys carried the body back to the House, placing it on a trestle table in the dining hall. Fred Lodge had been alerted and was in the hall. The master told him to take the pony and trap and ride to Colonel Shepherd's house and tell him he was needed urgently.

What could not be established was the exact timing of the murder. The witnesses in the kitchen who had said they saw Enderby return from the garden and pass their window mid-morning couldn't be any more accurate. There were other points that needed clarification, such as the real purpose of Enderby's visit to the garden in the morning, and why had he bothered to tell the women in the kitchen. It was out of character for him to actively carry out minor supervision of the boys and to take such a time about it. As it turned out he hadn't gone anywhere near their end of the garden. Also, he'd been seen returning to the House before the midday meal, but no one was certain where he went at that point. He must have returned to the gardens in the afternoon but no one saw him and for what purpose we had yet to discover. He couldn't have returned to the Calmans' living quarters after the women had seen him because the master and matron had returned there themselves by midday and had noted his absence, assuming he'd left the premises altogether.

Daniel Ollington adjourned the inquest so that these questions could be investigated, although he did authorise Enderby's burial in the interests of decency. The weather was becoming warmer and it was difficult to maintain the decomposing body in a decent state for interment. As local JP I was nominated to begin an internal enquiry the next day, questioning fully all those who had been present and involved at the time. There would be three of us officiating – myself, Jack Shepherd and the lawyer Robert Bignell. Following any outcome, we would report to the coroner and to an extraordinary meeting of the board the day after.

After the session at the magistrates I was in need of a quiet drink and some time to mull over events. I made my way to the Fleece where I was surprised when the landlord asked if he could have a quiet word. He pulled me a pint of ale and came across to the other side of the bar. Fortunately the place wasn't busy. We found a corner and Michael came straight to the point.

'Merry Mary says she has some information about Robert Enderby, but wants money for it. She came in here on Saturday night just after his body was found and seemed anxious when everyone was gossiping about what had happened. When I asked what was up she went all mysterious on me and said she knew quite a lot about Bob's last night and it might be of interest to "certain parties". I told her in no uncertain terms that if she knew anything she had to tell a magistrate or the coroner or even Colonel Shepherd. At first she flatly refused to speak to any of you, especially Mr Ollington and the colonel. Then she said she'd speak to you as you were fair and "comely"!'

I didn't know how I should take a compliment from the local whore, but I was certainly interested in anything she had to say.

'She'll have to meet me here,' I said. I had no intention of any clandestine meetings with the parish prostitute.

'I'll tell her, sir, but what about payment? She mentioned money. Would you be prepared to give her something?'

'She shouldn't expect money for doing her duty, but I won't

quibble – a half sovereign and no more. I'll leave the money with you. It wouldn't do for me to be seen handing cash over to the local harlot. Tell her I'll meet her here tonight at six o'clock.'

'She'll be in later – I'll let her know.'

Promptly at six I walked back into the Fleece. Sure enough Mary was at the bar, spruced up I noticed, which surprised me because on her innumerable appearances in court she generally made no effort to impress. The grubby woollen shawl had been replaced with one of poor-quality black lace and she had brushed her fine, mousy hair, which hung limply below a small soiled cap. I also detected the remnants of soap on the fringes of her face. But her faded blue dress, possibly the only one she possessed, didn't bear close inspection. In fact, I was forced to avert my eyes from the indecent bulge over the top of her bodice, where her breasts were squeezed tightly together, forming a platform that I thought could probably support a couple of pint tankards. It was likely she wasn't necessarily laying out her selling points but had simply grown out of the garment, which was tight in many other places. She bobbed a curtsy.

In spite of his reputation for meanness, Michael Jameson poured us both a brandy, waved away my offer to pay, and I took Mary to one of the booths. There were some looks exchanged between a few of the regulars, but my reputation was so secure that I returned their stares and simply raised an eyebrow, which was a signal for them to mind their own business. I wanted the meeting to be a brief as possible and had already rehearsed tactics in my mind. There was no point in badgering her for information; she had to give it to me in her own time. So we sat down and I thought to open the conversation with a few generalities, as though we were acquaintances meeting up for a routine drink together.

'Well, Mary, how are things with you?'

As soon as I said it, I regretted it. The last thing I wanted to hear was an account of Mary's business activities. But some innate intelligence on her part recognised that my question was simply an opening gambit and to my relief she played the game.

'It's fair, sir. I make my way. But I know you're a busy man and will want to get on with the business. Michael's told me the deal and I accept.'

'So what exactly do you want to tell me?' She leaned forward, and I was momentarily distracted by the two grey bulges spilling out of the top of her bodice, both of which were in danger of exploding into full view. I hoped she wouldn't draw a heavy breath.

'Bob Enderby was a regular of mine; we had an arrangement twice a week. He was a drunkard and a bully, but he always paid me. On the night before he was killed – that was a shocking way for him to go, sir, whatever kind of man he was – anyway, on that night he'd been with me. He was very drunk, as usual, having been in the Fleece for at least three hours before we met up at my place at about one in the morning. The usual arrangement was that he came across and stayed the rest of the night, returning to the House sometime during mid-morning.

'This night he seemed different. He wasn't particularly interested in what I had to offer, more inclined to talk.' She took a long pull at her drink and I could see that there would be several refills before the tale was told. 'What came out was this: he said he had a good thing going up at the House – new blood he called it, exceptional he said. I knew he was always on the lookout for a good feel—' I winced but let her continue. 'I reckoned he was having one of the inmates. But that wasn't all. He let slip there was a very young one he was inter-ested in and he was working on how he could, as he said, "manage it". I took notice because he never normally talked about the women in the House – called them all whores and trollops – which is funny really when you think who he was talking to. Fortunately I don't take offence – can't afford to.'

By this time I had to signal to Michael to bring over another brandy. Mary was clearly beginning to enjoy herself. When the brandy arrived I asked her, 'What did you make of it?'

'It, sir?'

'What he said. Did he mention any names? Did you think it was the drink talking, or was there really something going on?'

'Oh, sir! I know – knew – Bob. He was, as I said, a bully, but he knew women and how to get round them. He'd been quite a good-looking man once – a bit like yourself, sir. I wasn't surprised when he told me he'd found possibilities up at the House. But then he worried me. From what he was saying it seemed as though the woman was very unwilling – "playing hard to get" he said, but he was certain he wouldn't be denied. Now, my experience is that when a woman says "no", it's red rag to a bull to some men – yourself excluded, sir, I'm sure. In my game, as you might imagine, sir, I get to read the signs and can make a quick getaway. I've only been caught out twice, very nasty, but what I think you gentry might call a hazard of the occupation – am I right, sir?' I looked at Mary, at this regular feature of my court, and realised for the first time that she was a vibrant, funny and utilitarian woman – a true example of the 'enlightenment' indeed! She offered an inherently chancy but necessary service, while accepting those risks with sanguinity. Had she been born under different circumstances who knew what she might have achieved. But she was making the best of what she had and above all honest to her own principles.

'I can only agree, Mary. But it shouldn't be this way. Men who treat women thus are no better than animals. What you've told me confirms my own suspicions and this information is an important part of the picture I've been building up. You may have supplied a solid motive for his murder.' Her podgy, open face became pink with pleasure and importance. 'Sir, if ever you feel inclined—'

I rose quickly before she could finish the sentence. 'Thank you for what you've told me. I've left your money with Michael behind the bar. One thing I must warn you of. You must say nothing about this to anyone – you haven't already discussed it, have you?'

'Oh no, sir! I knew you should be the first to hear of it. You can trust me. I've got lots of secrets about many of the men in this town. That's why they keep coming back to me; they know I can keep my mouth shut. It's one of the tricks of my trade. Only I hope you can get to the bottom of what has happened and catch the bastard who did this. I may not have liked Bob very much, but no one should get away with what they did to him afterwards – besides he was a good customer and I'll miss him!'

'Good. Now, Mary, I imagine we'll meet again in court – only try to make the appearances less frequent, will you? The law will tolerate so much – but if you try to make a mock of the process it has a habit of hitting back!'

'Yes, sir. God bless you, sir, and thank you.' She gave me the full worth of her gappy grin and remained seated in the booth. As I passed through the bar I nodded to Michael. Mary would immediately make a claim on the money.

As I rode home I had a great feeling of relief. It dawned on me that Mary's information had effectively saved me from exposing Fred's letter to the enquiry. Both were allegations and hearsay, but I could safely introduce Mary's evidence as an anonymous verbal source, which simply replicated what Fred had been told by the women. She had had it from Bob Enderby himself, which made it all the more potent.

At ten o'clock on the following day Shepherd, Robert Bignell and I gathered in the House dining hall, where a table and three chairs had been set out for us. We'd been given a list of the inmates who could have no possible knowledge of any of the events and there would obviously be no value in interrogating any of the young children. The majority of the inmates, men and women, had been oakum picking for most of the morning and the afternoon. The most valuable witnesses were the women in the kitchen who were probably the last to see Enderby alive. They'd been questioned individually by the coroner and would be unlikely to change their statements, but we might pick up something from them that had been missed. There were the two boys, Samuels and Tuttle, who had been working in the vegetable gardens and whom Enderby had said he was going to find. Close questioning might reveal something about Enderby's motives for saying he would be visiting them. We would also want to speak to the Calmans, and the porter and his wife, who could confirm whether or not Enderby had left the premises before or after the midday meal.

We prepared to question the nine inmates who were most likely to confirm the schedule of events, and who might be able to throw additional light on the hours when Enderby was missing. Although no one would be asked to swear an oath – this was not another inquest or a court of law – we tried to impress on all the witnesses that they should tell the truth. The first we called was Rosa Hinds, one of the five women working in the kitchen. She was middle-aged, a widow who had been in the workhouse for three years. According to Calman she was a hard worker who kept herself to herself. Physically she was a large handsome woman and stood very straight and stiff before us, giving her account clearly and unhesitatingly. She had no timepiece, so could not be accurate as to when Enderby came though the kitchen, but she judged it to be around ten thirty as they were still peeling vegetables and hadn't started the cooking, which they routinely began three quarters of an hour before serving at twelve. Enderby had come in and definitely told them he was going outside to supervise the boys in the garden.

'Did it seem strange to you that he told you this?' I asked.

'Well – I didn't take much heed of it. I could smell drink on him, and thought he was just trying to be more sociable than usual because of it. All the women heard him say it, but it wasn't till afterwards that we gave it any mind.'

'So what did you think – afterwards?'

'What d'you mean, sir?'

'Well – you obviously remembered he'd had some conversation with you all, what did you make of it?

'Like I say, sir, we thought it was the drink talking – he was never one to be friendly with any of the inmates. He just came through, told us where he was going and left.'

'You say you next saw him in the middle of the morning – after eleven o'clock. Where was he going?'

'That's right, sir. We saw him coming past the kitchen window back from the garden and towards the main building.'

'You didn't see him return to the garden anytime after that?'

'No, sir, and we never saw him to speak to again. What happened to him after we last saw him I couldn't say.' I caught finality in her words, as though she felt she had nothing more to explain. I wanted to ask one final question.

'What did you think of Mr Enderby?'

Jack Shepherd fidgeted in his seat and leaned forward. 'I don't think that's relevant, Mr Lawes. Whatever the inmates thought of the man can't possibly throw any light on events.'

I wouldn't be denied and pursued my question. 'You and the other women must have had some view of the man. You've already said he wasn't usually sociable, not willing to pass the time of day –

yet here he was explaining to you his intentions – quite out of character as you say. Was he a fair man?'

'Fair, sir? I'm not sure what you mean.'

'Did he treat people well? Would you speak to him if there were
any difficulties or problems, either personally or connected with the
running of the House?'

She looked bewildered. 'No, sir. That kind of thing doesn't go on
here. We simply get on with our work. No one ever passed the time
of day with the overseer or anyone else in charge if it comes to that.
Mr Enderby was a man in charge – and acted in that way.' That was
final and so we dismissed her. After she left Colonel Shepherd rounded
on me.

'Look here, Lawes, we can't have this kind of thing. This is an
enquiry into a murder; whether or not the inmates esteem members of
staff is immaterial. I think you're going completely down the wrong
path. It seems to me that no one on the premises could possibly have
had anything to do with the overseer's death. It has to be someone
from outside.'

'Really, colonel? And how can that be? Are you trying to say that
someone randomly climbed over the wall, met Enderby in the garden, knocked him over the head, castrated him and tipped him into
the pigsty – all alone and unaided? What would be the motive? I don't
think that holds up at all.'

'A madman – someone outside with a grudge against him. I
admit he wasn't a popular man locally; he could have had any number
of enemies. I don't want to speak ill of the dead, but he did like a
drink, perhaps he got into a tavern argument with someone.'

'It doesn't explain the method. Someone with a grudge – and a
knife – would surely just stab him and get away as soon a possible –
why spend time mutilating him?'

'You've never been in a war have you, Lawes? Men with a blood-
lust do frightful things sometimes. I knew soldiers in the Peninsular
War who did terrible things to bodies afterwards – Spanish, French,
Portuguese and even English infantrymen – couldn't help themselves.'

'The workhouse is not a battleground, colonel. Much as it would
be convenient for the board for it to have been a complete stranger
with no link to the union, I still think it very unlikely that was the

case. In my opinion this was a murder committed by someone inside the workhouse and the sooner we get to the bottom of it the better.' With a sigh of frustration Shepherd sat back in his seat.

One by one we called the rest of the women who had been in the kitchen, but they could only repeat almost word for word what Rosa Hinds had told us. We moved on to Peter Samuels and William Tuttle, the two young boys who had been working in the garden in the morning and then returned at four o'clock to feed the pigs. The older one, Peter Samuels, who I understood was about fourteen, appeared to have some intelligence and gave his answers plainly. I recognised him as the boy I had seen on my first visit who had suffered isolation for some misdemeanour. A tall, thin, wiry boy, he seemed to have withstood the physically straitened conditions imposed by his incarceration. He confirmed that he and William Tuttle had been hoeing in the vegetable garden until dinner time. They were far out of sight and hearing of the pigsties, working right at the bottom of the garden near the midden heap, hoeing around young carrots. Robert Bignell took on the questioning.

'Did Mr Enderby come down to see you at all during the morning?'

'No, sir, we never saw anything of him – that is until we found his body.'

'What time did you return to the House in the morning?'

'Just before dinner, sir.'

'I take it you don't own a watch?'

'Oh no, sir!'

'Then how did you know it was dinner time?'

'We can hear the church clock from across the fields. When it chimed the quarter we knew it would soon be time to start packing up for dinner.'

'You must have passed the pigsties on your way back to the House – did you notice anything?'

'No, sir – although we thought the pigs were making quite a noise – but they'd been grunting and snuffling a lot when we fed them first thing. The slaughter men had been the day before and I think they could still smell the blood and it got them excited.'

'Did you go over to the sty to see what was happening?'

'No, sir, it's like I said, they can often be very noisy. We walked straight up the path to the back door. You have to make a detour to get to the sties from where we were coming from. We just heard some noises, but thought nothing of it. Anyway, we were hungry.'

'So you saw no sign of Mr Enderby. He didn't come down to the vegetable garden to see you? That's what he told the women in the kitchen he was going to do.'

'We never saw him, sir – at least—'

'Yes?'

Samuels looked apprehensive. 'Until we went out to feed the pigs later on and found Mr Enderby in the pigsty.'

'Where exactly were you both after dinner?'

'Picking oakum in the workroom, sir. We always work there in the afternoon until it's time to feed the pigs.'

I intervened at that point. 'Tell me, what do you normally do when you feed the animals?'

'We take the bucket of slops, which is left outside the kitchen door, and just tip it into the trough in the sty.'

'Tell me exactly what you found when you looked into the pigsty.'

'It was like I told the gentleman yesterday: the pigs were making a great noise but we just thought they'd heard us coming and knew it was feeding time. Pigs are very smart animals and get to know when we're there with the bucket. I told William to open the sty gate and get the trough ready – sometimes they've tipped it upside down. He went to unfasten the catch and gave a little scream and said, "A body! – A body!"'

'What did you do?'

'I thought he was playing the fool at first, but when I looked I saw bits of a body being snuffled by the pig.'

'Could you tell who it was?'

'No, sir – but I didn't look too closely. It was a horrible sight; there was lots of blood everywhere and we were both scared.'

'So, what did you do then?'

'We ran back to the House to tell the master.'

'So you were there for only a few seconds? Did you touch anything? Did you notice anything unusual – apart from the body that is?'

Samuels shook his head. It was clear that the recollection had been painful and he looked close to tears. Nothing more could be gained from further questions so I assured him that he had acted perfectly correctly, had done nothing wrong and had given his account very well. He went off gratefully.

The younger boy, William Tuttle, confirmed every detail in his evidence. He was a malnourished, undersized lad, unprepossessing in appearance and with a tiny, pale face already pinched and marked by privation and distress. In the spirit of mercy we didn't question either of them about their involvement later when they returned to the scene with the master and matron. We would leave that to the questioning of the Calmans.

When William Tuttle left, Robert Bignell observed that it was still not established that Enderby had been in the pigsty at midday – the pigs were, according to the boys that knew their habits, making no more unusual noises than they would have expected, besides which they hadn't gone over to the sty to investigate on their way back at to the House at midday. So that still left the time of the murder to be established. It could have taken place at anytime between mid-morning and just before four o'clock in the afternoon.

Our next witness was John Calman. His evidence was unchanged from his account given at the inquest. His movements were unequivocal. He and his wife had left the House at ten fifteen, after Enderby had arrived to deputise for them. They had driven into Seddon and returned at midday. On arriving back at the workhouse, his wife had asked where her brother was but no one could give a definite answer. He had a key to the secure door in the wall at the farthest end of the garden, which enabled him to come and go without disturbing the porter, who would have to open up the main gates. John Calman presumed he'd walked across the fields, probably to visit the Fleece; his horse was still stabled. It wasn't until four o'clock when the two boys ran back from the pigsties that he knew what had happened to his brother-in-law. He described how he and his wife had run down to the sty, how the boar was in a ferocious state and that it had to be coaxed out of the sty and into another with the aid of food and a stick. His account then went on to confirm what we had already heard. Well aware of the effect such a gory sight would have on his wife, he was intent on protecting her from it. She was close to fainting and he himself was feeling very ill. Calman said he was in such a state of shock he more or less left Edward Willis and Henry Millhouses to deal with the body. Enderby was then carried up to the House on the stretcher. By this time Fred Lodge had been alerted and was in the hall. The master ordered him to take the pony and trap and fetch the colonel. John Calman supported his wife back to their quarters where he stayed with her for a while before returning to the dining hall. There was nothing more he could add.

When it came to her turn, Mrs Calman more or less confirmed everything he had said. But from her perspective I was most interested in why she hadn't taken more rigorous steps to find her brother on her return to the House. Her answer was plain. 'We returned just before midday and I was immediately required to supervise the midday meal.'

'But weren't you at least curious as to where your brother was? I understand he was deputising for you. Wouldn't you expect some kind of report from him as to how things had been since you left him in charge?'

Her little tongue darted out like a lizard's as she moistened her lips.

'We were only gone a couple of hours, sir. I didn't expect anything much to happen in that time.'

'When he hadn't put in an appearance after the midday meal didn't you begin to worry as to his whereabouts?'

She looked slightly annoyed – as though she had already anticipated where my questions were leading.

'My brother had much to do as overseer and was often away on union business – particularly seeking out tradesmen and workers to take on the practical maintenance of the building.'

'But I understand it was his day off – that he was doing you a service by standing in, even though he needn't have been on the premises at all?'

'That is correct, sir.'

'Was he always so amenable?'

'My brother went out of his way to be helpful to me, my husband

and the board of guardians. He is – was – a good man...' Her voice tailed away and she looked directly at Jack Shepherd, who nodded encouragingly.

'Good man – good man!' he echoed. 'Couldn't do enough for us – very grateful – very sorry about your loss too, ma'am – damn disgrace the way he went – must have been a madman.'

I continued. 'But, as helpful as he obviously was, it doesn't explain why he seems to have remained unaccounted for from mid-morning until he was found later in the afternoon. Had you no idea where he might've been? Your husband thought he'd left the premises by the wall door and walked over to the town – possibly to the Fleece.' She had recovered her stern demeanour and now seemed rattled, but agreed reluctantly that that might have been a possibility.

'I believe your brother has – had – a reputation as a – how shall I put it? Well, someone who liked a drink – or two?' I raised my eyebrows questioningly.

She bridled. 'Whatever you've heard is gossip, sir, and I wouldn't have you speak ill of my brother, especially at this time.'

'No, by all means, but as a customer of the Fleece myself I had heard from others there that he was a regular. I'm simply trying to establish why anyone would want to do such a wicked thing to such a sociable man. Colonel Shepherd has suggested it was an outsider, so I'm investigating how your brother – this sociable man – could have made such an enemy who would do a thing like this to him. The murder is bad enough, but frankly it was taken beyond an act of revenge or dislike to one of significant loathing. You were close to him; have you any idea who it might be?'

I wondered if I'd gone too far, but I wanted a reaction from the woman. Her inscrutability was difficult to countermand and even now her face had returned to its usual impassivity. It was as though all emotion had been drained out of her and she was simply an automaton. But I guessed that deep inside she was angry and, in her own way, grieving for a brother she'd doted on.

'I can't say, sir. I only know my brother had friends in the town and was well respected. I wouldn't know whether he had any enemies, either inside or outside the House. I can't imagine why he would.'

The colonel intervened. 'Quite right – quite right! The man was respected – did his job here well. So what if he did like a drink? Perfectly proper for a working man to take a glass or two at the end of the day. I must say, he did some beating at some of our shoots and George Stenning had nothing but praise for him.'

Between Jenny Calman's staunch defence of her brother's qualities and Colonel Shepherd's reverence for the man on the grounds of his abilities at country sports, it was clear we would never get to the bottom of his true character in that forum until we were able to ask the perpetrator of the murder himself, which seemed unlikely at this stage of the investigation.

We called Fred Lodge next, who was clearly nervous. He stood before us, his hands to the front clasped tightly together. I began by saying, 'Mr Lodge, I believe you or your wife opened the main gates to Mr Enderby at about ten o'clock on the morning of his murder?'

'It was almost exactly that, sir. Our clock in the lodge had just struck the hour and I noticed it was in chime with the church clock across the way.'

'He rode in – did he say anything?'

'He dismounted and gave me the reins. He asked me to stable the horse for him as he was expected up at the House and was late.'

'Did you notice anything about him – anything different? Was he his usual self?'

'He was drunk, sir, or at least partly. He certainly smelled of liquor.'

'Not unusual, I believe?'

Fred shifted awkwardly from his right to his left foot.

'No, sir, he liked a drink. I wasn't surprised that he still smelt of it. He is – was – known to be one of the late drinkers in the Fleece and other taverns locally.'

'Still, he was able to stay upright on his horse and to arrive in one piece at the union House?'

'Oh yes, sir. Mr Enderby could handle a horse. He was a good steeplechaser – reckless but very practised. People always put money on him to win.'

The colonel saw his chance. 'Enderby was a first-class rider. He regularly turned out for the Seddon and was usually first in at the kill – he was an all-round good countryman.'

I ignored him and resumed my questioning. 'As far as you were concerned, that was the last you saw of him. He evidently didn't return out through the main gate?'

'No, sir, his horse must have remained in the stable all day. The only people who went in and out were Mr and Mrs Calman, who left at ten fifteen – by the church clock – and returned before twelve. Neither my wife nor I opened the gates to anyone else until after four o'clock when I unlocked them to let myself out with the trap to go for help.'

'So no strangers, or anyone else, came through the main gates after Mr and Mrs Calman returned?'

'No, sir.'

Having established these facts, I moved on to the more delicate area of what Fred knew of Robert Enderby's predilections. I'd thought hard about how I would frame the questions without compromising his integrity. I knew he wouldn't lie, but I was certain that I didn't want him to be involved in any concealment.

I drew a breath. 'You say you know that Mr Enderby liked a drink? Did you also know he had the reputation as a womaniser?'

The colonel was up out of his seat. 'Look here, Lawes! Are you going to impugn a dead man? Damn it – he's not here to defend himself – what right have you to make such an allegation?'

'Colonel, certain allegations have come to light. There have been complaints from some of the inmates about Mr Enderby's behaving improperly towards the women.'

'Where have they come from? Who's made such accusations?' the colonel demanded.

Fred stiffened in apprehension.

'I have a source from the town, one that I trust, who claims that Mr Enderby admitted to them himself that he had desires on some of the women in the House.' Fred's eyes widened and he raised his eyebrows and looked momentarily puzzled. 'I wondered, Mr Lodge, if you had heard such rumours?'

'There has always been gossip about Mr Enderby, sir. He leads – led – a rackety life and everyone knows he liked the ladies. There was talk that he sometimes made comments about some of the female inmates and I'm sure they sometimes took exception to it.'

'Would it be serious enough for someone to want to kill him?'

'That I couldn't say, sir. If someone took a real exception to him acting wrongly, then there might have been a reason to do him harm.'

'Would you make a connection between his reputation – by no means established, of course – and the brutality with which he was killed?'

'Someone might, sir, but you as a lawyer would know that couldn't necessarily be used as evidence to blame someone.'

An intelligent point well made! Fred was evading the question very neatly and I didn't pursue that line. Instead I moved on to confirm that he hadn't seen Enderby at all after ten o'clock and that he and his wife had been about their duties as normal. While Mr Enderby should have been overseeing the whole of the building, Amy Lodge was deputising for Mrs Calman while she was out and had spent the whole morning in the oakum room minding some of the young children. She had returned to the lodge after the midday meal was finished to feed her own children. The rest of her day was spent in the women's area. As their information was very much in tune with each other's it was not felt necessary to call Amy Lodge in person to give an account of her movements.

The last witnesses were Edward Willis and Henry Millhouses, the two inmates who had appeared on the scene and helped transport the body to the House. Since we'd been in session for over an hour I felt we should stop at this point before we had them in, for refreshment and an evaluation of what we had heard. Amy Lodge appeared with biscuits and poured the sherry. The colonel was looking aggrieved and I presumed he was still angry at my line of questioning.

'Y'know, colonel, we have to get to the reason why Enderby was murdered. That means some hard questions have to be asked and we may uncover things that are distasteful.'

'I'm fully aware of that, Lawes,' he said stiffly. 'I don't have to be reminded of my duty. I just don't like hearing a man who can't speak for himself having aspects of his character called into question. Where's your proof? Who spoke to you of these things? It seems to me you're on shaky ground if you can't produce them to give evidence.'

'I think things will become clearer as time goes on. People aren't yet ready to talk about things here. Putting it bluntly, there's still much to investigate – and I don't just mean this murder. We've already uncovered wrongdoing in the organisation of our supplies, for instance.'

Robert Bignell, who up to this point had remained mostly silent, spoke up in support. 'I think Mr Lawes has a point, colonel. None of us like to hear that an officer of the union may have been guilty of serious misdemeanours; neither are we happy about the contracts for provisions as they stand at present. We must pursue whatever line leads us to the truth – however unpalatable – although,' he added, 'we mustn't confuse the two enquiries. After all, we're here to investigate something much more serious than the adulteration of flour.'

Jack Shepherd went quiet and knocked back another sherry.

'Shall we get on?' he grunted and resumed his seat.

I asked Fred Lodge, who was still in the hall, to call Edward Willis and Henry Millhouses. A few minutes later they both entered. We signalled to Willis to speak first, while Millhouses stood waiting at the back of the hall.

Edward Willis was a small, rat-like man, made even more so by his grey workhouse apparel and wispy grey hair and beard. He sniffed continuously throughout our interrogation, occasionally wiping his nose on his cuff. He was able to give very little in the way of new information. He said he'd been walking back to the House from the privy when he heard the commotion. He saw the Calmans running with the two boys towards the pigsties and could see something was up. Henry Millhouses was coming out of the House to visit the privy himself. Together they ran after the foursome. As they got close they saw the matron and master in evident distress; the two boys were trying to coax the boar out of its sty into an adjacent one using a bucket and stick. As they looked over the sty wall they saw the remains of a man face up, naked from the waist down, and a great quantity of bloodied straw. It was clear that the boys were not able to control the boar on their own, so Millhouses had jumped in to help them. Having successfully removed the boar to new quarters, the boys stood back while Millhouses cleared the face of muck and straw. Immediately they could all identify it as Robert Enderby. Willis shuddered. 'Dreadful end for the man! I've never seen anything like that – makes you want to vomit just thinking about it! Who would do such a thing – even to him?'

I was anxious to avoid speculation and prompted him to continue. He went on to describe how Millhouses had dragged the remains close to the wall, lifted them up and he, Willis, had pulled them over on to the grass. Together the two men took the shed door off its hinges to make a stretcher. They rolled the corpse on to the door and Millhouses took one of the blood-stained aprons from its hook in the shed and covered the mutilated body with it. With the help of the two boys they carried the stretcher and its contents up to the House, where Calman ordered it to be placed on a table in the dining room. They were then told to return to their quarters.

Having heard his completed account – and weary of his sniffing – I sent him away and beckoned Henry Millhouses forward. If Stenning was rat-like, then Millhouses was positively lupine. Tall and rangy, he held himself upright as he walked towards us with long strides from the back of the hall. There was nothing servile about him; he looked straight at us. He stood with his arms at his sides, hands open. The colonel began the questioning. I could see that he was also aware of the man's physicality; Millhouses was mentally alert and clearly ready for the chairman.

'Look here – you went with another inmate to the scene – is that correct?'

'Yes.' The monosyllabic answer was not what the colonel was expecting. But he ignored the man's absence of due deference.

'What made you both go across?'

'I believe that Mr Willis has already explained where we were and that we were alerted by the noise coming from the pigsties. It was a matter of seeing whether we could help.'

The colonel looked at us both for assistance. The man was not forthcoming with any additional information. I decided to change the tenor of the questions. Henry Millhouses was no fool. If there had been anything untoward going on in the workhouse he probably had a good idea what it was.

'Tell me, Mr Millhouses, how long have you been an inmate?'

'Since the beginning of last March – I make that three months.'

'Therefore you must have got to know Mr Enderby quite well?'

'Know, sir, it depends what you mean by it. He was the overseer and we saw him irregularly. When he was in the place his position was such that we simply took his orders. There was no question of "knowing" the man.'

'What about his reputation?'

'Can you be clearer in what you mean, sir?'

'We've heard that he was something of a womaniser.'

'If that was the case, I can't see how any inmate would know of it. Whatever he did outside the workhouse was unknown to me.'

'What about his relationships with the women in the House?'

'Do you mean the staff or the inmates?'

'The inmates.'

'I believe he was prone to make what might be called salacious remarks to the younger women occasionally. Whether these came to anything or not I couldn't say.'

'Do you know if the women took offence?'

'I imagine they were sometimes offended – but there would have been very little they could do about it. Mr Enderby held all the power.' He looked Shepherd squarely in the face. 'There's no system for complaining here.'

The colonel looked uncomfortable. 'We have a monthly visit when inmates can speak to us.'

Millhouses raised his eyebrows and the corners of his mouth twitched. He continued to gaze questioningly at the colonel. 'When was the last time anyone complained to any guardian, sir? I imagine the regulations insist on all conversations that pass between the inmates and the guardians being logged for the record. In all my time here I've never heard any man make a complaint. Of course I can't speak for the women, but I'd hazard a guess that it's much the same for them. Correct me if I'm wrong.'

'Good God, man! We're always willing to hear genuine grievances. We assume because no one complains that all is in order.'

'Then your assumptions are weak, colonel. There are many things that are wrong with this place; the fact that no one complains says more about their lack of opportunity to do so than it does about their contentment with how it's run.'

The colonel was up on his feet, his features flushed and contorted with anger. 'Look here, Millhouses, I haven't come to bandy words with a blackguard who's content to live off the backs of others. This union has been efficiently run according to the law since it opened. Inmates should be grateful for a roof, food and clothing.'

Henry Millhouses stood silent. Having made his attack, he was content to allow Jack Shepherd to bluster, increasingly tying himself in knots of justification. Seeing which way the enquiry was leading I attempted to wrest it back to its essential purpose – to discover a motive for Enderby's murder.

I looked the man fully in the face and asked him straight out. 'Mr Millhouses, can you think of any reason why anyone would want to murder Robert Enderby in such a way as he was killed?'

'I can hazard several guesses, sir, but that wouldn't be evidence. Mr Enderby wasn't popular with anyone – man or woman – but evidently someone had a serious grudge against him. It seems to me that the mutilations committed on his body must indicate the motive. But you have probably worked that out for yourselves.'

The colonel looked confused, but Robert Bignell and I exchanged glances, realisation dawning that we'd both been thinking along the same lines.

Bignell addressed Millhouses. 'Are you saying that cutting off his genitals was some sort of message about the overseer's behaviour?'

'Well, it doesn't take a genius to work out that this was some kind of retributive action for a perceived injustice. I can't say any more since I've no proof to offer that this was the case, but it was the first thing that struck me when I saw the body.'

He was right – there could be no question that whoever had planned the murder had also determined to make a significant connection with Enderby's philandering. The second point that struck me was Millhouses's skilful articulation. His rhetoric was above the common kind and he was evidently an educated man. I recollected the first time I'd met him on my visit when I'd been struck by the openness of his features and the quizzical look in his eyes as he had stared directly into mine. This was no labourer and I was just about to probe a little deeper into his background when he completely took the wind out of our sails by saying, 'If you'll excuse me now, gentlemen, you won't know but this morning at eight o'clock I gave three hours statutory notice to the master that I wished to leave the House. The time is up and I'm now free to go. I believe I've told you all I saw last Saturday afternoon, which I know replicates Edward Willis's account and I have nothing further to add. I would now like to vacate the premises as is my right.'

The three of us were shocked into silence for a moment, then the colonel opened his mouth to speak but I cut in quickly. 'This is most unexpected, Mr Millhouses, but surely you must have your reasons and I presume somewhere to go?'

'Yes, sir, I'm well able to accommodate and feed myself – even provide myself with a decent suit of clothes. I thank you, gentlemen, for your charity during the last three months; it's been an education.' He gave a short bow of his head. 'Now, I wish you all good day!'

He turned on his heels and walked back down the hall towards the door. For some reason I was anxious not to see him go so soon. I called after him. 'Have you money – is there anything you require of us?'

He stopped, turned to face us and took from his trouser pocket a small black book, which we could see from the gold cross on the front was a Bible. He waved it aloft. 'I have all I need here, thank you!'

And with that he loped through the door and disappeared into the main lobby. The colonel, with his impeccable sense of the immaterial said: 'The man's no business going out that way.'

We sat in silence for a few moments. Robert Bignell was the first to speak. 'Well, that was a surprise!' he said inconsequentially. 'And as far as our enquiry is concerned we seem to be no further forward than we were at the inquest.'

I considered we'd gathered a little more information than the coroner and said, 'But we have established that Enderby had enemies – probably connected with his philandering. I'm also certain that this crime was committed by someone in the House itself – it was certainly not an outsider.' I looked purposefully at the colonel, daring him to disagree, but he nodded reluctantly. I proposed that we try to construct a proposition for the murder with the information we had; in other words, to conjecture how the deed was done and exactly when. Within twenty minutes or so we had provided ourselves with the outline of the crime.

Firstly, we looked at the timing. Although it was agreed that Enderby could have been killed any time between approximately eleven fifteen and about three forty-five in the afternoon, closer examination showed this was probably not the case. It was most likely that he had been killed before the Calmans had returned. Surely he would have sought them out in their quarters to report to them. Even though Mrs Calman was not surprised at his absence, it had only been about thirty minutes between him being sighted outside the kitchen and their return. There was also the question of the supervision of the men. Until the master returned, in effect there had been no one overseeing the male quarters; that meant there was opportunity for someone to slip out unobserved. The women on the other hand were supervised by Mrs Lodge who'd been with them in the oakum room all the morning. They were fully supervised again in the afternoon by the matron herself. The only unsupervised female group were the five working in the kitchen during the entire morning and each had confirmed that none of them had left the premises.

The other question we asked ourselves was what had prompted Robert Enderby to go down to the garden in the first place. He'd already made one visit there as reported by the women. Evidently he returned again, unseen, at some point before midday. We agreed that he must have arranged to meet someone there and, given what we now knew of his predilection for young women, it was most likely someone pretending to seek an assignation. How that was managed and who arranged it we hadn't yet fathomed; possibly it was by a note or word of mouth. Bignell pointed out that no note had been found in any of Enderby's pockets.

Whatever the method, Enderby fell for it and arrived at the sties at about eleven forty-five. The assailant or assailants were waiting for him there and as he approached – still partially drunk – he was probably attacked with a heavy object, which knocked him unconscious. If that was the case it must have been something brought from the House as there was nothing to serve such a purpose in the shed. The small wooden outhouse contained only three blood-stained overalls, which were used the day before by Thomas Lewis's men who had come to stick a couple of fattened pigs. They had brought their own slaughtering equipment with them and taken it away again. It seems that Enderby was then stripped of his boots and breeches, leaving him completely naked from the waist down, his genitals were excised and his body tipped over into the sty. The boar was still fairly wild with the smell and sight of blood lingering from the day before and what happened next could be guessed at from the state of the body when it was found. Whoever carried out such butchery must have put on the aprons to carry it out. Enderby's breeches and boots had been thrown in a corner of the shed. Before its discovery the body had been inter- mittently under attack from the boar for several hours.

The timing was very tight if the murder had been carried out before the midday meal. Whoever had committed it had to be back in the House just before twelve when a head count was taken. It was extremely well planned and executed by someone or some people with cool heads driven by an implacable sense of hatred and revenge.

This was as far as we could surmise – and still only conjecture. There were weak points that we could not get around. The main one again being the timing – we always came back to that. If it had taken place when we suggested there was barely enough time for it to be carried out so effectively. But we felt the planning had been meticu- lous and details probably worked out to the second, so we stayed with our timescale. By the time we'd completed our working theory we'd convinced ourselves – at least Bignell and I had – that this had been the modus operandi. Even Colonel Shepherd, who had clung obsti- nately to his hope that it was the work of an intrusive madman, had to concede eventually that our account rang true on many fronts. We jotted down our notes, which I said I would write up for the board meeting due to take place the next morning.

The timing of the murder had disrupted Colonel Shepherd's own timetable for meetings. The killing had taken place on the Saturday. With the inquest on Monday and our investigation on Tuesday, it was necessary to hold an emergency meeting on the Wednesday so that a full report from our small enquiry could be presented. On the day every guardian attended in expectation of details and gossip.

As I rode up to the open gate Fred stepped out of the lodge and met me.

'I have a message for you, Mr Lawes. I don't know whether you'll understand it – it seemed puzzling to me, but Henry Millhouses asked me to give you Ambrose Hudson's regards and to tell you he'll be writing to you very soon.' I was puzzled. But suddenly, in the back of my mind I recalled the name. I'd had a conversation with someone who'd mentioned an Ambrose Hudson, but I couldn't remember who or when. I was still speculating as I entered the boardroom.

Shepherd took his place at the end of the table and we arranged ourselves in our usual seats. Of the officials, Calman was there, as were the surgeon and the relieving officer. Understandably Mrs Calman remained indisposed in her quarters. Habits die hard and the usual trays of sherry and Bath Oliver biscuits had been placed on the occasional table for our refreshment at the end of the meeting.

Colonel Shepherd opened proceedings by asking the chaplain to say a short prayer for Enderby, and ask that the Almighty would bring the culprit to swift justice and a condign punishment. It had already been agreed that, as well as a full discussion of the crime, the meeting would be a practical affair as to how the efficient running of the House would continue while investigations were still active. Even the chairman, dispensing with usual protocols, got straight down to business.

'Firstly, since our matron's likely to be indisposed for some time I suggest we ask the porter's wife Mrs Lodge to step in temporarily and oversee the female inmates.'

'I hope she'll be suitably remunerated,' said Ted.

'A small honorarium will suffice. It might only be for a few days – Calman?' Shepherd raised his eyebrows.

'Indeed, sir.'

'As for a replacement for the overseer, since most of the poor-rate had been collected so efficiently by Mr Enderby, we can probably afford to wait a week or two before advertising the post. Are we agreed?' There was a general murmur of assent from round the table. The colonel cleared his throat. 'Moving on to the main point of today's business, as you know three of us met yesterday to try to get to the bottom of this dreadful murder of one of our officials. We heard testimony from all those who'd been involved with the discovery of the body and after a long discussion came to the conclusion that the murder had been perpetrated by someone on the premises – that is, someone who is connected with the House. It pains me to say it since I can't possibly imagine anyone connected with the union could be capable of carrying out such a dastardly crime. But – there it is. I'll leave Mr Edgar Lawes to inform you of our supposition – and remember it is only that; we have as yet no evidence to substantiate our conclusions.'

He sat back in his seat and nodded to me. I read our findings from a document I had produced from our notes, which the guardians listened to with rapt attention. When I invited questions, Ted Lake was first on his feet. In his astute way and as quick as a flash he'd picked up on the weak element in our account.

'It seems to me that the blighter – or blighters – had to be very quick to carry all this out in your timescale. They had to get from the main building – wherever they were – down to the sty, waylay the man with a few pleasantries, whack him over the head, cut off his balls and tip him into the sty, all in fifteen or twenty minutes, and without being seen; not to mention the fact that he must have returned with a deal of blood on him and would need time to clean himself up. If he put the slaughterer's apron on, that would've taken even more time.'

I admitted that this had presented us with the same problem, but given the fact that according to the women he had passed by their window around eleven fifteen, it was just possible, and must have been very smoothly done within the timescale. But Hugh Bradshaw and William Marchant both agreed with Ted that it seemed almost impossible for the thing to have been carried out in such a short space of time. Hugh also asked how it was the women in the kitchen hadn't seen Enderby pass the window a second time. We conjectured that they were to and fro from the kitchen to the dining room at that time, and therefore not always within sight of the garden. Enderby must have been very surreptitious. Hugh looked sceptical.

No one proposing an alternative theory, I continued with our findings. I told the board that we felt the murder was directly connected with Enderby's reputation and that there was a good deal we didn't yet know about his relationships with the women in the House. As Henry Millhouses had suggested, this seemed to have been an act of retribution by someone, or some people, who had a vehement grudge against the overseer. Unless someone in the House was prepared to come forward and enlighten us more on Enderby's behaviour we would remain in the dark as to who might have carried out the attack. It was agreed that we would continue to investigate and interview every inmate if necessary until the truth was revealed. It was an unsatisfactory conclusion, but all we could do under the circumstances. Discussion continued for a while but it was not long before it dwindled down the path of wild speculation, which was getting us nowhere.

Seeing how things were moving the colonel suggested it was an appropriate time for refreshments. Will Harbey poured the sherry and took the tray of biscuits to the far end of the table. The chaplain, an ever-hungry bachelor, leaned forward from his chair and removed the cover of the large oval salver, which was spread with a good number of biscuits, thin, round and brownish-grey. He stretched out his hand towards the centre of the plate to take the largest one and picked up a misshapen object between his finger and thumb. He gave an immediate squeal of horror, dropped it back in the dish and drawing his hand away rubbed it vigorously on his coat-tails.

'Good God!' he exclaimed.

'Blaspheming, chaplain? That's not your style – what's the matter?' asked Ted Lake, who was sitting on the cleric's left-hand side.

He stood up and peered into the tray; all eyes were now drawn to the plate. Ted took his pencil and, with its sharp point, poked at the object with surgical precision.

'Fuck me! It's a set of bollocks in among the Bath Olivers!'

The cleric shuddered and waved his hands weakly in the air. 'Really, Mr Lake!' he protested, putting his hands to his face. But sure enough, lying in the centre of the salver surrounded by the biscuits was a complete, if shrivelled, specimen of genitalia.

Ted was roused. 'A guinea says we all know whose they are!'

'I'm sure we all know whose they are,' I said.

'Of course we do! They're Enderby's private parts presented on a platter! I wondered where they'd gone, although it was my guess that the pigs had had them.'

Ted was in his element with schoolboy delight and I braced myself. He continued to explore the exhibit with the sharp end of his pencil then, neatly sliding it between penis and scrotum, hooked the whole lot out until they lay across it like a pair of saddle bags. He waved them gently to and fro in the air before placing them on a piece of paper for everyone's closer scrutiny, while he restrained from further forensic use of the pencil. There was a collective gasp of revulsion from round the table and all the men who considered themselves in full working reproductive order must have instinctively crossed their legs, clenched their buttocks and squirmed in their seats – I certainly did.

I looked down on the grey, flaccid objects, which were void of life, desiccated and of reduced dimensions. As if reading my thoughts Ted observed, 'Look at that John Thomas! Poor old Merry Mary! Even she wouldn't take money for that!'

Shocked into silence at first, Colonel Shepherd now attempted to bring the group to order in his usual blustering way.

He turned on Ted. 'Look here, Lake, this won't do. I won't have coarseness. This is a serious matter.'

'Certainly was for this blighter – cut off in his prime!' I noticed that most of the board had turned a sickly shade of grey to match the object itself. Several had reached for the sherry decanter, which was now almost empty. Ted turned to Patchin. 'This silver salver thing – what price John the Baptist, eh, reverend?'

The chaplain could take no more, put his hand to his mouth and rushed from the room for the privy. The only person unmoved was the professional butcher, Thomas Lewis, who was presumably more used to raw offal than the rest of us.

Shepherd, now visibly angry and flustered, lost his temper. He brought his fist down on to the table with a thump that made us all start. 'Lake, enough!' he roared. 'Remember, the man's brother-in-law's present.'

Ted sat back, chastened. 'Apologies, Calman. I'm out of order. You're right, colonel, this is a serious thing and we need to get to the nob – sorry – the nub of the matter.'

I was beginning to agree with the chairman; Ted's levity was misplaced. It was clear that the chairman had no idea what to do next and I felt it was time the gruesome exhibit was put away. I swept the biscuits off the tray on to the table, picked up the paper and replaced them with Enderby's tackle, covering it with the lid.

'We need to investigate this immediately,' said Shepherd, 'starting with the women in the kitchen. Calman, perhaps you'll ask them if they know anything, although I can't imagine even a workhouse woman doing such a thing. Anyone could tamper with these biscuits. They're put out long before we arrive and the room's not locked.'

'Good idea, Colonel,' retorted Ted. 'Can't let this kind of thing go on – whose will be next I wonder? One thing, though, he won't want them where he's gone.'

I flashed him a warning look. His wiseacre comments were really getting the colonel's back up.

'I suggest Burgwin takes them to the coroner and lets him decide what's to be done. I imagine he would want them reunited with the rest of the body before burial.'

Ted looked at the salver. 'We're sure they're... ?'

'Of course they are – who else's could they be?'

There was another frozen silence while the board considered the awful possibility that there was another man in the vicinity incomplete in that area, then a mutter of assent and general relief that the objects were now under cover.

The chaplain returned and I explained our decision. Clearly grateful that he could soon return home he nodded agreement to my proposal. I glared at Ted, hoping he would keep his flippant mouth shut and not suggest that Patchin might say a valediction for Enderby's balls.

Finally it was pointed out by William Harbey – always ready to steer us in matters of correct procedure – that the board really ought to alert the Poor Law commissioners of the unprecedented events at our union. The colonel was very reluctant, thinking, I imagined, that we might be invaded by officials from London who would certainly disturb his carefully organised regime and, more worryingly, might uncover the aspects of the running of the House that some of us were beginning to question. But as the rest of the board considered Harbey's suggestion a sensible one, the chairman was forced to agree. A letter was composed there and then in the form of a formal résumé of circumstances and how the board was managing them.

We didn't think it necessary to go into the full details of Enderby's gory end. We just informed them that there had been a suspicious death, which, following an adjourned inquest, a group of guardians headed by a JP was in the process of investigating thoroughly. Finally the colonel swore everyone to complete secrecy. Nothing of the discussion – and particularly the graphic exhibit – was to be discussed with any person outside the board; the meeting was closed. Still shaken, the guardians filed out in silence into the main hall.

Calman, looking intense, was waiting to speak to Colonel Shepherd. But he had had enough for the day and waved him away. 'Not now, Calman, I'm sorry. I understand your concern and obviously it will be best if you don't mention any of this to your wife. It will be necessary for us to speak very soon, but not at the moment. Perhaps you could resume your duties as normal – for the time being.'

The master nodded and walked back through the main hall and into the kitchen area. The rest of us assembled at the entrance waiting for various conveyances.

Ted Lake took my arm. 'Have you any idea what's going on here? First a suicide, then a murder, now a practical joke; this is a nasty business.'

'Damn right it is!'

But on this occasion I wasn't prepared to have a serious talk with Ted until I had turned over all my thoughts into something coherent. Besides, he hadn't been helpful in the meeting, and although I knew his intentions were fundamentally sound and he was passionate about putting the House in better conditions, he'd shown that sometimes he could be a liability. I was beginning to have doubts as to how he might be handling his committee – for I knew he'd made himself chairman. I'd been pleased initially that he was assigned a crucial role, but was now uncertain whether he could take it seriously enough, or even stick to it.

While I was considering Ted's mercurial nature, Fred Lodge

brought my horse round. I tipped my hat to Jack Shepherd who was mounting his own, called across that I would be in touch and left.

I rode away with a feeling of deep confusion. What started out as a desire in me to do some good had subsequently developed into a muddle. I felt I was fighting on two fronts. The most important task, which was to improve the welfare of the inmates, had now become subsumed into a murder enquiry that I didn't feel confident to lead. The more I considered Enderby's death and the manner of it, the more I felt it led to a conclusion that there were dark forces in the House that had sprung directly from the way the lives of the inmates were governed. The poor food, clothing, bedding, lack of stimulation and education for both adults and children, all put together made a sorry situation. If this ghastly crime had been committed by any of the inmates in retribution for any perverted acts of Enderby, then it might be squarely put at the door of poor supervision of House officials and laxness in welfare arrangements for the inmates. The evidence of Fred's letter, confirmed by Mary Wilcox's statement and the manner of Enderby's death all pointed in that direction. The board of guardians might have a lot to answer for – Colonel Shepherd more than most. What I could not foresee was that the progress of the two strands of our investigation would be accelerated from a totally unexpected source.

Part Two

Part Two

Ambrose Hudson's Account

It goes without saying that a journalist must keep a journal and for my purposes it is certainly essential. The effective reporter must endeavour to keep the personal out of the purely objective record and without written prompts his memory plays tricks and is a poor guarantee of accuracy, especially when he's trying to recall the chronology of events and the idiosyncrasies of people. I have been reporting through the press for almost twenty years and been to some strange and very unfamiliar locations; the situation I placed myself in Seddon workhouse in Suffolk was one of the direst. How I arrived there requires a little background and some explanation.

I was born in a small village in that county and was the second of two boys; my father, Arthur Millhouses, owned a small yet successful milling business and could afford to have high hopes for us both. We were put to school at about the age of five and encouraged to read and learn. By the age of twelve, acknowledging my lack of interest in the flour trade while recognising a certain skill in writing, my father indentured me to a printer in London; the family had connections there and I was apprenticed to an uncle. For seven years I was trained in the arts of printing, during which time I had access to books, journals and pamphlets covering the widest range of topics. I met authors and writers and, as I progressed, was able to discuss with them not only ideas about printing styles and presentation, but also the content of their work. This stimulated an interest in reportage and politics and I began to write, and had accepted small pieces for journals and broadsheets, mostly concerning daily life in and around the city – the writers I met advised me to write about what I knew. As a journeyman myself with the good fortune to be indentured to a fair master, I began to observe the variation in practice in trade apprenticeships locally, and I soon noted how young boys and men were often badly treated and physically misused. I persevered with my own apprenticeship on the advice of my uncle and father, who were doubtful whether I could make a sufficient living for myself – and hopefully at some time a family – simply with the use of my pen. However, having achieved the level of 'master printer', I remained fortunate in my contacts and, with the not insignificant body of writing I'd produced, was encouraged by my friends to apply for a post as a journalist with a weekly broadsheet journal, the *Escritoire*.

In a great act of faith, the editor James McNiece, a shrewd Scot from Edinburgh, immediately set me my first major assignment, which was out of London. He was somewhat of a radical himself and took a great interest in the waves of social unrest that had occurred since the end of the Napoleonic Wars. Although he was taking a risk with a young, untried journalist, he seemed to have confidence in my abilities and sent me to Manchester to report on Henry Hunt's speeches on electoral reform. This was a baptism of fire and my first taste of the consequences of political unrest. It was here that I reported first hand the events in St Peter's Field in the year 1819 when Englishmen were mown down by mounted soldiers with sabres, simply because they had turned out to listen to a radical orator.

On my return McNiece and I settled into a long and very effective partnership. The editor had a keen interest in Westminster politics and a detailed knowledge of the workings of parliament. For almost ten years he followed particularly closely the tortuous passage of parliamentary reform until it reached its conclusion with the Great Reform Bill of 1832. Four years later the reduction of stamp duty on newspapers was an obvious bonus, not only for the owners but also the burgeoning radicals who were pressing for yet further electoral and social reform since their demands could now be more widely disseminated. But McNiece's main passion, and one that I absorbed from him from the beginning of our relationship, was that of the iniquities of child labour. Recognising the poisonous mix of new technology with ingrained inhumanity, we had long discussions about what we knew of the working conditions of children in the textile factories in the north-west and north-east. By the late 1820s we decided we couldn't continue simply talking about it; if improvements were to be made, the conditions must be exposed to a general public, which, by and large, was in ignorance of how its cotton and woollen clothing was produced, and at what human cost.

As I was young, single and with no ties – by now my parents were both dead and my brother was away in the army in India – I was sent up again to Lancashire at various times to investigate the cotton mills and the conditions under which children – and women – were working. I questioned, took notes and kept journals. As might be expected, from the outset I met with much suspicion and hostility from the owners and managers of the mills, to the point where I was on occasions threatened with physical harm. For my own protection I had to devise ways to acquire information covertly. Ultimately it occurred to me that the best observations would come from practical experience of working in the conditions I was investigating. In the year 1835 I spent several months as a factory hand working alongside men and women, and children as young as four who were constantly at risk of harm from their close proximity to heavy machinery. I took copious notes and, when I returned to London, wrote up these experiences, which were published under my pseudonym 'Ambrose Hudson', my maternal grandfather's name. Although my exposés produced small flurries of outrage at the time of printing, changes to the law were very slow in coming – too many vested interests, and mill owners dominating politics in the North. I quickly learned to my frustration that it would be a continuous struggle to overcome the power of the wealthy to obtain some justice for the poor.

However, pleased with my efforts, McNiece next turned his attention to the new Poor Law, which was now fully in place. Together we recognised the weaknesses within the new regulations and the possibilities for maladministration and bad practice. Our conclusions were based on our experience of other recent social legislation, for example, the 1831 Ten Hour Bill introduced by the MP John Hobhouse, which was supposed to secure the exclusion of children under nine in the factories and limited the working hours of children less than fourteen to forty-eight hours per week. Children under thirteen were to attend school for not less than two hours a day. But my own experiences in the mills of the north-west had taught me that such legislation was very narrowly observed, often ignored and abuses remained widespread.

McNiece and I decided we should investigate how the new Poor Law arrangements were being implemented. I was prepared to undertake another long-term assignment and volunteer my way into a union workhouse to ascertain how the new rules were being applied. I have a journalistic hero – Daniel Defoe – a man who's mainly remembered now for his engaging novels, but was primarily an observer and reporter of facts, one who actively followed his sources. In that regard I would acknowledge him as our first journalist. He struggled with bankruptcy and accusations of sedition and was imprisoned for both several times. While I had no desire to emulate that aspect of his biography, I was prepared to travel, like him, but also spend time incognito to bring back a first-hand account of my experiences.

The plan was for me to volunteer myself into the Seddon Union workhouse in Suffolk. It had to be Seddon because, under the admission rules, I could only apply for relief of any kind in the parish in which I had been born. There would be no danger of anyone recognising me in my village. I'd left home as a callow youth aged just twelve and my parents had been dead ten years. Since neither my brother nor I had been trained to take it over, the mill at Kettlebaston was sold as a going concern and we shared the cash inheritance.

It was necessary for me to concoct a story by which I could infiltrate the workhouse system. The first contact and first major obstacle would be the parish relieving officer who held great power over the poor of his district. In order to convince him and all concerned of my absolute need I had to make careful preparations.

I had spent years in a professional occupation and had hands to show it. For several weeks, therefore, I lent myself to my old master where my hands received a roughening from the wood and iron presses, producing broken fingernails, skin stained with oil and showing many calluses and blisters that I allowed to age and harden, I hoped convincingly. Literally rolling up my sleeves my arms soon became brown, ingrained with dust and dirt, until they were passably workman-like. I also lost a few pounds in weight since I could hardly turn up at the workhouse gates looking hale and healthy; I practised what I hoped was a convincing cough. My story was that I'd lost my job as a carpenter in London because of ill-health and tramped the south-east looking for a job. Unsuccessful, I was finally reduced to applying for relief in my home parish. I hoped this would be sufficiently plausible – I was concerned that they might question a single man in his thirties as to why he would want to incarcerate himself in the workhouse. But as long as I stuck to my story about tramping for work over several months I hoped this would be enough to persuade the union authorities.

Of course, as well as preparing myself physically, I researched and noted all the regulations prescribed in the new Poor Law, which governs union arrangements. They were certainly an indigestible read, but I was most struck by their attention to detail. Life for the inmates is prescribed minutely; every aspect of daily routine is regulated to the nth degree. Supervision is supposed to be constant and this presented me with a practical problem. I would need to take careful and continual notes of my observations in order to report them fully, but retrospectively, when I finally discharged myself; I couldn't carry it all in my head. A notebook and pencil – tools of my trade – were out of the question. My uncle the printer came up with the solution. He would compile a small Old Testament Bible, but with every verso page blank. To all intents and purposes it would look like a normal Bible, but one I could use as a notebook. The spine would be sufficiently loose so that I could place a quantity of small pencils inside it. I would have to be disciplined in keeping notes relevant and succinct. I wasn't sure as to when I would be free to scribble down these thoughts, but was optimistic that there would be some parts of the day when I could find some privacy – even if it were only in the privy.

I had deliberately chosen the very beginning of March to begin my investigation because regulations decreed that the current board of guardians of all unions would disband at the end of that month and new guardians would be elected; I'd read that process was tightly regulated. The first meeting of the new board of guardians had to take place as soon after 15 April as possible. I would therefore make my entry as this process was unwinding.

Set up with what I hoped was a credible story, physically prepared and with the means to record my findings, I set out from the city to travel to my home village of Kettlebaston, which was within the compass of Seddon Union workhouse. I took the mail coach from London to the Ipswich post-house where I would spend the night. That evening I had what was probably going to be my last substantial meal and a bath, before turning in and enjoying a peaceful and solitary night's sleep. The next morning I changed into workman's clothes, bundled up my good shirt, jacket, breeches and boots in my travelling bag and paid the innkeeper a half sovereign to leave it with him at the post-house. I obtained a receipt, placing it with my money in a small leather purse, which I kept on my belt. I told him that if I hadn't returned by six months he was welcome to sell the contents of the travelling bag and pocket the proceeds.

Over the next two days I made my way on foot to Kettlebaston, sleeping the night in an empty barn, and reached the village green on Thursday, 1 March, from which date I kept brief notes in my Bible, from which this full account was devised.

March

Thursday, 1 March 1838

A frosty March morning, with rime spreading over the bare twigs and branches of trees and hedgerows. I was told by a villager that the Seddon Union relieving officer was probably working on his smallholding, but that he was due a regular visit to the neighbouring village of Chelsworth on union business early in the afternoon. Immediately I could see that his movements were logged by locals, as were strangers to the district. The man I asked looked me up and down, half suspicious, half sympathetic; it must have been clear to him what my business was.

Chelworth is only about four miles away and I made it there just after midday. On enquiry again I found Mr Carrick inside the local tavern. I was hesitant about coming between a man and his drink, so I withdrew to the village bench and waited. Within an hour he appeared and I approached him. This was my first taste of the embarrassment a proud man must endure, but he did have the decency to take me inside to enjoy the warmth of the inn and we sat in a quiet corner where I explained my situation. He asked me straight out if I was looking for an 'offer of the House', in other words a place in the workhouse. Then as I professed ignorance about the process for admission, he laid it all out for me very clearly. If my situation fitted the requirements, he could give me a provisional order of admission, but I would have to use it within six days or it would expire. If he thought I was in immediate need, he could recommend that the workhouse master should admit me there and then. That seemed the only option. My circumstances were applicable – I was without a home, without work and had not been in the best of health; clearly there was no prospect of anyone taking me on. I told him I had no family either to support or to support me and for days had been without money for food, and certainly could not afford a bed for the night. He agreed I was clearly destitute and signed the ticket for admission. So, with that in my pocket, I set off to walk the eight miles or so to the workhouse.

I walked briskly in the cold air. Whatever my story to Thomas Carrick, in my purse I had actually twenty sovereigns and a substantial quantity of small change, which I intended to secrete away until I eventually discharged myself from the House. About a quarter of a mile from the workhouse I deviated off the road on to a small track. Part of a field wall had broken away and I hid the purse deep within its tumbled stones, taking careful note on the first empty page in my Bible as to its exact location. I now had nothing in my pockets other than the Good Book. I was wearing the bare minimum of clothing, well-worn boots through which I felt both the stones of the road and the cold of the frost, and an old felt hat. I was acutely aware that my situation was false, unlike all the other inmates and those on outdoor relief I could opt back into society at any time of my choosing. I was not destitute, neither was I in the deep despair that chronic dependency must instil. But I had to imagine the thoughts and feelings of those who were, and try to enter the spirit of the enterprise whole-heartedly.

Walking further along the road I came to a pair of large iron gates, well described by the relieving officer, and pulled the bell rope. A young, fresh-faced, tow-haired man peered through the bars.

'I've been sent with a ticket from Mr Carrick. He says I should be admitted today.'

The porter or lodge-keeper, as I presumed he was, stretched his hand between the bars and took the ticket, which he read aloud.

'Henry Millhouses of Kettlebaston. No means of support and no abode. To be admitted forthwith while searches are made as to his situation.'

He unlocked the gates and as I walked through he shut and relocked them behind me. To my surprise I could see at the end of a drive an attractive country house, four-square with a Georgian pediment over the main door. If this was the workhouse then it didn't present as the forbidding place I'd been led to believe. But before I could take in much more the porter signalled for me to follow him. He told me his name was Mr Lodge and that he would be responsible for my admission. We walked on to a large, new-brick building attached to the lodge house. Ushering me through the door I found myself in a substantial whitewashed room with wooden floors and a couple of beds, tables and chairs. There was a small fire burning in a grate at the far end of the room.

'This is the receiving ward. You need to undress and have a good wash. You will then be issued with workhouse clothing. At some time in the next couple of days a doctor will come and examine you to make sure you're not infectious or anything. Your own clothes and belongings will be stored here. If you leave, they'll be returned to you. Have you anything valuable with you?' I took the Bible out of my pocket. This would be the test – whether or not he would take it upon himself to inspect it.

'This is all I have. I hope there's no rule against a man keeping his mother's Bible?'

'I should think it most unlikely, but I'll ask Mr Calman; he's the master here – the one in charge. Keep it for now.' He left me to undress and, as there was no bath, I took a strip-wash in some warmish water from a wooden tub. As I was rubbing myself dry with a coarse towel he returned with a bundle of clothing. All was grey cotton – trousers, shirt, jacket and undergarments, linen vest and long-pants. On the top was a pair of thin black boots. He picked up my own clothing, which I'd stacked on a chair and asked me to put my signature, or mark if I couldn't write, on a receipt. I signed my name.

Now dressed in workhouse garb I stood waiting for instructions. I was hungry. I'd had my last good meal before I reached Kettlebaston and since then subsisted on a piece of bread and some cheese. As though reading my thoughts, Mr Lodge said I was fortunate I had arrived when I did as I was in time for supper, which was at six o'clock. He would make arrangements for something to be brought to me. Sure enough, about an hour later a woman who introduced herself as the porter's wife came in with a tray. The meal was poor – some thin vegetable soup, and bread that was sour with a chalky consistency – washed down with very watery small beer. I saw no one after supper until at eight o'clock Mr Lodge came in to tell me I should go to bed as it was lights-out for all the inmates. When I asked him about the lavatory, he pointed to a large tub at the end of the room that was there for my use. I lay down on a straw palliasse and reflected on all that had happened. There was little light in the room, just a couple of candles and a faint crack of moonlight between the shutters. I took my Bible from under my pillow and shook out a pencil. Totally alone, I was able to make notes freely. One word summed up my first impression – 'bleak'.

Friday, 2 March

I slept badly and was relieved when dawn came and I took advantage of the increasing daylight to embellish my notes. Within the hour the porter entered to tell me to get up as it was seven o'clock. The fire, which I'd tended the day before with wood piled in the corner of the fireplace, was well and truly out, and Mr Lodge indicated that it was my job to relight it and later to go out into the yard and chop more wood. Some breakfast of gruel, that is thin oatmeal soaked in lukewarm water, and bread was sent across, and then I was left to my own devices for a couple of hours. Some time in the late morning – I was already beginning to lack all sense of time as there were no clocks – the surgeon, Mr Burgwin as I later found out, came to assess my health. His examination was cursory, although he made me strip and glanced over my physique. As I have explained, in an effort to look the part I'd taken steps to lose some weight and was now on the thin side. This seemed to impress him, as did my cough, which I presented from time to time, although fortunately he made no attempt to listen to my chest. He nodded to Mr Lodge and signed a certificate confirming I was free of any infections. I imagined this would be my admission endorsed, but the surgeon told me I would still have to go before the board of guardians for approval for entry to the main House. They were not due to meet until the following Wednesday. He said I was lucky because they only met once a fortnight and I could have been incarcerated in the receiving ward for as long as two weeks. I would still have to wait here for five more days.

My next visitor was the master, Mr John Calman: a shortish man, but of significant bulk and with an unhealthy complexion.

He rolled into the ward and looked me up and down. 'Henry Millhouses – no fixed abode, no employment I understand?'

'That is so.'

'Sir.'

'Sir.'

'I expect Mr Lodge has explained that you must stay here until the next meeting of the board of guardians, which takes place this Wednesday at eleven o'clock. You'll be expected to appear before them in order that they can authorise your admittance.'

'What happens if they don't… sir?'

He frowned and then answered wheezily. 'Then they'll authorise outdoor relief, which will keep you going until you find work. Given you're single, not old and in fairly good health, that's quite likely. You'll have to make a case as to why you should be admitted as an inmate.' This was a setback and one that I hadn't expected. For my purposes I needed to be admitted. Between now and Wednesday next I would have to think up a good story. The master continued. 'I gather you came in with no possessions, only a Bible – which you can keep. It mustn't be said we dissuade our inmates from their religion, but there can be no evangelising here, if that was in your mind. We leave that to our chaplain. You're not a Methodist, are you?'

'Certainly not, sir!'

He nodded, turned on his heel and waddled out.

Later in the day I was sent outside to chop wood, a therapeutic exercise as far as I was concerned, but as I split logs and kindling I wondered how I could sustain over any length of time the energy required for such manual work on a diet of vegetable soup and porridge. The rest of the day passed quietly and, apart from Mrs Lodge bringing in my meals, I saw no one. Bed time at eight o'clock was a real novelty but night was already becoming long, uncomfortable and lonely.

Sunday, 4 March

I spent what was probably one of the most tedious weekends of my life. I met one other union official, Mr Patchin the chaplain, who called in to the receiving ward in the morning, on his way to take Sunday service with the inmates. He offered to say prayers with me, and as I needed to be seen as cooperative it was expedient for me to

On the House

agree. I knew he would be canvassed at the board meeting for his opinion as to my character and consequently I sat back and stroked his professional pride by listening intently to his proselytising. I went as far as to risk opening my Bible at a text that I knew would augment his topic. This clearly impressed him. The rest of the day I pondered on the difficulty of recording accurately what I saw. It was obvious that I would be entering a situation of almost permanent supervision, not only overseen by officials, but also running the gauntlet of other inmates' curiosity. These few days of isolation would be my only opportunity to record fully and accurately what I had experienced so far.

Monday, 5 March

At around eleven the porter entered the ward with a man, probably in his mid-thirties.

'Millhouses – you have a companion. This is Richard Alfrey, who's in the same situation as you – that is, he's waiting to be admitted.'

I looked into the bright blue eyes of a man who exhibited all the signs of misery and despair. His pale face was devoid of emotion, blank and bewildered. He was of average height and build and I noticed immediately he had a deformed left leg that he dragged considerably. Uncertain as to the courtesies required in what was for us both a unique situation, all I could do was hold out my hand. 'Henry Millhouses – good day to you!'

He took my hand apathetically. 'Alfrey – Richard.'

He said no more and Mr Lodge went through the admittance procedures and left him with the bucket of water, his bundle of workhouse clothes and a couple of blankets. As there was no mechanism for privacy I lay on my bed with my back towards him, so that he could strip and wash himself down with as much dignity as the situation allowed. When I judged he was probably in a decent state I turned to face him.

Trying to initiate a conversation I said, 'Welcome to Seddon, I've been here since Thursday. I make sure I keep a note in my head of the days. It's easy to lose complete track of time here. Hours of the day are really difficult, apart from the routine of meals and bedtimes. It's important to keep one's mind alert – don't you think?'

He shrugged wearily. I could see my effort would be thwarted and that conversation was going to be difficult. I judged it wise to let him make it in his own time. I went across to the fire, threw on a few logs and drew up a couple of chairs. He sat down and put his hands to the heat. We continued in silence for a few minutes and then, look-ing into the fire, he said, almost to himself, 'I can't believe I'm here. I keep asking myself how I could let my family down like this.' I nod-ded sympathetically and he went on. 'Perhaps I won't ever see my wife and daughter again. As we walked through those iron gates this morning they went one way, I another. I've been told that men and women are permanently separated in this place. How can I live with-out her? She's been the most constant support of my life.' He put his head in his hands. 'I don't think I'll be able to go on if she's not with me.'

These were statements of fact and any response would seem trite. He went quiet again and I thought I would engage him with a little of my 'history', while being sympathetic at the same time.

'I'm single, so can't begin to imagine what you're feeling. But the fact that we're both here shows we have things in common. I lost my job in London and tramped back to my birthplace – which is Kettle-baston by the way. You must be local too?'

He looked up. 'Boxford – we come from Boxford.' I knew that the village was just within the compass of the Seddon workhouse, but a good ten miles away.

Having broken the ice I felt confident to probe a little deeper. 'How old is your daughter?'

'Fourteen.'

I pressed on. 'What's her name?'

'Caroline – her name is Caroline – and my wife is Emily. We've never been parted all our married life.' He looked up at me. 'How am I to manage?'

I felt it was necessary to get the man to talk – it might relieve his distress. I sought to distract him by asking about his work, which was possibly an easier topic for him than his family.

'What was your trade?'

'I was a leather dresser – cleaning hides for clothing, furniture and saddlery – that kind of thing. My problems started last year. At the end of November I had an accident at work because I made a stupid mistake. As a result I damaged my leg, which, although it didn't stop me working, slowed me up. At the same time work at the tannery was drying up and I knew the boss was eying up a young lad in the village to take on as an apprentice. Employing him would cost the works very little, not even half of what I was earning and I was soon on my way – at the age of thirty-six officially out of work. Boxford's an average-sized village and, apart from labouring on the land, the tannery's all there is. We had no savings, and neither my wife nor daughter could find work, so eventually we were forced to give up our cottage. We're homeless and this is our last resort. That's my story, which is probably true of everyone else here – you included, I suppose?'

'That's right. As I said I've tramped from London to get here. I was a carpenter but the works closed and we were all out of a job. I'm not in the best of health and have found it hard to get work. But at least I'm single.'

We both fell silent, retreating into our own thoughts. I tried to imagine how he was feeling. Probably the most overwhelming emotion was guilt that he was responsible for bringing his family so low; no wonder he was in despair. There was very little I could say or do that would alleviate his misery so we sat brooding together in silence in front of the fire. During the rest of the afternoon we exchanged very few words and I was unable to draw him out any further.

At six o'clock promptly, Mrs Lodge came in with our supper. This evening it was a piece of cheese with bread and the same watery beer. How I longed for the comfort of a proper drink. I noted never to take ale, brandy or wine for granted again. The porter's wife, whose name I gathered was Amy, was a pleasant and friendly woman. I noticed she was aware of Alfrey's depressed mood – easily ascertained by his listless demeanour and monosyllabic responses. She guessed rightly that he was brooding about his wife and daughter.

She took his arm and led him to a chair. 'Mr Alfrey, Emily and Caroline are well and safe. They send their love and are thinking about you. Emily said to be sure to tell you it's not your fault – please don't blame yourself. She and Caroline will get through as best they can, but she said to remember they're always thinking of you.'

The change in the man's face said more than words. It was as though the spark of life, and with it hope, had regenerated his spirit. He took her hand and I thought he was going to kiss it. Instead he looked into her face and simply said, 'Thank you and God bless you!'

I was impressed with the woman, who was probably breaking all the rules of the House by interacting with the inmates so closely. I took her to one side said quietly, 'That was a kind thing to do. The man's been almost out of his mind. I can see he was very comforted by your words.'

'The rules here are too harsh to my mind. Separating families is cruel and unnecessary. But we're told the point of these places is to make them as unwelcoming as possible – to keep people out. But I can't see why husbands and wives shouldn't be in contact. I can see that sleeping arrangements would be difficult – this isn't an inn after all – but there's no harm in them being allowed regular contact during the day.' She stopped and looked as though she regretted her comments. 'There now, I've said too much. I'm not supposed to have unnecessary conversations with inmates, let alone give my opinions. Please ignore what I said!'

I held up my hand. 'Not at all! From what I've seen so far I agree with you – but that's also between ourselves. I'm always willing to listen if you need to get anything off your chest, although I suppose you talk freely with your husband.'

'Oh yes! Fred – that's my husband – thinks exactly as I do. I know he's got concerns about how things are run here.' She laughed. 'There I go again – there must be something about you that invites confidences. I'll avoid you in future.'

'Please don't. I can see I'm going to need all the conversation I can get!'

She left us with our meal and I felt optimistic that I might have found an unexpected source for information – and one that was in tune with my own first impressions.

Wednesday, 7 March

The morning of the board of guardians' meeting was sunny and crisp. We would be called sometime after ten o'clock and neither Alfrey nor I knew what to expect. The porter told us there were fourteen guardians as a rule, although not all of them turned up regularly for meetings. Some union officials would be there – the relieving officer, the surgeon, the master and matron, and the chaplain – who would all be called upon to give reports. The chairman was a Colonel Shepherd who had held the post since the union was established in 1834. His approach was efficient and brief; that is, according to Mr Lodge, he didn't like meetings to go on for too long.

We were taken across to the boardroom by Mr Calman who, having walked us up the gravel drive led us through the main door – an experience I wouldn't have again for some months. From the well-decorated lobby we walked into a large, plainly whitewashed room, which I presumed was used as a dining and meeting hall as I could see quantities of tables and chairs stacked up against the walls. We were told to stand outside the boardroom until called. Whether keeping us waiting was intentional – another way to reinforce our status – I couldn't say, but it was some while before the master showed me in.

My journalistic instincts made me alert to all the features of the room. Unlike the hall, this room was warm with an ample coal fire glowing in the grate. It was large enough to accommodate a substantial rectangular table that occupied the centre, with chairs on either side and one each top and bottom. Trays of glasses, sherry and biscuits had been placed on a small occasional table. I was aware of at least fourteen pairs of eyes appraising me as I walked up to the end of the table. The chaplain, the back of whose head I recognised, turned in his chair and peered at me myopically. At the other end a ruddy-faced man occupied a large captain's chair. Even though sitting he was clearly tall and I presumed he was the chairman, Colonel Shepherd. I stood, trying to look unconcerned, with my arms hanging loosely against my sides. I found myself looking down at the company – I'm a tall man – but not knowing on whom I should focus. In the end I gazed at a hunting print on the wall above the chairman's head. He had a sheaf of papers in front of him that he consulted.

'Name?' He had a booming voice, a feature of his army background as I found out later.

'Millhouses, Henry Millhouses, sir.'

'From Kettlebaston I see. I have your birth details here – father, Arthur Millhouses, miller, and mother, Annie Millhouses – both dead. You were christened in the parish church. You've come up from London, I understand, because you couldn't find work. The surgeon says you're very underweight and have a weak chest.' Mr Burgwin nodded in agreement. 'The relieving officer has checked your background and everything seems in order. How much effort have you put into trying to find work?'

'I tramped around London, Kent and Surrey for many weeks, sir – that's probably how I came to have this bad chest. Food was scarce and I often had to sleep rough. In the end I knew things would only get worse and so I decided to volunteer myself into the union. I really had no choice.'

'Well, that's as maybe.'

The chaplain intervened at this point. 'May I put in a word here, colonel? I've spoken at length to this man. He seems to be a very good Christian – in fact, he carries his mother's Bible with him and was able to converse with me over certain Old Testament texts quite knowledgeably. I believe the man is in genuine want and it is our Christian duty to provide him with relief as an inmate – at least until he can fend for himself.'

'Little do you know,' I wanted to say, and also: 'By what means am I supposed to get back on my feet once incarcerated in here?'

The colonel said, 'The man's not a Methodist is he, Patchin? We don't want any subversives here!' It seemed there was a concerted objection to non-conformity among officials and guardians.

'Oh, I think not, colonel. He just has a deep – and I might say – commendable appreciation of the Old Testament prophets, who, after all—'

Shepherd quickly intervened and thanked the chaplain in order, I think, to shut him up. He looked round the table. 'Has anyone else anything to add? Are there any objections? The relieving officer's report says that he is a genuine resident of the union area by virtue of his birth there. We have spaces I presume, master?'

Mr Calman nodded. 'Yes, sir, four beds for men and three for women, although there are three further applicants for the board to discuss this morning – one man and his wife and daughter.'

'Well, Hillhouses – er, Millhouses – we're minded to grant you admission. We would draw your attention to the rules of the House, which are posted up in the dining hall. Also, there's a list of punishments for breaches. If you can't read, the master, Mr Calman, or the overseer, Mr Enderby, will read them out to you. But, as you carry a Bible, I understand that will not be needed.' He looked at me almost suspiciously, as though a literate inmate would be an impediment to good order.

'No, sir – thank you, sir!' I replied and tried to look grateful and humble at the same time. Colonel Shepherd nodded to the master and waved me away. The interview was over.

As I came out of the room and closed the door behind me, Richard Alfrey stood up. At the same time, in through the main door came the matron, with two women. The three were facing me and I momentarily gasped at the contrast between the hatchet-faced woman in black and the beauty of the other two. In spite of their drab grey garb, their faces, which bore marked similarity, had such symmetry of features, intensified by a remarkable quality of luminescence, that it almost took my breath away. They were obviously mother and daughter and I presumed the wife and offspring of Richard Alfrey. The matron, who quickly realised that contact between families would be very awkward and should have never been possible, physically interposed herself between the three and manoeuvred the women to the back of the hall. But Alfrey instinctively moved towards his wife just as the boardroom door opened and John Calman came out to fetch him. Looking at Mrs Calman the master immediately apprehended the situation and grabbed Alfrey's arm, pulling him through the door into the room. The women clung to each other very distressed and Mrs Calman ushered them to some seats and stood sentinel over them. Alfrey's interview was soon over and he was speedily escorted out by the master who indicated to me that I should follow them both. Alfrey looked over to the women and I have rarely seen such a look of longing and love – it expressed more than any words. Mrs Alfrey smiled at him, her face lighting up. She was holding her daughter's hand tightly but her whole attention was on her husband. In the fleeting seconds the exchange took place, Richard Alfrey seemed to grow taller. He squared his shoulders and threw his head back as he limped behind Calman and alongside me.

We were escorted through a back door of the hall, which led directly to the men's quarters. Walking in silence we passed the kitchen and went through a corridor to what was obviously the workroom. My immediate impression of the interior of the House was always of plain limed walls, wooden floors and small, high barred windows. The workroom was littered with bits of rope, baskets and fibres. Infinite flecks of dust floated and danced in shafts of sunbeams that poured in through the small, dirty windows. It occurred to me that soon I wouldn't have to feign my cough; regularly inhaling these particles, I would soon achieve one with a genuine provenance.

Next we were taken up a flight of stairs to the dormitory, which housed sixteen wooden bedsteads, and Alfrey and I were allocated beds opposite each other. Here were the same straw palliasses and union-issue blankets as we had become used to in the receiving ward. The room stank of stale urine, the source of which was a large bucket in a corner, which we were told served the whole dormitory during the night. We had no possessions to arrange and, after a brief appraisal of our sleeping quarters, we were ushered back into the dining hall. By the time we'd been interviewed and allocated our beds it was almost dinner time. The board meeting was evidently over and all the guardians had left.

Some of the male inmates were setting up the trestle tables and chairs in two clear sections at the back and front of the hall. Promptly at midday the women filed in from one door and occupied the rear tables. At the same time the men came in from another and took their places at the front. Row upon row of inmates all faced frontwards. There was no contact between men, women or the older children, but everyone was aware of each other. Consequently there was an underlying tension in the hall that was almost palpable. Very young children sat with their mothers who were constantly distracted in trying to keep them quiet. Richard Alfrey and I had to wait to find vacant seats because, as I soon learned, most of the men returned to claim the same places territorially. Meals were taken in complete silence, as in a Trappist monastery – but with no accompaniment of biblical texts. This was the rhythm of the House; habit and custom drove the monotony of daily life.

When everyone was seated the master said a short grace, then five women entered from the adjoining kitchen at the back of the building; they carried large vats of soup and trays of bread, which were placed, with wooden bowls and spoons, on a table at the front of the hall. Tin mugs were filled with small beer or water, according to choice. Line by line the inmates queued up to be served and returned to their places.

My friend and I were in luck. This was a 'flesh day', apparently the only one in the week when the House provided some kind of meat; I never did identify its variety confidently but thought it might have been pork. The serving women always endeavoured to share the fatty lumps out fairly from among the vegetables in the vats of soup, often slipping extra pieces into the young children's bowls. To my surprise not one of the adults made any objection to this, although they could plainly see what was happening. I assumed the basic animal instinct to feed the young was as compelling here as anywhere. Most of us finished our food – however unpalatable, and there was little left over for the pigs. Within fifteen minutes the meal was over, cleared away and the tables and chairs restacked. Males, females and children filed back to their separate areas, where we all had a further thirty minutes recreation time, which was mostly taken up with queuing for the privy. I mentally assessed the mealtime experience overall as more than disagreeable – it was dehumanising.

Like new boys at school, Richard Alfrey and I were inclined to stay together. As far as I could tell there were about a dozen male inmates of varying ages. Queuing up outside the privy I tried to gauge age and condition of as many as I could see. Most of them were of indeterminate years. Their incarceration had had such an effect on them physically that it was hard to tell whether they were old men by chronology, or young men ageing quickly. Poor diet, lack of exercise and fresh air, but above all the infection of despair, had combined to sap their energy and life force. A man who cannot look into the future with hope and expectation has almost nothing to live for. Physically some had developed an institutional shuffle – scraping along on the flats of their shoes with heads bent and rounded shoulders. Others adopted blank expressions that encouraged no interaction with the rest of us, and their thoughts were most likely mired in resentment or confusion.

Since we had a few minutes before the one o'clock bell, I took Richard back into the dining hall to have a look at the regulations governing the behaviour of inmates, which were, in conformity with the Poor Law Act, posted up on the wall. I wasn't sure whether Richard could read, but standing in front of the notice he immediately rehearsed aloud the first few edicts. Apparently punishments could be applied for many kinds of offences ranging from making a noise when silence was ordered to be kept, playing cards or dice, climbing over the walls and malingering. There were also clear sanctions for any physical violence. The punishments varied according to the severity of the misbehaviour. Apart from bread and potatoes, food could be withdrawn for as long as forty-eight hours. Inmates could be isolated in a separate room for up to twenty-four hours. Corporal punishment was considered necessary in the reining in of recalcitrant children, but no male thought to be over the age of fourteen could be beaten. For serious crimes the offender would appear before the local Justice of the Peace. What was most interesting was the way the word 'REFRAC-TORY', which I understand means 'unruly' and 'perverse', appeared in capital letters at the bottom of the sheet. Its presentation in 'upper case' revived in me memories of my printer's apprenticeship; it was the style we used for titles or to reinforce a word or idea. Here it was clearly designed for the latter purpose, drawing attention to the list of prohibited behaviours.

'Well, Henry,' Richard Alfrey said as he scanned the notice, 'this pretty well covers all aspects of refractory behaviour a human being can commit. We'll have to watch our step.'

By one o'clock we all assembled into the workroom. Richard and I took places on the end of a bench against one of the walls and were introduced to the intricacies of oakum picking. I'd read that this was a widespread occupation in union workhouses. It started with the 'junk', which was old, frayed rope from sailing ships, sent in large crates from the ports. Most of the Seddon junk came from Felixstowe and Yarmouth, and some also from Tilbury. The inmates' job was to untwist it into the raw fibres called oakum, which was bundled into sacks and sent back to the ship-builders. It provided a steady income for the House – 'money for old rope' as far as boards of guardians were concerned – but was a dusty, mind- and finger-numbing occupation for the inmates.

I tried to engage Richard in conversation, but he'd relapsed into a subdued mood, so I left him to his thoughts and turned my own to a journalistic review of my first full day. I decided a brief description would centre on the words 'grey', 'routine', 'inertia', 'degrading' and 'dehumanising'. I had no necessity to prompt reminders about the food, which was as dire as I'd ever tasted, even while living in hovels on my investigations up north. But I constantly returned to the mien of the inmates. I was beginning to accept that I would have to rely on my own observations; it was unlikely the men would volunteer any useful information, so self-absorbed were they. But I determined to persevere over the next few weeks to encourage some social interaction.

Several sacks of oakum later we stopped for prayers and supper at six o'clock. The former were on the agenda twice daily, at breakfast and supper time and were read by the master who was fortunately brief about them. Tables and chairs were reassembled as at dinner time and we took our customary places to be delighted with bread, cheese and small beer again. As the House timetable determined we were still under the influence of winter; bedtime was at eight o'clock so we had an hour of 'recreation' time. We couldn't linger in the dining hall, which was cleared immediately after the meal, so some of us took the opportunity to get some fresh air in the yard designated for use by the men – the women and young children had their own area. In spite of the chill in the March air eight or nine of us walked around the cobbled ground, which was partly covered with a roof supported by large beams. The atmosphere among the men, once they were outside, was significantly more relaxed. They passed the time of day with each other – admittedly with superficial conversation because there could be little exchange of news from an institution that followed a monotonous routine – certainly the only gossip that passed between them mainly concerned the officers and was generally negative. One or two attempted to engage with myself and Richard Alfrey, a positive state of affairs for me, but painful for Alfrey. He resisted all their attempts at conversation and eventually they left him to his own devices. He was a brooding man; of that there was no doubt.

I forgot to mention that the routine of the day was governed by the bell, which roused us from sleep, informed us of mealtimes and indicated when it was time for bed. I kept returning to thoughts of my schooldays, which were governed by the same auditory imperative. While they had been for the most part a positive experience, I was reminded that certain aspects were less pleasurable – sharing a dormitory being one. I was anticipating the coming night with some nervousness. How would I find sleeping in a room that stank, with thirteen strangers of unknown nocturnal habits? I thought of the straw mattress and the universal bucket in the corner and inwardly shuddered. But then I reminded myself that this is what I had come for – the real experience. I thought of my hero, Defoe, and remembered he'd been incarcerated in places far worse than this, but survived and told the tale. We filed into the dormitory as the bell rang at eight o'clock and I steeled myself for the night ahead.

Thursday, 8 March

It was not as bad as I'd feared. As well as school, I had some experience of sharing rooms with strangers in coaching inns, and one advantage of an alcohol ban – and the union had a strict abstinence rule – was that the consequences of getting drunk, that is snoring and having to get in and out of bed to visit the bucket several times, were less apparent. On that account I had a relatively peaceful night. Some of the inmates did snore at different pitches, which at first was amusing but later irritating, until the culprits involuntarily turned over and stopped of their own accord before I was tempted out of bed to push them over myself. A few had brief conversations with themselves while sleeping; five I was aware of got up to relieve themselves in the bucket and many farted loudly, with various lengths and tones of release. I'd taken steps beforehand to ensure I didn't have to get up and use the bucket. Apart from my sharp awareness of sleeping on prickly straw, which did its best to escape from its containment, mostly what

kept me awake was the oppressive darkness. The dormitory was shut-
tered tightly and candles extinguished by eight thirty; not a beam of
star or moonlight could squeeze itself through the tiniest cracks. I had
therefore just half an hour to write up some notes, while testing my
companions to see what their reaction would be to my scribbling in a
Bible. But either they were uninterested, or just unobservant. No one
expressed any curiosity as to what I was doing.

An aspect of this closed community interested me very much.
The French have a saying: 'In the night all cats are grey.' In the
anonymity of the dark, men who had hitherto been morose and taciturn with each other in their daytime exchanges seemed to come to
life in the dormitory. For at least an hour after the lights had been
extinguished, they talked to each other across the room. I thought
of it as the confessional of the darkness and realised that, like a sup-
plicant disclosing to a priest, it was the absence of face-to-face, eye-
to-eye contact that made these anonymous exchanges possible. The
conversation mostly concerned memories, experiences – common or
individual – and, most interestingly, their thoughts about the future.
These varied from one individual who was positive he would be
relieved by relatives sometime, to the majority who had apparently
given up all hope of restoration to the outside. A few fantasised that
their luck would turn and a job with a house would be found. Those
with wives and children in the House were most likely to keep their
optimism in that regard. Having experienced the racy conversation
of a boys' dormitory, as far as their carnal needs were concerned, I
was surprised that it was a subject they seemed to avoid. The enforced
withdrawal of conjugal relations was perhaps not a topic for sharing. How many of them comforted themselves under their blankets
I didn't even guess, but I would have been surprised if that had not
been so. By and large, when they did discuss women it was often with
surprising warmth and respect, fulfilling the meaning of the old adage
'absence makes the heart grow fonder'.

An aspect on which we were all united was food. The monotony
of a diet that lacked variety and substance stimulated us all to dream
and fantasise about the taste, smell and look of an array of dishes.
Universally top of our list was a craving for pastry with meat inside
running with juice. Savoury dishes were more favoured than sweet,

although no one would have turned down the offer of custards or cakes. We tantalised ourselves making lists and discussing favourite dishes. It did us no good at all; those exchanges simply made the desire stronger and more out of reach. But we couldn't help ourselves and conversations more often than not developed into competitions as to who could devise the most mouthwatering meal.

We rose at seven o'clock at the ringing of the bell and dressed and tidied what little bedding we had. I noticed one of the two young boys who had been placed here because there was no room for them in the children's quarters looking tearfully at his bed and I guessed he'd had an accident in the night. I knew that he should be at least ten years old to be placed with the men, but he looked younger. Pathetically he tried to soak up the puddle with his towel, and given there was no heat in the room it would take some hours for the straw to dry naturally. If he was lucky and the air warmed up it might dry by bedtime. The other boy, who was older, came across to try to help and between them they were able to disguise the wet mattress by turning it over and covering it with neatly folded blankets.

One of the men took the bucket and walked with it carefully down the stairs and out into the yard, grumbling because there were two turds floating on its surface that nobody would own up to. Alfrey and I followed the rest sheep-like into the yard where we queued for the privy and the pump. There was no bathhouse at Seddon: some men cursorily splashed their faces with cold water; braver souls stripped to the waist and put their heads under the spout. I felt I had to make some kind of gesture of competence and self-respect, and immersed my head and trunk under the freezing spring water. It was certainly stimulating in spite of the darkness of the hour and the temperature. I towelled myself dry vigorously with the rough piece of flannel I'd been allocated, dressed myself again and, as the seven thirty bell rang, lined up with the rest for a daily head count and breakfast.

I was interested to see that the master was not present for morning prayers as I assumed he should have been. Instead, Mr Lodge the porter was standing in for him. The whole company sat again in specified rows, and this time we were served thin oatmeal porridge, made with half milk, half water in the same wooden bowls, along with a piece of bread. Then it was oakum picking from eight o'clock.

I was slowly developing some companionship with Richard Alfrey. At one point in the morning he actually instigated conversation by telling me, as he unpicked the hemp rope, how he missed the feel and smell of the hides he used to work with. We agreed that all trades have their own familiar smells and textures; for a carpenter it's not only the smell of wood and sawdust, but also the polish and the glue. I was heartened that he was beginning to unbend, although I still steered clear of any mention of his wife and daughter as I felt these were touchstones that might produce a serious reaction from him.

The day passed much as the day before and, I anticipated, the days to come. I took note of when Mr Calman finally appeared at about eleven o'clock. An important part of the duties of the master and matron was a daily inspection of the House from top to bottom and I was told they always undertook this together. For the first time I was able to appraise them as a pair. When I studied them the nursery rhyme 'Jack Sprat' came to mind – as her husband was rotund so she was the opposite. He was slow-moving because of his great bulk; she was like a percipient bird forever on the lookout and, if she was a bird, it was a falcon. My first impression was reinforced; she was a pitiless woman.

There were harsh punishments for infringements of the rules. Mrs Calman was responsible for the state of the linen and bedding and became incensed with bed-wetters and there were a few in our dormitory. I learned that the youngest regularly soiled his bed and was duly chastised for it. Today I saw Calman exercising one of those punishments. After the inspection he came down to the workroom and hauled the boy out in front of us all. Holding him by his arm he brought his face down to the level of the boy's ear and wheezed, 'Again, you foul boy – won't you learn?' The boy trembled and hung his head. Calman brought out the rod that he carried under his arm. Almost automatically the boy held out his hand and received six vicious strokes across his small thin palm.

Friday, 9 March

This morning I saw Robert Enderby for the first time. He swaggered

into the workroom dressed in jacket, breeches and riding boots looking somewhat dishevelled as if he had had a hard ride, a hard night, or
both. The overseer had taken some days off but returned this morning
at around ten o'clock. As he entered I noticed an immediate change
in the atmosphere; where it had been calm and almost relaxed it now
became tense. This was a man who evidently wielded a power that
went far beyond his official remit. His intimidating appearance made
him ideally suited to the task of collecting the poor-rate, backed up
by his reputation as a bully. But to my mind his employment as a
tax collector was about as sound as employing Mr Richard Turpin to
gather in the nation's income tax. I doubted whether all the money
found its way into the union coffers, although I had as yet heard nothing to suggest he was dishonest with money. Enderby was a jack-
of-all-trades who lived outside the House in rooms above a shop in
the town and came and went from the workhouse at his pleasure and
often stayed the night when he and Calman returned inebriated from
the local inn. Everybody knew that Bob Enderby was worshipped by
his sister and she could deny him nothing. In so far as she held sway
over her husband, the overseer dominated the pair of them.

How best to describe him? He was in his early thirties, just under
six feet tall, with dark curling collar-length hair. But I flatter him too
much – his physique was unquestionably good, but his face exhibited all the dubious aspects of his character. He was obviously a heavy
drinker – the contours of small broken veins were mapped out in
the areas under his eyes; they had lost their sclerotic clarity and had
become bulging and bloodshot. There was the same hardness about
his mouth that I'd noticed in his sister, Jenny Calman, and, overall,
there was a considerable likeness between them. It appeared to me that
Enderby was drinking and fornicating himself into dissipation, and
both addictions were having an equally damaging effect to his physiognomy.

I picked up some gossip about him. He was considered reckless in
all things, particularly as a rider; he regularly hunted with the Seddon
hunt – the Master of Hounds was Colonel Shepherd – and was always
favourite in steeplechasing events. But it was his relationship with
women that caused most comment. He was unmarried, but it was said
partial to other men's wives. In earlier times, before he became dis-

solute, there were plenty who wouldn't refuse him. As his looks and superficial charms faded his choices became more limited, until his only permanent port of call for relief was as a regular customer at the home of the local strumpet, Mary-Ann Wilcox.

More disturbingly were the rumours that Enderby was known to have designs on some of the women inmates. I could find no one who would swear to it, and when I asked for gossip about specific incidents there was no corroborative evidence. I saw nothing to support the conjecture, but we were segregated from the women and I'd no notion of what went on at the opposite side of the building. What I was certain of was that I disliked the man on sight.

Wednesday, 14 March

It was time to take stock of what I had seen and experienced now I'd been an inmate for seven days. In my mind I compared the conditions of entry to the House with what I know of prisoners in jails. Unlike them, volunteers to the workhouse don't have prescribed dates for release. Prisoners are at least assured that once they've carried out the sentence they'll be free to come and go and make their own decisions and choices once again. Inmates here can, for the most part, no longer look forward to release, although ironically they are legally free to go whenever they like. However, unless a relative or sponsor on the outside comes forward with offers of support, they are more or less abandoned and with no possible outcome other than continued dependency.

The other aspect that I'd quickly appreciated in the brooding atmosphere of the House is the lack of imperative by which most males of the species seek to dominate any situation in which they find themselves. In other similar institutions that I can think of – schools, workplaces, prisons – there is always a pecking order. Newcomers are immediately tested and as a result established in an appropriate place in the natural order. In prisons, in particular, men are often highly emotional. They have, barring some miscarriages of justice, been fairly caught and are either resentful of the fact or resigned to it. But they are there for a reason – they've put themselves outside

what are considered acceptable social codes of behaviour and therefore society punishes them for it. Those who are irredeemably unrepentant will fight against the system, with each other and those in
charge. They soon establish their place in the power structure of the
institution and seek to maintain it against challengers.

Here that imperative seemed to be strangely absent. Each man
was bound within himself, his own thoughts and needs of subsistence,
showing very little interest in anyone else. The place was imbued
with an aura of apathy and the normal drives of social compulsion
were not evident, at least not to me. Men were content to accept, for
example, their regular places to sit, to sleep and to work; they also
appeared to leave newcomers more or less unchallenged. The impo-
sition of long periods of silence and discouragement of conversation
had a significant effect on the men's ability to socialise. Although I
wasn't well acquainted with them, asylums possibly engendered the
same response. When each patient lives within his own head and has
little appreciation of time or circumstance, then institutional apathy
becomes ingrained.

The physical aspects of this place were egregiously grim. I understood it was so because its main purpose was one of deterrence. But
the dehumanising effect of the regime currently conducted here was,
to my mind, unforgivable. The over-harsh punishment meted out to
the young boy for an accident was a vivid example of unnecessary
cruelty pitilessly administered. I made a mental list of all the privations we suffered purely as a result of our personal misfortunes. Cold
dormitories with no fires even in winter; cheap, uncomfortable, inadequate bedding; and food of such dubious quality that I sometimes
hesitated to eat it. There was also personal dehumanisation in the lack
of means to keep ourselves properly clean. The tedious and stultifying employment and absence of any means for proper recreation and
association with others added to the degradation of our spirit. Above
all the oppressive silences we must keep and the constant reinforce-
ment by the officials of our dependent status. This was particularly
true of some of the guardians, and also the chaplain who preferred to
emphasise the harsh dogma of the Old Testament over a New Testament Christian message.

Truly there was little to comment on the daily routine – one day being identical to the next, with the exception of Sundays of which I will write later. But that very repetition allowed my mind to wander without difficulty and I have had plenty of time to study my companions closely, although conversation was more difficult to induce. The oldest male inmate was probably Jacob Fearnley, although I couldn't be completely certain as no one knew his exact age. He was an inmate in his parish workhouse before the amalgamation and transferred to Seddon with two women of equal vintage. He was a prime example of what long-term incarceration does to the human spirit. When I engaged him in conversation about his life previously, he had very little memory of the immediate past, although he could recall aspects of his childhood. Physically he exhibited all the consequences of long-term exposure to poor diet, lack of exercise and absence of mental stimulation. His gnarled, grey face, with watery blue-grey eyes set wide apart, produced an image of flat mental dullness that was matched by the monotone of his voice.

'I used to work on the land as a young boy – crow-scaring and picking stones. The best job was keeping the gate because I could just lie about doing nothing.'

I probed a little. 'What did you do for a living when you were a man?'

'Difficult to say, sir.' I ignored the civility – I didn't wish to distract him. 'I think I might've been on the coasters for a time up at Felixstowe, but I'm not sure.'

'How did you come here?'

'Walked, sir.'

'Certainly, but can you remember from where?'

'No, sir. It's all blank. I'm happy here – I get fed and it's quite warm.'

'What about your family? Were you ever married?'

'That I couldn't say, sir – I might have been – there again I might not.' I was not getting very far. It seemed as though he had blanked out any existence before he came into the House. In the end I gave up and left him methodically unravelling junk rope and letting the fibres fall into his lap.

I spent most of the time with Richard Alfrey, who I found increasingly interesting. He'd become more relaxed as the days went by and we spoke about many things. He was not a totally uneducated man; although unread, he had a quick mind and grasped ideas readily. I still hesitated to speak of his wife and daughter, but kept to general topics. He was most interested to hear about my life in London.

'It's a place I always wanted to visit; our capital city – everyone should visit it at least once. I hear there are all kinds of new things happening – like these new gas street lamps. I'd like to see them lit up.'

'I suppose we take them for granted now. But what you'd really like to see are the new railways; lines are opening up everywhere.'

'There's real opposition to them in the countryside. Nobody other than the landowners wants them. But it's my guess they'll push them through anyway!' He sighed and shook his head. I imagined he was thinking he would probably never see a steam locomotive.

Tuesday, 20 March

There was a small and puzzling incident today that at the time did not occur to me as significant, but would be explained as events to come revealed themselves. At about mid-morning we were working among the oakum as normal when the overseer came in. We generally only saw Enderby when the Calmans were otherwise engaged. It was coming close to Lady Day, 25 March, when all payments of the poor-rate were due, and he was most often found circulating round the parish collecting in the tax. So this visit was out of the ordinary.

He stopped at the end of the bench where Richard Alfrey and I were sitting and then deliberately moved across to face Richard directly. He looked him up and down and I caught a look of triumph in his face. Richard stiffened beside me, sensing trouble, and I could imagine his fists beginning to clench. I couldn't understand what Enderby's purpose was, but there was a palpable air of self-satisfaction about him. He stood looking at Richard for what seemed minutes, but I was sure were only seconds; his intimidating stance was obvious – he was challenging Alfrey, but for what purpose or reason I couldn't guess. As quickly as he had come into the room, he left it.

'What was that all about do you think?' I asked.

He shrugged. 'You never can tell with a man like that. He's a devious bastard.'

'Why single you out? He doesn't usually take notice of any inmates.'

Richard sighed. 'I can't make head or tail of anything here; everything seems out of kilter to me.' We fell silent and continued with our work. Neither of us mentioned it again, but neither of us forgot it.

Wednesday, 21 March

I knew it was important to identify what the date was but soon appreciated how quickly one grey day merged into another. Fortunately I had my Bible notebook that enabled me to record all dates day by day. From my early research in London, by my reckoning the meeting of the board of guardians on this day would be the penultimate of that particular constitution. Annual elections were due on 5 April for changes to the board. Having only been confronted by the board on one occasion, I wasn't familiar with the current set of personalities, other than Colonel Shepherd. What interested me was what the composition of the board would be after the elections.

Much of my information about the running of the House, its officials and occupants was coming from the porter, Fred Lodge, who, like his wife, was often willing to talk, especially when Calman was absent and he was deputising for him. Even in my short time here I recognised Lodge as a man with a conscience who, while he wouldn't be overtly critical of the union, particularly to one of the inmates, had concerns about the shortcomings of its administration. I was sufficiently experienced in quizzing witnesses for their observations that it presented no difficulty for me to persuade him to talk, but I was sure to keep the conversations just short of indiscretion; I'd no desire to jeopardise his position.

Our ritual on days when the board of guardians met was somewhat disrupted. For our part we were required to be even quieter than usual. Fred told me that once a month the board made a tour of inspection. I wait expectantly for the next one to occur.

Sunday, 25 March

At last, a break with routine! I hadn't considered there would be any reprieve from the daily grind to which I'd quickly become accustomed, let alone a chance to leave the House for a while, but once a month there was provision for those who wanted to attend morning service at St Mary's on the outskirts of Seddon town. Now, I'm not an avid church-goer, but as I'd presented myself as a keen reader of the Bible, I'd no hesitation in joining the dozen or so inmates who were keen to participate. In total, eighteen men, women and children lined up in three grey files under the supervision of the matron and Mr Lodge, whose wife and two children followed behind us during our walk across three fields to the church.

It was pleasant to walk into the dimly lit Norman church, which was cold but not unwelcoming. All the inmates were directed to four rows of pews at the back, two on each side of the aisle. Mr Lodge and his wife and children sat up in the main body of the church. Mrs Calman placed herself at the end of the children's pew, ready with a frown, a pinch or a poke for any of them tempted into 'refractory' behaviour. The rest of the pews were taken up with local folk who mostly ignored us. Dressed in their Sunday best, their finery made our workhouse garb seem even shabbier and just another form of humiliation. I noticed the backs of a few gentry sitting in the front. It was a service with all the trappings of High Anglicanism and I sat back and enjoyed the aestheticism of its ritual – the smell of the incense and the tinkle of the bell. The sermon was mercifully short and even more quickly forgotten and, after waiting for the rest of the congregation to leave in their strict social hierarchy, we were soon outside in the early spring sunshine. In spite of the cool air many worshippers had stopped to gossip with their neighbours out in the churchyard; I took the opportunity to try to identify any of the guardians I'd seen at the board meeting, but they must have been dispersed across the union parishes today for none were here that I recognised.

I took note of the local squire – if that was what he was – a young man almost as tall as I, well built with a pleasant face who was talking to the rector. I gathered that he owned the estate of Seddon Hall and was the local Justice of the Peace. I thought he was young for such a role – possibly mid to late twenties – but I might have been wrong. I hoped my powers of discernment were not diminishing in the stultifying atmosphere of the House.

The walk back across the field was a tonic. For the first time since I entered the House I felt warm sunshine on my face, heard birds singing and other sights and smells of the countryside. Late snowdrops, crocuses and clumps of early daffodils were in full bloom among the graves; many had escaped the churchyard and found further sanctuary in the surrounding field. Never had air smelled so sweet. Another reminder not to take any gifts of nature for granted in the future. I wished Richard Alfrey had agreed to come with me. As I walked towards the lychgate it occurred to me that if we could get a message to his wife next month she could attend with her daughter, and the family would at least see each other, even if they couldn't converse.

Monday, 26 March

Last night there was another incident of bed-wetting that might have resulted in predictably nasty consequences. As before, it was the younger of the two boys who occupied beds that were in the full draught from the door. Although I'd not noted it specifically, I'd been mentally taking account of how they were treated. My understanding of the position of younger inmates was that they should be receiving some education on working days or, if they were over nine, might be indentured as an apprentice to a master in the locality, but only if they could read and write. The boys, Peter Samuels and William Tuttle, were not occupied in anything that could be construed as education or training. Their tasks were oakum picking, gardening and looking after the domestic animals and fowls, particularly the small herd of pigs kept on the union's smallholding.

I took it upon myself to try to extract some information about both boys. William, the younger of the two, was most resistant to conversation and I could get very little out of him. When I asked him his age he said he thought he was nine but wasn't sure, and I couldn't gauge it. The older boy, Peter Samuels, was more forthcoming. He told me he was thirteen and he thought that his companion was about ten. Peter was more physically robust that his friend; his face was imprinted with the cunning and shiftiness that results from the imperative of self-preservation through lack of care. This young man had lost all confidence in the world around him and particularly the people who were mapping out his future.

I manoeuvred myself next to him during a work session and set about engaging him. He wasn't averse to answering my questions, but was clearly on his guard.

'I saw you in church yesterday, did you enjoy the service?'

He looked suspiciously at me and then thought for a moment. 'What do you mean "enjoyed it"? I go because it gets me out of here for a while.'

At least he would talk to me, so I went on. 'How long have you been here?'

'About two years – I came with my mother, but she died sometime last year. I'm on my own now.'

'Have you no relatives to go to?'

He looked at me witheringly. 'You should know that no one here has relatives or family, leastways any that is interested in us. If we did, we wouldn't be here.' He looked me boldly in the face. 'Where are your relatives? I'd be surprised if you had any!'

I nodded. 'Quite right – I don't. So what happens when you're grown up? Surely you won't stay here forever?'

He shrugged. 'Can't rightly say. One of the men told me I should be put out for a 'prentice, but I have to be able to read and write my own name for that to happen – and I can't' – he shifted on his seat – 'never been taught.'

I frowned. 'I thought all boys and girls in the House had to be taught to read and write – someone told me you should have learning three hours a day.'

Again, he looked pityingly at me. 'You don't know much about this place, do you? I thought you'd been here a few weeks. Things don't operate by the rules. I know, I ask questions. There're people here who can tell me what's what and they say this union is bad – 'specially for children.'

I could see he was becoming flushed and angry. I backed off and brought up the subject of his friend. 'Even if I'm stupid about some of things going on here, one thing I noticed is that you're a good friend to William.'

He looked into the middle distance as though embarrassed by any show of appreciation. 'Will's a good boy. He's a bastard – doesn't know his mother or father. He's been here since he was born – well, not exactly here – he was left outside one of parish workhouses where he stayed until it was shut when this place opened. Whoever owned him at least gave him a name. He had a label pinned to his blanket that said "William Tuttle". He's still got it somewhere; he sometimes looks at it and cries. He only has me and I stand up for him against some of the bullies – although I can't do it against the master or Enderby. I try to protect him, especially with the bed-wetting, which he does regular. I sometimes switch his mattress for mine. Those whacks across the hands sting bad. He's not a big chap and sometimes I think he might faint if Calman knocks him too hard. I hate the man – and his wife – and her brother – the whole fucking pack of them.' For the first time he was animated, clenching his fists and contorting his face. He spoke quietly, though, able to maintain, even in his anger, the requirement for low-pitched conversation. The vehemence of his response told me more than words, as did his ability to bring himself back under control. This was a boy who obviously thought more than he spoke. 'The only decent people here are Mr Lodge and his wife. She does little things for us that make a difference.'

'What do you mean?'

'If I tell you, you mustn't let on?' I nodded encouragingly. 'She sits and talks to us when she's standing in for the matron and best of all, she brings in books for us to look at and she reads to us. She knows it's against the rules, but she does it all the same. She's got children of her own, lucky sods; they've got a good mother. Those times are the best – apart from walking to church on Sundays and feeling the sun. I also quite like being in the garden for the same reason. This is a good time of year because we're planting the vegetables. Will and I work outside on our own some days and that's a relief – no one breathing down our necks.'

Having tacked cautiously down the coast, I made a break, hoisted full sail and turned out into uncharted waters. 'Do you know anything about your father?'

His reaction was surprisingly moderate. 'The bastard upped and left us all when I was about Will's age. My mother was left with me and two younger brothers, but they both died. We never heard from my pa again – Ma said he ran off with another woman. Anyway, it wasn't long before we were homeless and forced into the House. The shame of it all broke her heart and that's what I think she died of – a broken heart. She's buried in a pauper's grave on the edge of the churchyard. That's one of the reasons I like going there each month. If Mrs Lodge is in charge of us she lets me go and stand by the grave for a few minutes. Mrs Calman just rushes us back as fast as she can.'

I maintained a respectful silence for a little while and then returned to the matter of his future and also Will's. He was ambivalent about what might happen – almost resigned to being in Seddon for the rest of his life – although I hoped that wouldn't be the case. As for Will – apart from his self-appointed protector – he was completely alone. His future was bleak: no family to take any interest, no means to better himself, and no education or even apprenticeship. I was appalled at the waste, but reminded myself that this was not a unique situation. The position of the children working up in the textile mills in the north was similarly desolate with the added risk of early mortality through industrial accident.

I felt I had gone far enough; besides it was almost midday and time for dinner. We resumed our untwisting but in a more companionable silence.

Tuesday, 27 March

Today my self-respect was somewhat restored. For the first time since my arrival I challenged the matron. During the previous night young William Tuttle woke whimpering and I immediately sensed what was wrong. Having no wish to see the boy chastised yet again, I got up, went over to his bed, which was soaking wet, took off his soiled night shirt, lifted him up and moved him to an unused mattress at the other end of the room. Carrying his poor, naked little body I could feel his ribs and long bones, which were stick-like. As I laid him on the clean palliasse he woke, saw me and looked scared. I told him to go back to sleep and I stayed with him until he drifted off. This morning, as the bell went at seven o'clock, I dressed and went across to his soiled mattress. The straw, which had clearly not been changed for days, was a stinking foetid mass. I pulled the whole mattress off and, together with his nightshirt, carried it down the stairs, walked across the yard and down to the pigsty where I shook the straw out. I came back to the yard, washed the cover and William's night shirt under the pump and hung them both up to dry across a low beam.

Mrs Calman was already up and supervising at the pump. Seeing my activities she immediately challenged them. I told her that the mattress was in no fit state for anyone to sleep on, let alone a small child.

She stood in front of me, hands on her hips. 'Inmates don't take it upon themselves to organise the linen – that's my job; I say when covers are to be changed or washed. Straw's expensive at this time of year and we keep what we have for bedding the animals. The boy must learn to control his bladder. God knows he's been beaten enough times for bed-wetting. Don't you realise you're breaking regulations and can be punished for it? Perhaps you'd like a taste of isolation and forty-eight hours on bread and water.'

I was moderate in my response – up to a point.

'Mrs Calman, this is a boy of nine, parentless as far as I know, sleeping in a dormitory full of men who care nothing about him. In spite of your beatings he can't help himself. Now listen, I'll deal with the outcome of any accidents he may have – including washing soiled covers and garments and refilling his mattress. That's one less job for you.' I was robust and Jenny Calman stepped back a pace. 'There's no point taking the rod to a small boy for wetting the bed. There are other ways to cure his weakness.' Her sharp pale face began to redden in anger and to my surprise she turned on her heels and walked away. Just as quickly, as though she'd made up her mind, she came back.

'So – what's in it for you?'

I caught the undertone of her remark, shocked that a woman should have thought it, but didn't rise to the obvious insult. 'All the men have to endure the persistent smell of piss in the dormitory. It's not always William at fault; some of the older men have accidents, but they manage their own needs quite effectively under the circumstances. William's a boy who just needs some training – that's all – nothing else.'

'I don't believe you, but very well, we'll try it your way. From now on, you're responsible for the boy's accidents. But take note – there's little straw available, so you'll have to dry it and reuse it, which is our normal practice at this time of year.' She walked off and, in truth, I was as surprised at her acquiescence as the other observers of this curious confrontation.

I had now undertaken a responsibility that I really didn't relish, nor knew how to manage – but, after all, I had plenty of time on my hands.

April

I'm a bachelor with no experience of young children; my nephews and nieces are away in India and I've never met them. Training small children in these matters is most certainly a job for a woman. But having made the commitment to remedial action, and in front of witnesses, I now had to find ways of fulfilling it. Immediately I thought of Amy Lodge. She was the mother of two small children and their training must be fresh in her mind. Seeking her out at a quiet moment I explained my and William's predicament. She was very obliging and gave me explicit instructions, which she guaranteed – if I used suitable encouragement and reward – would solve the problem.

During the following nights William and I struggled together to keep his bed dry. I adopted in full all Mrs Lodge's techniques, ensuring that he didn't drink any water for at least two hours before he went to bed, that he made a visit to the privy just before bedtime, and then used the bucket before the candles were snuffed. I lay awake for any signs of restlessness on his part and as soon as he started to stir I went across and lifted him out and, almost in his sleep, stood with him while he used the bucket and then put him back to bed. Apart from two nights when I'd not been quick enough to catch him, the regime had been successful. As Amy Lodge had also suggested, to sweeten the pill, I promised him that every time he had a dry bed I'd give him a piece of my cheese from supper. At first the other men viewed my activities with suspicion, thinking, I imagined, along the same lines as the matron. But after it became obvious I had no vicious intention towards William – and the stench of stale urine was reducing – they curtailed their comments and eventually their interest. Fortunately William was very cooperative. He was old enough to feel ashamed of his accidents and the inducement of extra food really clinched our whole arrangement. I also canvassed Peter Samuels to encourage rather than tease, which, although not malicious, hadn't helped William's confidence.

Wednesday, 4 April

I was fully imbued with the monotony of life at Seddon by the time April was with us. My spirits were only lifted by nature's gifts of warmer sunshine, drifts of yellow daffodils and buttercups, purple crocuses and, above all, the unconfined smell of spring itself. That at least the House couldn't contaminate.

The board of guardians in its current format met for the last time today. Mr Lodge told me later that there had been much back-slapping and toasting with the union's sherry, although some of the members had absented themselves, most noticeably those who'd resigned. Elections were underway and the first meeting of the new board was due on Wednesday, 18 April.

Friday, 13 April

As I'm not a superstitious man I had no qualms about it being the thirteenth – neither did my companions, who by and large were completely unaware of the date, only that it was Good Friday and a religious holiday. Apart from compulsory attendance at the Reverend Patchin's service in the dining hall, we were left to our own devices. Unfortunately the weather was poor and we mostly sat around the covered area of the yard, resting and gossiping. The Calmans had gone to church and then off elsewhere and Fred Lodge was deputising as master. When there was a break in the cloud and the sun shone briefly, Richard and I walked down to the vegetable patch to admire William and Peter's handiwork. They'd made a fair attempt at a patch of carrots, turnips and onions, all of which were beginning to show through. I rather envied them their task, as it took them out of the dusty confines of the workroom and enabled them to taste the fresh air. On this day, with the Calmans away, they were with Mrs Lodge, who had brought one of her children's books to show them.

Sunday, 15 April

The church bells ringing across the fields reminded me it was Easter
Sunday. In spite of the fact that our next visit to the church would not
normally be until the end of the month, we had a special dispensa-
tion to attend morning service today. Unfortunately it was not a glorious spring day – rather the air was steel grey and full of rain. For
many of us this was no deterrent – anything to escape the boredom of
the House, which retained its cheerless atmosphere regardless of hol-
idays. On this day I was pleased that Richard Alfrey had agreed to
attend and it was soon clear why. His wife and daughter were walking
in file behind Mrs Calman. The bad weather meant we didn't try to
linger either on the walk there or back. An opportunity to appreciate
different surroundings was never to be missed, but on this occasion
we walked with heads bent against the wind and were relieved when
we finally entered the porch. The church had been beautifully decorated with spring flowers, which immediately raised my spirits, and
although the air was cool – it was not unpleasantly so. Mrs Alfrey and
her daughter managed by some stroke of good fortune to find a place
in the pew directly opposite her husband. For the whole service their
attention was completely absorbed by each other. Sitting in front of
them all, the matron had no knowledge of the silent contact between
them.

The service was orthodox and the sermon tedious, but I took
great notice of the finery in which the locals were arrayed. The Easter
service is traditionally a time to impress, and hats and bonnets of all
shapes and hues were on display. Inevitably this contrasted acutely
with our grey uniform, making us feel all the more shabby and
unkempt. However, we didn't have to suffer the usual indignity of
being routinely scrutinised at the end of the service since there was
no loitering for social pleasantries at the door of the church. Umbrel-
las were up as protection of their wardrobes from what was now
driving rain. As a consequence they moved quickly to their various
conveyances, while we walked at an equally urgent pace back across
the fields, Richard Alfrey with a genuine spring in his step. The difference contact with his family had made to his mood was startling;
for the first time I saw him smile.

Wednesday, 18 April

Fred and Amy Lodge were deputed to supervise the House between ten and eleven o'clock while the Calmans and other officers attended the board meeting. Fred Lodge had seen all the guardians through the main gates; some had come in carts, others on horseback and one in a carriage, among them the local JP Edgar Lawes, whom I had caught sight of in the churchyard after Sunday service. Amy told me a little about him. He was, apparently, a good friend to her uncle, the farmer Ted Lake who had himself been newly elected. He'd told Amy that it was he who persuaded Mr Lawes to consider joining the board.

The main business of the meeting had been to set the poor-rate for the year, and this meant that Enderby would continue to be out and about on collection business. Some rate payers made an annual payment, others on the quarter days. But once the rate was set it was the overseer's responsibility to bring in the money. In an earlier semi-interrogation of Fred Lodge he had told me that the clerk to the board, one William Harbey, was a master at book-keeping, and the accounts were considered pristine. It seemed as though Enderby would have no chance of pocketing monies illegally, but what would be certain was that his intimidating presence made people pay up swiftly to get rid of him. This was one of his busy times and on the rare occasions he'd been in the House he sought no further confrontations with Richard Alfrey.

Although a full list of the guardians had been posted up in the town, and a copy was available in the House, off-hand Mrs Lodge could not remember the names and occupations of all the new members, although she said that the landlord of the local tavern, Michael Jameson, was one of them. As far as I dared, I asked her if she could find out more about them. She was surprised by my request and asked me why I was so interested.

'I just think we should all know who are making decisions about us. If you think about it, the inmates' lives are in the hands of a few men – some almost self-selected by the sponsorship of existing members. Colonel Shepherd, for example; I heard that his bailiff, Mr Stenning, is on the board. Now, how did he come to be involved?'

'I really couldn't say, but should you be asking such questions? I wonder about you, Mr Millhouses; sometimes you don't seem like the normal sort of inmate we get here.'

I raised an eyebrow. 'And they are?'

She smiled. 'Poor people who don't ask any questions!'

I thought it time to close the conversation as I felt sure she was ready to turn the tables and interrogate me more fully. But I knew I was right. The constitution of the board was very important as far as the recipients of Poor Law relief were concerned. They set the rate, and if it was too high then local folk would become resentful, which would have political implications – as well as being rate payers, some of them now had a parliamentary vote. On the other hand, if the rate was too low, then the union paupers suffered gross and unfair deprivation, something I was sure was happening in Seddon.

Tuesday, 24 April

This was a day of domestic triumph for both William Tuttle and me. It had been three weeks since we embarked on our plan together to eliminate his wet beds, and he had now woken on a dry mattress for the last two. Indeed, one of the unintended consequences of the regime was that he started to learn his numbers. Every occasion of a dry bed was entered on a blank page in my Bible, and as we went along I taught him the names of the figures. By yesterday he had remembered up to the number sixteen, because we included all the dry nights he had accomplished overall. His success quickly produced a marked change in his appearance and confidence. His little pinched and worried face had cleared and he became more talkative. I was now sure that he had established good personal habits and I would no longer have to be awake and vigilant throughout the night.

Sunday, 29 April

Perhaps it was the better weather that tempted us out, but today's Sunday service was very well attended by the inmates of the House and to my satisfaction again included Richard, Emily and Caroline

Alfrey. Although they walked in separate groups and sat in different pews, they were in full sight of each other and able to communicate by glances, which I was sure made a great difference to Richard's state of mind. Peter Samuels was also in better spirits, having been allowed to visit his mother's grave by Amy Lodge, who with her husband had been in charge of the group.

I had been here almost eight weeks and conjuring up thoughts about food for at least five of them. The subsistence diet I was experiencing was just adequate for survival, but not in any way satisfying. By this stage I was permanently hungry and on some nights I dreamed of rich meats, pies and sweet cakes, which came into my mind in many strange guises. Our food is prescribed by the Poor Law commissioners from London, who send out dietary plans that the guardians and officers are to follow. Our union fare was basically bread, a thin porridge gruel made up with milk and water, meat once a week, vegetables, soup thickened with rice or barley, and cheese, which was a regular at supper time. Children under the age of nine should have had extra milk and meat, but I hadn't seen them catered for in this way in Seddon. Those over nine should receive an adult's fare. For my part I knew my stay wasn't permanent, but wondered at the stamina and fortitude of long-term inmates who daily faced such dietary deficiencies. I thought of sailors on long voyages in the past, those who often died because of want of proper sustenance. It wasn't always for lack of bulk but more usually the absence of all the balanced dietary constituents needed to sustain life. How long could a man last on a restricted workhouse diet? Well – judging by Jacob Fearnley – many years, but it had left him and men like him weakened and unfit, certainly for manual work. In this way the commissioners' regime in the union workhouses was self-defeating of their objectives. They sought to make inmates fit for work outside, but denied them the proper nourishment by which that could be achieved.

May

Poor Peter Samuels fell foul of Robert Enderby this morning. The overseer, stinking of alcohol, swept through the workroom on some errand or other. As he passed by Peter he swung his arm and, with the back of his hand, caught the boy a severe clout across the head, which went back with a crack against the wall; I think the boy must have seen stars. As he came to, he pulled himself on to his feet and yelled out 'Fucking bastard!', clenching his fists. Fortunately the nearest man restrained him, pulling him down on to the form. But Enderby came close and, putting his face down to Peter's, growled, 'What did you say?'

Peter's eyes filled with tears of rage and pain. 'What was that for?'

'Because I felt like it! You're a cheeky young guttersnipe and need pulling down a peg. Now I'm going to report you to the master for swearing at an officer. Let's see how you like isolation and bread and water.' He strode off back into the main building and, sure enough, he returned with his brother-in-law who was carrying the punishment book.

Calman pulled Peter to his feet and confronted him. 'Mr Enderby reports you for obscenity to an officer. He said you called him a bastard.'

Peter had recovered himself, and with dangerous insolence replied, 'No, sir, he's lying. I called him a fucking bastard.'

I couldn't fault his spirit, but I feared for his safety. Without comment, the master entered Peter's comments in the book and Enderby grabbed the boy by the arm and hustled him out.

I heard no more until the afternoon when, after I'd enquired after the boy, one of the inmates told me that Peter Samuels was in isolation on a reduced diet of bread, potatoes and milk for twenty-four hours. He had also received twelve strokes of the rod across his back.

Friday, 4 May

A subdued boy returned to the dormitory last night. I couldn't say he was chastened, but as he undressed I could see the raised livid weals made by the rod across his young back. He spoke to no one, not even William, but I heard him quietly crying himself to sleep. I was incensed by such wanton cruelty. These two men are a couple of monsters. It struck me that the members of the board of guardians were also implicated because of their lax supervision of the officers they'd appointed. Neither Enderby nor Calman would have got away with such tyranny had they been properly overseen.

Peter was miserable, but William was blossoming. He stuck to me like glue at times and, although I was touched by his evident fondness for me, I began to keep my distance. Knowing I would be taking my leave of the place in the not too distant future, I had no wish for him to become reliant on my friendship – I most certainly didn't want him to view me as a father-figure who could only disappoint him. But I did resolve to try to do something for him once I was able. In the meantime, I was friendly but made sure he spent most of his time with Peter. This was not difficult because they were now more often than not working down in the vegetable garden sowing and planting out this year's crops. Before he went to sleep we rehearsed what he had remembered of his numbers and he was very proud when he reached three figures unhaltingly. I still slipped him pieces of my cheese, but simply to satisfy myself that he was getting some extra nourishment.

Monday, 7 May

We had an unexpected visitor today. Sometime mid-afternoon the master, with matron following behind looking even more sour than usual, came into the workroom with the JP, Mr Edgar Lawes. I was puzzled because an ad hoc visit such as this was unheard of.

As he entered we stood up directly and, like a military inspection by a visiting general, the master led Mr Lawes down the line. It was left to Mrs Calman to explain what we were doing. The JP signalled to us to sit down and standing in front of us he seemed to single out Peter Samuels, who was sitting at the end of the form. He asked the master what the boy's age was and was told it was fourteen. Calman was very keen to describe Peter's recent misdemeanours and the punishments that had been inflicted – although he didn't mention the strokes across the boy's back. Mr Lawes seemed shocked at the idea of a boy of such a young age being isolated and virtually starved, but he had to concede that the master had the authority of parliament to administer such discipline now the boy was over twelve.

The JP caught my eye and we looked each other over. The impression I gained from a brief obscured view of him in the churchyard was now confirmed. He was a young man slightly shorter than I, with blue eyes and light, Byronically curly brown hair. Lacking the aquiline shape I would associate with the class, his nose was at first sight snub, but on closer viewing I counted it retroussé. Neither did he have the haughty expression of the true aristo, his face being open and his expression friendly. He asked me my name but, just as he was about to engage me in conversation, Mrs Calman intervened and guided him to meet Jacob Fearnley. I liked the courteous way he talked to Jacob, giving him time to speak and listening attentively to his answers. Lawes asked one or two incisive questions, prompting a speedy response from Mrs Calman, who drew Mr Lawes to one side and explained how Jacob was completely conditioned to life in the House and anything he said was unreliable.

Almost as soon as it began the visit was over and the group moved on to inspect the women's and children's quarters. I heard later that it was brief and well controlled by Mrs Calman, who gave the JP no opportunity to engage with any of the inmates. I pondered on what the outcome of this visit would be. Days later I found out and was not disappointed.

Tuesday, 15 May

For some reason, after the day's work we were ordered to make the place exceptionally clean and tidy. Floors to be swept and surfaces wiped free of the oakum dust. We inmates are to be equally spruced up; this evening we have been issued with clean clothing and told to make sure we wash our hands and faces first thing in the morning, like children ordered to make a good impression when wealthy relatives are due.

Wednesday, 16 May

All has been revealed. Nine days after Mr Lawes's visit, today we had an official inspection from the new board. At least thirty minutes before it was due to meet, ten of the members who had arrived made their tour, led by Colonel Shepherd and John Calman. When they arrived in the workroom the master got us to our feet. The colonel proceeded to harangue us and impress on us the need for gratitude towards our neighbours who had kindly fed, clothed and sheltered us. As I remember it he advised us to 'work hard, love God and obey the rules'. I could hardly contain my desire to respond with a retort to the effect that he should listen to his own exhortations, but controlled myself, looking blankly forward and not catching Edgar Lawes's eye, even though I could feel he was looking at me with curiosity. Unlike his visit, none of the guardians attempted to pass the time of day with us, let alone ask if we were content, or otherwise. They passed through the workroom and disappeared into the kitchen.

What happened at the meeting that followed did much to raise the spirits of all the inmates. Mr Lawes somehow arranged for the committee to try the workhouse food for themselves and their response was revulsion. However, the outcome was positive from the point of view of the inmates. A small committee was set up to look at provisions and procurement. The news flashed around the House immediately, and there was much lightening of mood and Mr Lawes came in for some heartfelt expressions of gratitude. I began to like the man. To me this was more than just a single act of common sense; I hoped it signified a move towards improvements generally. It seemed certain that the JP was on our side. Who knew what other enterprises he might have up his sleeve? We all went to bed with expectations of possible change.

Tuesday, 22 May

The lightened mood for me was quickly destroyed today. Enderby returned to the House yesterday evening and by this morning Richard Alfrey had been ruthlessly destroyed by him. As I discovered later, around mid-morning Richard went outside to take a privy break. At the same time Enderby came into the workroom, looked everyone up and down and asked where Richard was. On being told, the overseer went outside. What happened then I was only able to ascertain that night after supper. Throughout the day I could see the man was obviously in a state of complete shock, anger and panic but that he wasn't yet ready to share. When I heard what he had to tell me I was amazed that he'd been able to keep it to himself until the evening.

What Enderby said to him no husband should hear. He had cornered Richard in the yard and, being a few inches taller, loomed over him. When Richard asked him what he wanted, Enderby said straight out, 'Your wife. I'm going to fuck your wife – Emily, isn't it? Or had you forgotten, you being so long apart? I noticed right away, as soon as I saw her, she's a looker; particularly fine figure she's got, well-rounded but firm no doubt – but I've yet to find out. I'm going to screw her rotten and, you know what, there's nothing you can do about it.'

Richard said he was so shocked at the man's foul cold-blooded aggression, and the confidence with which he made his threat that he couldn't respond for a few seconds. He just stared into Enderby's eyes, which were boring back into his seeking some kind of reaction.

'Come on, man, don't you know what I'm saying? I'm going to have your wife. I won't tell you when, but you can keep thinking about whether it's happened or not. When it has, I'll let you know. Who knows – she may like it enough to come back for more!'

At that moment Richard came to and took a swing at him, but Enderby was prepared. Knowing he must by now have goaded the man beyond endurance, he hit him hard in the stomach so that Richard immediately doubled over and, being unsteady on his bad leg, fell back on the ground. Looking down, the overseer left a gob of spit close to Richard's face and then, laughing, swaggered from the yard down into the garden and out through the wall door into the fields beyond.

My first reaction was one of astonishment, then I was frenzied with anger. The more I considered it, the more likely it seemed Enderby would do as he said. How could it be prevented? What could Alfrey do? If he reported the confrontation, the overseer would simply deny it. His sister would undoubtedly give him full support; we all knew she doted on him. If it came to a complaint to the board, and that was unlikely given their obvious uninterest in the inmates' welfare, she would provide suitably outraged denials. How could an inmate accuse a man like her brother of such a thing? etc., etc. It occurred to me she might be colluding with Enderby. After all, it would need someone with access to allow him inside the women's quarters. I felt wretchedly impotent, and couldn't begin to imagine how Richard was feeling. This was a man I knew was besotted with his wife, who already felt ashamed that he'd reduced her to the desperate state they were in. As he'd grown more relaxed in my company he had begun to talk about her more readily, and it was obvious that he was as in love with her now as he'd been when he courted her nearly twenty years before. For her part she'd been loyal, loving and never blamed him for their current plight. He spoke constantly of her exceptional beauty – which was not just a husband's idealisation, but obvious to anyone who saw her. She had a rare beauty, inside and out. This explained Enderby's actions. When he had first come across her he must have thought her too good to miss. It also accounted for the incident back in March when he had come into the workroom and silently confronted Richard – obviously assessing what kind of man he was. This meant that he'd been plotting his move since then. It was only because he'd been away from the House collecting the dues that he'd had to postpone his lechery. Now he was back there was no reason for him to wait.

I urged Richard to try to be calm and keep a clear head. Then I thought of Fred Lodge. Perhaps I could get this information to him and maybe he could tell someone – or even let Enderby know that he knew. It might just make the man reconsider. I resolved to seek out the porter and tell him everything. My opportunity came in the evening. Mr Lodge was acting master from the afternoon until lights-out and I was able to take him to one side after supper while we were free to walk in the yard and garden. I ushered him as far away from the building as I dared and told him frankly what had passed between the overseer and Richard Alfrey. Although he was extremely shocked and disturbed at Enderby's behaviour, he said he already knew from general gossip that the man was a serious womaniser. He confirmed there were rumours that he had had relations with some of the women in the House, a few of which had been welcome. But Amy Lodge had picked up information of Enderby's attentions and this was not the first time he'd heard that the man's name had been connected with the act of rape – for that would clearly be the outcome since Mrs Alfrey would be a totally unwilling participant. Enderby's movements at the weekend were already planned, as far as anyone could ever be sure of them. The overseer had informed Fred that he'd be staying in the Calmans' apartment overnight and Fred was not on duty until Sunday. It seemed highly likely that Enderby would make his move this weekend.

Saturday, 26 May

Unfortunately this was the case. Today the bastard made it known to Richard Alfrey himself; not only that he took his outrageous design one step further. Finding his opportunity that evening he isolated Richard. 'Not only will I fuck your wife tonight – but then sometime very soon I think I'll have your daughter too.'

What to do? I couldn't go to Fred Lodge as he was on leave for the day and Mrs Lodge had told me he'd gone across to visit his uncle's farm twelve miles away where he would be staying the night. He wasn't due back until late tomorrow morning.

Sunday, 27 May

Richard had a bad night. Several times he cried out in conscious agony of thought, or in his sleep. I sat up with him and we both saw the faint light of dawn through minute cracks in the shutters.

Trying to calm him I said, 'This man Enderby – I know his sort – all bluff and bluster. I can't imagine he'd risk such an assault on these premises. Town prostitutes are more in his line.'

'You didn't see his face, Henry. He pushed it right into mine and his eyes never blinked. He described in detail what he would do to my wife – and Caroline – and was relishing every word. I can't bear it! I've now got pictures in my mind of Caroline struggling with him; those images won't ever go away! Almost as bad are the thoughts in my head. I'm useless to both of them. What kind of a husband is it who can't provide for his family? The man that's led them here and – worst of all – can't protect them? Henry – I'm going mad! I want to kill the bastard, but don't know how to. I'll never know if he's even carried out his threat. What will happen to Caroline? How can I protect my daughter? I must go to them!' He swung his legs over the side of the bed.

'What are you doing? You can't get into the women's quarters – the outside doors are locked and the windows barred.' He sat back on the bed with his head in his hands.

By this time some of the men were awake and asking what was going on. I told them that Richard was having a nightmare. 'Moody bastard!' grumbled one of them. 'Keeping us awake. Tell him to shut his mouth.'

It occurred to me that whenever Enderby carried out his boast, he would be quick to let Richard know of it, but I said nothing of that. I felt for him so strongly it briefly crossed my mind to seek out Enderby at some point and kill him myself, but I knew that was a fruitless idea. Justice lay elsewhere and I made a promise to myself that I would seek it as soon as I was able.

I didn't want the whole dormitory woken up and, enquiring as to the substance of his trouble, I tried to soothe him quietly with stupid platitudes that had no effect. I lay awake for hours listening to Richard tossing and turning.

As he filed into the hall for breakfast he seemed only semi-aware of his surroundings and I struggled to get him to take some food. I suggested we went to church where we might see Emily and Caroline – it might be that Enderby was just a braggart, and that nothing had happened. But I knew I was fooling myself. Robert Enderby was a risk-taker; if there was a challenge, he wouldn't shy away from it. No doubt he saw Emily Alfrey as just such an attraction. Would she put up a fight? That was the inducement for him – it would be a power struggle and one he was certain of winning.

He hardly heard my suggestion, but when I repeated it he shook his head and muttered almost inaudibly, 'No, Henry, I'll stay here; I can't face seeing them and not knowing.' Reluctantly I left him with the remainder of the men in the House. How he passed his time I would find out the next day. It happened that neither Mrs Alfrey nor her daughter attended church and, as the tight-lipped matron was in charge this morning, I couldn't ask Mrs Lodge how matters stood with them.

When I returned, Richard was sitting on a form staring into space in the workroom. I tried to engage him, but he remained withdrawn and silent, even until we went to bed, where he had less of a disturbed night, but I knew he wasn't sleeping. God knows what was in his head throughout those dark ten hours.

Monday, 28 May

There was a hanging today, although it was more of a strangling – demonstrating the practical difference between being hung and being hanged. A hanged man will have a regulation knot and a measured drop through a trapdoor to ensure a cleanly broken neck for a swift exit. All this is officially overseen by the services of a professional hangman, a doctor to certify death, and a chaplain to pray the man's soul into heaven.

This was not official, just a home-made plait of odds and ends of rope with a small but stocky bundle dangling from its noose, slowly swinging this way and that under its own momentum until finally coming to a stop, like the pendulum of a clock whose mechanism has run down. Having expended all its energy, it hung still in the sweet May air; the supreme imperative of gravity by which the body should reach the earth only denied by the stout hook to which the carefully measured rope was tied, and the resulting tension as it pulled against the beam.

A wooden crate had been kicked away by feet clad in poor, thin shoes. The legs, arms and body were straight as an arrow, but the head hung down impotently, chin on top of chest. The neck was squeezed by the rope, turning the skin beneath purple. The face was the same hue, as was the tongue that had protruded through the lips, grotesque and swollen. No colour could be determined from the bloodshot eyes that bulged expressionless. The man was of average height and build, dressed in meagre grey clothing: cotton shirt, jacket and trousers – grey in every particular. *Ecce Homo*. What would lead a man to end his existence this way? Undoubtedly this is a house of misery, where all dignity has been extinguished and nothing is left but black despair.

At about three in the afternoon I found the body hanging from a thick wooden beam across a corner of the yard. I'd gone out to find him as he seemed to be taking an inordinate time in the privy and I was increasingly worried about his distracted and moody behaviour. As soon as I surveyed the scene I could tell that he'd planned it well; it would have taken time and secrecy to put together enough hemp rope to plait into a strong enough length to do the job. His main difficulty would have been keeping it secret and finding time and an empty yard. On the other hand, it would only take a minute to attach the rope and throw it over the beam, slip on the noose and kick away the crate that was found lying on its side nearby. I presumed he'd spent Sunday morning putting it all together. Very few men had stayed behind from church and Richard was always one to keep himself to himself. Strangely I wasn't all together surprised; the level of his grief had been almost unbearable to watch and I knew that he saw only hopelessness. When it came to it, he was unable to protect his wife and daughter from the most foul of crimes perpetrated by a man steeped in wickedness. In the end the thoughts that must have prevailed in his head sent him temporarily out of his mind. But on reflection I thought a man hanging himself quietly in private was probably the first and last independent action he could choose to take in this place. I guessed that his mind was far from deranged.

I rushed back into the workroom immediately and called for help, then returned to the scene. One of the inmates went for the master, who was close at hand and came wheezing into the yard. I took the weight of Richard's body and Calman – gracelessly – stood the crate upright and clambered on to it. Taking the rope now made slack, he cut it in one stroke with a sharp knife. The body fell into my arms and I looked at the face, the features so contorted I barely recognised them. Two men lifted a door off its hinges from one of the stables and gently I laid him on it. Four of us carried him to the dining hall where a trestle table had been erected and where we placed the door and its contents. Mr Calman positioned himself sentry-like over the body. We all stood for a long time in awkward silence until it was broken by the arrival of Edgar Lawes, Fred Lodge and Colonel Shepherd. All had been called and ridden hard together from Seddon Hall. Soon afterwards the surgeon came in with the coroner, a man called Ollington. A fast rider was needed to summon them and who else would it be but irony of ironies, Robert Enderby. Mr Burgwin looked carefully at the body, noted the contusions on the neck, the protruding tongue and bulging eyes, and declared the man died of asphyxiation caused by strangling with a rope.

The coroner was keen to hold the inquest immediately since the surgeon could, without hesitation, certify cause, and those who would be involved as witnesses were all present. The verdict would be a formality. The brief inquest was held in the boardroom; the only witnesses attending were myself who'd found the body, the master who'd cut him down and Emily Alfrey. There was a swift exchange between the coroner and the master about the probable time of death, but no questions as to why the man might have taken his own life and whether anything in particular had triggered his action. Mrs Alfrey was questioned as to what she knew of her husband's state of mind, but could give no coherent answer. She hadn't spoken to her husband for nearly three months. No other inmates were called who might have an idea why he did it. The master was clear that the workhouse staff were certainly not responsible and the institution was completely absolved from any implied negligence by the coroner's verdict of 'suicide by hanging while temporarily mentally deranged'. The whole affair was wrapped up within twenty minutes; the death certificate was signed and witnessed and permission given for burial of the corpse as soon as a grave could be dug.

Obviously it crossed my mind that I should tell the inquest why the man had taken this course of action, but I hesitated. I had no proof that Enderby had carried out his threat. He could have simply been playing games with Alfrey – although I doubted it. In any case someone would need to speak to his wife and find out the facts before levelling charges. Also, I knew I had the luxury of time to investigate further and then plan any action that would be appropriate. I kept quiet and let the formal procedures of the inquest take place uninterrupted.

We carried the body, still on its stout door, to an unused stable to be placed in a workhouse coffin. Mr Ollington expressed the hope that burial would be swift. As a suicide Richard Alfrey's body would be buried outside the churchyard. Four of us volunteered for a work detail to dig a grave.

Wednesday, 30 May

Reaction to and comment on Alfrey's death was muted in the dormitory last night. The news of his suicide had settled like a black miasma and the men seemed reluctant to acknowledge it, let alone gossip and speculate. The question was asked as to why he had done it – but no one had any explanation other than the observation that he was 'a moody sod, anyway'. As I was recognised as his friend, they looked to me for reasons, but I was vague and non-committal and they didn't pursue their questioning. I perceived that self-slaughter was not a topic they wished to examine too closely. Perhaps in the past it had crossed the minds of some of them to take that route themselves.

We heard that at the regular board meeting Richard Alfrey's suicide was on the agenda, but just another piece of union business. There were those on the board, so my source Amy Lodge told me later, who pressed for more clarity to be sought as to Mr Alfrey's state of mind. To that end I was called and found myself back in the boardroom quizzed by some of the guardians. Colonel Shepherd set off in his usual hectoring manner, which didn't get him very far with me. In the end I was mostly questioned by Mr Lawes and Mr Lake, who both enquired after Richard's state of mind generally and in the last few days in particular. I was as vague as I dared to be. I dropped them a few bits of information, like Richard's nightmares and brooding behaviour, but that was as far as I went. Although they were no nearer to discovering the truth, they seemed satisfied that they'd done all they could.

Thursday, 31 May

The funeral took place this morning as the church clock was chiming ten. The board of guardians and the coroner wanted him buried as soon as possible; a suicide was – is – very unsettling. As I was told by one of the long-standing inmates, under the normal circumstances of death by natural causes, more often than not union officials didn't like to waste time or money on individual burials, particularly in very large institutions. They would wait until there were several bodies to be disposed of and then have a mass burial in a designated corner of the local parish churchyard. Carpenters did a brisk trade in coffins for workhouses, making them of the cheapest wood with a sawdust lining. The corpse was often naked or, if they could run to the expense, had a cotton shroud. The name of the deceased was chalked on the top of the coffin, which was buried in an unmarked grave. To be fair, the officials did try to contact any relatives to see if they would take on the funeral arrangements, but given that most of the deceased were paupers, there was little chance that any family on the outside would defray any costs.

Richard Alfrey was trundled off in the workhouse wagon in his chalk-marked pine coffin, his wife and daughter walking with silent dignity behind. Even in this moment of acute grief, they both maintained a steadiness and grace, mutually supportive, holding hands. As a suicide Alfrey had to be buried without benefit of clergy. Noticeably there were no representatives from the board of guardians. Our work detail, which had dug a deep grave in an adjoining field the evening before, now pushed the cart to its destination and we lowered the coffin with rope – junk rope – into the pit. Before we replaced the earth Mrs Alfrey and her daughter were allowed a few minutes privacy at the graveside and I saw them murmuring prayers together. Then there was a repeat of the small, sad procession that had walked to the grave-site as everyone returned to the House, apart from two of us who remained to fill in the grave. Here it was business as usual, although I was told by Mrs Lodge that Emily and Caroline Alfrey were excused work until the afternoon and had been allowed to sit together in their dormitory.

I now had all the time in the world to grieve for my friend. Although we'd only known each other for a short time, I'd grown to like his reserved demeanour and quiet, unassuming manner. Silently I promised myself that I'd seek out Enderby and get the truth out of him. Then I'd bring him to book. For as surely as if he had wielded a knife and killed Richard, he was guilty of his death. In the event it wasn't left for me to apportion justice, someone got there first.

June

Saturday, 2 June

This day was much like any other; we worked our normal hours, Sunday being our only day of rest. The Calmans had gone out for the day just after ten and we were told that Enderby would be in charge. We'd not seen him during the whole of the last week – perhaps he was keeping out of the way in case anyone sought to implicate him in Richard's suicide. Now that the man was buried he must have thought himself safe. However, we saw nothing of him, although someone noticed his horse in the stable. I was still pondering what to do about the circumstances of the suicide, and trying to solve the problem of contacting Emily Alfrey. I hadn't had the opportunity to speak to Fred Lodge for many days.

Late in the afternoon, one of the inmates, Ed Willis, went out to the privy and I followed soon afterwards. As he was coming out and I was about to enter we heard a hullaballoo from the area of the pigsties. Running towards them were four figures, which turned out to be Mr and Mrs Calman, Peter Samuels and William Tuttle. There was obviously something up, so Willis and I ran after them. We reached the sties to find Mrs Calman in a state of hysteria, clinging to the wall of the building and almost fainting. Mr Calman was trying to keep her upright and the two boys were occupied in the sty, from which there came a frenzied grunting and squealing. At the same time as trying to support his wife, the master was screaming at the two boys. 'Get the fucking pig out! Get the bastard out!' Peter and William at either end of the boar and obviously also in a state of panic were attempting with difficulty to coax and prod the fat beast through a gate into the adjoining empty sty, Peter tempting it with a bucket and William tickling its backside futilely with a stick. A gruesome sight confronted Willis and I as we looked over the sty wall. There was a half-naked body, stripped from the waist down and face up, covered in dung and straw, with blood everywhere. The animal had clearly been feeding off the corpse that lay straddled across the middle of the sty; its snout and trotters were bloodied. I jumped over the wall and with William's help started to push the boar through the gate that Peter was holding open. The master continued to shout and rave while Mrs Calman had all but fainted against the wall. At last the boar, still reluctant to desert his prize, squealed and snuffled his way into his new quarters, where he discovered Peter's bucket. Now more or less satisfied he turned his attention away from the grisly contents of the corpse's crotch and put his head in the bucket with a satisfied grunt. Peter quickly closed the gate on him.

I went over to the remains of the body and cleaned the face, which, although filthy from the dung and straw, was virtually untouched. I could immediately identify the corpse as Enderby's, or what was left of him. His eyes were mercifully closed, but his mouth was open and still a faint whiff of spirits floated up to me as I leaned over him. My eyes roamed downwards until I came to the naked area below the waist and I nearly vomited. The man's genitalia had evidently been sliced off and there was a bloody expanse of raw flesh that the boar had enlarged while gorging on it. Other parts of the exposed lower torso were studded with deep bites and scratches.

Feeling utterly sick, I manhandled the body to the side of the sty and, taking it under the arms, heaved it up so that the head and torso hung over the wall. From the other side Willis pulled it unceremoniously to the ground. By the time we had finished our hands were sticky with blood. I noticed a trail of blood to the water trough. As in the case of Richard Alfrey's body, we made a stretcher of the shed door and laid Enderby on it. In consideration of Mrs Calman's proximity, I immediately covered the body with one of the blood-stained leather aprons that were hanging in the shed. I noticed the overseer's breeches, underwear and boots were in the far corner. I recommended to Mr Calman that he took his wife back to the House for a brandy and said that between us – the two boys, Willis and I – we would carry the corpse up to the dining hall immediately. I placed Enderby's clothing on the stretcher, which we hoisted and carried back across the yard, up the passage and into the main hall. There we deposited the door and its contents on to a trestle table and then returned to the workroom. Mr Calman, having seen his wife up to their quarters and there being no one else, had no choice other than to return to guard the body. Mr Lodge had been sent to fetch some of the guardians and the surgeon.

Tonight members of the dormitory parliament all had much to discuss and relish, apart from Jacob that is, who in his normal fashion started to snore as soon as his head hit the mattress. Unlike their reticence over Alfrey's suicide, the murder of Enderby generated detailed discussion among the inmates, much of it salacious. It seemed every inmate was intensely hostile to the man; there were no expressions of sorrow. Firstly, there was obvious and intense speculation as to who the perpetrator was. Some went with the idea of an outsider, but most scoffed at that as completely unfeasible. The consensus was that two men had done it to get their own back for some malicious act by Enderby. But no one could offer a coherent scenario as to exactly how it had been carried out and when. Having gone swiftly round full circle and exhausted all the possibilities, they turned their attention to the two immediately available witnesses. Peter Samuels and William Tuttle were at the forefront of demands for information of what they'd seen. As I say, no man had any pity for Enderby and none were frightened to express their feelings about him. But I was concerned about them quizzing the two boys, particularly William who was obviously still very shocked and frightened. Peter was older, and while he was less impressionable and more hardened to the distressing aspects of life, even he had never been confronted with such as sight as the state of Enderby's body. Earlier in the evening, as soon as I had an opportunity, I took them both to one side and calmed them down from what was developing into a mutually generated frenzied state. It had spread like wildfire that Robert Enderby had not only been castrated, but totally excised and the conversation was dominated by discussion of how that might have been achieved.

I hoped I could protect them from the inevitable questioning from men thirsting for information, but when one of the men asked the boys what the body had looked like Peter wasn't averse to filling him in with a gruesome description.

'When we saw him he was face up but covered in blood and stuff. Mr Millhouses cleaned off his face and we saw it was Enderby, although we'd guessed that's who it was. We'd already seen he's had his bits sawn off.'

'Was it right he'd been castrated?' asked one of the men with relish.

William chimed in immediately. 'Peter – what does that mean?'

'What?'

'Castri—?'

'Castrated – it means what I just said. He had his whatnots taken off, you know, his cock and balls.'

I stepped in and said as calmly as I could, 'Mr Enderby was attacked and parts of him were cut off – parts that are very, er, very precious to a man.' As soon as the stupid words were out I wished them unsaid. But William pursued them. 'What's precious about them? They're only used to piss out of.' Peter sniggered along with some of the men.

One of them said, 'They might be as far as you're concerned – the rest of us get a lot more use out of them than just pissing, young Tuttle. Hasn't anyone ever told you? Perhaps someone should, and soon.'

I intervened again before William responded with more graphic questions. 'Will, I suggest you try to forget what you saw – it won't be easy, but the pictures in your head will get less and less as time goes on. What happened to Mr Enderby was very unusual and strange – I've never seen anything like it and I've been around lots of places.'

'I heard that castration goes on in Italy with young boys,' observed Ed Willis to no one in particular. 'When I was younger I used to go into the Fleece Inn and I remember a boy – not much older than Will – used to read out from the daily broadsheets that they pinned up inside. He charged us, mind – something like a penny a story. What he did was to spread the paper out on the table and then read what people asked him to. I remember one of the stories was about these Italian boys who were sold to musicians and had their balls cut off. I think they were called "castratis", or something like it. I've never forgotten it; it made me shiver. The story said they did it because it let them carry on singing like a girl and they could make a lot of money at it. Well, I'd be buggered if I'd let anyone take my balls off so I could sing like a wench.'

Now I was really worried. Details of such anatomical interventions were likely to inflame William's already heightened curiosity.

I said quickly, 'I don't think they do that any more. It's gone out of fashion because they allow female singers now.'

'Why did they want boys to sing the women's parts? Why couldn't the girls do the singing?' asked the practically minded Peter.

'Because in the Bible St Paul said "let women keep silent in church". But most of us think that women have every right to sing anywhere they please. Anyway, it's a barbarous thing to do to a boy.'

'What's "barbarous"?' asked Will.

'Never mind – it's time you were asleep.'

I hoped that would be an end of it, and by and large, apart from a few stray reminiscences about Enderby's rakish life, most lapsed into drowsiness, no doubt many clutching protectively at their manhood as thoughts of the fate of Enderby's produced indelible pictures in their minds. Finally it went quiet – until ten minutes later the silence was broken by a disembodied voice that said, 'Tell you what, though.'

'What?' came back out of the darkness.

'It's put me right off pork!'

Sunday, 3 June

The chaplain said a few words today at the Sunday service in the dining hall about both Robert Enderby and Richard Alfrey. For Enderby he delivered a eulogy about the man's contribution to society, how he was held up in the community as a man of action and energy. The suicide of Richard Alfrey was of a different substance. Something about God's will being observed and the wickedness of cutting short a life without His sanction; nothing about the man's misery, or any expression of sympathy for his widow and child – just a lot of cant. As he droned on my mind wandered.

Patchin was deluded. He couldn't really imagine that anyone can sustain a belief in God's providence once they've walked over this threshold; for we were in one of the most godless places, where a man was stripped not only of his own clothes, but of his identity, dignity and pride. It was a punishment for poverty and locked the destitute in for good. What was really most galling was that they had to apply to come in – actually to have an interview to see if they met 'all the requirements of pauperism.' Welcome to the twilight world of the workhouse, where existence was subsistence and the reverse. A setting that brought the unfortunate face to face with their lack – lack of money, lack of anything to sustain their spirit, but above all a complete lack of control of their own destinies. While there was provision for subsistence there was nothing that allowed the promise of a future, let alone planning for it. Richard Alfrey went one step beyond subsistence; in his case, knowing that rock-bottom was exactly how it sounded, there was no point in further excavation.

I pondered on how I could arrange matters so that I might speak to Mrs Alfrey and decided that my best hope lay with Amy Lodge. I would find a way to ask her if an interview with Mrs Alfrey could be arranged. Mrs Calman was still indisposed, resting in her apartment, and would be until at least a couple of days after her brother's funeral. Robert Enderby was to be interred the next day on account of the warm thundery weather and a lack of appropriate storage arrangements. He was apparently at rest in a rather smart oak coffin on the rosewood dining table in the Calmans' apartment. In view of her continued absence, Amy Lodge had been deputising for the matron since the murder and would continue to do so until Jenny Calman felt able to return.

The regime under which Amy Lodge ran the women's section bore no resemblance to Mrs Calman's. Amy actively encouraged conversation between them, played with the young children and made sure they were given adequate time with their mothers. Whether Mrs Calman knew of this I didn't know, but the women certainly never told her and we learned in the men's quarters that there was a collective sigh of relief when they heard that Amy Lodge was now on duty for the foreseeable future. Also at this time Mr Calman was particularly attentive to his wife up in their apartment and consequently, now the overseer was no more, Fred Lodge had stepped in to fill the breach as deputy master. This made mobility around the House much more flexible. For a few days, although still in separate areas of the building, there were opportunities for men and women to meet for snatched conversations. I took my chance and during this afternoon was able to take Mrs Lodge to one side and ask her if I could speak to Mrs Alfrey.

She looked at me with curiosity. 'Can I ask you why you want to speak to her?'

'It's simply that I was Richard Alfrey's friend and probably one of the last people to speak to him before he died. I thought I might be of comfort to her. She may wish to ask me questions – after all I saw more of him that she did in the last three months.'

She frowned slightly as she considered. 'That sounds reasonable to me, Mr Millhouses. But I'll have to speak to her first, though – she doesn't seem to want to talk to anyone. She's very withdrawn and silent, to the point where I am thinking of calling in Mr Burgwin. If you can do some good and get her out of herself, that would be friendly indeed. At supper time, if you both remain behind after the tables are cleared I'll unlock the boardroom and you can speak to her there in private, but only for a few minutes, mind.' I thanked her profusely and thought that if ever I was in a way of doing her some good in the future, then I would do it.

That evening as the last inmate filed out of the dining hall Emily Alfrey remained behind with Mrs Lodge, who signalled to the pair of us to follow her as she unlocked the door of the boardroom. 'I'll come back for you both in about half an hour.' I thanked her and she left, closing the door behind her. I pulled out two seats from the long table, and put them adjacent to one another, inviting her to sit. For the first time I was able to take a close look at her face. It was indeed exceptionally beautiful. The privations of the House, although making it paler than it should have been, couldn't eliminate the perfection of her features. I wondered from where this loveliness originated. The physical harmony of her face remained immutable, but the sadness in her eyes and her generally troubled demeanour filled my heart with concern. Over the last few hours, although I'd rehearsed the prospective conversation, it was impossible to guess what her response might be. I had two thoughts: the first was to try to provide some comfort for her loss and to tell her all that had taken place between her husband and I since he arrived at Seddon. The second was to try to get to the root of the rumours surrounding Enderby's designs on her, whether he'd carried them out and what risk there had been to her daughter's safety and honour. This would be difficult. She might not want to revisit such appalling events. It was quite likely the overseer had revelled in telling her how he had taunted Richard; grief for her husband may also be burdened with guilt if she thought he'd taken his own life because of it.

I broke the ground with some customary civilities and asked her if she realised that Richard and I had been friends. She looked into my face. 'Mrs Lodge has always tried to keep me informed about Richard and she told me you'd been a good friend, indeed, probably his only friend. Richard had some acquaintances, but didn't make close friends easily. I heard that you talked together and had become quite close.' Encouraged I asked her if there was anything she wanted to know about Richard's last three months.

'Only whether you think he was bearing it well. When we made the decision to come here in early March, he was as low as I'd ever seen him. I expect he told you the circumstances we found ourselves in after he lost his employment. Neither of us had any relatives who could help us and we certainly had no savings to fall back on. This was the last place we expected to find ourselves and it took at least three weeks before we made the final decision to apply for admission.' I listened intently and what she was saying reinforced what I already knew about Richard Alfrey's state of mind. He was in despair even before Enderby metaphorically plunged in the knife. She went on.

'Mr Millhouses—'

'Henry, please.'

'Henry – I'll come to the point. Given that I know that he was in a very poor state of mind when we came, what was it that finally drove him over the edge? I'm very anxious to know because his suicide seemed to come out of nowhere. We'd been rubbing along here for a few months and I was always thinking of ways by which we might extricate ourselves and thought he might too. I know lack of contact with Caroline and me must have played on his mind – we've never been apart until we were forced to walk through separate doors into divided lives. But I know there's something else, something unknown to me that happened. He would never have felt so helpless unless something very serious was on his mind. I'm convinced this is so. Have you any idea what it was?'

So now we came to it. Should I tell her plainly what I knew – that Enderby had had designs on her, had taunted her husband with his intentions, and had threatened his beloved daughter? That on the same night before Richard hung himself, the overseer had said he would be making his move against Mrs Alfrey later on.

I manoeuvred the question round. 'Mrs Alfrey – Emily, there have been rumours about the behaviour of the overseer, Robert Enderby.' She immediately stiffened and was on her guard, so I proceeded very carefully. 'There have been complaints about his improper language towards some of the women inmates, and, worse than that, his lascivious behaviour around them. I know that Richard heard these stories and worried for your safety. To put no finer point on it – and begging your pardon for speaking plainly – you are an exceptionally beautiful woman. Were you ever in any position of being insulted by Enderby?' I left the question hanging in the air.

She was silent and became slightly pinker in the face as she drew breath. Her response surprised me in its directness.

'Enderby was a vicious, evil man. It was common knowledge about the House that no woman under the age of fifty was safe from him. Some of the others warned me about him when we arrived and told me to steer clear; also to watch out for my daughter. But he was too clever for me. Quite soon after we came here he saw me in the dining hall and swaggered across to where I was sitting. In front of the other women he made such lewd suggestions that I was shocked into silence. I'm not a shrinking violet by any means, but I immediately realised any retort would simply encourage his lechery, so I didn't complain. In any case, who was I to report him to? I'd been told that the matron was his sister. She was apparently enamoured of him and would do anything he said. The master's a weak man, particularly with regard to his wife – I believe he's scared of her. So, I had no one to tell and hoped that, as far as Enderby was concerned, I'd be a passing fancy. Indeed, for several weeks he was fortunately not around the House. But he started to drift back in April, and by the first weeks of May he was here regularly.' She stopped and began to twist her hands in her lap.

I wondered if I should divert her from any revelation that might be forthcoming. The journalist in me wished fervently for a full, unmoderated account; my humanity wished her to stop before painful memories overcame her completely. I remained silent and she continued in a low voice.

'During those weeks before his death he harassed me continually. I did my best to avoid all places where I thought he might be but finally, on Saturday, 26 May – oh yes, I've made sure I took note of the day and date – Enderby cornered me in the women's yard in the afternoon and told me, in so many words, he would be seeing me later on. What was worse was that he said that if I didn't cooperate, then he would assault Caroline instead. I became extremely distressed and eventually told two of the older women who, although sympathetic, seemed to think this was part of House activity – perks for the officials. I asked them how this could be and my suffering was such that they began to feel pity for me, and when I told them about his threat against my daughter they became really angry. I think their attitude was one that reflects the degradation which occurs here; women might be seen as fair game – after all some of the inmates have been women of the streets and are inured to the vile attentions of some men, but their collusion stopped short of the contamination of an innocent girl. Besides, Enderby was universally hated by the inmates for his posturing, foul mouth and casual cruelty.' She fell silent as though recollecting the man.

I asked her if she was well enough to carry on and she nodded. 'The women advised me that my only course of action was to acquiesce if I wanted to save my daughter, and in spite of my own abhorrence at the idea of Enderby touching me in any way I came to the same conclusion.'

'Later that evening, about nine, Mrs Calman, who connived with her brother and procured women for him, unlocked our dormitory door and Enderby came in behind her. She led him directly to my bed and he leaned over me.' Her face contorted and I felt very uncomfortable. 'I could smell the drink on him. He put his hand over my mouth and pulled me out of the bed and, wrenching my arm round my back, walked me to the door and upstairs to where the children were sleeping. This was his most cynical ploy because none of his victims would cry out as they passed by their children's beds for fear they would wake, see what was happening and be frightened and cry out. At the end of the girls' dormitory is a small door to an area of roof space; this was Enderby's secret hideaway. Only his victims and his sister know what it existed for. Inside was just a straw mattress on which he threw me.' She stopped and in respect for her feelings – and my embarrassment and shame for my sex – I didn't pursue my questioning of events to their inevitable denouement.

We sat silently together, immersed in our own thoughts. This was the time I would have to tell her about Enderby's cruel and insulting behaviour to her husband. I took her hand and forced her to look up at me. 'Enderby is dead and probably deservedly so. Whoever killed him was seeking revenge for innumerable heinous acts of which we know few details – probably we'll never know all of them. But you have nothing with which to reproach yourself. Indeed you did everything you could to protect your daughter – making the ultimate sacrifice of your own body. Your honour is intact and wherever Richard is he knows it. But I admit, the rumours of the overseer's lechery towards female inmates had reached his ears and he put two and two together that you would be irresistible to Enderby. It was confirmed when, a week ago, the brute told your husband he had designs on you, and your daughter. I know Richard killed himself because he thought he should be able to protect you and Caroline against the man, but he was impotent to do it. I also know that he was still as in love with you as he'd been when you married. On the occasions when he felt like talking, it was always of you and Caroline – nothing else mattered to him.'

Her hand tightened in mine and she looked back at me with cornflower blue eyes full of tears. 'You've confirmed what I suspected, Henry. I was certain that Richard killed himself because somehow he knew of the man's intentions.'

My heart leapt at the purity in her face. I recognised immediately that a woman such as Emily Alfrey could never be degraded by a monster like Enderby, whatever he had done to her.

Before there was any opportunity for her to start delving for more information about her husband's state of mind, Mrs Lodge tapped on the door and entered. The conversation was over and we went our separate ways.

Monday, 4 June

Shortly before the inquest Peter Samuels and William Tuttle sought me out. They were in some distress as they thought they might in trouble because 'important gentlemen wanted to talk to them'. I reassured them both that they were really very important themselves, and known as 'crucial witnesses'. William repeated the phrase several times and drew himself up a couple of inches. My only exhortation to them was to give their evidence clearly and as accurately as they could remember and try not to gossip to the other men before they were called for. They wanted to go over their story with me, but I said that was really against the spirit of the enquiry. Good men, like Mr Lawes, would want to hear their account fresh from themselves, without any input from me. Besides, I'd be giving evidence too and my story would tally completely with theirs. As it turned out Peter was a good witness and very accurate as to timing; the soundness of his evidence reinforced by his observations of the chiming of the church clock. The questioning of William was very brief. Knowing the board's intention to hold a full enquiry the next day, I warned them both that they would be called again – but there was no need for concern because it would be a repetition of today and they'd already done so well. William was delighted with his performance and even the usually cynical Peter managed a little smile of satisfaction.

I was feeling disingenuous about this conversation. I kept to myself the fact that I had been making plans over the last few days that I thought would probably leave them both feeling very let down.

Tuesday, 5 June

We rose as normal at the summertime bell at six o'clock. No wet bed for William who, as always, came across while I was dressing to chant his numbers – now up to four figures in tens. His face was pink with pleasure, but I felt wretched knowing how deflated he would probably feel by the end of the day.

Those of us due to appear before the enquiry were told by Mrs Lodge that it would open at ten o'clock in the dining hall, and we would be called individually. In the meantime it was work as usual. There was a tension in the air that hadn't evaporated since Enderby's death. The manner of his end had been so horrific that it was irresistible to persistent gossip and speculation.

There were nine inmates to be questioned: the five women in the kitchen, the two boys, Edward Willis and me; Mr and Mrs Calman and the porter were also to be called. At about ten thirty Mrs Lodge came in to collect Peter and William who, in spite of my encouragement, looked apprehensive. Ten or so minutes later they came back – looking relieved. I had a chance to ask them what had happened and how they had held up under the guardians' questioning. Peter, obviously relishing all the attention, strutted about the workroom full of self-importance. William was more subdued and almost immediately picked up a hunk of rope and began to unpick it. I gathered that the questions had been routine and they had both been able to answer them easily, their young memories accommodating times and facts with accuracy.

Edward Willis and I waited for a full half-hour while the Calmans gave their accounts – it was obvious the enquiry was picking its way methodically through events as they had happened. The last official to be called was Fred Lodge who faced questions for almost twenty minutes. When he had done he came to fetch Ed and myself to the dining hall.

A trestle table had been placed at the top of the hall and behind it sat Mr Lawes, Colonel Shepherd and Mr Robert Bignell, who I knew was a local lawyer. They had sheaves of papers in front of them and, I thought, looked business-like.

I stood at the back of the hall as Edward was called forward first. Their questions to him were fairly brief and predictable. His sniff, which always appeared when he was nervous, was very much in evidence. He explained how we came to be involved with rescuing the body and laying it out on the door. Ed was finally dismissed and ushered towards the door by Fred Lodge as Mr Lawes beckoned me to the table. I stood in front of the interrogators trying to look more relaxed than I felt. The colonel opened with some rhetorical questioning about how I'd gone down to the sty when I saw the master and matron running with the two boys, which was simply a repetition of what Ed had already told him. Mr Lawes evidently perceived the way the enquiry might go and intervened. He began to probe me about Enderby's reputation as a bully and a womaniser. I could see Shepherd squirming in his seat, but the JP persisted. The nature of his questioning led me to assume that, for his part, he'd already given credence to the notion that the manner of Enderby's demise was retributive. My purpose was to keep a balance between what I knew and what I suspected. In the end I was able to substantiate the overseer's reputation with women – and the universal antipathy with which he was regarded. At some point during this part of the exchange I enjoyed a small sense of triumph over Colonel Shepherd and felt I had put him on the ropes. I manipulated our dialogue to bring home to him the fact that Enderby's behaviour went unchallenged because there was no facility for inmates to make complaints. In typical blustering fashion he tried to justify the system he himself had instigated, but his logic failed and he began to tie himself up in polemical knots. Mr Lawes brought proceedings back to its purpose, but he was beginning to probe too deeply. Looking me straight in the eye he asked me directly who might have wanted him dead and why I thought the overseer had met such a grizzly end. I went as far as I was prepared to go by orchestrating a scenario that might explain the murderer's motive.

At that point I delivered my coup de grâce. I explained that three hours previously, in accordance with regulations, I'd notified the deputy master, Mr Lodge, of my intention to quit the House and, as it must surely be well past eleven o'clock, I now proposed to leave. My announcement was met with an amazed silence. Mr Lawes was the first to speak and asked me if I had somewhere to go. I replied that I was well provisioned, thanked them graciously for their hospitality and turned to walk back down the hall. Calling after me, the JP asked me whether I had the wherewithal to sustain myself. Turning to face them all, I produced my Bible from an inside pocket and told them something to the effect that I was well catered for. With great deliberation and thorough relish, I strolled through the bottom door of the dining hall, through the tastefully furnished lobby, then unlatched the main studded door and passed through to the gravel drive. It would have been ideal had it been a glorious warm June day. Unfortunately it was raining hard and I ran down the drive towards the lodge with some lack of dignity.

Why did I choose to leave the workhouse at such a moment? In truth I had from the outset always planned to remain only three months, or even less if circumstances allowed. From previous experience of covert work I knew that it was generally possible to gauge the essentials of a bad situation in less than that time. The monotonous routines of daily life in the mills of Lancashire were such that nothing much changed from day to day. It was simply necessary to observe the characters within their setting and find a few useful sources. Once trust had been achieved, information followed naturally. I usually found I was able to make an accurate journalistic assessment of circumstances within the first couple of weeks.

So it had been at the Seddon Union. Indeed, if anything, the routine was even more stultifying than the factories. As far as collecting evidence of malpractice by the officials and guardians, I really had no need to stay longer than a month. But I'd become inextricably involved with some of the personalities in the place and the suicide of Richard Alfrey had led me to stay for the full duration. Enderby's murder had been an added complication, but I felt that Edgar Lawes was an intelligent man and this, together with his status, would probably get him to the truth at some point soon. The manner of the murder gave an obvious clue to the motive; I still had no idea who had actually done the deed. Before the enquiry I'd already decided I would write to Mr Lawes and lay out what I knew. The testimony of Emily Alfrey had confirmed in my mind that it was an act of retribution for Enderby's treatment of the females in the institution. But her information had been given to me in confidence and I'd no wish to abuse her trust.

Leaving was difficult. I don't like loose ends, neither did I relish leaving the two boys to the cruelty of the Calmans. But I'd been heartened by the JP's actions to correct some of the more egregious aspects of the running of the workhouse; moves that I was sure would progress at a good pace. I had confidence that the positive steps he'd taken so far would eventually lead on to better conditions for all the inmates, especially the children. My own report could only enhance that process.

I saw Fred Lodge peering through his window. He came out to meet me and I asked for my clothes, passing over my ticket. I'd no quarrel with the porter; he and his wife had been of inestimable help to me, and I recognised that at times they may have put themselves at risk of punishment or, worse, losing their position by divulging information. The motives of the pair were unclear to me, but I had a distinct feeling that they were good and just people. Possibly they simply abhorred casual cruelty and gross unfairness. If my later revelations put them at any risk I would be sorry for it, but it would be for the greater good.

I took my bundle of clothes and Fred unlocked the receiving ward door. I recollected it was almost exactly three months since I'd entered here and spent a miserable week adjusting to privation. It was also where I first met Richard Alfrey and I stopped to reflect on his suicide. Had it been really necessary to take his life, or was it ultimately an empty gesture? But perhaps not – perhaps it had been the catalyst for Enderby's murder. It was not difficult, even for a bachelor, to appreciate the panic, fear and, most distressing, the frustration he must have endured knowing it was likely that Robert Enderby would carry out his threats to his wife and daughter, and there was nothing to be done to prevent it. Male pride would have combined with that frustration, which finally distilled into black despair and utter hopelessness.

Although the clothes I'd been wearing when I entered the House were rough, I was distinctly relieved to get back into them. The House uniform, thin and grey, was not only inadequate but also a badge of shame. Our sorties to the church where we were exposed to the full view of the neighbourhood had brought this home to me. We must have been a sorry sight to all those in their Sunday best as we mustered into our respective files to walk back across the fields.

I folded the House clothing and tucked it under my arm. Checking I'd transferred my Bible to my own jacket pocket, I walked to the lodge door and rang the bell. I received a cheerful smile from Mr Lodge who took the bundle of clothes and gave me back my certificate of leaving, which he countersigned in receipt of union property. I held out my hand. 'Goodbye, Mr Lodge. I'm grateful to you!'

He looked puzzled. 'Grateful? I'm sure you've nothing to be grateful for – three months in here – I'm surprised you feel gratitude!'

'Our talks have kept me sane – will you also thank your wife for all her assistance as well? Please tell her that I know how much she does for the children; Peter Samuels and William Tuttle are particularly grateful for her kindnesses.'

He nodded and said, 'But I hear you've also made their lives a little easier – especially William's. Amy's been very impressed with the way you solved his bed-wetting – oh yes, word soon got round! In fact, she told me that there were some mothers she knew who've never really mastered the problem of training their children into clean habits. She reckoned you're a natural with children. Perhaps you'll have some of your own one day!'

I smiled and raised an eyebrow. 'Perhaps!'

He asked me to wait while he returned to the lodge. As he came out I could see he was carrying a small parcel. 'My wife made this up for you when she heard you were leaving. It's just a few bits of food to keep you going until you find somewhere to stop.'

'Please thank her for her kindness. Now could you do yet one last favour for me?'

'Certainly, anything I can do that doesn't break the regulations.' He winked and for the first time in three months I realised we were equals. I could have a normal exchange with a fellow human being, nuanced and with banter, without being considered insolent.

'I'd like you to give Mr Lawes a message,' I said. 'Tell him Ambrose Hudson sends him his regards and will be in touch.' He looked puzzled, but nodded, took the key chained round his waist, unlocked the gates and swung one open. I touched my cap to him and walked through on to the lane.

During our conversation it had briefly stopped raining, but now it began again quite steadily and I stepped up my pace. I'd made meticulous plans for my departure and rehabilitation into the 'real world'. The first task was to retrieve my purse from the stone wall where I'd secreted it. Sure enough it was still hidden, slightly damp but untouched. The weather was uncomfortably wet and I walked briskly along the road heading towards Ipswich. It had taken me two days to walk from the county town to Kettlebaston but my journey back from Seddon would be somewhat shorter. I planned to reach the small village of Aldham, which was just under halfway, and spend the night at its small inn. Arriving late in the afternoon, I was relieved to find it a rough and ready place; my appearance, which was unkempt and shabby, would go unremarked. There were no other customers and the landlady showed me to a small, poorly furnished room but with, joy of joys, a feather bed! To her credit she also provided reasonably clean sheets for a local hostelry that I imagined had few guests. After a frugal meal of cold meat, cheese and unadulterated bread, which I washed down with several pints of acceptable ale, I went to bed and for the first time for ninety-seven days, excepting the four days before Alfrey arrived in the receiving ward, I slept alone.

As I was trying to calculate the numbers precisely it reminded me of William and I thought guiltily of how he and Peter had received the news of my departure. I found it very difficult to think of the younger boy's reaction. For the first time he'd found an adult to trust, but now he would have all his previous experience of them reinforced. I would be seen as just another person who'd walked out and let him down. It was the one aspect I was most ashamed of. I'd not even said goodbye because I couldn't explain the circumstances of my leaving. I determined that I would get messages to them – probably via Edgar Lawes – and that I would make sure I did something for them in the future. In the meantime I prayed that Amy Lodge would recognise the void in their lives my departure had probably left and do her best to ameliorate their confusion.

Wednesday, 6 June

In the morning, after a better breakfast than the evening meal, I was preparing to set out again when the landlady mentioned that her husband was driving to Ipswich to collect stores and he'd be pleased to give me a lift. This really raised my spirits because I'd estimated the walk to the town would take me all day and into the evening; travelling by horse and cart I would arrive sometime before midday. Also, although it wasn't raining heavily, the weather was still damp and conditions underfoot were very soggy from sustained downpours. I had thin boots and doubted they'd survive too much soaking. Gratefully I climbed up next to the innkeeper and he flicked his whip to the mare between the shafts and we were off. Fortunately my driver was of a taciturn nature and apart from a few pleasantries seemed singularly reluctant to gossip – a handicap I would have thought for an innkeeper, but perhaps his wife was more accomplished in that regard. Immersed in his thoughts throughout the journey, he kept the horse at a lively pace and we reached the centre of Ipswich just as a church clock was chiming eleven. I offered him some recompense for his kindness, which he accepted with a grunt.

My plans had been laid carefully and thanks to the unexpected lift I had much more time to carry them through. Firstly, I needed some food as I'd not eaten since breakfast. I sought out a suitable pie shop and found one from where the smell drifting through the door made my mouth water. From here I bought two large meat pies and, for the first time for months, having yearned for them, relished the taste of good, juicy lamb surrounded by soft, smooth pastry. As I bit into it my taste sensations were almost on fire, substantially enhanced in consequence of the deprivation they'd suffered for so long. I rolled the fibres of meat around my mouth and the saltiness of the gravy hit the front of my tongue, producing a wonderful sensation. I tried to eat with decorum, but I'm afraid once I'd enjoyed the initial tantalising experience I couldn't get the food in fast enough.

Having gorged myself and now with a satisfied stomach I set about achieving my next priority. This was a haircut and shave. Washing and bathing in the House had been primitive and it was up to each man to establish a level of hygiene acceptable to himself. This didn't always mean it was acceptable to the rest of us, and for those less assiduous in their personal grooming our only recourse was to apply pressure and shame until they relented and took appropriate action. There were no baths at Seddon, only the cold-water pump in the yard; neither was there sufficient hot water to shave properly. Most of the men let their beards grow. We occasionally cut each other's hair and beards when they had grown too long for comfort. Lice, of course, were endemic and itching scalps were endured by us all, however much we plunged our heads under the pump. Now, before presenting myself at the coaching inn, I sought out a backstreet barber where my appearance would cause no comment. As I settled into his chair I anticipated the pleasure of hot water on my head and face and I wasn't disappointed. Even Defoe himself might find it difficult to describe the exquisite feel of warm foamy water running through the hair after months of cold sluices and hard soap. With a newly stropped razor the man deftly rid me of my stubble and I emerged from his shop with a feeling of lightness about my head and a spring in my step.

My attire had a down-at-heel air about it and I needed to present a more civilised appearance at the coach house. I found a small outfitter and purchased a pair of trousers, a shirt and coat. Three doors down the street a cobbler had a selection of working boots on display outside his premises and I bought a decent pair. Taking my purchases beyond the town I found an empty barn where I changed old for new. The boots fitted well and took me comfortably back to the centre of the town. There was an old lady begging from a shop doorway and I handed her my bundle of old clothing for which she was sadly overgrateful. Before reaching the coaching inn I sought out a stationer's shop and bought ink, ten sheets of good-quality paper, a pen and a quantity of metal nibs.

There were a few people coming and going in the yard of the inn but it was quiet inside. Seeing the innkeeper, who was serving a table of travellers in the front bar, I waited until he appeared in the hallway and presented the receipt for my valise, which he retrieved from a cupboard under the stairs. I booked a room for the night and, passing over a decent tip for himself, asked him to make sure it was the best he had. He called a lad to show me up to a spacious room that, although on the front of the building over the main street, was not as noisy as those at the rear which overlooked the stables. It was well furnished, but I looked especially at the bed, which was a large four-poster, without curtains but with a thick down mattress and good coverings. As I sat on it to test it out I sighed with pleasure and the boy gave me a puzzled look.

Smiling I said, 'I've been on a long journey and haven't seen a bed such as this for many months!' I dipped into my purse. 'There's a generous tip here if you can supply me with a bath tub, as much hot water as you can carry and all the towels the inn can spare – as fast as possible.'

Within the hour I was up to my neck in hot soapy water with plenty more standing by. My generosity was rewarded with the swiftness and regularity the boy replenished my tub. If the pies had been a highlight, then this was the acme. I soaped myself slowly all over, including my hair, which received its second wash of the day that I hoped would see off any lingering lice, and luxuriated in the heat of the water, the tips of my fingers and toes eventually starting to wrinkle. I must have wallowed for almost an hour, for the boy ran up and down the stairs with more jugs than I could count. Eventually I stood up and rinsed myself with a jug of warm water, stepped out and wrapped myself in clean soft towels. I heard the mail coach arrive from London and reckoned it must be about three o'clock. The next coach to London left at six the next morning and I'd booked a place inside as I meant to be as comfortable as possible.

Now in my original clothes – which a young maid had pressed – bathed and shaved, I made my way downstairs to the public bar where I found the landlord moving barrels. He came across and I ordered a pint of ale and also arranged for my meal to be served in my room. I intended to start on my notes as soon as possible, but my first task when I returned upstairs was to take up pen and paper and write a letter to Peter and William. Wishing them to receive it as soon as possible, I addressed it care of Mr Edgar Lawes, Seddon Hall, along with a short note to him also. By ten o'clock I could do no more to my journal, having run out of paper, although I had completed a draft account of my first three weeks in the House. I tidied the manuscript and put it between two pieces of card, stoppered the inkpot and wiped the nib clean. Putting on my nightshirt I looked with pleasant anticipation at the clean white sheets now invitingly exposed by the maid who'd been up and turned down the bed. I dowsed the candles and climbed in.

Wednesday, 7 June

One of the best night's sleeps I've ever had. I commended the landlord on his mattress and left a generous tip for the maid and a further reward for the boy who'd been equally attentive to me at breakfast and taken responsibility for my letters, which he promised to send post-haste. The journey to London was uneventful and, apart from a hefty companion who took up some of my seat, endurable. The coach arrived very late in the evening at the Bull and Mouth inn on London Wall and I took a fly back to my rooms in Gresham Street, close to St Paul's. It was later still when I knocked on my landlady's door – I hadn't taken my key – and after a short delay she opened up and peered out nervously. 'Who is it? Whoever you are it's very late to come calling!'

I stepped forward so she could see me. 'It's me, Mrs Bridie – Ambrose – I'm back! I'm sorry to disturb you at this hour but I don't have my key.'

I was met with such a show of welcome – she took my hand and pumped it up and down, all the while saying, 'It's been three months, and not a word. Where have you been?' She pulled me into the hall and I put my bag down and she embraced me. Agnes Bridie was a doughty Scots woman and the older – much older – sister of my editor James McNiece. In fact, I sometimes wondered privately if she'd been an early mistake or he a late afterthought. I was her only tenant and she treated me like a son, going far beyond the domestic responsibilities of a landlady. I'd always paid her a retaining fee when I was away on long assignments and she was content not to sublet the rooms to strangers.

'I've been out of anyone's reach. I'm sorry I couldn't let you know when I was returning.' She looked me up and down anxiously. 'My! How thin you are. You look like a matchstick! What have you been doing with yourself?'

'I'll tell you all about it in the morning!' It was neither the time nor place to begin explaining. I picked up my bag and asked her if my rooms were in order.

'I've kept them as you left them – only cleaning occasionally. Fortunately I gave them a good dusting last week. The only thing I haven't done is air the bed, but a good warming pan will soon fix that.

While I get the coals from the kitchen range can I get you something to eat and drink? You've obviously had a long journey from somewhere.'

'I had a good dinner at the last coaching stop before London Wall, but a glass of wine would be very acceptable, thank you.'

She hurried into the kitchen and returned with a tray on which she'd placed a carafe of wine and some little sweet cakes. 'Sit down and enjoy these while I tend the bed.' Under her arm she carried a package of letters. 'Here's your post. There are three letters from India – I suppose that's your brother.' Taking the letters I was too tired to look at them closely – they could wait until the morning. I would spend tomorrow organising my affairs before I went to find McNiece and delivered my story.

I took a sip of wine and sighed with content to be home at last under my own roof. Finally, Mrs Bridie having prepared the bed, I went up to my rooms and saw all was in order. What relief I felt to see my own bed. I stripped off, poured warm water from the jug into the wash bowl, rinsed my face and hands and undressed. I slipped gratefully into the warmth of the sheets, and as I drifted off my last thought was, *What a pleasure it is to be mothered – but only sometimes!*

I make no apology if these domestic details appear insignificant and of no purpose. For me to record them accurately is to make plain the acute contrast to all the deprivations I'd experienced in the workhouse, and which others were continuing to undergo as I enjoyed my rehabilitation. Simple domestic comforts like a good bed and copious hot water which many of us take for granted are, by the whim of the state, denied to the poorest, only adding insult to their already dehumanised condition.

Part Three

Mr Lawes's Account continued

Seddon Hall, Suffolk, 1838

Part Three

Chapter 7

Dear Ted,

I am still reeling under the shock of all that has transpired at the workhouse in the last few weeks. My mind is so suffused with thoughts and images to the point I find I am unable to make any sense of it. The suicide and murder are of course uppermost in my mind, but Henry Millhouses's dramatic departure simply added to my confusion. To that end I feel it would be useful for us to meet as soon as possible. Besides these immediate concerns, we should discuss the progress of your procurement committee. Unfortunately I have much court and estate work to catch up with that I can no longer postpone. The earliest available date would be sometime late on Saturday next. I'll send this note by the stable boy who will wait for a reply.

Your friend,

Edgar Lawes

Rushie Farm

Thursday, 7 June

Dear Edgar,

Your note was timely and I thank you for it. Like you, I am very troubled by recent events, especially Millhouses's departure, which, as you say, was certainly 'dramatic'. I feel there is a lot more to that man than we'll ever know. I am anxious to discuss these matters with you, particularly the report of my committee before we present it to the board at the next meeting. Our findings cause us much concern and

I would welcome your advice on how we must proceed.
There are serious implications for the whole board and the
chairman in particular. In that regard I will ride over early
on Saturday evening. There's no need for a reply if these
arrangements suit.

    I remain your friend,

    Edward Lake

Later that same afternoon Foster entered the library with a sealed
packet, which had just arrived marked post-haste. Opening it I found
two letters, one addressed to myself, the other to Peter Samuels and
William Tuttle, who I remembered were the two boys who'd been
witnesses at the inquest and the House enquiry. Now, with my
curiosity roused, I opened my own letter. It explained the cryptic
message Fred Lodge had relayed to me earlier in the week.

Post-house,

Ipswich

Wednesday, 6 June

Dear Sir,

I am aware that this letter will come as a surprise to you.
My first consideration is that by now Mr Lodge will have
passed on to you my message as I arranged with him at the
time of my departure from Seddon Union. My second is
to tender my apologies for the deception I have played on
you and the rest of your colleagues during the last three
months. You will remember me as 'Henry Millhouses' –
which, in fact, is my correct name. The sobriquet I have
adopted for the purposes of my professional life is that of
Ambrose Hudson.

    For now I will be brief as I intend later to inform you
fully of all the events with which I have been associated
concerning the House at Seddon. Consider this as a written
introduction and one I sincerely hope will eventually lead
to a meeting between us. My knowledge of you, ascer-

tained from our brief contacts during my stay as an inmate, has been most positive. Instinctively I feel we are on the same side – that is to procure some justice for the paupers who are unfortunate enough to find themselves in the House at Seddon. This ambition I have found is in contrast to some of your companions on its board of guardians. Thus it was necessary for me to practise such artfulness in order to gather evidence for the exposure of the cruelty and deprivation that I uncovered. All this I will share with you in due course.

You will find a second letter within the package and note it is addressed to the two boys, William Tuttle and Peter Samuels. I would be very much obliged if you would ensure that it is delivered and that someone reads it to them as soon as is possible. It is my one regret that I left the House without saying farewell to either and I wish to offer them an explanation that might go some way to mitigating my unavoidable omission.

Within the next few days I hope to have finished the draft of a full journalistic account of my sojourn at Seddon House. Before it is published, I will ensure you have a copy to read; also that the board of guardians are made aware of my intentions to expose their maladministration. Unfortunately this implicates you as member of the board, albeit newly appointed. However, I feel confident that you are a man of integrity who will not shy away from such exposure and am sure you will fully support the intentions behind my investigation, which is to bring everything to a satisfactory conclusion for the welfare of the inmates.

It is my fervent hope that we may meet in the not too distant future. In the meantime:

I remain your humble servant,

Ambrose Hudson

As I considered the contents of Millhouses's letter – or as I should now prefer to call him, Hudson – many things fell into place. I immediately took his point and wondered how far I could be considered complicit in the maladministration of the House. I decided, as a board member, I must accept the principle of collective responsibility. As to the rest, I had always considered Hudson to be a man of a different stamp to the other inmates. There had been an air of quiet confidence and almost defiance about him that didn't correspond to the normal disposition of paupers who sought union assistance. Like my correspondence with Lake, Hudson's letter was timely since I could share its contents immediately with Ted. I hoped it would open up yet more avenues of enquiry for us both.

On Saturday Ted arrived close to five o'clock. As he furnished us with brandy in the library, I told Foster we were not to be disturbed. Taking my first sip and before Ted could get underway I took out the journalist's letter and passed it to him.

'Ted – what do you make of this? It arrived two days ago and will surprise you, I'm sure. I always knew there was something odd about the man.'

He took the letter, unfolded it and read it quickly. 'Well – good God – the cheek of the man! All that time an imposter!' Then, as if something was stirring in his mind, he exclaimed, 'Wait a minute! I know that name. Ambrose Hudson is the journalist who writes articles about factories up north. If you remember I told you about him when I came here to dinner months ago. You know, the one who was at Peterloo. Of course! That's why the name was familiar.'

I did remember. During that meeting Ted had been fulsome in his praise for Hudson, especially his work in exposing bad practices in textile mills; I seemed to recall he'd described the man as a 'crusader'. The journalist had, for whatever reasons, now turned his attention to the small and insignificant Seddon Union. It seemed we'd been covertly investigated.

'He believes he's uncovered a good deal of bad practice at our workhouse – which comes as no surprise to you, I'm sure, any more than it does to me.'

'Damn right it doesn't!' said Ted warmly. 'I'll be very interested to read this journal he's been keeping – that is if you'll allow me to share it?'

'He's asked that all the guardians are made aware of its contents

– it'll be interesting to see if your committee's findings are in agreement with his. So tell me, as briefly as possible, what have you and your investigators found?'

To my surprise he took out a sheaf of notes, paused to gather his thoughts and drew breath. 'I can sum it up in a very few words – food, clothing, bedding and cleanliness – the lack of the last. Starting with the victuals, the adulteration of the flour we already knew about thanks to you. But after that our committee closely investigated the miller in question and found the practice of adding chalk to the bags in large enough quantities to taste but not enough to poison, has been going on since the House opened. Rastons of Bury St Edmunds were given the contract in '34 through James Keen, one of the original guardians; Raston's a relative. Keen was able to persuade the board that his price would be the lowest. The inmates have been eating spoiled bread for four years. Keen was not party to this deception I hasten to add, and was very shocked when he found out. Fortunately your exposure enabled us to put matters right immediately, as you know, and we can guarantee the bread is now fit to eat, as we reported to the board on' – he consulted his papers – '30 May. At the same time we asked to inspect the kitchens.' He referred to his sheet again. 'This we did on 4 June, when fortunately, because of her brother's murder, Mrs Calman was indisposed and Amy was able to give us free rein. What we found was very disturbing. We knew the allocation of food to the inmates didn't follow what's laid down by the commissioners; we couldn't find any type of food that gave more than a semblance of nourishment and the quantity they get is inadequate.'

He paused and I asked him directly before he could continue, 'What are your recommendations then?'

'Our committee feels, firstly, that the meal plans need a total overhaul; secondly, there should be an immediate increase in the meat ration – I'll say more about the source of meat in a minute – and all inmates, especially the children, should have fresh milk daily, as well as fruit at least twice a week. By God, Edgar! If Captain Cook could order sailors to be given limes to eat to prevent scurvy in the last century, then it must be within our enlightened times to ensure our inmates receive the same consideration.' His face began to flush with passion.

Bringing him back to the issue in hand I said, 'Tell me about the meat supply – what's going on there?'

'As we all know' – he controlled a smile – 'the union maintains a piggery and Thomas Lewis – a name you'll recognise – has the contract for slaughtering and butchering the pigs. The arrangement is that he slaughters the animals on site and then takes the carcasses away to butcher in his shop. The proceeds – both financial and in kind – are supposed to come back to the union. There's no question that the money that Lewis pays for the meat, minus his expenses for slaughtering, comes back into the union coffers – Harbey's books show that. What's uncertain is where the pork, hams and sausages go. The pork is meant to provide "fleshdays" for the inmates at least three days a week. We spoke to the women in the kitchen who cook and serve the food on a permanent basis – most of them have been there since the place opened so are well aware of what the inmates are getting in the way of meat. It was clear from them that fleshdays only occur once a week, and the quantities of meat supplied to the kitchen are very meagre. That left us with the question, where does the rest of it go? As yet we have no answer. I can tell you Thomas Lewis is not implicated in any cheating – we're sure of it. But damned if we know where the meat's going.'

I moved on to his second concern. 'What's the problem with the clothing?'

'You could see for yourself it's inadequate – especially in the winter. The cloth is the cheapest cotton that could be procured and – you might have guessed – is supplied by another of our esteemed guardians – the cloth merchant, John Newton. Admittedly he was given the contract before he was elected to the board two years ago – but the board's choice of weight and quality was steered by him on the grounds of his "practical knowledge". Let's face it – Colonel Shepherd would know little and care less about the difference between calico and cheesecloth. The inmates are therefore clothed in the cheapest, poorest-quality material Newton can supply. The same goes for their footwear. I think Newton should consider his position.'

'That's for later,' I said. 'I admit I'm not surprised at what you've found. The whole atmosphere in the House is one of shortcuts and life on the cheap. It all originates in Shepherd's obsession with keeping costs down to keep the rates low.'

He nodded, referred to his sheet and began again. 'Bedding next – which is fucking dire.' I was wondering how long it would be before his language lapsed, but let it pass. 'Would you like to sleep on a stinking straw palliasse, with only a couple of blankets? We have to order in flock mattresses with some waterproofing and at least another blanket each. As regards the washing facilities – they don't exist – just a pump in the yard. What is needed is a bathhouse where everyone can have a weekly bath in hot water. Anyway – that's another of our recommendations.'

'Costly, I imagine?' I observed.

'Certainly – but the money's there if we can get access to it.'

I raised an eyebrow. 'How's that then? I thought the union operated hand-to-mouth on the equivalent of a single candle.'

'No it doesn't! One thing we did find out, which is good news, is that William Harbey is an excellent clerk – totally honest, and his books are exemplary. Not a penny unaccounted for. It's not his fault if contracts are dubious and the suppliers crooked. What he did show us, and none of us could have guessed it existed, was a "contingency" fund of £2,492.16s.8d!'

'Where on earth did that come from – and why didn't we know about it?' My next questions were: who else knew and why was it kept so quiet?

'It's a remnant from the monies collected from the sale of all the workhouse buildings in the parishes when the amalgamation took place back in '34 and all the proceeds were devolved into the union coffers. The fund was set up to provide money for emergencies – fire and flood, damaged roofs, things like that. You would call it good housekeeping if it wasn't such a large amount. Under no circumstances would we ever need all that cash – even if the place was totally destroyed and had to be rebuilt. There's the answer to the bathhouse problem – we've plenty of money in hand to build one – if we can get *our* hands on it. According to Harbey, Colonel Shepherd hasn't only kept that information to himself, but wants to keep the money intact as a hedge against raising the poor-rate if union costs rise.' I might have known. 'Although I think our committee has done a thorough job – it's one thing to find the problems, another to solve them. We can build all the bathhouses in the air we like – but unless Jack Shepherd gives us backing we can't proceed.'

I was already mentally spending the money myself – as well as a new bathhouse, improved diet and clothing, new beds – there would be enough for the wages of a schoolmaster, the matter dearest to my heart. As regards Shepherd, he would have to be confronted with some uncomfortable facts, but I kept quiet and allowed Ted to finish his account.

'I think that's all I can report at the moment. One thing that surprised me was how well our small group worked together. The guardians really got into the spirit of investigation – almost like bloodhounds. Robert Bignell was especially impressive and got quite heated once or twice – unusual for a lawyer!' He winked at me. 'Once they took hold of anything suspicious they wouldn't let it go. William Harbey was quite intimidated at first, until I was able to congratulate him on the quality of his book- and minute-keeping.'

Ted Lake as a diplomat was a novel concept. 'Is there anything else?

'Only small details that can wait until the next meeting.'

'When did you last hear from Fred?'

'Damn it! Thank you for reminding me – I meant to tell you. He came across to see us a few nights ago. He says the atmosphere in the House is very tense. The Calmans are nowhere to be seen – they keep themselves shut away in their rooms. Fred and Amy are the only ones able to keep the routine going. Fortunately the inmates are so habituated they act like sheep. But there are some elements – mostly the women – who are bolder and show it. Even Amy, who has a good reputation with them, is careful what she says. The next guardians' meeting is not until Wednesday. I think we should ride over before then, perhaps Monday or Tuesday, to see for ourselves.'

'I agree. It's hardly surprising given all the events of the last week or so. Maybe we should go tomorrow if it wouldn't inconvenience you; I know it's Sunday, but we still have a responsibility to the place. Monday's my morning in court and I already feel I've neglected some of my duties as JP. Look here, why don't you dine with me this evening and then stay the night? I can send the groom over to the farm to let your people know and we can ride over to the House together in the morning.'

'That sounds like a good idea! My boys have got used to managing without me these last few weeks. Anyway, Garth O'Brien and his family are about – and very reliable.'

It was agreed and we continued our discussion late into the evening on the best methods of remediating the House.

We breakfasted and left the Hall just after ten, arriving at the gates of the workhouse by ten thirty. On first sight the place appeared to be very quiet, but just as Amy Lodge came out to open the gates a huge hullabaloo erupted at the main door and crowds of men and women burst through on to the drive. Then the men seemed to hesitate, hanging back in the lobby and allowing the women and young children through; they began to form two columns either side of the gravel drive. Suddenly from within the grey interior the familiar figures of a man and a woman were pushed forward into the sunshine. There was an ominous silence. Hostility was undisguised and flanked by their guard of dishonour the couple were forced to walk the gauntlet of the women and children who now stretched either side of the drive as far as the main iron gates.

It was the Calmans. Jenny Calman was tattered and dishevelled. In contrast to her usual impeccably neat appearance, her dark brown hair was capless and awry, she had no shoes and her stockings were about her ankles. The top of her dress was torn and in order to protect her modesty she had flung her left arm across her chest to hold up what remained of the bodice; her normally immaculate cuffs and collar had been wrenched off. Bruises to her face, blood from her nose and the start of a black eye were evidence she'd been physically attacked. She stumbled down the path, followed by her husband who was cowering in the face of palpable malevolence. As they staggered one behind the other all twenty female inmates remained in formation down the drive. Equipped with wooden bowls, they tapped them with wooden spoons in a regular and sinister beat. The Calmans were being drummed out of the House. It reminded me of the stories I'd heard about 'Les Tricoteuse', the women thirsting for blood who took their places – and their knitting – to the foot of the guillotine during the terror in the French Revolution.

Rosa Hines, who was nearest the gate, was carrying two light leather travelling bags. Amy Lodge, who had come out of the lodge house to let us in, squared her shoulders and handed over the key without a word. Unlocking the gates Rosa flung them both outwards with some force and they defined their widest arc, which almost reached the lane. Fortunately Ted Lake and I were standing back from where we had a clearer view of what was happening, although we still had to manoeuvre our horses to avoid the ironwork. By now having reached the end of the lines Jenny Calman almost fell on to the road and Mrs Hines threw the two bags after her as the spoons rattled faster against the bowls, until their sound reached a climax, then stopped, producing a chilling silence. Hitting the ground, the bags burst open to reveal two sets of male and female workhouse clothing, intermixed with handfuls of stinking wet straw. Mrs Calman stumbled and fell over completely.

Instinctively I dismounted and held out my hand to her.

Her response was unequivocal. 'Fuck off! Fuck you and damn you to hell!'

From those who heard there came a mighty roar of derision, which was captured and echoed all along the lines until it reached the group of men in the porch and reception room who were craning to see what was happening. I continued to hold out my hand, but she ignored it, glared at me and pulled herself up by means of the gate, while still attempting to keep a semblance of dignity with one arm holding up her bodice.

Mr Calman, whimpering, was frantically stuffing the clothing back into the bag. His wife hissed through lips like rail lines, 'Leave it!' But practicality overcame fear of his spouse and he rapidly stowed away the garments and caught up the bags by their handles. Then, obediently, he waddled after her with a bag under each arm and stray wisps of damp straw sticking to his breeches. By now they were fully out on the road. As Jenny Calman turned left and started to disappear round the wall of the House, with the pathetic figure of her husband trailing behind, there was another tremendous rally from the inmates: men, women and children all rushed to the road as though to confirm their enemies' departure. Only when the pair was out of sight did the crowd turn towards the main door and disappear through it to the interior.

I remounted and Ted Lake, half with shock, half with pleasure, asked, 'You're the lawyer, how do we stand reading the Riot Act in a workhouse?'

'This doesn't look like a riot to me, more a well-planned strategy to expel the enemy – it was almost military! If I do have to read them the act, remind me to add "God Save the King" – many a prosecution for riotous assembly's been overturned because the wrong reading was given.'

'Don't you mean "Queen"?'

'Of course – thank you, I keep forgetting! It's been so long since we had a woman on the throne. Anyway – this is no more a riot than a village football match. Let's go on inside and see what it's all about. Your nephew was very perceptive; there's certainly a mood of rebellion but it must be kept in check, otherwise any advantages the inmates secure by getting rid of the Calmans will be meaningless. If violence does break out inside the House, I don't want to order in the militia. Let's see what we can do to calm things down and avoid that at least!'

We rode up the drive together and as we approached the main door Ted exclaimed, 'Well, fuck me – will you take a look at that!' He pointed above the door, but at first all I could see out of place was a ladder propped up against one side of the pediment. 'Do you see that? I know a pair of drawers when I see one! A guinea says they're Jenny Calman's. I swear she didn't have any on when she fell on the ground!' Sure enough there was a garment hanging limply in the warm still air; adorned with quantities of lace and startlingly white, it clung decoratively round the base of the spike topping the pediment.

Somewhat apprehensively we dismounted at the front of the House and were able to secure an inmate to deal with our horses. We passed through the lobby into the dining hall to be confronted with what must have been the total complement of the workhouse. The women had laid down their bowls on a table and now sat resting in chairs, which were set out randomly. For the most part the men remained standing. As we approached all fell silent. I was surprised there was no hostility. It seemed as though the expulsion of the Calmans had acted as a catharsis, purging and dissipating all the anger and resentment contained within the walls of the place and which was substituted by an overwhelming sense of relief and exhaustion. It was time for us to seize the initiative and set the House back into some semblance of order. I cleared my throat and addressed the whole group, explaining that we were already aware of many of their grievances and that Mr Lake, indicating my companion, was in the process of making many recommendations for improvement.

There was a universal growl of cynicism and a shaking of heads in disbelief. One man stepped forward, as spokesman I presumed. 'How do any of you know what's been going on here? You never asked. Begging your pardon, Mr Lawes – you was the only one who began to question what happens here, and we're not ungrateful, but it wasn't enough. You say changes are going to be made – but all the time that fucking bastard Shepherd's in control nothing will change. We needed some action and by God we've had some today, but it was of our own making. We don't trust any of you and if you say the Calmans have to come back then you guardians have got a fight on your hands. Having got rid of the buggers we'll never allow them back in!' The women picked up their bowls and began to rattle the spoons in them again.

I held up my hand and said, 'First of all, I understand why you feel you can't trust us, and I include myself in that. I've been too slow in responding to what I was aware of, but I wanted to do things legally so that any changes brought in could never be challenged or upset. I can assure you the Calmans will never set foot here again, I give you my word.' This time there was a more receptive murmur. I went on. 'The events of the last few weeks have ensured that the board has to take a close look at every aspect of how this union conducts its affairs. It's clear from Mr Lake's investigations that there have been gross breaches of the regulations, to your detriment. Many on the board are seeking to put that right. Those that don't cooperate will have to consider their positions.' I knew I was sticking my neck out, but I was certain we could push through all the remedies Ted and his committee had recommended. As chairman Shepherd had overseen serious violations of persons and regulations. The results having now culminated in a near revolt they would have no choice other than to resign.

My final comment was to recommend they returned to their work and normal routine for the time being until new arrangements for their welfare could be established. At first, having seized such a grand initiative, they were reluctant to relinquish their control, but it slowly dawned that they had no option. Their own welfare depended on the normal running of the House – for example meals had to be prepared. Finally, to my relief, they seemed to accept my word and slowly drifted back to the safe monotony of their daily routines. Whatever had been the motivation for their group enterprise, nothing they'd done could change their individual material condition – they all remained destitute with nowhere else to go.

I realised that much had gone on here before the final triumph at the gates. It was a pity, I thought, that Ambrose Hudson had left. Not only would I have obtained a coherent and balanced account, he would have had an excellent story for his paper. Instead I had to consult a couple of the more able men, including Edward Willis who – in spite of his persistent irritating snuffling – was not unintelligent. I beckoned them to remain and, with Ted Lake bringing up the rear, led them into the boardroom, where I sat them in the best oak chairs and got straight to the point.

'What happened to Jenny Calman? I could see for myself she was manhandled and roughly treated. Good God! She barely had any clothes left!'

The men shuffled in their seats. Ed Willis spoke first. 'It was the women, sir. They were all fired up about Emily Alfrey and what Enderby had done. But it was Jenny Calman what allowed it to happen. She's the one who let him into the women's quarters. She's no better than a pimp. The women decided to give her a dose of what some of them had suffered.' He hesitated.

'Go on,' I prompted. He looked very uncomfortable and I went on. 'Look, Willis – nothing you tell us will ever be laid at your door and it's most likely that nothing further will come of any actions by the women. The Calmans have left and I'd put money on it they won't be returning to report any assault – there's too much about their own behaviour that was unlawful for them to want to give evidence in court.'

Willis looked at his companion for encouragement. The man had been listening intently and nodding now and then in agreement.

Ed Willis continued his account. 'Naming no names, it was the older women – the ones who had been on the receiving end of Enderby's whoring in the past. They decided Mrs Calman ought to know how that felt, so when she came into the hall to go through to the kitchen there was a party of about ten to meet her. At the same time the men had found the master and brought him to watch.' He hesitated again. 'Do you really want to know the rest?'

I told him it was better we knew exactly what had happened and as men of the world we weren't easily shocked. He drew a deep breath, wiped his nose on the cuff of his sleeve and continued.

'They grabbed her and laid her across one of the tables, held her down, ripped at her dress, rolled it up and whipped off her drawers. Then one of them hit her full in the face. But what was worst of all was that none of the women, including those who held her down, said a word while this was going on. There was no sound apart from Mrs Calman trying to swear and scream – but one woman had her hand over her mouth until the end. It seemed to make it all the worse. But no one interfered with her – you know, there.' I took his meaning. 'After it was over and one or two more had thrown in a few punches, she was dragged to the front door and – I think you must've seen the rest. Someone found a ladder and stuck her bit of linen on the spike over the door.'

Their account ended where we had entered. Clearly relieved as we let them go they stumbled as quickly as they could out of the boardroom back to the workroom.

'Well, damn it! Some kind of justice I suppose,' Ted observed. 'It makes you think what women are really capable of when they take their minds to things that matter. I wouldn't have wanted to be on the receiving end of those Furies.'

I said nothing, but a thought flashed across my mind – what would they have done to Enderby if they'd been able? Then a second thought was – *did* they do something worse than that to the overseer? Could women contemplate and carry out such a savage act? I kept my thoughts to myself. There was no point at this particular moment in distracting Ted with such ideas.

We turned our attention to how the House should be managed without either a master or matron. We considered bringing in the relieving officer, Thomas Carrick. As the most experienced officer he'd be invaluable – if he was prepared to cooperate. The other obvious solution was to continue with Fred Lodge as deputy master and Amy Lodge as temporary matron. It would need authorisation to pay them all honoraria – something that would stick in Colonel Shepherd's craw – but if we could hasten the chairman's resignation that would be our salvation. The guardians must be informed of the latest events and our emergency decisions for staffing the place. Ted volunteered to ride into town and organise contact with as many of the board members as he could. We decided on a meeting in the House the next day at two in the afternoon. We drafted a letter together, which was brief and to the point: that the Calmans had left; the House was orderly but lacking necessary staff; and that, for the time being, I would stay on the premises until the receiving officer could be contacted to take over. Ted went off and I went into the kitchen.

The five stalwarts were still there – chopping and peeling as normal. Rosa Hines bobbed a curtsy as I entered. I had a plan in mind that I immediately put in train. 'There's been much upset in the House today and many of the inmates are still angry. My experience is that a good meal goes a long way to calming things down. When we have a full belly we feel better about things – don't you agree, ladies?'

Rosa Hines seemed to be the spokesman for the rest. 'Chances of a full belly here are rare, sir,' she said sourly. 'With other things, that's what set us off.'

'It would be a good idea if I knew all your names – I remember three of you who were so helpful to me at the meeting – Rosa, Edith and Aggie, but I don't know you two.'

Rosa nodded towards the two women, both in their thirties. 'This is Lizzy Edwards and Jane Moss, sir.' They gave me a cursory nod.

'Now, I want the inmates to have a good midday meal. Two of you come with me to the Calmans' quarters to see what they've stored away. I've heard rumours that they received food that you should have. I suggest we go on a raiding party to see if it's true. Bring a crate each.'

I wasn't surprised at what greeted us as we entered the Calmans' apartments. But Edith and Aggie stood open-mouthed as they looked around the living quarters. It was very comfortably furnished, with good-quality furniture, ornaments and pictures, which must have been in the House when it was originally sold to the union. I understood that it went on the market with all its contents so, by some devious means, the pair had acquired many of the items before they were put up for general sale; likewise, the two bedrooms contained large beds with deep mattresses and heavy coverings. One of the women jumped on the bed and lay fully stretched out – luxuriating in its comfort.

We moved into the kitchen where immediately we could see flitches of salt pork hanging from hooks in the beams. We walked to the far end and opened the door into a very large walk-in pantry; on the shelves, under numerous fly-covers, were plates of ham, bacon and sausage. In boxes on the floor we discovered fruit and fresh green vegetables, along with loaves of newly baked bread. Other items included eggs from the House hens, which, according to the women, never saw their way into the House larder, and many varieties of cheese. There were cakes and pastries, although not in large quantities but enough for most of the inmates to have a taste. The women found empty boxes and began packing. It would take several visits to clear out all the hoarded stock and transfer it to the main kitchen. I puzzled where all this food had come from and where it was going; it couldn't be imagined that the Calmans might eat all this. They were obviously selling union produce and supplies at local markets and pocketing the profits.

I left the women to it and returned to the others in the kitchen with orders for them to make what they could from the provisions we'd found and ensure that all the inmates shared a plentiful and nourishing meal. I hoped that years of preparing root vegetables and bad bread hadn't in any way diminished their culinary skills.

My next move was to find Fred and Amy and ask them to take over the House for the time being. Amy was in the women's quarters and said she could speak for Fred; they would be willing to cooperate.

Word had come through that Thomas Carrick was prepared to come in immediately and be resident master for a while. He promised he would arrive within the hour.

Rustling in my pocket was Ambrose Hudson's letter to Peter Samuels and William Tuttle. Having settled the immediate running of the House, and thankful for the cooperation of both officers and inmates, I went off to find the boys. They were in the garden, supposedly weeding between the vegetables, but actually both were lying fully stretched out and asleep in the sunshine, obviously taking full advantage of the general air of relaxation.

I crept up on them and leaned over Peter's right ear. 'No work to do then?'

He jumped like a rabbit and as confused. William rolled over and seeing me also leapt to his feet.

'Sir, sir! Sorry! We didn't see you there. We're just taking a rest – we've finished the weeding – honest, sir!'

I noticed how they both instinctively put their hands behind their backs as though in anticipation of punishment. I pointed to an old garden bench tucked into the hedgerow. 'Come and sit down, I want to talk to you both.' I took out Hudson's letter. 'I've received a letter for you from Mr Millhouses.' William particularly seemed to reanimate. His small emaciated face lit up at the mention of the name. Peter said, 'Mr Millhouses? But he's left – we don't see him no more. We don't know where he went – he didn't say. He's like them all; they all leave – my pa and ma…' His voice dropped and he sounded resentful.

William nodded. 'And my ma!'

Peter's mouth formed a thin line; William's eyes welled with tears.

I looked down at the letter. 'I'm not sure if either of you can read?' I asked, raising my eyebrows.

'No, sir, we can't – we've never been taught. I told Mr Millhouses – perhaps he's forgotten.'

'Not at all! I asked you out of politeness, but he said I'd probably need to read it to you. Would you like to hear it now, or shall we go inside first?'

'No, no!' cried William. 'I want to hear it now – read it now!'
I opened the letter and read the following:

> Post-house,
>
> Ipswich
>
> Wednesday, 6 inst.

My dear friends,

Firstly, I want to apologise to you both for leaving the House without at least saying goodbye. There were very good reasons why I went without speaking to you. I hope quite soon to be able to explain them to you face to face.

I want you both to know that I value our friendship and will always do so. It is my intention to do whatever I can to help you both in the future. Mr Lawes, I'm sure, will vouch for my promises, although as yet he and I do not know one another as well as I would like, but I'm sure that will be changed very soon. In the meantime I am certain you can trust him.

I intend to visit Seddon and its House in two or three weeks' time and you will be the first I shall seek out. But for now I hope all is well at night, William, and that you are well advanced in your numbers. When we meet I shall insist you chant them to me all the way through. Peter – I hope you still look after our young friend and will continue to protect him well as you have always tried to do.

Until then I remain your affectionate friend,
Henry Millhouses

For a while they said nothing. Then William asked me to read it again and point out each word as I did so. Peter asked when Mr Millhouses would be likely to come back, but I couldn't tell him exactly, although I assured him he was a man of his word and if he said two or three weeks that would be the case. They'd have to be patient; I was sure he would explain everything when he saw them. In the meantime I promised to write to Henry and tell him that his friends were well, sent their regards and looking forward to his visit. I folded up the letter and held it out to them. Peter took it, but seeing the disappointment on William's face, folded it again and, with a wink, slipped it into the boy's jacket pocket.

I felt immensely satisfied having completed my errand. The physical change in William especially was remarkable. He literally jumped with joy all the way back to the building and even sceptical Peter, infected by his friend's obvious delight, allowed himself a smile as he ran after him.

Chapter 8

I returned home to find the normally imperturbable Foster very rattled. 'Colonel Shepherd is waiting to see you, sir. He arrived about half an hour ago and, I regret to say, was most ungentlemanly in his language. I have seated him in the drawing room. I must say, sir, his temper has not improved with waiting.'

'Thank you, Foster. I apologise for the colonel; I'll go in straight away. Perhaps you could bring in some brandy when I ring?'

'Certainly, sir.' He inclined his head and opened the drawing-room door.

Jack Shepherd was sitting on a straight-backed chair, his face as brick-red as sandstone. He stood up, but I waved him back into his seat.

'At last! Damn it, Lawes, I've been waiting here half an hour! Look – I'll get straight to it. What's all this business up at the House? I received a message from that radical Ted Lake via my bailiff. He told him there'd been some serious incidents with the inmates and that you wanted to call an emergency meeting of all the guardians tomorrow afternoon. Is that the case?' I opened my mouth to confirm, but just pausing to draw breath he continued, 'Well, firstly, I object to being disturbed on a Sunday and, secondly – and let me make myself quite clear – it's not your business to call meetings – emergency or otherwise. That's my prerogative as chairman. We've already had this out. I wouldn't be at all surprised if this pandemonium up at Seddon is the result of your recent meddling. I want a full explanation of what's been happening. If I think it necessary to call the guardians out specially, I'll notify them myself.'

Ringing the bell for Foster, I let Shepherd run on for a while to draw his bluster. Then I said, 'Colonel Shepherd, as I've told you in the past, I've never sought to undermine your authority as chairman. I am, however, primarily concerned about the welfare of the inmates – for which we all have a responsibility – and the good name of the union. Something I feel sure you're passionate about also.'

Foster knocked and entered with the brandy. I poured two glasses and handed Shepherd one.

'Thank you,' he said, and cleared his throat. 'Of course, I'm concerned that the board is respected by all the rate payers of the parishes. Since the union was formed four years ago, I've tried to make it a model for all the others in the county by building up its reputation as one that takes value for money very seriously. You, on the other hand, seem to have done nothing but try to weaken that intention. Your pantomime with the soup, for example, only served to stir up the inmates and make them discontented –' He took a gulp of his brandy. 'The Calmans reported back to me what some of them said and it verged on the revolutionary. Now I think about it, I'm not surprised there's trouble; it's been brewing for some time. Once you give these people an opportunity to whine there's no stopping them. If you'd left well alone – well, it's obviously too late now. I want a full account of what's been happening.' There was a spark in his pale, watery eyes as he threw me a challenging look.

Briefly, and omitting the more lurid details, I told him how the inmates had ejected the Calmans from the House and that inspection of their quarters showed they'd been regularly cheating the union out of food stuffs and money over a long period. He blustered again and was very defensive of his two protégés. He also rounded on me and asked why I hadn't read the Riot Act. I told him that, if on the occasion they wouldn't disperse, it would mean calling out the militia. 'Do you want to be involved in the possibility of more bloodshed?' I asked him. 'Anyway, in my judgement it hadn't been a riot, more an organised and orderly expulsion.'

Sitting back in his seat, brandy in hand, he retorted that he couldn't understand how a man in my position and with important aristocratic connections could hold views that were a danger to the state. 'Radicals upset the peace and produce revolutions,' he declared. I smothered a laugh but couldn't bring myself to give him the satisfaction of an argument.

At that point I suggested we moved into the library where I had some documents to show him – most importantly a copy of the procurement committee's final report, which Ted Lake had left for him. I rang the bell for my manservant. 'Please take the drinks into the library, Foster,' I said as I ushered Jack Shepherd out of the drawing room.

Settling him into a comfortable armchair and with a generous helping of spirits at his elbow, I went to the desk and produced Ted's résumé of his committee's findings and recommendations. Suggesting he take a few minutes to read them through, I left the room on the pretext of speaking to my housekeeper on some domestic matters.

When I returned ten minutes later I found him still reading – obviously going over the document again. I sat opposite him by the fireplace and said quietly and seriously, 'You see, Jack – there are real problems here that can no longer be overlooked. The guardians have to deal with them quickly, otherwise there'll be serious consequences, both for the board and the inmates. You can't deny there's been a succession of disasters – beginning with our discovery of the adulteration of the flour, and the corrupt practice by one of our suppliers, who—'

'Yes, yes! I know all about that; what of it?' He reached for the decanter and generously refilled his glass. His drinker's face was pinker than ever, his bulbous blue nose a notable feature in a rubicund landscape.

'There's much to be made of it, Jack, as you'll have read.' He said nothing, just stared back at me. I continued, 'Then there was the inmate's suicide, the appalling and brutal murder and mutilation of a House official – to say nothing of the insult to the board at our last meeting. Now we have acts of what you'd call potential revolution and what I'd describe as extreme frustration.'

He began to bristle and, pointing to Ted's report, he said, 'These findings are beyond belief – are you sure this committee's got its facts right? I can't credit the Calmans and others connected to the guardians as being complicit in such fraud and mismanagement.'

'Well, they're true, Jack. But have you nothing to say about the treatment of the inmates – their poor diet, lack of facilities for good hygiene? Did you never question any of those things? To put it bluntly, you seem to have been prepared to accept the status quo without any regular and close inspection of day-to-day practice. My short time on the board has revealed to me that its only priority has been to maintain the poor-rate at the lowest level possible at the expense of—'

'What's wrong with that? Local tax payers expect us to be careful with their money. The poor-rate's a very unpopular tax. People see it as giving money to idlers who won't work – like the damn tinkers.' He was almost out of his seat and in danger of knocking his brandy glass over.

'I think you'll find that they're the best example of self-sufficiency in the neighbourhood. Garth O'Brien would no more ask for a place in the House than you would yourself!'

Somewhat regaining his composure, he leaned back in his chair. 'I don't know how you can say such things – thieves and vagabonds the lot of them. I'm sure those boys of his poach my coverts.'

'As the local JP I can tell you honestly that none of the family has ever appeared before me on any charge – poaching or otherwise.'

'That's because they're too clever. They know the land as well as I do – George Stenning swears they're regularly in my woods.'

'Ted Lake employs them on his farm and has no complaints. In fact, he says he misses them when they leave after harvest.'

'To my mind, Ted Lake's a damn radical who sails close to the wind – I've heard he talks near-sedition in the tavern. These new ideas are dangerous. Good God, Lawes! Why is there so much agitation to change systems that have been with us for centuries? If no one knows their place anymore, the confusion will surely bring on a revolution. When it comes down to it there are too many who expect the rest of us to pick them up when they fall over.'

'Not all of us see it like that, Jack. Some of us know from experience that people become destitute for all kinds of reasons that aren't necessarily their fault.' I paused and watched his face, which had taken on a dogged expression. 'Where do they go when they've no further means of survival? I agree the workhouses were never set up with the intention of encouraging fecklessness, but neither should they be seen as opportunities for the punishment of the poor by means of their humiliation.'

He leaned forward, now very animated. 'That's all very well – you and your Whiggish ideas. If you got about a bit more and came down from your high horse, you'd hear different views. Most of my estate workers are against the union. They see it as a drain on their wages and unfair. They all say they'd do anything rather than volunteer as an inmate. It's really those wastrels at the bottom of the heap who take advantage of union handouts.'

I couldn't let that go unchallenged. 'So what happens if you have to sack one of your workers and take his cottage? What does he do and where does he go?'

He looked back at me squarely. 'Back to his family – let them sort him out. His contract for a tied cottage is that he works on my estate. If that's no longer possible, the cottage will be required for someone else. That's how it works, as you well know. What do you expect me to do – build places for old retainers to live in until they die?'

'That's what I'm planning to do, Jack,' I said quietly.

His head came up with a jerk. 'What?'

'I'm building almshouses for my retired workers to live in if they can't make any other arrangements.'

'Good God, man! Whatever are you about? You must be mad! This is an extremely dangerous precedent. Every worker in the district will expect the rest of us landowners to do the same! You're trying to upset the whole natural balance of things. Look – we've had the same system of rule here for generations and it works. Those that own the land hold the power. Consequently, we've had no revolution here – leastways not since Cromwell and his cronies. It's that tradition that gives us the right to continue. It's almost—'

'Divine?' I asked.

'Well, of course not! But seeking to overthrow it will certainly bring chaos and possibly the wrath of God.'

'You'll be telling me next you believe in the divine right of kings.'

'Well – if you put it like that – no harm in the king having a direct connection to the Almighty.' I stared back at him, for the first time shocked and almost speechless. But on reflection this man was echoing the thoughts of many of our class. No wonder change would be at a snail's pace. However, I didn't want to continue down the route of a discussion on the arcane points of the English constitution, so I simply said, 'Change is coming, Jack, whether you can cope with it or not. If we don't address some basic truths, like how we treat those who can't help themselves, there'll be trouble quite soon, believe me. Have you never considered that the poor of the parish are unsuccessful in our terms mostly because they lack money, skills and, above all, education – especially education – which would help propel them out of penury and distress?'

'I suppose you mean teaching them to read and write. Now, I ask you, what use is book-learning to a shepherd, for instance? Are they going to read to the sheep? There's no need for them to have book-learning. The only book they need understand is the Bible, and the parson'll read that to them. Once you have them able to understand newspapers, for example, then the cat's out of the bag. There'll be revolution and we know what that leads to – look what happened in France!'

'I hardly think teaching youngsters the letters of their native language will trigger blood in the streets, Colonel. Besides, if we don't start acting to reduce poverty and ignorance, we'll all suffer.'

'What do you mean?'

I thought carefully for a little. 'You must know we're in the middle of the greatest changes we've ever experienced – industry and commerce are growing almost faster than we can control them. The new steam revolution is pushing everything forward at a pace we've never known before. As I see it, the people are like one of the new giant steam engines. As one body they have the potential for enormous power if they wish to wield it. All the time people like us – who we could call the engineers – keep stoking the boiler with actions that produce the steam of resentment. Unless we're prepared to adjust the valves regularly and let off some of the tension within the boiler, the whole engine of state will explode and bring us all down. The ruling class is at significant risk from forces the like of which we've never seen.'

'What are you talking about? Boilers and valves – poppycock!' He snorted. 'Fanciful nonsense. What the ruling class need to do is hold the whip hand and maintain tradition and custom.'

I realised reasoned argument, let alone metaphor, was lost on him, so I played my ace. 'I'm afraid as far as Seddon Union is concerned, using your own expression – the cat's already out of the bag.' I passed him Ambrose Hudson's letter, which he read and then put into his lap with a sigh, almost of resignation.

'I knew that blackguard was more than he seemed to be – too

insolent for a pauper. What's this evidence he's got? Where is it? Have you seen a copy?'

'I expect it any time this week. Be assured I know this man is a thorough journalist who investigates and exposes what he considers wrongdoing. My judgement says he'll have discovered things about the running of the union that will be unfavourable to the board and to you in particular. I've already mentioned the sustenance and care of the inmates as being derelict, but I think he lays the responsibility for the other serious matters – suicide and murder – at your door. Not' – I added hastily – 'that he thinks you carried out the murder – but rather your poor lack of leadership and judgement allowed these events to happen. There – that's being as blunt as I wish to be. But better you're prepared than not for the storm about to be unleashed when he publishes.'

For the first time he looked totally stunned and could find no mechanism within him for a reply, either defensive or aggressive. I went on. 'Again, plain speaking is probably best now – you have to consider your position.'

Eyeing me sharply, he said, 'You mean, resign?'

I was surprised. I hadn't expected him to even consider that as a possibility. In fact, I thought he might prolong the argument by trying to justify further his principle of supporting the rate payers. But however much of a backwards-looking man he was, Jack Shepherd wasn't stupid – after all he'd survived a tough war – but simply stubborn; he was a man who could recognise when his back was against the wall. I pointed out to him that if he continued as chairman, he would take the full force of exposure of Seddon Union's maladministration in the press; inevitably there would be a top-level enquiry by the board of commissioners in London, and he personally would have to accept their findings and all the notoriety that would accompany such an investigation. Ultimately, when he'd suffered all that humiliation, he'd have to resign anyway. It required a pragmatic decision, although he wouldn't have recognised it as such. It was a fine line I was treading, between encouraging him to go and yet not pushing him into a decision that could only be his.

He surprised me a second time when he said, 'Well, Lawes, I see I have little choice. After four years of doing my best it's come to this.

My intentions were, I thought, correct for the parishes and the tax payers. It seems I was a victim of circumstances – as well as less honourable people. So no need for further discussion; I recognise there's nothing for it but to tender my resignation as both chairman and a guardian. I'll write to the board within the next few days.'

'We have the extraordinary meeting tomorrow afternoon. Perhaps that would be a good time. In fact, you could write your letter here and I could take it with me. I don't want to be seen as forcing your hand, but from a practical point of view the board does need to be in a proper constitutional state to appoint new officers and start implementing Ted Lake's committee's reforms.'

Having made the decision, he seemed to cave in altogether. 'Very well – leave me to it. If you could find me paper and pen, I'll do it now. But before I do I want to say one thing to you. I've never understood you, and even less your father, who I thought was a misguided fool – you seem to be following him. I tell you, young man, people with ideas such as yours cause endless trouble. All this will end badly and it'll be your responsibility if we all have to arm ourselves against cutthroats and ne'er-do-wells with ideas above their station.'

I wouldn't dignify that comment with an answer, so I set out the necessaries and left him to it. Returning to the library twenty minutes later, on the desk was an envelope addressed to the Seddon Union board of guardians. Of Colonel Jack Shepherd there was no sign.

The night was disturbed with thunder and heavy rain, and the summer storm continued through the morning. Cases in the court were light and were over by midday – enough time for me to have some food and ale in the Fleece. Because of the weather I'd used the carriage and after leaving the tavern I was driven straight to the House for the extraordinary meeting that afternoon. I gave orders for my driver to return in under three hours. Amy came out of the lodge to greet me looking tired, but there was no sign of the anxiety that had seemed to haunt both her and Fred when the Calmans had been there. We walked up the drive together and I asked her how she and her husband were managing with so few officials. It wasn't as bad as I'd feared.

'We've been lucky, sir. The inmates have been very cooperative.

Now they feel they've had some success getting rid of the master and matron, they seem to have calmed right down.'

'I understand the relieving officer has arrived?'

'Oh, yes, sir. He's been very good. He moved into the Calmans' quarters last night. Mr Carrick's strict – but very fair.'

'Not like the Calmans then?'

She smiled. 'Certainly not like the Calmans! The surgeon, Mr Burgwin, has been to visit several times. For the first time I've been able to get him to really look at the children – not because they're ill, but so undernourished. He's a kind man and I think he wants to talk to the board about a new infirmary. As things stand we've never had one – but we've been lucky because there's never been any infection here since the House opened, so we've never needed to isolate anyone.'

I realised this was an area I hadn't thought about. Surprisingly, the general low state of the inmates had not, as far as anyone reported, developed into any serious illnesses. I asked her what the arrangements would be at the moment if there was an outbreak of anything contagious.

'When the place opened it was decided that the receiving ward could be turned into a small infirmary if necessary. As I say, fortunately we've never had to use it.'

'What would've happened if there'd been some new admission there already – and it was then found necessary to use it for other purposes?'

'We'd have to turn them out and put them on poor relief outside – that would be to protect them from the infection and to keep them going until we could offer them a place again.' I could see all this was a piecemeal attempt by the board to save money by not building a separate infirmary, which was an essential under the circumstances; there were no other infirmaries in the immediate district – the nearest was in Ipswich.

As we walked through the hall I noticed the same lack of sound as had struck me on my first visit. The House seemed calm and orderly; there was no sign of the inmates who, I presumed, were all at work. Amy walked towards the kitchen and I entered the boardroom to find almost a full complement of guardians already assembled, along with the surgeon, Thomas Carrick and Fred Lodge. The only man missing was John Newton who, as I found out later, had resigned following the allegations of fraud in the procurement of cloth. Most were sitting round the table, in their customary places, reading Lake's full report in silence. The only unoccupied seat was at the table's head. It had already occurred to me that Thomas Bennett, the vice-chairman, must officiate until a new chairman was elected and quietly I passed the colonel's letter of resignation to him to read out to the board, although I realised that Jack Shepherd would have at least informed the deputy of his intention and that Bennett had probably told everyone else already. But just as Bennett was about to take the top seat, the door opened and Jack Shepherd walked in.

There was a muffled gasp of surprise from the assembly; some guardians stood awkwardly to their feet, but Colonel Shepherd signalled to them to resume their seats. I could feel the tension and embarrassment mounting and waited for him to say something. He walked to the table and stood by his old seat and began to speak, but without his distinctive military bark. 'Good afternoon to you! Well – it's come to this. I've spoken to Mr Lawes and decided that I should resign as your chairman.' A low murmur rippled round the table and he held up his hand for silence. 'I've read your report, Lake – in detail' – and he looked at me – 'and see that your committee has been thorough and uncovered some shameful behaviours. As chairman it's on me to take final responsibility – so I've no choice but to resign my position.'

To my surprise no one dissented and I wondered if he was disappointed. Even his cronies who would have supported him on most other occasions remained silent. The evidence of negligence contained in the report in front of them was damning and the primal urge for self-protection was evidently stronger at this time than loyalty to their colleague. He went on. 'One thing I want to make clear. My resignation doesn't imply that I feel any guilt for my overall chairmanship of the board and the way I have conducted myself. I had no knowledge of what was being done in our name – perhaps I should have been more assiduous in my enquiries – but you should know I consider my intentions to maintain the poor-rate at an acceptable level was in the best interests of our local tax payers and the union itself. Unlike some of you' – and he looked hard at Ted Lake and myself – 'I think we are becoming too lax in our attitude towards those who hold out the begging bowl. There's plenty of work for those who want it. But I've been told I'm out of step with new ideas, and people like me must move over or bend to them. I have no wish to dance to anyone's new fiddle! I'll continue in my own way – maintaining traditions that I believe are inimitable to ensuring the country's future well-being.'

I was anxious that this disquisition shouldn't develop into a political colloquy and so, politely, I stopped his flow. 'Colonel Shepherd, I'm sure we all appreciate you coming here today to explain your position once again and in person. We recognise you as a man of principle and one who sticks to what you believe in.' A few of the members banged their hands on the table in agreement, not appreciating, I thought, my subtext. 'I would ask Mr Bennett as vice-chairman to express for all of us the board's gratitude.' Thomas Bennett got to his feet and gave a short valediction, followed by a toast. As graciously as he was able, Jack Shepherd thanked us all, gulped down a sherry in one and turned to leave. His bailiff, George Stenning, left his seat as though to follow him, but the colonel turned and waved him back, growling, 'No need for that, George! You're your own man. Never let it be said I keep a lackey.' Stung, Stenning sat back in his chair. William Harbey held open the door and the ex-chairman passed through.

Apart from John Newton, no other members of the board sought to offer their resignations, so it remained almost as it had been. All we needed was to elect a new chairman. After discussion with Ted I'd privately canvassed Robert Bignell as to whether he'd be prepared to take on the responsibility. His measured approach to the Enderby enquiry, and Ted's appraisal of him as an assiduous investigator were positive indications that he'd make a first-class chairman. Although nothing was said, I guessed Ted was disappointed that I'd not suggested him and later, when we were alone, I told him the board needed him as the grit in the oyster – just as he had once described himself. I assured him he'd be much more effective as chairman of the new visiting committee overseeing how things were running and ensuring that all his reforms were carried out to the letter. He didn't disagree and seemed mollified.

There was only one item on the agenda and that was the committee's report and its recommendations. In spite of that the meeting was long and sometimes heated. For the first time all the members wanted to be heard and take a full part in deliberations. The urgent question of a new master was first to be raised. Robert Bignell, now in the chairman's seat, asked if anyone knew of likely candidates who could be available as soon as possible. I felt awkward for Fred and asked him if he would like to be considered, but he seemed relaxed and forestalled any awkwardness by telling us that he would not be applying for the post as he was content for the time being to continue as porter. In spite of deputising in the running the House for the last weeks, he felt as yet insufficiently qualified to take it over permanently. I was quietly relieved as I had ideas concerning him that at present I was still mulling over. Thomas Carrick's salary as relieving officer was so far in excess of the master's that it wasn't feasible he would want the position permanently, but he knew a mature married couple who might suit. Although not experienced in running a workhouse, they had managed a large country house with a great number of staff. The pair were of good character and well respected in the district. Carrick felt sure they would be acceptable to the board if he could persuade them to apply. In the meantime he would continue to officiate as master with Fred's help.

We moved on to discuss material changes to the House. Robert Bignell was particularly incensed at the amount of money discovered lying unused in the contingency fund. 'I don't understand why we never questioned this. I'm in no way blaming Mr Harbey – it's not his fault. But for us to have been sitting on such a large amount of money is iniquitous.'

'Jack Shepherd was always concerned we should hedge money to offset changes in the local situation,' declared James Keen. 'I must say I'm inclined to agree with his view that the poor-rate must be kept at an acceptable level, otherwise they'll be complaints.'

'It depends what you mean by acceptable, Keen,' said Ted robustly. 'Looking at the way the poor buggers here have been treated, I don't think even the most miserly rate payer would begrudge them some comforts, do you?' He looked challengingly around the room. Most of the board nodded.

Ted then put it to the vote that we should spend large amounts of it immediately to bring the living conditions of the inmates up to a 'reasonable standard', although, of course, 'reasonable' is open to interpretation.

'I suggest we open up requests for tenders for new buildings.'

The surgeon found his voice at last. 'Gentlemen, we must have an infirmary. There can be no challenge to that; regulations demand it!'

Everyone agreed that the present ad hoc arrangements were unsuitable and it made me wonder why they had previously been so lax in providing what was, after all, a regulatory requirement. It was decided to build in combination a new three-bedded infirmary and an adjoining bathhouse.

Then it was my turn. 'Members of the board I propose the immediate appointment of a schoolmaster. As Mr Burgwin has pointed out, the infirmary is a regulatory requirement – and so is education for the children. The board has been most derelict in its duties to its youngest inmates and we can no longer ignore the fact that we're in breach of the Poor Law Act and have been since the Seddon Union opened.'

My proposal was passed unanimously and it was agreed that advertisements for master, matron, overseer and schoolmaster should be drafted by three of the guardians as soon as the meeting was over. Ted Lake offered to take them immediately to the local printer and have them distributed and displayed in the usual places around the district – he hoped, given the urgency, within two days.

Discussion had continued over almost three hours. Nutrition, education, clothing and sleeping arrangements all came under close scrutiny for the first time; the board had covered all aspects of the running of the union and agreed on reforms that now closely satisfied the regulations. By the end of the meeting most of us were content we'd achieve the improvements we sought. We celebrated with another glass of sherry – no biscuits – and prepared to leave.

I took Fred Lodge by the arm as we walked together down the drive towards his house. 'I was glad to hear you say you didn't want to be considered for the office of master. However, I think you're very well qualified for it. But it suits me to hear you turn it down. Come up to the Hall – bring Amy – I've something to discuss with you. Shall we say this Thursday, midday? Will that be possible – with your duties?' He looked confused and a little worried. 'I'll ask Thomas to take over for me. Will it take long, sir?'

'An hour, that's all.'

Four days later Foster entered the library carrying a substantial package, well sealed. 'This arrived by special courier from London, sir. There was nothing to pay, but I signed for receipt. I hope that was correct, sir?'

I took the packet and immediately recognised the handwriting as Ambrose Hudson's. 'There was no requirement for an answer, Foster, thank you.'

Breaking the seal I emptied the contents on to my desk. There were innumerable sheets of paper bound together and a separate letter. Sure enough it was from the journalist-spy, as I'd come to think of him.

Gresham Street,

London

Wednesday, 13 June

Dear Mr Lawes,

I promised you sight of my full journalistic account of the conditions that I observed during my stay at Seddon. My intention is to extract from it such information as I think necessary to write a full article, which will expose the shortcomings on the institution. My editor, James McNiece, is keen to publish as soon as possible.

I wish to do you the courtesy of allowing you to examine these findings before they come into the public domain. I would also press you to agree to a meeting between us. Apart from discussing what clearly are urgent matters for you as one of the board of guardians, I would like to meet you on your own account, having only exchanged brief words under difficult circumstances.

Since my work on my journal is now complete I intend to visit Seddon as soon as possible, not least to keep my promise to William Tuttle and Peter Samuels. I will be arriving by mail coach in Ipswich, where I will spend the night, on Thursday, 21 inst. I will find a conveyance to bring me to Seddon the following day. Will you be so kind as to receive me at or about midday of the twenty-second?

I remain –

Your humble servant,

Ambrose Hudson

I immediately wrote a short note, thanking him for his enclosure, which I said I'd study carefully and insisting he stayed at Seddon Hall. I would send a coach to Ipswich on Friday morning to convey him here.

As arranged Ambrose Hudson arrived at the Hall late Friday afternoon. As he alighted from the coach, in smart breeches, jacket and boots, with a beaver and carrying a valise, I hardly recognised him. He looked very well indeed. When I'd last seen him he was thin as a lath, pale-faced and unkempt – with a stubbly beard and untrimmed hair. Now, as well as being smartly dressed, he'd lost the beard and his dark brown hair was fashionably cut. It was also evident that he'd put on some pounds in weight and the addition suited him admirably.

I came down the steps and held out my hand. 'Welcome to Seddon Hall, Mr Hudson – not Mr Millhouses I take it?'

He laughed and shook my hand. 'Ambrose – please. I prefer my professional pseudonym, although I've no shame in my patronymic. It's just useful sometimes to use an alias and one I can remember!'

We walked inside together and Foster took his bag and showed him immediately to his room. I had drinks prepared in the library and when Hudson returned from refreshing himself, I offered him a sherry and we sat down. After exchanging a few very English pleasantries concerning the journey and weather, I asked him if he'd be prepared to visit the House the next day, in spite of having just made an extensive journey here. I understood he was anxious to see William Tuttle and Peter Samuels and thought he wouldn't want to delay a visit to them. He readily agreed. Then I broached the matter of his journal.

'I've read your account minutely. I must say it gives an entirely different perspective which, of course, is what you intended. It's clear that you have experience in this kind of clandestine approach. I understand from a friend that you've worked in a similar way in the north of England.'

'Yes, that's true. My maxim is that to find the truth you have to live the truth. Absorbing the life of the people you're endeavouring to help is the best way of obtaining the evidence that change is needed. It's served me well in the past, and I think I'm right in assuming it'll produce results here?'

I thought for a moment then said, 'Your report was certainly accurate and supported everything that some of us already thought or knew. We've not been entirely inactive ourselves, though; we've put into place many of the omissions you observed.'

He nodded. 'When word circulated round the House that you'd intervened – with your "theatricals" as it was called – I knew that it wouldn't be long before further improvements would be made. But I asked myself how fast they would come into play.'

I gave him details of the board meeting at which the chairman had resigned and Ted Lake's committee had reported and all its recommendations agreed. He was impressed at our speed of action and went on to enquire how else conditions would be improved, especially education for the children. With some pride I mentioned that I'd been instrumental in filling that void by insisting the board hire a full-time schoolmaster. That led him to ask after Peter and William. I assured him I'd been swift to deliver his letter and described their delight – which obviously pleased him. He still felt awkward about leaving them without any explanation and hoped he could rectify that as soon as possible.

We moved on to discuss the fate of inmates, officials and guardians. Resignations and forced removals interested him greatly. Of the Calmans he commented that their ejection could be compared with the driving out of the Gadarene swine – a well-defined analogy under the circumstances, from a true wordsmith. I described how to the end Jack Shepherd had resisted responsibility for the grave outcomes of his chairmanship. Ambrose likened him to a fossil – absolutely petrified in his own antiquated principles. But, he acknowledged, while men like Shepherd held the reins of power, change would be hard fought for and step by step.

I gave him full details of the infamous board meeting – which has entered union mythology as 'the board of the biscuits', which he was both shocked and amused by, as one 'who appreciated black humour'. As far as Enderby's murder and mutilation were concerned, he asked me how the investigation was progressing and I had to admit the chances of apprehending the culprit – or culprits – were receding and the coroner's inquest remained open.

Foster rang the first bell for dinner, but just before we left the library to change I said I had a serious issue to take up with him – something I'd read in his journal.

'Oh, yes – and what's that?'

'I've no objection to the Byronic comparison – at least from the point of view of the "dangerous to know" allusion, not the others – but my nose, my nose is not retroussé! You make it sound like a girl's. Look! A man has his pride and if you intend to publish this journal widely—'

He broke in. 'Let me confess – it wasn't my first impression,' he laughed. 'I thought at first it was snub – but revised my opinion on a second viewing!'

Our catching-up was done and now it was time to eat.

Following my customary practice of not discussing local affairs in front of the servants, during the meal we left the topic of Seddon workhouse. Instead I was keen to discover more about my companion's life. I'd read his own account of course, as he'd laid it out in his journal. But he'd mentioned little about his life and work in London, which had not been relevant to his account. He told me something of his experiences in the textile mills of the north, but was more inclined to want to discourse on the new ideas circulating the capital – particularly the new sciences. He began to outline some of the recent developments of applied science as a motive force.

'I'm particularly interested in the new railways. They're beginning to cover large parts of London, as well as up in the industrial north of the country. I can foresee the whole of the country being on one network. Soon it'll take but a few days to get from London to the northernmost coast of Scotland. If I'd spare money, that's where I'd put it – in railway stock!'

'I don't visit the capital that often so I'm interested to know how it's changing.'

'Well, you might not recognise it at night – it's all lit up with the new gas lighting. Twenty years since it was first introduced, but now it's widespread in most of the streets. Walking at night's much safer and easier as you can imagine. Of course, there are parts of the city that remain forever in the dark; these are places where no sane man would walk alone! But again, I can foresee that they will one day share illumination – not only gaslight, but taking on new thoughts and ideas.'

As he was speaking with great enthusiasm I began to feel woefully ignorant. Of course I'd some idea of these discoveries and their application, but in many areas of new scientific research and experiment I was certainly behind the times. It was all very well for me to sit in my library reading the classics and absorbing new moral philosophies, but I could see that technical progress was advancing much faster than I had appreciated.

Ambrose talked of men in the forefront of science. 'Have you heard the names Humphry Davy and Michael Faraday?' I had to confess I hadn't. 'Both are instrumental in the founding of the new British Association for the Advancement of Science – and there's John Dalton, whose work on chemical elements is considered fundamental to that advancement. I wonder at their discoveries, which I confess I find hard to understand. I've been to a few open demonstrations of Faraday's work – it's a modern miracle as far as I'm concerned!'

As he spoke enthusiastically about the development of electricity it became clear to me that as one of the landowning gentry I had a responsibility to explore much more thoroughly such new ideas.

'Ambrose, I can see that many new techniques might be practically applied in the context of the countryside.'

'Certainly! I suppose you have one of the new threshing

machines? Not universally accepted, especially by the farm labourers, but they must inevitably be embraced by landowners, especially those with a large acreage like yourself.'

'I'm in the process of investigating the possibility of introducing such a machine, but as yet haven't made any move to purchase one. I'm still mulling over the consequences. As with all controversial innovations I see both sides of the argument. I recognise that machines will reduce or even eliminate laborious tasks and speed up all the processes, which must, as you say, advantage the landowner in terms of profit. On the other hand, and taking it to its logical con- clusion, introducing them will mean the labourers must eventually find themselves surplus to requirements. How then will they feed their families? There's never been a time when rural folk can't find some work on the land; they rely on it – even if it's only casual or seasonal. They can earn enough to survive. Take that away and there can only be one outcome for them; if they can't find work, it's the workhouse. I'd find it more than ironic if any of my workers were forced into Seddon Union because I had decided to mechanise their labour!'

'You're right, Edgar, it's a dilemma. But the force for progress in mechanisation is irresistible; we're living in a time of frantic change. The moral questions are important, but it's the practical management of such upheavals that should be regarded as a priority by those with power.'

Dinner came to an end and we took the port back to the library and returned to matters concerning Seddon Union and its inmates. Acknowledging the invaluable help Fred and Amy Lodge had been to him, he also was keen to know what their prospects were.

'Fred and Amy have refused to be considered for the post of mas- ter and matron because, as they've told me, the whole regime and rationale of the Poor Law is disagreeable to them. They're certain that no matter what reforms the new board would be able to introduce, officials would still have to conform to a rigid set of harsh government regulations that they feel they could no longer administer.'

'What are they going to do then? Bearing in mind they'll lose not only their employment, but their home.'

'They came over to discuss things and Fred was very clear. He said he'd rather try his hand on the land than stay where he was. His uncle, Ted Lake, had already promised he'd take care of them in those circumstances. It was at that point I put forward my proposal.'

'Which was?'

'My estate manager, Sam Saunby, is approaching seventy and wants to retire—'

'Don't blame him. Poor chap! Do you always keep your managers on so long?'

'I'm talking about a man who's never stopped working for almost sixty years. He lives and breathes this estate. I'll admit I'll be sorry to see him go. However, this is where Fred comes in. I've offered him the post of under-manager for six months while he learns all he can about running the estate. He's very alert and a quick learner. He reads and writes well – taught by Amy to produce a fair hand – and Sam has agreed to take him on and give him a proper training. He'll stay on for a further six months to keep an eye on Fred's progress. Fred seemed delighted with the idea, but said they'd like to talk it over. I'm waiting to hear from him.'

'I presume there's a house goes with the job?'

'Oh yes! A substantial one – perhaps over-large for his family, but I've further ideas concerning that. You might be interested in them.'

'I would be – go on.'

'They concern the two boys, William Tuttle and Peter Samuels. I know you've a desire to do something for them too.'

'Certainly, I don't want to abandon them now. Tell me what you have in mind.'

I went on to outline my ideas, which we would put to the boys the next day when we visited the House. Ambrose was delighted with the proposals, and equally warm in his regard for the Lodges. 'Fred's very honest: down to earth and fair-minded; his wife also – she's a real asset.'

'The Lodges and Lakes are good examples of the best in country folk, open-minded and generous. Ted Lake's occasionally over-excitable in his approach, but I can't fault the man for his passion for wanting to put things right.'

Ambrose smiled over his glass. 'We need men of spirit at this time, Edgar. Exuberance is something to be celebrated not discouraged – it gets things moving.'

'He does that all right! By the way, Ted rates you as a first-class journalist. He talked a lot about your crusading work. His report to the board completely surprised me, not only with its attention to detail, but most importantly its succinct grasp of the problems and prescription for reform. His presentation was masterly – in complete contrast to his behaviour at the infamous board meeting, where at times he was so cheerfully indiscreet and childish I could have throttled him!'

We talked some more about a few of the individuals Ambrose remembered. When he enquired over specific inmates I could be of little help. To my shame I'd never really got to know any of them. He raised the subject of Emily and Caroline Alfrey and what would happen to them. We discussed it at length and, as a consequence, together came up with an idea that would need careful organisation and the cooperation of others – but by the end of the evening I was optimistic we could improve their future situation significantly.

Without realising it we'd been talking until past midnight, when Foster came in to enquire tactfully whether he should bolt the doors. Agreeing we should have an early start we each went to bed with our heads full of plans.

Chapter 9

Planning to ride to Seddon Union, as I called to give instructions to the groom I remembered I'd forgotten to ask Ambrose what kind of rider he was. It transpired he was a poor one – at least very out of practice. As he reminded me, living in London he had no need to keep a horse. Apart from the expense, it was unnecessary with the convenience of public transport, particularly the new and safer hansom cab that was taking over from the less stable fly. We were able to find him a quiet mare who, if she was blindfolded, would know her way all around Seddon and required no great horsemanship.

Stopping off at the gates of the House – which were both wide open – I dismounted and tapped at the door of the lodge, but there was no reply. Curious as to why the gates were unattended, we continued up the drive and round to the back of the House to the stables. On approach, we heard many voices and, coming round the corner of the buildings, saw three large carts and inmates pulling off what looked like mattresses. In the middle of the activity stood Robert Bignell, Thomas Lewis and Fred Lodge, who were directing matters. Other inmates were bringing out the palliasses, which they took to an empty stable and shook out all the straw, bringing back the empty covers and throwing them into a corner.

Dismounting, we handed our horses to a couple of inmates and walked over to Robert Bignell. I held out my hand. 'Good day, Robert! I didn't expect to see you here this morning. What's all this?'

'As you can see, the board hasn't let the grass grow. One of the bitterest complaints from the inmates was the bedding. As soon as I realised there was spare money available, I instructed Thomas here to search around for a reputable supplier who could provide fifty mattresses as fast as possible. He obtained two sealed tenders, one of which we chose on account of speed of delivery. The man was slightly more expensive but we felt we needed to show the inmates we were doers not just talkers!'

'I'm impressed, Robert. This is a new departure for the institution to have a chairman who's active in its running.' Then, realising I'd

completely forgotten my manners, I turned to Ambrose and introduced him. 'Apologies – Robert Bignell, may I introduce Ambrose
Hudson?'

Bignell looked at him with a flicker of recognition and turned to
me questioningly, 'Haven't I met him before?'

Ambrose smiled and held out his hand. 'You'll remember me as
Millhouses – Henry Millhouses – the man with the Bible!'

Bignell looked even more confused. 'So who are you – Hudson
or Millhouses?'

Before we were side-tracked into long explanations, I took
Robert to one side and said, 'Robert, I'll explain everything later. First,
Ambrose and I have some unfinished business with the two boys
William Tuttle and Peter Samuels.' I turned to Fred Lodge. 'I imagine
they're down in the gardens somewhere?' He nodded and offered to
send for them, but Ambrose said he would like to find them himself.
So while he strode off down the path to the vegetable patch, I took
Robert to one side again and described the circumstances that had led
Ambrose to become an inmate. At first he baulked at the idea of a spy
in the House – but eventually I was able to convince him that the
journalist had only justice in mind. Partly mollified, he went back to
supervising the unloading.

Some minutes later, I heard the shouts of excited boys and turned
to see Peter running alongside Ambrose, who was carrying William
pickaback. Young Will was in fair danger of falling off as his arms
flailed around. The three came into the yard and Ambrose gently
dropped his burden to the ground. Peter and William immediately
became subdued and awkward as they looked from Robert to me.
I held out a hand to Peter, who wiped his own on the back of his
trousers before taking it in a warm, sweaty grip. William put his hands
behind his back and shuffled from foot to foot, refusing to look me
in the eye. Ambrose pushed him gently forward and said, 'There's no
need to be frightened. You probably recognise Mr Lawes, who's often
visited the House. I'm staying with him for the moment; I've already
told him a lot about you both and he wants to talk you.'

Shyly, William gave me a limp handshake, but immediately hid
behind Ambrose and Peter. I suggested that, in order to speak to them

in private, we should take them both into the boardroom where we wouldn't be disturbed.

We moved chairs into an informal arrangement and sat the boys down. Riding across to the House, we'd rehearsed our plan and how we'd put it to them; so, as arranged, I sat back and let Ambrose lay out our main idea. The boys were very nervous – I sensed they anticipated some kind of punishment for bad deeds they were unaware of – but he immediately put them at their ease.

'Firstly, I'm sorry I left without telling you I was going; I've been worried about you both ever since. When Mr Lawes and I have finished talking to you, I hope you'll ask me any questions you like. But for now we have some suggestions to make about your futures.'

William looked puzzled. 'What are "suggestions"?' he asked. I could see that Ambrose was going to have to choose his words carefully.

'Ideas – things to do,' he explained. Then he went on. 'Neither Mr Lawes nor I want you to stay in the House a minute longer than you have to.'

'What do you mean?' asked Peter suspiciously.

'We'd like you both to live outside the House in a proper home with a family.'

'How can we?' asked Peter sceptically. 'We don't have no families – you know that. I told you.'

'I remember everything you told me. That's why we're trying to help.' He turned to William. 'William, how would you like to live with Mr and Mrs Lodge? They have two children who are younger than you and they'd like them to have an older brother.' William looked confused and said, 'Would I have to work there – gardening or doing the oakum?'

'Certainly not – they'd bring you up just like their own children. You'd be treated just the same. Mrs Lodge will teach you to read and write. I know you're good at your numbers, so perhaps you could teach her children what you know. What do you think?'

I have a limited knowledge of children, and naively expected an enthusiastic response at such an offer. I was disappointed. William continued to look worried and, as if reading his concerns, Peter said,

'How long would it last? Would it be until he can be sent somewhere as a 'prentice? I've heard that fostered boys are badly treated.' This boy was worldly-wise.

Ambrose responded quickly. 'William will stay with the Lodges until he's ready to leave home himself. He'll go to school with the other boys and then he can choose a profession.' He turned immediately to William. 'Profession means a good sort of job – like I do or Mr Lawes here. To get such a job you need some good learning – we want you to have that.'

Peter then completely took the wind out of my sails by asking, 'Who'll pay for it? We can't just be got out of the House – that costs money.'

'That's a very sensible question, Peter, but you don't have to pay to get out of the House. Mr Hudson and I are prepared to pay for all Will's education. Mr and Mrs Lodge want to help by providing William with a good home.'

'No one does things for nothing – what will you get out of it?'

I looked at Ambrose for help. How could I explain to a thirteen-year-old the concept of doing good for its own sake – especially one who'd known nothing other than a dog-eat-dog kind of world?

Also scratching around for an honest answer, Ambrose simply said, 'We want nothing in return – we need nothing, you can see that. I hope William will accept the offer from someone who thinks of him as a friend – that's all. Now, while Will's thinking about it, this is what we would like you to consider, Peter. Mr Lawes is offering you an apprenticeship with his stable master at Seddon Hall. You'll be taught everything he knows about horses – and that's everything anyone knows! You'll lodge at the Hall with the groom and his wife – they're nice people but they've no children of their own and the idea of a ready-made son is something they're looking forward to – if you agree.'

Peter looked positively alarmed and said quickly, 'Am I to be separated from William then? I can't leave him. I've looked out for the poor little bastard since I came here. We've put up with this place, but always together – I can't see him managing without me!'

Endeavouring to calm him, I explained that, although he wouldn't be living with William, the Lodges would be moving to a good-sized house on my estate and there would always be room for him to visit and stay. I was also proposing that he join William for lessons so that he could learn to read and write too. I assured him there was no intention of splitting them up – I was sure they would always remain friends and try to keep together.

Peter then raised a second and possibly most serious concern for him, which was his mother's grave and how far away from it he would be. 'I'm not going anywhere away from her!'

Again, I was able to assure him it was not far; perhaps even closer than where he was now. Also, he could visit whenever he liked – not just on one Sunday every month when Mrs Lodge happened to take him to church. He could take fresh flowers from the Seddon Hall gardens each time he visited. I think that might have been the tipping point. He visibly relaxed and, for the first time, a little flush of anticipated pleasure coloured his cheeks.

Ambrose and I had discussed whether we should leave them for a couple of days to think over our proposals – or take their answer there and then. After we'd laid out our suggestions, William came up and nervously took hold of Ambrose's sleeve. 'Will you come and visit me often?' he asked. 'Peter says you live in a place called London, which he says is far away. Can't I come and live with you?'

Ambrose had anticipated this suggestion. 'Will, it wouldn't be practical. That is, it wouldn't work for a young boy to live with an old bachelor – that's a man who isn't married. I'm often far away working and couldn't look after you in the way you should be. But I promise that on every occasion I can I'll come up and visit you both. I'll also write every week. I'm sure you'll soon both learn to read my letters. Anyway, you wouldn't want to live far away from Peter, would you?'

The two boys looked at each other. I said they could have as much time as they needed to discuss it. Peter said they should talk together now and we left them looking slightly bewildered.

Outside in the hall Ambrose said, 'Peter's been incarcerated here for too long; he's overly cynical for his age. If he were let loose in the streets of London I wouldn't say much for his chances. He'd end up a very successful criminal – or dead very young. If he grabs the opportunity you're offering, I think his native cunning and quick wits, guided by some good examples, will lead him to a solid and worthy future. That's why it would be a pity if he turns you down.'

'Do you think that's likely? I can't see why he'd refuse – it's a good offer.'

'You know, he's deeply suspicious of anyone in long boots and a top hat! And rightly so. His question about your motives should have told you that. But my guess is they'll both accept the offers.'

He was right. Within a few minutes they crept cautiously out of the door. Peter extended his hand to me, looked me in the eye and said, 'We'll take it.'

It remained for us to make arrangements for the boys to be officially discharged from the House, and there was no difficulty for me as a JP to sign an order that gave them both into my care. In anticipation, Amy Lodge had already prepared a bed for William in the lodge and, as she had forged an almost motherly relationship with him during his time as an inmate, he was very willing to take up his place within her family. Later that day, when we said goodbye to him, he was already dressed in a smart jacket, new white shirt, trousers and a pair of stout boots. As he came out of the lodge he took Ambrose's hand with a grave expression and, in a grown-up way, wished him good afternoon, as though he was already adapting to his new role as the elder brother. Ambrose promised to visit him every day until he returned to London. William and Peter said a stiff, awkward farewell to each other, but I swear there was a glint of a tear in Peter's eye as I pulled the boy up onto the back of my mount.

Peter's destination was with me to Seddon Hall, where my stable master and his wife, Harry and Mary Valentine, were waiting to welcome the newcomer. I had warned them that Peter was rough and ready – sometimes free with foul language – 'but not malicious, spiteful or dishonest'. I described his relationship with William and how he'd taken it upon himself to protect the boy – as best he could in the environment of the House. I said I hoped they would appreciate his difficulties and make allowances. While they recognised the first few weeks might be difficult, they promised to persevere. Mary Valentine – a substantial lady in girth and heart – declared she had a nephew who was wild in spite of having a pair of loving parents – perhaps too loving as they had managed to spoil him badly. With that experience, she was confident she could persuade Peter that he was in the right place with people who would care for him – if he let them.

Ambrose remained at the Hall for almost ten days. He was true to his word and allowed the docile mare to amble him across to the lodge house every day to visit William. His stay incorporated a guardians' board meeting where he was given the opportunity to read extracts from his journal and provide some graphic evidence of the lives of the inmates. Most of the board were shocked and a few expressed their shame at their ignorance of conditions. No one actually blamed the colonel for his style of chairmanship, but I believe many thought it. When we left the meeting I described to Ambrose the difference in style, tone and intensity of the meeting in comparison with the first one I had attended back in mid-April. He had already apprehended the heightened interest that the guardians showed in every aspect of the agenda. It appeared to him that all were determined never to be accused of dereliction while they were a board member. The sea change was obvious to me. Also, biscuits were back on the table – gingerbread replacing the Bath Olivers.

Early in his stay, in a package of letters sent on from London, he received an edited copy of the article he had prepared for the *Escritoire*. James McNiece had left it virtually untouched, with a few cautious amendments to names that might have brought the broadsheet in conflict with the defamation laws. But it would be obvious to anyone who read the paper in our small community who the references described, however much they had been obscured. By and large the article was a fair summation of all the negligence that Ambrose had noted and endured himself, and we both hoped it would stir consciences, particularly of those with the power to change legislation. However, we were realists and knew it would take much time and sustained patience before real reforms were likely to be introduced.

By the end of his stay Ambrose had visited all those whose curiosity had demanded satisfying. Ted Lake was the first to invite us over to Rushie Farm, having become extremely excited when he heard that the great journalist was among our society. He invited the Lodges – who brought William with them – and even one of the O'Brien boys who had been working in the yard. Ambrose received a rapturous welcome and enjoyed one of Sarah's huge farmhouse spreads. Feasting, drinking and quizzing went on all afternoon and I was finally forced to send for the carriage – I wouldn't risk my friend on any mount, however gentle.

The enthusiasm to meet Mr Hudson the Whig journalist – as he was now known – was even embraced by the Tory Somersets. Lady Somerset was predatory in her pursuit of spouses for her daughters, and the combination of a bachelor on the loose in the district – whatever his politics – and the chance of good stories and gossip from London was irresistible. We had two invitations – one for cards, the other for dinner. Warning my friend of the Somerset girls' determination, he managed to maintain a polite but safe distance throughout both visits.

We also dined with my friend Hugh Bradshaw and his sister Deborah. We were able to sound them out as to their willingness to help Emily Alfrey and her daughter. There were many inmates in Seddon we would like to have taken out and helped on their way, but we felt that what the Alfrey family had suffered so egregiously was a direct consequence of the bad management of the House and deserving of recompense. Hugh and Deborah were only too willing to offer work and a home to Emily and Caroline.

I knew I would miss Ambrose when he returned to London. I would feel the lack of his intellect and knowledge. We'd spent many evenings discussing widely differing topics – never really coming to any conclusions, like the good Whigs we were – but nonetheless each recognised in the other mutually agreeable qualities that we had no doubt would ensure the friendship endured. We arranged to communicate frequently by post and he invited me to visit him in London. His house, he said, was not grand, but his landlady would give me a warm welcome and I could be sure she would never serve me pork unless I particularly requested it!

Postscript

Seddon Hall,

Suffolk

1 October '38

My Dear Ambrose,

Thank you for your letter, which, although arriving five days ago, I received only yesterday. I have been away on the other side of the county for the last few days engaged in legal work.

Congratulations on the completion of your own work. I am delighted that the journal will now see the light of day as it fully deserves. Rumours circulate the district that Seddon and its environs will soon become famous – if not notorious. When pressed for information about what you might write – as I am constantly – I try to warn that your observations about us may not necessarily reach that height of flattery which they often feel they deserve! I know my warnings go unheeded. They are received – to paraphrase Dr Johnson – as the triumph of hope over probability!

You ask me for news from the district, particularly concerning William and Peter, although I know you have been writing to them both regularly and, as you say, William is now in correspondence with you. The first thing to tell you is they are both well and happy. William continues to lose his wispy thinness and has filled out now that he is enjoying the Lodges' substantial meals. Several visits to Rushie Farm since I last wrote have also aided this process; Peter likewise. The combination of good food, fresh air and hard work in the stables has done great service to his physique. He seems to have grown considerably and

I think will end up rather tall. We have also confirmed his age. In fact, Calman was right – Peter is fourteen, a month off fifteen. We found his baptismal record in his parish church.

Both William and Peter have acquitted themselves very well at Amy's little school – set up in a spare room of their house and now accommodating seven young children from the village, plus her own three. I say three because William is fully included as one of the family. Fred tells me that his younger boy idolises William – as William still idolises Peter. Anyway, their progress with reading is notable and both of them can now make a fair hand with their writing. Seeing what William can do has spurred Peter to greater effort and he says he will be corresponding with you once he has enough letters together to form all the words he would like to say. Aside from his education this young man is in a fair way to becoming an excellent horseman. He was terrified on his first mount, but my stable manager Harry Valentine kept him at it and, even when he fell off and went away in tears, persuaded him to remount and try again. He can now handle a beast that you would probably baulk at and all in less than four months! I think you can be proud of both your protégés.

Further news of others of our acquaintance. As you will remember, Hugh Bradshaw and his sister Deborah offered to provide employment for Emily and Caroline Alfrey. A position as a seamstress and under-cook was found for Emily, and Caroline serves at present as a parlour maid. But shortly after they moved into the Bradshaws' residence there was an interesting development. Fortuitously Hugh discovered that Caroline had exceptional brains, as well as much beauty. To her confusion he found her looking through his books in his beloved library one day and, in his usual generous way was unperturbed – indeed he told her she could borrow any book she liked – provided she told him which one as he is still very jealous of his first editions! Apparently her father had taught her to read but she had been limited to the Bible and a few books borrowed from a kindly curate in their village at Boxford, who also recognised she had intelligence. She admitted she could not write, so Hugh has taken it upon himself to teach her. He told me she was becoming very proficient and he is hoping she will soon be able to help him in his task of cataloguing his books; in which case she will cease to be a parlour maid and become his assistant – instrumental in placing orders for books and cataloguing the library efficiently. Her love of books is such that he feels she has now become a soulmate with whom he can share his passion.

Emily has been in the path of a well set-up local man who, struck by her unusual beauty, has been attempting to court her, but she was badly damaged by the Enderby affair and staunchly, but with great politeness, eschews all approaches of a romantic nature. However, she has found a true refuge with Deborah Bradshaw whom she takes care of in the matter of her mistress's various ailments. The pair have become very close.

You ask about the Calmans but their fate and whereabouts still remain a mystery. It was rumoured that immediately after their ejection they found their way to a relative who was happy to accommodate them until they found employment and their own accommodation. Some say they had secreted the illicit gains made during their stay at the House in a London bank and, immediately after leaving Seddon, were thereby able to afford passage to the New World, where they have set up a very successful 'boarding house'; this is thought to be a euphemism for 'bawdy house', which given Jenny Calman's history, is more than likely closer to the truth. But in any event it is said they will one day retire rich on the profits. Alternatively it is put about that they became so degraded and reviled they were unemployable and ended up as inmates in a workhouse, where they will remain – separated – until they die. I think this last possibility reflects more wishful thinking than actuality, but it is a nice conceit.

After his long sojourn in the workhouse institution, Jacob Fearnley was finally laid to rest last week. It seems that he so relished his new mattress that he found it more and more difficult to rouse himself and eventually was found under the blankets with his face in the flock, smiling but stone dead.

I am pleased to hear that local undertakings keep you occupied, but understand that a man of your energy and talent must thirst for other adventures. I wait to hear with keen anticipation that another exciting assignment is in the offing.

I would be delighted if you would join me at Seddon Hall for the Christmas festivities. You will be inundated with invitations – and I promise I will filter out the less attractive ones. Ted Lake will throw his usual bash at Rushie – which is an experience not to be missed. If you need persuading, I'm sure I could ask William and Peter to write and invite you themselves.

In anticipation of your reply I remain your great friend and honourable servant,

Edgar Lawes

New South Wales

October 1842

Dear Mr Lawes,

You will be surprised to receive this letter after four years. I was one of the women in Seddon Union workhouse at the time of the death of Robert Enderby. Since I am safely on the other side of the world, and the main perpetrator of the crime has lately deceased, I feel I owe it to you and others connected to close the account of the events in June 1838.

Firstly, those involved express no remorse for what happened. Enderby was a monster and deserved the treatment meted out. He had assaulted and demeaned women in the House for some time, but his threat to attack Caroline Alfrey was the straw, as they say, which broke the camel's back. She was but fourteen and innocent and beautiful – as was her mother, who did not escape Enderby's attentions and the violence of his actions. These, I believe, led to her husband's suicide. Enderby was stupid because, in a typically drunken state, he had boasted of his intentions to one of the women the day before.

There was no question of clearing her conscience before she died – Rosa Hinds remained unrepentant. But in the month before her end she gave me permission to send you her confession to her part in the murder and I enclose it with this letter. The plan was devised between we five women working in the kitchen, but only two of us carried out the killing, the rest were responsible for confusing you all with its timing. For all I can be certain, you may have already worked it out for yourself, but if not let me lay the events out for you.

On that day, as he often did, Enderby came swaggering into the kitchen, as we said, around ten thirty. I passed him a note purporting to come from Emily Alfrey saying she had changed her mind and would meet him in the shed next to the pigsties as soon as he was able. She had nothing to do with any of this and, as far as I know, is still unaware who killed Enderby and why.

You may question why a man would want to meet a woman at ten thirty in the morning at such a location for a casual encounter, but remember Robert Enderby was invariably semi-drunk and, begging your pardon, like any male animal sniffing a female on heat, he would never throw up such an opportunity. He went off for the assignation; Rosa was already in the shed armed with a heavy iron skillet from the kitchen. I followed him at a distance. If you remember, the pigsties are out of everyone's sight, except if you are coming up from the bottom of the garden and pass them, or have to visit them for a purpose – as the two boys did who found his body.

Enderby went into the shed and Rosa hit him over

the head with the skillet. I arrived to find him out cold but still breathing in a shallow way. She hastily put on the butcher's full-sized apron and indicated I should do the same. What she did next completely shocked me. I knew she hated Enderby with a passion – I was never certain exactly what he had done to her in the past, but she obviously still bore a heavy grudge, which, considering what she did, is an understatement. Without a word she started pulling at his boots and breeches and, almost mesmerised, I helped her strip him from the waist. With cool attention to detail she searched his pockets for the note, which she retrieved and kept with her until she could destroy it in the kitchen range. We threw his clothes into the corner of the shed where they were later found. When he was half naked and exposed she took a sharp paring knife from the fold of her dress and proceeded to leave him in the state you found him. She savagely carved his private parts off his body, wrapped them in a cloth she had brought for the purpose and concealed them in her dress along with the knife. As he was just alive, the blood was pumping furiously from the wounds hence the protection that was needed from the aprons, already blood-stained from the killing of the pigs the day before. You would have seen a tremendous quantity of blood when the body was discovered. She then took Enderby under the arms, indicated I should take his legs, and we manhandled him to the side of the pigsty and tipped him in with the boar. We took off the aprons and placed them back on their hooks. Our arms and hands were fouled with the blood and we washed them in the water in the trough inside the sty. Obviously no one bothered to look in it later when the body was discovered, or they would have seen that it was bloody. We walked quickly back to the kitchen where we resumed our duties. Rosa was calm and collected from beginning to end. I was shaking with fear and shock, but was now so implicated I could only try to act normally. We told the other women the deed was done, without going into detail and reaffirmed our collective story that we had all seen Enderby well after eleven o'clock. That was the confusion we wished to cause. Five of us with the same story would not be doubted, and neither was it.

I think that Mr Ambrose Hudson, or Henry Mill-houses as we knew him, may have guessed the truth. Either he sympathised and felt it was rough justice, or, and most likely, he had no significant evidence or proof. He certainly did not know who the main perpetrator was. We knew he was aware of Enderby's predilections and, perhaps if we had been more patient, the overseer would have eventually been brought to face a court of law. But the threat to Caroline Alfrey was imminent and we could not wait for Justices and investigations.

A stroke of good fortune and a loyal sister now sees me contentedly married to an engineer and resettled in the colony of New South Wales – as a colonist, not a transported convict. Rosa Hinds, as I said, is dead; the other three women who were guilty of perjury and conspiracy I doubt you will ever find. Before writing this I investigated their whereabouts but could find no trace. They are either dead or in places they cannot be found – if you are minded to search for them that is.

I hope I have been able to set the record straight and that you will consider the case now closed. However, what you do with this information is obviously for you to decide. We would have no objection to you sharing this letter with Henry Millhouses if you know where he is. He is a decent man – we all thought there was more to him than meets the eye, as they say. As you will see, I choose to remain anonymous. You may guess which one of the four other women I am, but I hope you will now let the matter rest. As far as we were all concerned justice was served.

Your obedient servant...

Post scriptum

The business with the biscuits was Rosa's idea. She had a violent dislike of all the guardians and an utter loathing for Colonel Shepherd in particular. She thought it would be a message you would all understand.

London

January 1842

To whom it may concern,

I, Rosa Hinds, freely confess to the murder of Robert Enderby at Seddon Union Workhouse, Seddon in Suffolk, on Saturday, the second day of June 1838. While I was willingly assisted in this action by one other, it was my intention and mine alone to kill Mr Enderby in order to stop his attack on Caroline Alfrey. I have no remorse, in spite of the fact that I will shortly meet my maker. I will leave it in His hands to mete out any divine punishment I am owed.

Your humble servant,
Rosa Hinds

Afterword

Between 1864–5 in his great classic *Our Mutual Friend*, Dickens writes explicitly about the abhorrence of the poor towards the thought of the workhouse. Mrs Higden, a childminder and washerwoman, expresses her feeling vehemently when talking about her young protégé Mr Sloppy:

> 'He was brought up in the—' with a shiver of repugnance, —'the House.'
>
> 'The Poor House?' said the Secretary.
>
> Mrs. Higden set that resolute old face of hers, and darkly nodded yes.
>
> 'You dislike the mention of it.'
>
> 'Dislike the mention of it?' answered the old woman. 'Kill me sooner than take me there.'

She then goes on to explain her antipathy:

> 'Do I never read in the newspapers,' said the dame, fondling the child – 'God help me and the like of me! – how the worn-out people that do come down to that [the workhouse], get driven from post to pillar and from pillar to post, a-purpose to tire them out! Do I never read how they are put off, put off, put off – how they are grudged, grudged, grudged the shelter, or the doctor, or the drop of physic [medicine], or the bit of bread? Do I never read how they grow heartsick of it and give it up, after having let themselves drop so low, and how they after all die out for want of help? Then I say, I hope I can die as well as another, and I'll die without that disgrace.'

Acknowledgements

My thanks to Lesley Taylor, Kate Mcluskie, Carolyn Box and Oli Palethorpe for reading through the original draft and for their encouraging and helpful comments.

Patrons List

Gwyneth Adams
David Budd
Rachel Cullen
Christine Davies
Julie Hudson
Kathleen McLuskie
Antony Moon
Oliver Palethorpe
Lilian Vickery
Emma Whiteoak

Innocents to the Slaughter – A Preview

Foreword

There was a hanging today, a chilly May Friday overcast with threats of rain. They had provided all the trappings that made it an official execution. Surrounded by soldiers and officials, the main protagonist came out through the prison gates into its yard where the temporary wooden scaffold had been erected the night before. The woman's arms were pinned to her sides with a leather belt; her head was bare and her hair tied up in a neat knot on the back of her head. Pristine in her habits to the end, she had asked as her last request to have her linen cuffs and collar laundered and starched; but prison regulations denied her. Instead she made an unimpressive sight in a plain black gown with her neck bare in order to more easily accommodate the rope. She stood silent and expressionless, head erect and staring out into the sea of people. There was no twitching, fidgeting or resistance on her part as the soldiers on each side urged her along.

The waiting crowd of about five hundred, all of whom had previously been gossiping in the yard while anticipating the event, now fell silent, their attention drawn to the centrepiece of the spectacle. Tension became palpable; the atmosphere was imbued with hostility and loathing. As the prisoner mounted the steps of the scaffold and appeared into view, the militiamen, drafted in to provide a barrier against which the crowd could move no further forward, brought their muskets to the ready in anticipation of a surge. But it was not forthcoming; the crowd remained still, silent but watchful. As the executioner moved to place the prisoner over the trapdoor the spectators watched with intense curiosity. Standing behind her, he attempted to slip a small cloth bag over her head, but she vehemently shook it away and those closest heard her murmur, 'I will not have it!' With a shrug of indifference, the hangman took the noose already hanging from the main beam and placed it around her neck. The chaplain stepped forward with his book and opened his mouth to pray, but again she shook her head at him, 'There'll be no cant here!

I'll take my chances.' Then she cried, for all to hear, 'Take your God to the Devil and go to them both!' There was a gasp from the crowd, many of whom shook their heads in disgust; some crossed themselves.

Checking one further time that he had correctly positioned the noose, then tightening the rope and adjusting the knot until it rested on the back of her neck, the hangman moved to the side of the scaffold where he paused briefly until the clock in the prison tower struck the first of ten strokes; then at a nod from the prison constable he pulled the lever. The trap door opened with a clatter and the woman fell through the hole to oblivion.